Chapter 1: A Fateful Encounter

The boardroom is a pristine canvas of glass and steel, the sunlight filtering through the tall windows, casting sharp shadows on the glossy surface of the conference table. My heart races, not just from the urgency of my late arrival, but from the weight of what this meeting represents. I can feel the anticipation crackling in the air as I settle into the chair opposite the design director, a woman whose reputation for ruthlessness in her choices precedes her. As I adjust my notepad, I catch a glimpse of my reflection in the glass wall—a flurry of dark curls, a tailored blazer, and the ever-present pinch of anxiety nestled in the corner of my smile.

"Welcome, Scarlett," she begins, her tone clipped but not unkind. "Let's see what you've got."

I clear my throat, the sound echoing unnaturally in the space. My hands tremble slightly, but I open my portfolio with a flourish, revealing sketches that shimmer with the promise of elegance and innovation. The collection I've poured my heart into, titled "Rebirth," embodies the spirit of renewal. It's a mix of flowing fabrics and structured silhouettes, inspired by the delicate balance of nature's cycles. As I speak, detailing each piece, I catch a flicker of interest in her sharp blue eyes, and the tension in my chest loosens just a fraction.

"Interesting choice of colors," she remarks, her finger tracing the edge of one of the sketches. "Tell me about your inspiration."

"Spring, of course," I respond, leaning in slightly, emboldened by her curiosity. "It's all about new beginnings. The world wakes up from its slumber, and I wanted to capture that energy— the vibrancy, the chaos, and ultimately, the beauty in transformation." My voice gains strength as I speak, painting a picture of blossoming flowers and soft rains that bring life back to the world.

She raises an eyebrow, nodding slowly, and for a moment, I dare to hope. But then the door swings open, and in strides a man dressed in a tailored suit, his presence magnetic. My breath catches in my throat, a jolt of recognition hitting me like a bolt of lightning. It's him—the stranger from the street, the one who caught me before I fell. I'm momentarily stunned, unable to reconcile the cool, collected environment of the boardroom with the dizzying warmth of that brief encounter.

"Apologies for interrupting," he says, his voice smooth like dark chocolate, rich and intoxicating. "I'm here to discuss the upcoming campaign for Valleria."

The director's expression shifts from mild annoyance to calculated interest as she gestures him to take a seat. "This is exactly what we needed. Scarlett, this is Ethan Hawthorne, our marketing guru."

Ethan looks at me, and I feel that same electric charge crackle between us. There's a glint in his eye that suggests he remembers our collision, too. "Scarlett, right? You definitely know how to make an entrance," he teases, a charming smile breaking across his face, and my cheeks flush with heat.

I manage a half-smile, momentarily thrown off balance by the unexpected turn of events. The conversation flows between the three of us, and while the director's keen mind dissects every detail of the campaign, I find myself drawn into a rhythm with Ethan. He asks questions that spark deeper thoughts about my designs, teasing out ideas I hadn't fully realized were simmering beneath the surface. There's a chemistry here that feels utterly reckless in such a serious space.

As the meeting progresses, the air thickens with potential. The director leans back, crossing her arms with a look of satisfaction. "This is promising. I think we have the makings of something truly unique." Her gaze shifts between us, and I can't help but wonder if she senses the unspoken connection.

Once the meeting wraps up, the director dismisses us, her attention already drifting to her phone. Ethan and I are left standing together, the silence buzzing between us like a live wire. I'm acutely aware of the way the late afternoon light casts a golden hue around him, making him look almost ethereal.

"I hope I didn't steal your thunder back there," he says, his tone playful yet sincere.

"Not at all," I reply, trying to mask the thrill of being close to him. "You just added a nice touch to my show-and-tell."

He chuckles, and it's like music—warm and inviting. "You're quite the designer. I'd love to know more about your collection if you're free to grab a coffee. It seems we might just be working together."

The prospect is both thrilling and terrifying. On one hand, a chance to work closely with someone as talented as him could be an incredible opportunity; on the other, it's a collision course with the unexpected. My instinct tells me to play it safe, to keep my distance, but there's a magnetic pull that makes the thought of declining feel like a defeat.

"Coffee sounds great," I say, surprising even myself. "I'd love to talk about the campaign."

His smile broadens, and I can't help but feel like I've just crossed an invisible line. "Perfect. There's a little café around the corner. I promise it's worth it."

As we walk out together, my heart races not only at the thought of working with Valleria Couture but at the delicious twist of fate that has thrust Ethan into my path. The streets are alive with the sounds of spring—laughter, the distant clang of a streetcar, and the soft rustle of leaves unfurling in the breeze.

I step into the sunlight, and for the first time in what feels like forever, I allow myself to believe in the possibility of change. The world feels fresh and filled with promise, and perhaps this encounter is just the beginning of something extraordinary.

The café Ethan led me to is a charming little place tucked away between towering buildings, its exterior painted a soft mint green, complete with window boxes bursting with geraniums. The air inside is filled with the rich aroma of freshly ground coffee beans mingling with the sweet scent of pastries, creating a warm embrace that makes my pulse race with excitement. As we slide into a cozy corner booth, I feel a strange mix of nervousness and anticipation. It's not every day you find yourself discussing your dreams over coffee with a man who seems to effortlessly embody all the charisma of a classic movie star.

Ethan leans back, his expression relaxed, but there's a spark in his eyes that suggests he's been waiting for this moment just as much as I have. "So, tell me more about your collection. You mentioned something about capturing the chaos of spring."

"It's all about the contrasts," I explain, my enthusiasm bubbling over as I sip my cappuccino, the froth leaving a delicate mustache on my upper lip. "Think of the petals falling from cherry blossoms while new buds push through the earth. There's beauty in that tension, in the push and pull of life. Each piece is designed to embody that—softness combined with strength."

Ethan raises an eyebrow, clearly intrigued. "I like that. It sounds like you're weaving a story into your designs. Fashion isn't just about looking good; it's about feeling something."

I nod, grateful for his understanding. "Exactly! I want people to wear my clothes and feel empowered, like they're stepping into their own personal narrative."

He leans forward, his elbows resting on the table. "And what narrative are you hoping to tell? What does Scarlett want the world to see?"

My breath catches for a moment. It's not just my designs I want to share; it's the journey behind them—the struggles, the late nights, the moments of doubt. "I want to show that beauty is not just about perfection. It's messy, unpredictable, and sometimes, you have to embrace the flaws. That's where real life happens."

A soft smile plays on his lips, and I can't help but feel a flutter in my chest. "That's refreshing," he says, his gaze lingering on mine as if he's peeling back layers of me with every word. "Most people play it safe. They want to fit into a mold, and in doing so, they forget how to stand out."

Our conversation flows effortlessly, laughter spilling between us like the coffee from the barista's spout, and I'm surprised at how quickly I let my guard down. We talk about everything from our favorite movies to the best late-night food spots in the city. The tension that had initially gripped my chest melts away, replaced by a delightful thrill. I find myself leaning in, lost in the rhythm of our exchange, when suddenly, the café door swings open with a dramatic flourish.

In walks a woman who commands attention, her aura a mix of confidence and calculated elegance. She's dressed in a tailored black suit, the fabric hugging her curves with an unapologetic boldness. She scans the room, and I can't help but feel my heart sink when her eyes land on Ethan. Recognition flickers across her face, and she struts over with an air of authority that instantly fills the space.

"Ethan! I didn't expect to find you here," she says, her voice dripping with playful sarcasm. "I thought you were too busy charming clients to waste your time with coffee runs."

He straightens, his easy demeanor shifting slightly as he regards her. "Is that how you see it, Ava? Or are you just jealous I'm not fawning over your latest campaign?"

I watch their exchange, a mix of amusement and apprehension swirling inside me. This is clearly not just a casual encounter; there's history here, and I can't quite determine if it's competitive or flirtatious. Ava's eyes flicker to me, and for a moment, I feel like an intruder in their private world.

"And who is this?" she asks, her tone softening slightly but still laced with a hint of challenge.

"Scarlett," I reply, forcing a smile and extending my hand. "I'm a designer, hoping to collaborate with Valleria on the upcoming collection."

Her gaze sharpens, and I can sense the shift in the atmosphere. "A designer? How quaint," she says, her voice dripping with false sweetness. "What's your angle, then? How do you plan to stand out in a sea of talent?"

I feel the warmth drain from my cheeks, but I refuse to back down. "By being honest and authentic. My work isn't about following trends; it's about creating something real."

Ethan watches me with an unreadable expression, a hint of amusement dancing in his eyes. Ava tilts her head, considering my response, and for a moment, I wonder if I've made an enemy. But then she offers a sly smile, the kind that makes me question if she's impressed or merely amused.

"Well, Scarlett, good luck. You'll need it," she says, a flicker of something—perhaps jealousy?—crossing her features before she glances back at Ethan. "Don't keep her too long. We have a meeting to prep for."

As she walks away, the tension dissipates like smoke in the wind, leaving behind an unexpected camaraderie between Ethan and me. "She's a piece of work," I mutter, shaking my head.

Ethan chuckles, his eyes sparkling. "You have no idea. But I admire your guts. Most people would crumble under her glare."

"Maybe I'm not most people," I shoot back, and we share a laugh that feels like a tiny victory.

"Definitely not," he agrees, leaning back in his seat, a glint of respect in his eyes. "And I think that's exactly what the fashion world needs right now."

Just as we dive back into conversation, the café door swings open again, and a group of students bursts in, laughing and joking, their youthful energy infectious. One of them, a girl with bright purple hair and a nose ring, locks eyes with me and waves enthusiastically. I can't help but smile; she's from my design class, a budding talent I've been mentoring.

"Scarlett! Is that you?" she calls out, bouncing over, her enthusiasm a burst of color in the muted café. "I didn't know you were here!"

I introduce her to Ethan, and the conversation shifts to a lighthearted banter about our favorite design projects, my friend's exuberance filling the space around us. Ethan watches, an amused smile playing at the corners of his mouth, and I feel a surge of pride as I share stories about my students and the joy of nurturing their creativity.

As I glance at Ethan, I catch the twinkle of admiration in his eyes. It's unexpected, this mixture of encouragement and intrigue. But the moment is fleeting, as the bell above the café door rings again, and my heart sinks when I see Ava step back inside, her expression stormy and determined.

"Ethan," she says sharply, cutting through the laughter, "we need to discuss the campaign—now."

The shift in the atmosphere is palpable, the lightness of our conversation evaporating into an uncomfortable tension. Ethan glances between Ava and me, and I can sense the weight of the moment bearing down on us. I know I should leave, but I can't shake the feeling that the thread of our connection is woven tightly, and I'm not ready to unravel it just yet.

Ava's gaze sweeps over me with an intensity that feels like a warning, and I take a deep breath, steadying myself against the brewing storm. Something tells me this encounter is just the beginning of a much larger adventure, one filled with unexpected twists and turns that could either bind us together or tear us apart.

Ethan's expression shifts, his previous amusement clouded by a flicker of unease as Ava strides closer, a whirlwind of determination. I can't help but notice the way she carries herself—like a predator sizing up her prey, ready to pounce at the slightest hint of vulnerability. The air grows thick with tension, and I feel the instinctive urge to retreat, to fade into the background like a forgotten accessory in a designer's closet.

"Ethan," Ava repeats, her voice sharp, cutting through the lighthearted banter like a knife. "We really need to discuss the campaign, and I'd prefer if we did it privately."

"Just a moment, Ava," he replies, his tone steady but strained, as if he's trying to juggle the weight of her request and the warmth of my company. "Scarlett and I were just—"

"Talking about your designs?" she interjects, raising an eyebrow. "How cute. But let's not waste time, shall we?"

I shift in my seat, a sudden wave of self-consciousness washing over me. It's one thing to share ideas and dreams over coffee; it's another to be caught in the crossfire of what feels like a corporate power struggle. "I should go," I say, forcing a smile that feels brittle. "I don't want to intrude on your meeting."

"No," Ethan protests, his gaze locking onto mine with a fierceness that ignites a flicker of hope. "Stay. This is important for both of us. Your designs could play a key role in the campaign, and Ava just needs to understand that."

Ava crosses her arms, her expression skeptical but intrigued. "Oh? And why would I want to incorporate your designs?" she asks, her voice dripping with sarcasm.

"Because they're fresh and daring," Ethan replies, his tone unyielding. "And that's exactly what this campaign needs."

"Daring," she echoes, casting a sidelong glance at me. "You think a few floral patterns and flowy fabrics can compete with the established names? Please."

"Why not?" I interject, a newfound defiance sparking within me. "Fashion is about breaking boundaries, isn't it? About embracing the chaos that inspires us? Just because something is new doesn't mean it's not worthy."

Ava looks taken aback for a moment, her perfectly manicured eyebrows arching in surprise. "Interesting perspective," she replies slowly, as if assessing the potential threat I pose to her carefully curated world. "But we'll see if you can back it up."

I hold her gaze, willing myself to stand my ground. The air crackles between us, and I can almost see the gears turning in her mind, calculating risks and rewards. "Let's set up a time for you to present your collection," she says finally, her tone clipped but begrudgingly respectful. "We can discuss how to align it with our vision."

Ethan's eyes flicker with approval, and I feel a rush of triumph. "Absolutely. I'll get my team to prepare a comprehensive presentation," I say, my voice gaining strength. "I'm confident we can create something truly memorable together."

Ava nods, her expression inscrutable, before she gestures towards the door. "I'll be in touch then. Ethan, you know where to find me." With that, she turns on her heel and exits the café, the door swinging shut behind her with a definitive thud.

Once she's gone, the atmosphere lightens, and Ethan releases a breath he didn't realize he was holding. "You handled that well," he praises, a grin breaking across his face. "I thought she was going to chew you up and spit you out."

"Thanks," I reply, the adrenaline still coursing through me. "I wasn't sure I was going to survive that encounter. She's intimidating, to say the least."

"Intimidating is putting it mildly," he chuckles. "But you surprised me. You've got guts, Scarlett. I like that."

We share a moment of camaraderie, and I can't help but feel a spark of something more—something that flickers between us, electric and charged with possibility. "So, what's the campaign about?" I ask, genuinely curious.

He leans back in his seat, his expression thoughtful. "We're looking to rebrand Valleria's image, to attract a younger, more diverse audience. The current direction is stale, and it's time to shake things up."

"Sounds like a big task," I say, admiring the confidence in his demeanor. "But I believe it can be done. Fashion has always been about evolution."

"Exactly," he replies, his eyes shining with enthusiasm. "And I think your vision can be a pivotal part of that evolution. Together, we could create something that resonates with people—something that feels real."

Just then, my phone buzzes on the table, breaking the moment. I pick it up to find a text from my best friend, Mia: "You'll never guess who's in town. Let's meet at our usual spot?"

I smile at the screen, eager to catch up, but I also feel a pang of reluctance to leave Ethan's presence. "I should probably get going," I say reluctantly, not wanting to end this unexpected connection too soon.

"Before you do," he says, a teasing lilt in his voice, "how about we exchange numbers? You know, for 'business purposes.'"

I laugh, feeling the butterflies swirl in my stomach. "Of course. I wouldn't want to miss out on this incredible opportunity, now would I?"

As we exchange numbers, the world outside shifts into the vibrant hustle of the city, but inside the café, time feels suspended, as if the universe is allowing us this precious moment of connection. "Let's meet up later this week," Ethan suggests, his eyes sparkling with mischief. "Maybe we can discuss our grand plans over dinner?"

"I'd like that," I reply, my heart racing at the thought of another encounter. "But just so you know, I'll expect dessert to be included in this 'business' meeting."

"Deal," he grins, the warmth in his expression igniting a flurry of hope within me. "And who knows, maybe dessert will inspire some new design ideas."

As I gather my things, I can't help but feel buoyed by the prospect of what lies ahead. With every step I take toward the door, my heart races with anticipation, the echo of our laughter ringing in my ears like a sweet melody.

Just as I push the door open, a commotion erupts outside, the cacophony of voices rising above the usual city sounds. I turn to glance back at Ethan, curiosity tinged with unease washing over me. A small crowd has gathered on the sidewalk, their expressions ranging from confusion to alarm.

"What's happening?" I ask, concern threading through my voice as I step back to peer over the heads of the crowd.

Ethan joins me, his brow furrowing as we try to make sense of the chaos. And then, through the throng, I catch a glimpse of a familiar face, pale and frantic—Mia, my best friend. She's pushing her way through the crowd, her expression wild and urgent.

"Scarlett!" she shouts, her voice rising above the noise, filled with a sense of impending dread. "You need to come with me—now!"

Panic washes over me, and I look to Ethan, who's taken a step closer, concern etched on his face. "What's going on?" he asks, his voice steady even as the world around us spirals into uncertainty.

"I can't explain here!" Mia gasps, grabbing my wrist and tugging me away from Ethan's side. "Just trust me!"

As we rush into the fray, I cast one last glance back at Ethan, uncertainty swirling in my chest. The connection we shared feels like a lifeline slipping through my fingers, and I can't shake the sense that everything is about to change in ways I never anticipated.

Chapter 2: Beneath the Surface

The music swells around me, a cascade of violins and soft piano notes that swirled through the grand hall like an enchanting spell. Valleria, ever the picture of elegance, glided beside me in a gown that shimmered like the night sky. Her laughter rang out, drawing attention as we moved through the throng of impeccably dressed guests. I clutched my champagne flute tightly, the glass cool against my palm, grounding me amidst the dizzying whirl of silk and sequins.

"Relax, Ava," she urged, her tone playfully teasing. "You look like a deer caught in the headlights. We're not here to save the world, just to enjoy it—well, at least until the bidding starts."

I forced a smile, even as my heart raced with each glance I cast across the room. It wasn't the high ceilings adorned with crystal chandeliers or the artful arrangement of flowers that captivated me. No, it was him. Caden Hawthorne stood at the far end of the hall, surrounded by a group of equally polished elites, yet he was an island of intrigue amidst the sea of familiar faces. His dark hair was tousled in that effortlessly charming way that made me think he could have just stepped off a yacht, and the tailored suit he wore clung to his frame, accentuating a physique that seemed sculpted for more than boardroom battles.

The moment our eyes locked, it felt as though the entire room faded into a blurred backdrop, the chatter and laughter dissolving into mere echoes. I held my breath, a rush of warmth flooding my cheeks. There was an intensity in his gaze that spoke of secrets—layers of complexity wrapped in a charming smile that suggested he held the keys to worlds I had yet to discover. My heart fluttered with a mix of excitement and caution, a thrilling cocktail that left me breathless.

Valleria nudged me playfully, her voice low enough for only me to hear. "He's the one, isn't he? The mysterious billionaire. Just look at how everyone fawns over him." I resisted the urge to roll my eyes. Yes, Caden was captivating, but I had long learned that appearances could be deceiving. In the world of wealth and power, charm often masked treachery.

As if sensing my hesitation, Caden's gaze intensified. There was a challenge in it, an unspoken dare that sent an exhilarating shiver down my spine. It was as if he could read the swirling thoughts in my mind, could sense the walls I had painstakingly built around my heart. And yet, as I remained anchored to my spot, a magnetic pull urged me closer.

With a sudden rush of adrenaline, I took a step forward, abandoning my drink on a nearby table. Valleria's startled expression was a fleeting moment of concern, but I didn't have the luxury to dwell on it. My heart drummed a frantic beat as I navigated through the crowd, each step an exploration of a territory I had never dared to enter. His smile deepened as I approached, a knowing glint sparking in his eyes.

"Glad you could join us, Ava," he said, his voice smooth and rich, like velvet laced with intrigue.

"You know my name?" I asked, trying to mask the thrill that surged within me.

He chuckled softly, the sound almost conspiratorial. "In a room full of power players, it's wise to know the names of those who matter."

I tilted my head, a playful defiance sparking in my chest. "And do I matter to you, Caden Hawthorne?"

He stepped a fraction closer, and the world around us seemed to shrink. "You could say I find you... interesting."

A ripple of laughter cascaded around us, but it felt distant and surreal. The truth was, I found him fascinating, but the cautionary tales whispered in the corners of my mind warned me against pursuing this curiosity. It was like dancing on the edge of a precipice, thrilling yet perilous. "Interesting how? I'm just a nonprofit worker trying to raise funds for a good cause."

His eyes glimmered with mischief, and I felt the air crackle with unspoken tension. "Just a nonprofit worker? I think you underestimate the power of your position."

I raised an eyebrow, intrigued. "And what power might that be?"

"Every story has layers, Ava. People often forget that the most unassuming can wield the strongest influence."

His words lingered in the air, and I couldn't help but feel the weight of his attention. "What's your story, then? I hear there are layers to Caden Hawthorne."

He leaned in slightly, the air between us charged with a chemistry I couldn't ignore. "Let's just say I'm not the only one with secrets. It's the nature of the game, and I play to win."

The heat of the moment enveloped us, but I couldn't shake the prickling sensation that danger lurked beneath the surface of our exchange. I was drawn to him, but the undertones of his life—the whispered rumors, the power plays—loomed like dark clouds on the horizon.

Before I could respond, the evening's host took the stage, and the crowd hushed, the spell momentarily broken. Caden's gaze shifted, and the vulnerability of the moment slipped away, replaced by a mask of charming confidence. I couldn't help but wonder how many others had seen that side of him—the enigmatic billionaire who ruled boardrooms and dominated social circles.

The auction began, and my thoughts danced between fascination and apprehension. As Caden returned to his circle of elite friends, I felt a sense of loss, a vacuum where the thrill of our encounter had ignited something within me. I shook my head, trying to dispel the feeling. This was all a game, a dance on a precarious edge. Yet, as I glanced at him, laughing and charming those around him, I knew I was in deeper than I had anticipated, caught in a web I hadn't even realized I was weaving.

The gala unfolded like a dream, the kind that leaves an unsettling mixture of enchantment and dread lingering in the air. As I navigated through the crowd, the rich aroma of truffle-infused hors d'oeuvres wafted around me, mingling with the floral notes of the elaborate centerpieces that adorned every table. I glanced around, pretending to admire the artful arrangements, but my thoughts were a chaotic symphony, each note pulling me back to Caden.

As he held court among a group of similarly powerful individuals, I couldn't help but steal glances. There was a confidence in his stance, a commanding presence that had drawn me in from the start. I observed how he effortlessly commanded attention, each quip eliciting laughter that sparkled like the diamonds adorning the guests. It was both intoxicating and terrifying, a reminder of the chasm that lay between us—one filled with wealth, secrets, and danger.

"Do you think he's as ruthless as they say?" Valleria asked, her voice a mix of intrigue and concern as she approached my side, her gaze fixed on Caden. "I mean, a billionaire in the Hamptons can't be that charming without a few skeletons in the closet."

I smirked, appreciating her perspective. "At this point, I think everyone has skeletons. Some just hide theirs behind designer suits."

Valleria chuckled softly, her eyes glinting with mischief. "True, but I suspect Caden's skeletons might have their own bodyguards."

I couldn't help but feel a flutter of excitement mixed with apprehension. It was easy to get swept up in the drama, the allure of the elite world that surrounded us. Yet, with every passing moment, I felt the invisible tether pulling me toward him, urging me to confront whatever dangerous game lay ahead.

"Why don't you go talk to him?" Valleria nudged me with a playful shove. "He's looking at you."

"Looking at me? Or at my drink?" I replied, taking a sip, savoring the bubbles that danced on my tongue.

"Go. I dare you." Her playful challenge ignited something reckless in me. The truth was, my instincts urged caution, but the thrill of the unknown was far more enticing.

With a deep breath, I set down my glass and made my way through the crowd, the rhythmic pulse of the music beating in time with my heart. Each step felt like a leap into the unknown, a plunge into a world I had only glimpsed from a distance. Caden stood with his back to me, the sharp lines of his profile silhouetted against the warm glow of the chandelier. I hesitated for a fraction of a second, caught in a web of my own hesitation before I could convince myself that stepping back now would only deepen my curiosity.

"Caden," I called out, the name rolling off my tongue like an incantation. He turned, and for a moment, time stood still.

"Ava," he replied, his smile widening, inviting. "I was hoping I'd see you again."

"Hope, is it?" I teased, stepping closer, reveling in the way his gaze warmed me from the inside out. "I didn't know you were the type to leave things to chance."

His laughter was low and captivating, wrapping around us like a secret shared between conspirators. "In my world, chance is often the only thing worth trusting."

"Then you must be a gambler," I said, tilting my head slightly, unable to resist the thrill of our playful exchange.

"A calculated one," he replied, his expression shifting, as if revealing a glimpse into a more serious side of him. "Life demands it, especially when you're dealing with high stakes."

I raised an eyebrow, intrigued. "High stakes like what? Corporate takeovers? Charity galas?"

"Both, and more," he said, his tone dropping, hinting at a depth beneath the surface. "But let's focus on what's right in front of us. What brings you to this circus?"

I hesitated, the mask of nonchalance slipping slightly. "I'm here to support Valleria's charity. It's a noble cause, and apparently, I'm just the plus-one who can help sell a few tickets."

"Ah, the unassuming hero," he mused, his eyes glinting with mischief. "We need more of those around here. Tell me, what's your superpower?"

I laughed, enjoying the banter, feeling more at ease. "I make a mean meatball. Not exactly superhero material, I know."

"Hey, I'm sure there are plenty of villains out there who would be deterred by your culinary skills," he countered, the glimmer in his eye making my heart race. "So tell me, Ava, are you one of those who believes in happily ever after, or do you think it's just a fairy tale?"

I pondered his question, drawn into the depths of his gaze. "I think it's a little bit of both. There's something beautiful about the idea of a fairy tale, but the reality is rarely as tidy as a storybook ending."

"Isn't that what makes life interesting?" he shot back, a hint of challenge in his voice. "The unpredictable twists that keep us on our toes?"

"Yes, until those twists come crashing down," I said, suddenly serious. "What if the fairy tale comes at a cost? What if you have to lose everything to find it?"

He regarded me, his expression shifting as if weighing my words. "Sometimes you have to risk losing everything to truly gain what matters."

The air thickened with unspoken tension, and I felt the weight of his words hanging between us. My instinct to pull back warred with an irresistible curiosity. What lay beneath his carefully crafted exterior? What haunted him?

As we stood there, the music shifted to a softer tune, a melody that wrapped around us like a warm blanket. I could hear the laughter of the guests, but it felt distant, a reminder that we were cocooned in our own world.

"I suppose we'll just have to find out," I said, an unexpected challenge slipping from my lips.

"Find out?" he echoed, an intrigued smile playing at the corners of his mouth. "You're not afraid of the unknown, then?"

"Afraid? Not at all."

His laughter rang out, rich and intoxicating, causing heads to turn. "I think you might be more dangerous than you realize, Ava."

With that, he took a step back, his eyes glinting with a knowing edge. The moment lingered, thick with uncharted potential and the electrifying possibility of danger. I realized then that I was stepping into a world that promised excitement and risk, a world where fairy tales were nothing more than illusions waiting to shatter.

The evening glimmered with opulence, an intricate tapestry woven from laughter, clinking glasses, and the soft swirls of satin and silk. The gala pulsated with life, but amidst the elegant chaos, Caden's presence anchored me like a lighthouse amidst a turbulent sea. As I navigated through the crowd, the tension between us crackled like static electricity, promising both danger and delight.

Just as I felt emboldened enough to confront whatever this connection meant, I caught sight of a group of socialites approaching Caden, their laughter bubbling like champagne. They crowded around him, vying for his attention as if he were the golden ticket in this exclusive game. My heart sank slightly, that familiar pang of insecurity creeping in. He seemed to radiate an aura that drew people in, and I was just another face in a crowd of admirers.

"Don't let them steal your spotlight," Valleria whispered, sidling up to me with a mischievous grin. "You've got the upper hand here; he's looking for depth, not just shallow waters."

"Right," I replied, unable to shake the gnawing feeling that I was out of my league. Yet, her words ignited a flicker of determination within me. I took a breath, reminding myself that I wasn't just any guest—I was here with a purpose. "What's the worst that could happen?"

Before I could second-guess myself, I strode toward the group. My heart thudded in my chest, an exhilarating rhythm that propelled me forward. "Caden," I called, my voice cutting through the laughter.

He turned, and for a moment, everything else faded into the background. The laughter around him diminished, and the look in his eyes—a mix of surprise and genuine delight—made my stomach flutter. "Ava," he greeted, his tone rich and inviting. "I was just discussing the virtues of philanthropy with these lovely ladies. Care to join?"

"Or are you trying to steal all the attention?" I shot back, the words tumbling out before I could reconsider.

He laughed, a warm sound that sent a ripple through the crowd, drawing curious glances our way. "A little of both, perhaps."

As the conversation flowed around us, I discovered that I could hold my own. I navigated the banter like a seasoned player, responding with sharp wit that matched his playful jabs. The other guests began to fade into the background, their voices a mere hum as we locked in our own world.

Just as I felt the tide of the conversation shift in my favor, a sharp voice cut through the air, cold and commanding. "Caden! We need to talk."

A woman with striking red hair and an expression that could freeze fire stepped into our circle, her gaze flickering between us with a mixture of annoyance and possessiveness. It was as if she had crash-landed in the middle of our moment, and the sudden shift in energy sent an icy chill down my spine.

"Give me a moment, Delilah," Caden replied, his tone dismissive, yet there was a subtle tension in his shoulders that caught my attention.

"Oh, I think this is important," she retorted, crossing her arms as she glared at me, as if daring me to challenge her. "We need to discuss the upcoming merger."

"Can't it wait?" he asked, his patience wearing thin, but the undercurrents of their exchange sent a shiver down my spine. This wasn't just business; there was history in the way they interacted, unspoken layers that hinted at complexities I didn't want to unravel.

Delilah stepped closer, her voice dropping to a low, conspiratorial whisper that felt like an intrusion. "You know how much is at stake. You can't just—"

"Excuse us for a moment," Caden interjected, taking my arm and leading me away from the crowd. His grip was firm, grounding, yet I sensed the tension rolling off him like waves crashing against a rocky shore.

"What was that about?" I asked, once we were out of earshot. "Is she your ex? A rival? A long-lost relative?"

"None of the above," he replied tersely, his brow furrowing as he scanned the crowd. "Just someone who doesn't quite grasp the concept of personal space."

"Or maybe she's just very protective of her territory," I suggested, teasingly.

He met my gaze, and I was taken aback by the seriousness in his eyes. "In this world, boundaries are often blurred. It's a game of power and perception. Trust me, you don't want to get entangled in this web."

The caution in his voice struck a chord within me, mingling with an intoxicating blend of intrigue and desire. "Yet here I am," I countered, unable to hide the smile tugging at my lips. "Entangled already."

He chuckled, a sound that warmed the chill in the air, but the worry flickered beneath his amusement. "And I'm afraid for you, Ava. You're not prepared for the risks involved."

"Maybe not, but I'm not here to play it safe."

"Playing it safe can save your life." His words hung in the air, laced with an intensity that sent my heart racing.

Before I could respond, the gala swirled around us, the noise and laughter crashing in waves as people drifted closer, eager to witness our private exchange. I could feel the pressure building, a sense that the moment was precariously balanced on the edge of something profound.

"Look, can we—" he began, but the words were cut off by the sound of glass shattering.

In an instant, the crowd erupted into chaos. A piercing scream rang out, and I spun around to see a woman collapse, clutching her arm where crimson pooled against the ivory of her gown. Gasps and murmurs rippled through the crowd, and the festive atmosphere shattered like the glass that had fallen from her hand.

"Call for help!" someone shouted, and the panic in the air turned electric.

Caden's expression shifted, the ease of the gala stripped away, replaced by a fierce determination. "Stay close to me," he commanded, scanning the crowd, his earlier levity gone as he took charge.

I nodded, adrenaline coursing through my veins. The thrill that had danced between us moments before had transformed into something far more dangerous. As guests rushed to the woman's aid, I felt the gravity of the situation pulling me into the heart of a chaos I had never anticipated.

Caden's grip tightened around my arm, and I realized that I was no longer just a spectator in this high-stakes game. I was in the thick of it, a player in a dangerous drama that was unfolding right before my eyes. The tension between us shifted again, now layered with urgency and an impending sense of doom.

"Whatever happens, don't let go," he said, his voice steady, but I could feel the tremor of something darker beneath.

As we pushed through the throng, the chaos closing in around us, I caught sight of Delilah again. Her eyes glinted, not with concern, but with something far more sinister—a knowing, calculating gaze that hinted at secrets ready to spill.

And in that moment, as the sirens wailed in the distance, I realized that the world I was stepping into was far more dangerous than I could have ever imagined. The pull between Caden and me had morphed into a whirlpool, threatening to drag me under, and the choices I made next could seal my fate forever.

Chapter 3: Torn Between Desire and Fear

The evening air is thick with the scent of rain-soaked earth and blooming jasmine, wrapping around me like an unwanted embrace. I stand at the edge of my tiny balcony, the city's pulse thrumming below, alive with laughter, the honk of car horns, and the distant notes of a street musician's serenade. My fingers brush against the wrought-iron railing, the coolness of the metal grounding me. Caden is a shadow against the glowing backdrop of the city, leaning casually against the doorframe of my apartment. His presence is magnetic, an electric current that makes my skin hum.

"Nice view," he says, his voice a low rumble, smooth and deep, a sound that drips with confidence. He steps closer, the warmth radiating from him like the sun breaking through heavy clouds. I turn my gaze away from the street below to meet his dark, stormy eyes, which are a vortex of emotions I can't quite decipher.

"You're just saying that," I reply, a smirk tugging at the corner of my lips, trying to inject some humor into the tension curling between us. "You've seen better."

"Not at all. I like it up here," he insists, the corner of his mouth quirking into a half-smile that reveals a hint of mischief. "It's nice to be away from all the noise, just you and the city."

"Just me?" I challenge, raising an eyebrow. "What are you, my personal tour guide now?"

His laughter is a rich sound, a warm balm against the chill of the evening. "I can be whatever you want, as long as it involves this view."

I roll my eyes, but the flutter in my stomach betrays me. Caden has this way of turning even the most mundane moments into something electric, something loaded with possibility. Yet, there's a shadow in his gaze, a flicker of something that hints at trouble—danger lurking behind his smirk. I can't ignore it. I shouldn't want to.

"Tell me, Caden," I say, leaning against the railing, forcing myself to stay grounded. "What's your story? You're not just another guy in a suit. There's more beneath that polished surface, isn't there?"

His smile falters for a split second, and a flicker of something darker crosses his features. "Aren't we all just collections of stories?"

There's an edge in his voice that pulls me in, daring me to peel back the layers. "Yes, but I want to know yours. You can't hide behind that charm forever."

"I'm not hiding," he replies, the intensity of his gaze making my heart race. "Maybe I just like the mystery."

"Or maybe you like keeping people at arm's length." I can't help but push back, needing to poke at that darkness I sense in him.

His silence speaks volumes. A muscle in his jaw twitches, and for a brief moment, the confidence fades, revealing a flicker of vulnerability. "You know, it's not easy letting people in. Especially when you've had... experiences that shape who you are."

"Is that a line?" I ask, half-teasing, half-serious. "Because it sounds a lot like one."

He chuckles, but it's laced with an undercurrent of something real. "What if it's not? What if I'm just trying to figure out how to be human again?"

The weight of his words lingers in the air, heavy and undeniable. I'm tempted to reach out, to bridge the gap that feels like a chasm, but the pull of caution wraps around me like a thorny vine. "And why should I care?"

"Because," he leans closer, his voice dropping to a conspiratorial whisper, "I think you might be the only person who can handle the truth."

My heart stutters in response, a treacherous traitor. I can't be the one to unravel him. I have my own demons to wrestle. "You don't even know me."

"Yet," he replies, that playful glint returning to his eye, "I feel like I do. You're like a firework, bursting with energy and potential. But you keep that spark under wraps."

"Maybe because it's safer that way," I counter, crossing my arms defensively.

"Safe isn't living, and I'm not sure it's what you truly want." His tone shifts, becoming earnest. "You don't strike me as someone who settles for mediocrity."

I pause, the truth of his words hitting home. I'm not mediocre. I'm ambitious, driven, a whirlwind of passion and dreams. Yet, the very thought of letting someone into that whirlwind sends a shiver down my spine. "And what if I'm afraid?"

"Fear is just a wall," he says, his voice softening, "a barrier we build to keep people out. But what if it's worth it to break through?"

I swallow hard, feeling the weight of his gaze like a physical touch. My heart thuds, and every nerve in my body is alive with a mixture of desire and fear. Caden is like a storm on the horizon, promising chaos and exhilaration all at once. The question lingers in the air between us, heavy with implication: What if I do let him in?

Suddenly, a siren wails in the distance, pulling me back to reality. The moment feels suspended, like the calm before a tempest. "We're not even friends, Caden. I don't know you, and you don't know me."

"Not yet," he agrees, stepping back slightly, but not completely. "But maybe that's the point."

The spark in his eyes is impossible to ignore, igniting something within me. It's reckless, dangerous, and yet so intoxicating. I can't help but wonder if maybe, just maybe, giving in to the storm is exactly what I need.

The next few days spiral into a haze of uncertainty and excitement, each moment more charged than the last. Caden's presence lingers like a ghost in the corners of my mind, a whisper that sends shivers down my spine. He seems to pop up everywhere, his laughter echoing in my ears and the lingering warmth of his touch igniting a longing I can't quite articulate. It's as if he's become a force in my life, pulling me into a whirlwind where the lines between desire and fear blur.

One afternoon, the sun hangs high in the sky, its golden rays filtering through the leaves of the trees lining the street outside my apartment. I stand in my kitchen, preparing a half-hearted lunch while listening to the soft jazz playing in the background, a welcome distraction from the chaos in my mind. Just as I set the kettle on the stove, my phone buzzes against the countertop, vibrating like a tiny heart trying to escape its cage.

The text is simple: "How about lunch? I know a great place. — Caden."

My heart stutters at the screen, and I fight the impulse to read his message with skepticism. I tell myself this is just another casual meeting, a friendly lunch. But deep down, I know the truth; it's anything but. I hesitate, biting my lip as I consider the implications. I have plans today, but they are vague and unstructured, much like the notion of my own feelings toward him.

After a brief internal debate, I respond with a coy, "I guess I could be persuaded. Where?"

A moment later, my phone pings again. "Meet me at The Greenhouse in thirty?"

A jolt of anticipation zips through me. The Greenhouse is a trendy little café known for its sprawling outdoor seating adorned with twinkling fairy lights and vibrant flowers. It's the kind of place that feels alive, an oasis amid the urban landscape. I can picture it now, the scent of freshly brewed coffee mingling with the fragrance of blooming plants. It's the perfect backdrop for the burgeoning connection that has formed between us, a blend of light and shadow, hope and trepidation.

When I arrive, the café is buzzing with life. Patrons sit at sun-kissed tables, laughter bubbling up like champagne. I spot Caden right away, seated at a corner table, his striking figure framed by a backdrop of cascading greenery. He glances up, and our eyes lock, an electric current passing between us that makes my pulse race.

"Glad you could make it," he says, his grin broadening as I approach. There's an ease about him, an effortless charm that makes my heart flutter, despite the lingering doubt that festers beneath my skin.

"Wouldn't miss it for the world," I reply, trying to sound nonchalant as I take a seat opposite him. "What's the occasion? Or are you just after my culinary expertise?"

He chuckles, the sound warm and inviting. "I figured it was about time we had a proper conversation, don't you think? The balcony vibes were nice, but I want to know you. Really know you."

The sincerity in his gaze sends another shiver down my spine. "And what if I don't want to be known?" I challenge, crossing my arms over my chest in a defensive posture.

"Then I guess we'll just have to figure that out together," he replies, undeterred, the corner of his mouth quirking up. "But I'm pretty persistent."

We order our meals—an eclectic mix of salads and sandwiches that mirror the café's vibrant atmosphere. The conversation flows easily, infused with humor and teasing banter that reveals glimpses of our lives, our passions. I find myself laughing, the sound bubbling up from somewhere deep within, startling me with its intensity.

"Okay, your turn," I say, my curiosity piqued. "What's the deal with you? You seem like the kind of guy who has a million stories tucked away, but I'm not buying the mysterious act. There's something there, something deeper."

He leans back, studying me for a moment, the light shifting across his features. "You're perceptive, I'll give you that. But I'm not sure I'm ready to share everything."

"Not everything," I assure him, "just enough to keep me from thinking you might be an undercover agent or something."

He laughs, the sound rich and genuine. "I promise I'm not an agent. Just a guy trying to figure things out. Life gets complicated, you know?"

I nod, my heart racing with an urge to push for more, to peel back the layers he guards so closely. "Everyone has baggage, Caden. But you can't keep people at bay forever. It's exhausting."

"Trust me, I know," he admits, his voice dropping slightly. "But sometimes it's easier to keep the walls up. It's safer."

The weight of his words hangs in the air, and for a moment, I feel a flicker of empathy. I want to reach out, to bridge that distance and show him that vulnerability can be freeing. "What if I told you that letting someone in might just be the best thing you could do?"

He meets my gaze, the tension shifting palpably between us, a delicate balance of desire and uncertainty. "What if I told you that I'm scared of what that might mean?"

"Then I'd say you're human."

His eyes flicker with something unspoken, a moment suspended in time where the world around us fades into a blur. Just as I'm about to lean in closer, to navigate the distance between us, the moment is shattered by a loud crash. A tray slips from a nearby table, glass shattering and coffee splattering across the concrete floor.

Instinctively, I look over, the distraction pulling us both back into reality. As the staff rushes to clean up the mess, I turn back to Caden, and the momentary spark has dimmed, replaced by an unsettling silence.

"See? Life throws curveballs when you least expect it," he murmurs, the intensity in his eyes giving way to a flicker of uncertainty.

"True, but we have to keep moving forward," I say, trying to reclaim the lightness we had moments before. "So, tell me, what's next for you? What are you really looking for?"

He opens his mouth, hesitates, and then looks down at the table, running his fingers along the edge of his plate. "Honestly? I'm still figuring that out. But I know I want something more than what I've had."

"And what's that?"

He meets my gaze again, a seriousness settling between us, something raw and unfiltered. "I want... someone who understands the messiness of life, someone who doesn't shy away from the dark parts, who can handle the intensity. Someone like you."

The words hang heavy, stirring a whirlwind of emotions within me. I want to be that person, but the shadows in my own life loom large, threatening to consume any semblance of clarity I might find in him.

"Caden," I start, but my voice falters, uncertainty flooding in as I wrestle with the weight of his declaration.

"Just think about it," he interrupts, his tone softening, almost pleading. "I'm not asking for anything right now. Just... let's keep exploring this, whatever it is."

A rush of warmth floods through me at his invitation, a promise of something exhilarating and terrifying all at once. I nod slowly, feeling both exhilarated and trapped in the beautiful chaos of it all.

As we leave The Greenhouse, the sun is beginning to set, casting a warm golden hue over the city. The sky is a canvas of oranges and purples, the colors bleeding together like watercolors in a novice's hands. Caden walks beside me, his presence both reassuring and unsettling, as if he's a magnet drawing me in yet threatening to pull apart the delicate threads of my well-ordered life.

"I can't believe I almost spilled my drink all over you," I laugh, recalling the chaos that erupted in the café. "You're lucky; I'm usually a complete klutz."

"Maybe it's fate trying to keep us from getting too comfortable," he replies, a glint of humor in his eyes. "Or maybe it's just a sign that you should let me be the one to spill things on you."

"Wow, quite the gentleman," I retort, rolling my eyes. "I'll keep that in mind for our next outing."

We walk in companionable silence for a moment, and I can feel the energy humming between us, a tension that feels both exciting and frightening. My thoughts drift back to his words over lunch, that he wanted someone who could handle the intensity. Did he really see that in me? The thought sends a thrill through my chest.

"So, what's next on your agenda?" he asks, breaking the silence and diverting my thoughts. "You've had your adventure for the day. Any wild plans?"

"Wild plans? You must have me confused with someone else," I tease. "I'm usually a fan of quiet nights in, perhaps with a good book and a pint of ice cream."

He laughs, the sound rich and unguarded. "I like that idea. But you should also try living a little dangerously. You know, mixing flavors of ice cream that don't usually go together."

"Rebel," I smirk, nudging him playfully with my shoulder.

As we stroll down the bustling street, I notice the way his hand brushes against mine, a lingering touch that makes my heart race. It's thrilling and terrifying, and I wrestle with the conflicting feelings that swirl within me.

"Tell me something," I say, a little more serious now. "What do you fear the most?"

He stops walking, turning to face me, and for a moment, I think he might laugh it off. Instead, he studies me, his expression turning contemplative. "I fear losing myself," he admits quietly. "I've worked hard to be who I am, and sometimes I worry that letting someone in means giving that up."

His honesty strikes a chord within me, echoing my own fears. I understand the weight of that sentiment; vulnerability can feel like standing on the edge of a cliff, a daunting leap into the unknown. "I get that," I say softly. "But isn't that also where real growth happens? When we allow ourselves to be seen?"

"Touché," he replies, a smirk playing on his lips, though I can tell he's grappling with the truth of it. "Maybe I'm just being a coward."

"Or maybe you're just cautious," I counter, shrugging as we resume our walk. "Nothing wrong with that. We all have our walls, but it takes real courage to let someone help tear them down."

The air around us crackles with tension, the kind that makes the world feel alive and electric. Just as I'm about to say something more, a sharp shout slices through the evening air, jolting me from the moment.

"Hey! Watch where you're going!"

I turn to see a couple arguing nearby, a man gesturing wildly while a woman stands with her arms crossed, clearly fed up. Their voices escalate, and I glance back at Caden, who looks intrigued rather than annoyed.

"Drama on the streets," he muses, a wry smile forming. "You think they're together?"

"Together or not, they need a better way to communicate," I reply, shaking my head. "But it's just a reminder that life is messy."

"True, but I'd rather deal with that mess with you than anyone else."

My heart flutters, and I meet his gaze, searching for a hint of what he really means. Before I can respond, the shouting intensifies, and I watch as the man suddenly storms off, leaving the woman standing there, her shoulders slumping in defeat.

"Wow, that escalated quickly," I mutter, half-laughing to diffuse the tension.

Caden chuckles, but I can see a flicker of concern in his eyes. "Life is unpredictable. You never know what someone is going through."

"That's true," I agree, my mind racing back to our earlier conversation. "But sometimes, the unpredictability can lead to something amazing."

He looks at me intently, and I feel the heat rising in my cheeks. "Like what?" he asks, his voice a low murmur, drawing me closer.

I hesitate, aware that the moment feels charged with unspoken possibilities. "Like new adventures, connections that could change everything..."

Before I can finish, the couple's argument resumes, and the man suddenly spins back around, his face flushed with anger. "What are you looking at?" he barks, his gaze landing on us, narrowing as he approaches.

Caden steps protectively in front of me, a tension rippling through his frame. "Hey, we're just passing by. No need to escalate things."

"Yeah? Well, mind your own business!" the man snaps, fists clenched, his eyes wild with emotion.

I step back slightly, my heart racing. "Caden, maybe we should just go," I whisper, anxiety coiling in my stomach.

"No, it's fine," he replies, his tone steady as he meets the man's gaze. "But you need to calm down. This isn't the way to handle things."

I can feel the danger thrumming in the air, a visceral tension that sets every nerve on edge. The woman, still standing a few paces away, looks on, her expression a mixture of fear and frustration.

"What's your problem?" the man snaps, taking a step closer, the threat palpable.

Before I can react, Caden raises his hands in a gesture of peace. "Let's just walk away. No one wants a fight."

But the man isn't backing down, his anger bubbling over. "You think you're better than me?"

I can feel Caden's body tense beside me, an unspoken understanding passing between us. There's no way to defuse this without getting caught in the crossfire, and my heart races as I scan the area for an escape route.

In that moment of uncertainty, something clicks in my mind—a realization that this is more than just an argument. It's a test, one that will determine whether I can truly embrace the unpredictability that Caden represents. And before I know it, I'm moving toward the man, adrenaline flooding my veins.

"Hey!" I call out, my voice steady despite the tremors in my chest. "This isn't worth it! Let's just walk away."

He turns to me, eyes flashing with surprise, but there's no time to gauge his reaction. The world around us seems to slow, the air thick with tension. Caden stands firm beside me, his expression a mixture of admiration and alarm.

And then, before I can catch my breath, the man lunges forward, a whirlwind of chaos erupting around us. Time freezes as everything descends into a blur, my heart pounding as I realize this is only the beginning.

Chapter 4: The Mask Slips

The sun dipped below the horizon, casting a warm golden hue across the sprawling estate that Caden called home, the kind of place where dreams seemed to blossom and wilt in the same breath. The air was thick with the scent of cedar and something sweet that I couldn't quite place—a floral hint that felt alive, almost whispering secrets in the fading light. I'd always imagined weekends like this to be idyllic; a chance to escape the mundane and bask in the glow of romance. But here I was, seated on the plush, overstuffed couch of Caden's living room, fingers nervously tracing the seams of the throw blanket draped over my legs, my heart racing with the growing tension swirling around us.

Caden was at the window, silhouetted against the dimming light, looking every bit the picture of casual elegance. His dark hair fell in soft waves over his forehead, his sharp jawline highlighted by the soft glow of the lamp on the table beside him. He wore a simple gray sweater that clung to his broad shoulders, a contrast to the manicured perfection that usually surrounded him. The air was filled with a silence that felt like a taut string, ready to snap, and it made me feel as if I were holding my breath underwater, longing for the surface.

"Are you even listening to me?" I finally broke the silence, my voice a whisper that barely carried across the room.

He turned slowly, his expression unreadable. "What's there to listen to? You're talking about the weather, Ellie." His tone was clipped, his eyes narrowing in irritation, and a chill washed over me. It wasn't the Caden I knew—the charming, attentive man who could talk for hours about anything and everything.

"Not just the weather. I thought we could go for a walk later, explore the grounds or—"

"Why do you always insist on making plans?" The sharpness in his voice cut through me, and I felt the warmth of the room evaporate as he stepped closer, the scent of his cologne mingling with the sweetness of the fading flowers outside. It was intoxicating, but there was an undercurrent of something dark—something I couldn't quite place.

"I thought you enjoyed it," I replied, my voice faltering. I fought the urge to back away, to shield myself from whatever this was turning into.

He stepped forward, and for a fleeting moment, I saw something raw in his eyes, a flash of anger that made my stomach churn. "Sometimes I just want to be. Can't we just enjoy the moment?"

His words struck me like a slap, and I felt the rush of adrenaline as a wave of panic surged within me. I'd seen glimpses of his temper before—little flashes during trivial disagreements—but this felt different. This felt dangerous. I forced myself to meet his gaze, and just as quickly as the anger appeared, it vanished.

"I'm sorry," he said, the corners of his mouth curving into that familiar, charming smile that had once disarmed me. "I didn't mean to snap. It's just... sometimes, being here reminds me of things I'd rather forget."

I searched his eyes for the truth behind the mask he wore, the one I was beginning to think might be painted with shades darker than I could comprehend. I opened my mouth, the question sitting at the tip of my tongue, but a rush of uncertainty flooded me. Instead, I chose to let it simmer, hoping for a moment of clarity.

"Let's forget the plans," I finally said, forcing a smile, trying to navigate the choppy waters of his emotions. "We could just... talk. Just you and me."

He moved closer, wrapping his arms around my waist and pulling me into him. The warmth of his body was an anchor in the storm of confusion brewing in my heart. "I'd like that," he murmured, his breath brushing against my ear, sending shivers down my spine.

As the evening wore on, the darkness outside crept in, wrapping around the house like a suffocating blanket. We settled into the soft glow of the lamps, but something about the intimacy felt precarious, like a house of cards poised to collapse at any moment. He filled the space with stories of his childhood, anecdotes that danced around the edges of something deeper, something that made me itch with curiosity. I leaned in, eager to hear more, but every time I pressed a little harder, I could feel him retreating.

I watched as he slipped back behind the polished veneer he presented to the world, the laughter that rang out felt hollow. It was as if he was performing, and the show was starting to wear thin. Just when I thought I'd deciphered the riddle that was Caden, he'd pull a new card from his sleeve, one that only left me more bewildered.

As the clock ticked closer to midnight, the tension snapped back into focus. I could no longer ignore the feeling that hung in the air like a thick fog, obscuring the path ahead. "What are you so afraid of?" I blurted out, the words escaping my lips before I could catch them.

His expression changed, shifting from playful to something that made the room feel impossibly small. "I'm not afraid of anything," he said, the words low and gravelly. "You have to understand, some things are better left buried."

The weight of his gaze bore into me, and for the first time, I felt the chill of warning creeping in. I'd stumbled upon a truth he wasn't ready to share, and the realization felt like stepping onto thin ice. I took a breath, steadying myself against the sudden cold that had seeped into the room.

But just as quickly, he brushed my hair back from my face, his touch featherlight, and I could feel the heat between us reigniting, a flame flickering defiantly against the shadows. "You're not afraid, are you?" he teased, his lips curling into a smirk that felt too effortless.

I managed a laugh, though it felt brittle in my throat. "Maybe I should be." I leaned back, letting the tension break for a moment, but the truth lingered like a specter between us, refusing to be ignored.

The night wore on, the conversation shifting, the laughter returning, but the edges were frayed, and I could feel the cracks in the foundation of what we had built together. And while I wanted to believe in the warmth of his embrace and the charm of his smile, something whispered that I was treading on dangerous ground. With every heartbeat, I could feel the distance growing, and as the moon cast its silvery light across the room, I was left with a gnawing fear that the man I loved was not the man I thought he was.

The next morning arrived with a crispness that felt like a reset button had been pressed. Light streamed through the tall windows, splashing across the room in golden patches, chasing away the shadows that had clung to the corners during the night. The scent of freshly brewed coffee wafted from the kitchen, mingling with the faintest hint of cinnamon, a reminder that Caden had promised breakfast. I could hear the clatter of pans, the soft hum of music playing in the background, as I pulled myself from the cocoon of blankets and headed toward the kitchen.

Caden stood at the stove, his back to me, clad in a black T-shirt that hugged his torso perfectly, outlining the contours of his body in a way that sent a familiar flutter through my stomach. The sunlight caught the edges of his dark hair, illuminating it like a halo. He turned at the sound of my footsteps, his face lighting up in that charming way that had drawn me in from the very start.

"Good morning, sleepyhead," he said, his voice smooth like the coffee he poured into a steaming mug. "I was about to send a search party."

"Ha! As if I'd let you escape that easily," I replied, leaning against the counter, folding my arms in mock defiance. "What's cooking? I hope it's not just toast."

"Your breakfast is a surprise," he teased, raising an eyebrow playfully. "But I promise it's more exciting than toast. It's a secret family recipe."

"A secret? Now I'm intrigued," I said, trying to ignore the echo of our earlier conversation lingering in my mind. I took a deep breath, attempting to shake off the unease. The charm was back; it was as if the previous night had never happened.

Caden moved with the confidence of someone accustomed to the kitchen, flipping pancakes with a flourish, the batter rising in golden mounds. I watched him, captivated by the effortless way he managed the task, my heart warming at the sight of him so comfortably at home in this space. "So, what's the secret ingredient? A dash of love? A sprinkle of chaos?"

"More like a heaping dose of good intentions," he shot back with a grin, pouring syrup over the pancakes like an artist adding the final brush strokes to a masterpiece. "The chaos comes later."

"Looking forward to it," I replied, but my voice had an edge of hesitation that I couldn't quite shake off. I took a seat at the breakfast bar, watching him as he set the food in front of me.

The pancakes were fluffy, adorned with fresh berries and a dollop of whipped cream that looked almost too good to eat. I took a bite, letting the sweet flavor dance on my tongue. "Wow, this is incredible," I exclaimed, my eyes widening. "You should be a chef instead of...whatever it is you do."

"Careful, or I might take that seriously," he replied, leaning closer, a playful glint in his eye. "And then we'd have to switch roles. You'd be stuck with my paperwork while I whipped up breakfast every day."

"Sounds like a fair trade," I said, feigning a thoughtful expression. "But I have to admit, I'd miss your charming smile during those long hours in the office."

His gaze softened, the moment stretching between us like a tightrope, and for a heartbeat, I thought we might find a way back to the ease we once shared. But just as quickly, the flicker of something darker danced in his eyes, and I felt the knot in my stomach tighten again.

"Speaking of the office, I've been thinking about our little talk last night," he said, his tone shifting as he retreated behind the shield of his carefully constructed persona. "I don't want you to worry about me. I'm fine."

"Are you really?" I asked, the question slipping from my lips before I could hold it back. "You seemed...different. It's okay to have bad days, Caden."

He straightened, his body suddenly rigid. "I appreciate your concern, Ellie, but I'd prefer to keep my issues private." The air grew thick with tension, and I felt the warmth of the breakfast fading, replaced by an uncomfortable chill.

"Caden, I care about you," I said, keeping my voice steady, determined to breach the wall he was so intent on building. "I just want to help. But I can't if you shut me out."

He regarded me for a long moment, his jaw clenched, and I could sense the storm brewing beneath the surface. "Sometimes, help isn't what I need. Sometimes, I just need to be left alone."

His words sliced through me, and I pushed my plate aside, my appetite gone. "Is that really what you want? To be alone?" The question hung in the air like a dare, and his expression shifted—an imperceptible crack in his facade.

"Not always," he said, his voice barely above a whisper. The moment passed, and in a heartbeat, he was smiling again, but the flicker of vulnerability lingered, begging me to dig deeper.

"Let's forget about this for now. I promised you an adventure today, remember?" he said, sliding back into his role with practiced ease. "How about we take a walk through the gardens? I have a surprise waiting for you."

I hesitated, weighing the balance between my heart and my head. Something deep inside urged caution, but my desire to keep him close drowned out the warnings. "Sure, a walk sounds nice."

He led the way outside, and I followed him into the crisp morning air, where the sun cast playful shadows over the manicured lawns. The garden was a masterpiece in itself, bursting with colors that seemed to rival the very canvas of a painter's imagination. Flowers bloomed in reckless abandon, each petal telling a story of its own, and I inhaled deeply, allowing the floral notes to wash over me, soothing my nerves.

As we strolled along the winding paths, I tried to absorb the beauty around us—the vibrant marigolds, the delicate orchids, the hedges trimmed to perfection. But the vibrant hues of nature faded against the unease still swirling within me. I caught glimpses of Caden's smile, but there was a distance behind it that made my heart race with confusion.

"Here it is!" he exclaimed suddenly, stopping before a grand oak tree that stood like a sentinel in the center of the garden, its branches stretching outward as if embracing the sky. Beneath its sprawling limbs, a blanket was spread out, adorned with an array of pastries and fruit.

I couldn't help but laugh, the tension in my chest easing slightly. "You really went all out, didn't you?" I stepped closer, taking in the spread with delight.

"Only the best for you," he said, his eyes glinting with something unreadable. He gestured toward the basket, "I even brought your favorite—raspberry tarts."

My heart warmed at his thoughtfulness, and I felt a rush of affection, the kind that could temporarily distract me from the shadows lurking at the edges of my mind. But as we settled down on the blanket, the uneasy feeling lingered like an unwelcome guest.

"Tell me about this tree," I said, hoping to steer the conversation toward lighter topics. "Is it part of your family lore?"

He chuckled softly, leaning back against the trunk. "More like a family legend. My great-grandfather planted it the day my grandmother was born. They say it's lucky."

"Lucky, huh?" I nudged him playfully. "Does that mean I'm lucky too, sitting here with you?"

He smirked, the banter flowing easily again. "Only if you promise not to bring up my dark past."

"Now you're just being melodramatic," I teased, settling beside him and reaching for a tart. "But I can keep the past under wraps if you share some secrets of your own."

His laughter was genuine, but there was still a flicker of hesitation in his eyes. "Maybe just one secret for now," he said, his gaze locking onto mine. "But promise me you won't judge."

"Promise," I said, my heart pounding in anticipation.

He took a deep breath, the lighthearted air between us shifting again. "I used to think I was invincible, that nothing could touch me or my family. But then life happened." The vulnerability in his voice was tangible, each word layered with unspoken history.

"I'm all ears," I encouraged, leaning in closer, determined to pull back the curtain he had drawn so tightly.

"Let's just say that when you grow up in a world where appearances are everything, you learn to keep your mask on. And sometimes, it gets exhausting."

I felt the weight of his words settle around us, and the warmth of the sun began to feel distant, overshadowed by the shadows that danced in his eyes.

The silence stretched between us, thick and expectant, as Caden's words settled into the air like a heavy fog. The light that had filled the garden seemed to dim, shadows curling around us, amplifying the distance I felt creeping back in. I set my tart down, the sweet taste suddenly sour in my mouth, and tried to read the expression on his face, but it was like trying to decipher a complicated code.

"What do you mean by exhausting?" I finally ventured, my heart racing with curiosity and a twinge of fear. "Are you talking about your family or something else?"

He looked away, his gaze drifting over the sprawling landscape beyond the garden, where the trees swayed gently in the breeze, their leaves whispering secrets. "It's all connected. The pressure to maintain this image, to live up to expectations—sometimes it feels like drowning."

I swallowed hard, wrestling with the knowledge that his struggles were woven into the fabric of his being. "But you're not alone, Caden. You don't have to wear that mask with me." I reached out, my fingers brushing against his arm, feeling the tension coiled just beneath his skin.

He turned back to me, and for a fleeting moment, I saw the real Caden—the man beneath the facade, vulnerable yet strong. "You think it's that simple? I've spent years building this life, and the moment I let my guard down..." His voice trailed off, and a flicker of something darker danced in his eyes, sending a shiver down my spine.

"It's not just a mask," he continued, his tone lower now, filled with gravity. "It's armor. And I'm terrified of what happens when I take it off."

A chill ran through me, a realization dawning that maybe the cracks I'd seen weren't just signs of wear but warnings of an impending collapse. I hesitated, weighing my next words. "What are you afraid of? Losing control?"

"More like losing everything," he said, his voice rough around the edges, as if each syllable was a battle. "I've worked hard to create a world that makes sense, and if I start showing weakness..."

"You're not weak for feeling, Caden. We all have our demons." I took a deep breath, hoping to bridge the growing chasm between us. "Whatever you're hiding, it doesn't define you."

He scoffed, the moment shattering like glass underfoot. "You say that, but you don't know what's lurking in my past. You think you want to see the truth, but the reality is messy and dark. People get hurt in that darkness."

I recoiled, the weight of his words pressing down on me. "You mean to tell me you've never had anyone who could help you carry that darkness?"

His expression turned serious, a flicker of something I couldn't quite name crossing his features. "I've always had to protect myself. Trust is a luxury I can't afford."

"Then let me be that luxury," I blurted out, desperate to reach him. "Let me in, even if it means facing those demons together."

The silence that followed was deafening, and I felt the tension wrap around us like a tightrope, poised to snap. For a moment, I thought he might reach out, that he might finally drop the armor and let me see the man underneath. But instead, he turned his gaze to the ground, the weight of my words hanging heavily in the air.

"I can't," he whispered, the finality in his tone making my heart plummet.

A part of me wanted to press, to push until he revealed the secrets I could feel festering just beneath the surface, but I could sense his reluctance to share anything more. "Caden," I began, but he stood abruptly, the blanket rustling around him as he moved away.

"I think I need some air."

"Wait," I said, standing as well. "Where are you going?"

He didn't answer, his steps quickening as he headed toward the far edge of the garden. The sudden distance made my heart race with panic, and I followed him, the vibrant colors around me dulling into a blur as worry surged through my veins.

"Caden!" I called out, but he didn't look back, the tension in his shoulders taut and unyielding. He stopped beneath a tall tree, its branches swaying gently in the wind, and I finally caught up with him.

He leaned against the rough bark, his arms crossed tightly over his chest as if trying to ward off the world itself. "I just need to think," he said, the edge in his voice cutting deeper than I expected.

"Think about what? About pushing me away? Because that's not going to solve anything," I said, frustration bubbling to the surface.

His head snapped up, his expression fierce, and for a moment, I saw the flash of anger that had startled me the night before. "You don't understand. This isn't just about you and me. It's about everything—my family, my life. You have no idea what's at stake."

"Then tell me!" I urged, my voice rising. "You keep shutting me out, and I don't know how to help you if you won't let me in."

He stepped closer, and the intensity in his gaze made my breath hitch. "You really want to know?"

"Yes," I replied, my heart pounding in my chest. "I'm tired of the secrets, Caden. I'm tired of tiptoeing around your past like it's a fragile thing that might shatter at any moment."

"Fine," he snapped, the anger boiling just beneath the surface. "You want to know? My family isn't what it seems. We have history—dark, twisted history. It's not just my past. It's the family legacy I've been trapped in."

"Legacy?" I echoed, my pulse quickening. "What do you mean?"

He ran a hand through his hair, frustration evident in the way he held himself. "Things happened. Bad things. Things I've had to bury so that I could survive."

"Caden, you're scaring me," I said, taking a step back. "What kind of things?"

His expression darkened, and the air between us felt charged with an electric tension. "Things that could ruin everything—my reputation, my family, even you. It's better if you don't get involved."

"Better for whom?" I shot back, my voice rising again. "For you? For your family? What about me? What about us?"

He hesitated, the shadows flickering across his face, and for a brief moment, I thought I saw a crack in his armor. "You don't know what you're asking," he said softly, almost pleadingly.

"I'm asking you to trust me," I insisted, desperation lacing my words. "But I can't do that if you keep pushing me away."

His eyes bore into mine, searching for something that felt elusive. "You're right. You deserve the truth. But are you ready for what that truth might bring?"

"Whatever it is, I can handle it," I promised, though a part of me trembled at the thought of the unknown.

"Then prepare yourself," he said, the weight of his words heavy in the air. "Because the mask I wear is hiding more than just a past. It's a warning of what might come."

Before I could respond, a sharp sound echoed through the garden—a crack like thunder. Caden's body tensed beside me, his eyes widening in alarm as the ground beneath our feet trembled slightly. I glanced around, heart racing, searching for the source of the noise.

"Did you hear that?" I asked, anxiety creeping in.

He nodded, his expression shifting from frustration to fear in an instant. "Stay close to me," he warned, his voice low and urgent.

"What is happening?" I whispered, glancing toward the woods that bordered the estate, the trees standing eerily still, as if holding their breath.

Before he could answer, a figure burst from the shadows, emerging from the thicket of trees. My breath caught in my throat as I recognized the silhouette, a sense of dread pooling in my stomach. The world around us fell silent, the vibrant colors of the garden fading into a blur of uncertainty as the figure stepped into the light, revealing a face I never expected to see.

Caden's hand gripped my arm tightly, his eyes wide with shock. "What are you doing here?" he demanded, the composure he'd worked so hard to maintain slipping away like sand through his fingers.

My heart raced, a whirlwind of confusion and fear swirling in my chest as I tried to comprehend the sudden shift in our reality. The mask had slipped, and in the moment that followed, I realized that everything I thought I understood was about to unravel.

Chapter 5: Into the Darkness

The wind whispered through the trees, a soft, eerie lullaby that danced around me as I stood on the balcony, staring into the star-speckled abyss. I could hear the distant hum of the city, a faint reminder of normalcy that felt worlds away from the whirlwind of emotions that raged inside me. Caden was down there, somewhere in that vibrant maze of lights and shadows, and the thought of him sent a thrill coursing through my veins. Yet, with every heartbeat, an unsettling realization tightened its grip on my chest—he was keeping something from me, something important.

I took a deep breath, letting the cool night air fill my lungs, but it did little to quell the growing storm within. Caden was a tempest, both intoxicating and destructive, and I was willingly adrift on his currents. With each stolen glance, each electrifying touch, I felt my resolve dissolve, replaced by a longing so profound it was almost unbearable. But the darkness lurking beneath his charming facade was a growing shadow, an inkblot on the canvas of our story.

"Hey, earth to Annie," came a voice that sliced through my thoughts, sharp and teasing, pulling me back to the moment. It was Tessa, my ever-loyal friend and the only anchor I had to reality. "You're looking at the stars again. Planning your escape to a galaxy far, far away?"

I turned to her, forcing a smile. "Maybe I am. Wouldn't it be nice to just float away from all this? To leave behind the secrets and the—"

"Caden?" she finished for me, crossing her arms and leaning against the railing. "You know he's not just some charming guy with a dangerous past, right? There's something off about him, Annie. You can't ignore that."

"I'm not ignoring anything," I snapped, a little harsher than I intended. I had been wrestling with my emotions, trying to piece together the fragments of Caden's life he had shared with me. It wasn't much—only glimpses of a world filled with money, power, and shadows. "I just think he has his reasons."

"Reasons?" Tessa raised an eyebrow, the skepticism radiating off her like an electric charge. "His reasons are likely to get you hurt. You're diving into the deep end, and I'm not sure you know how to swim."

I sighed, pinching the bridge of my nose, the tension in my shoulders creeping higher. "I know what I feel, and I know what he's done for me. He's been there when I needed him. More than anyone else."

"Yeah, but what about when you don't need him? When his past catches up with him, and you're the one standing in the way?" Her voice softened, turning almost pleading. "You deserve someone who's an open book, Annie, not a mystery wrapped in a riddle. Don't let the allure blind you."

Just then, the front door swung open, and Caden stepped out, his silhouette framed against the warm light spilling from inside. He looked like a scene pulled from a dream—his dark hair tousled, shirt slightly wrinkled, and those piercing blue eyes that held a universe of secrets. The sight of him sent a flutter through my stomach, a battle between desire and the dread of what lay beneath the surface.

"Annie," he called out, his voice low and smooth, like honey dripping from a spoon. "I thought I'd find you out here."

Tessa shot me a warning glance, her mouth set in a tight line. I met her gaze, the unspoken message clear: be careful. But the moment Caden was close, his presence suffocating any doubt, all I could think about was the way he made me feel—alive, electric, whole.

"Hey," I managed to say, my heart racing as he stepped onto the balcony, the tension between us palpable, like a taut string ready to snap. "Just enjoying the view."

He leaned against the railing beside me, his arm brushing against mine, igniting a fire that shot through my skin. "The view's nice, but you're the one who really stands out," he replied, his voice laced with that familiar charm.

Tessa cleared her throat, the sound sharp enough to cut through the moment. "Caden," she began, her tone tinged with an edge I didn't like, "Annie and I were just talking about—"

"I'm sure you were," he interrupted smoothly, his gaze shifting from Tessa to me, his expression turning serious. "Annie, I need to talk to you."

My pulse quickened, the words hanging in the air like a tightrope stretched across an abyss. "About what?" I asked, forcing myself to sound casual, but inside I was a tempest of nerves.

"About me," he said, his tone dropping lower, drawing me in. "There's something I haven't told you—something I need to explain before this goes any further."

Tessa shifted uncomfortably, the atmosphere thick with tension as she glanced between us. "I'll, uh, give you two some space," she said finally, her voice hesitant, as if she were sensing the storm brewing. She walked inside, leaving us in a silence that felt charged, alive with anticipation.

Caden turned to me, his expression serious, the lightness of his earlier demeanor slipping away like sand through fingers. "I never wanted to involve you in my world, Annie. It's dark, and I—"

"Caden," I interrupted, unable to hold back the swell of emotion. "I care about you. I can handle it. Just tell me the truth."

He hesitated, his jaw tightening as he seemed to weigh his words. "There are things I've done—people I've dealt with—that could put you in danger. I'm trying to protect you. You deserve a life free of this chaos."

"Protecting me by keeping secrets?" My voice shook, a mix of frustration and fear. "I can't build anything with you if I don't know who you really are."

He stepped closer, invading my space, his eyes dark and stormy. "What if knowing the truth tears us apart? What if I lose you?"

"Better to lose me now than lose me later when the truth comes crashing down," I insisted, my heart racing with the weight of what lay ahead. "Please, Caden. I need to know."

He exhaled slowly, the tension in his shoulders easing just a fraction. "You might regret this."

"Try me," I challenged, the fire in my belly igniting as I stared into his turbulent gaze, daring him to unravel the secrets that could change everything.

The tension hung in the air between us, a fine thread of unspoken truths and restless fears. Caden's expression darkened, his shoulders taut as if he were bracing against an invisible storm. I held my breath, caught in the moment, each heartbeat echoing like thunder in the silence that stretched out before us. He took a step back, shoving his hands into the pockets of his jeans, a defensive posture that made my stomach twist with anxiety.

"Alright, then," he said finally, his voice low and gravelly, the weight of his words sinking into the cool night air. "But you need to understand that what I'm about to tell you might change everything."

"Good or bad?" I replied, crossing my arms tightly against the sudden chill that settled over me. I could feel the air thicken, the atmosphere charged with uncertainty. "I mean, I'm all for revelations, but I'd prefer it not be a complete horror story."

"Life isn't a fairy tale, Annie," he murmured, his gaze flickering to the ground, the flickering light from the balcony illuminating his features. "Sometimes, it's more like a dark fable where the hero has to make hard choices."

"Hero? Are we sure we're talking about you?" I couldn't help but let a teasing lilt creep into my voice, trying to break the suffocating tension. "You're not exactly a knight in shining armor, Caden. More like a rogue with a questionable backstory."

He chuckled softly, the sound wrapping around me like a warm blanket, but it didn't hide the shadows lurking in his eyes. "Fair point. Let's just say I've made some deals that weren't exactly... above board. You've seen the people I work with, the kinds of businesses I'm involved in."

"Yeah, the kind that seem straight out of a mob movie," I replied, keeping my tone light, though my heart raced in response. "You really expect me to believe it's all just a game of poker and late-night calls?"

Caden met my gaze, his expression earnest yet guarded. "There are things in my past I can't discuss. Not yet. Just know that I've made choices—bad ones. And those choices have consequences that extend beyond me." He hesitated, the weight of his silence palpable, before continuing, "I never wanted to drag you into this mess. You deserve better."

"And you think I'd just run away because it's messy?" I challenged, stepping closer, my voice steady despite the turmoil inside. "You don't get to decide what I deserve, Caden. I'm the one in this with you."

"You're saying that now, but when the walls start closing in—" he began, his voice tinged with a hint of desperation.

"I'm saying I'm not afraid of the walls," I interrupted, my resolve hardening. "But I need you to be honest with me. You don't get to keep pushing me away under the guise of 'protecting' me. If you truly care, you'll let me in."

He raked a hand through his hair, frustration etching deeper lines into his brow. "You think it's easy for me? I'm trying to protect you from a world that doesn't give a damn about anyone. You think I enjoy this?"

"Enjoy what?" I asked, my irritation flaring. "Enjoy being cryptic? Enjoy watching me worry about you while you play this game of shadows?"

Caden's lips pressed into a thin line, and he seemed to wrestle with himself, the battle playing out across his features. "I'm involved in things that could put you in danger. You have no idea what kind of people I'm dealing with. If they knew about you—"

"Then I guess we need to make sure they don't," I replied, a steely determination hardening my resolve. "But don't you dare make this about me being weak or naive. I've faced my own darkness, Caden. I know how to fight."

His expression shifted, a flicker of admiration breaking through the tension. "You're incredibly stubborn, you know that?"

"Only when it comes to people I care about," I shot back, unable to suppress the smile creeping onto my lips. "So, are you going to keep talking in riddles, or are you going to spill the beans?"

Caden sighed, his gaze drifting towards the skyline, where the city lights twinkled like stars trapped on Earth. "I'm part of something... complicated. It involves people who don't play by the rules. There's money involved, power struggles—things I never wanted. But it's a part of who I am now, and it's a part I can't just walk away from."

"Are you saying you're in some sort of criminal organization?" My voice was a mix of incredulity and disbelief, the pieces of this puzzle clicking together in a way I hadn't anticipated.

"It's not that simple," he replied, his voice tight. "I didn't choose this life; it chose me. My father was involved, and it's been a cycle of obligations and loyalties I've been trying to break for years. I thought I could keep you out of it, keep you safe, but now..." He paused, his gaze locking onto mine with an intensity that sent a shiver down my spine. "Now, I don't know how to keep you safe from my past."

The vulnerability in his voice was like a soft knife cutting through the armor I'd built around my heart. I stepped closer, closing the distance between us, my fingers brushing against his. "You're not alone, Caden. Whatever mess you're in, we can figure it out together."

His expression softened, a flicker of hope igniting in his eyes, and I felt the world around us blur, leaving just the two of us standing on that balcony, suspended in time. "I wish it were that simple."

"Life rarely is," I countered, my voice barely above a whisper, the gravity of his past pulling me in deeper. "But you need to let me in. If you want me to understand, you have to show me the whole picture."

Caden took a deep breath, and for a fleeting moment, it seemed as if he might finally let the walls crumble. "There's a reason my associates are so dangerous. They won't hesitate to hurt anyone who threatens their interests, and if they discover you—"

"Then we'll make sure they don't," I interrupted, my determination unwavering. "I'm not about to let fear dictate our lives. If you trust me, we can navigate this together."

He looked at me, a mixture of admiration and disbelief reflected in his eyes. "You really mean that?"

"Of course, I do," I said, trying to sound braver than I felt. "I didn't fall for you because of the shadows; I fell for you because of the light you showed me. If you're willing to trust me, I won't let you down."

Caden's lips quirked into a half-smile, the shadows flickering in his eyes slowly dissipating. "You might be the craziest person I know."

"Crazy is my middle name," I shot back, relief flooding through me. "Now, let's tackle your darkness together. Just promise me we won't let it consume us."

He took a step closer, wrapping his arms around me, and I melted into him, the warmth of his body a balm against the chaos outside. "Deal," he murmured against my hair, and in that moment, the weight of the world shifted just a fraction, as if the tides were beginning to turn in our favor.

The moment hung between us, heavy with unspoken words and a fragile hope that seemed to glow brighter in the dark. Caden held me close, the warmth of his body igniting something within me, something fierce and unyielding. "If you're in this with me, you need to understand the risks," he murmured, his breath tickling my hair, sending shivers down my spine.

"I can handle risks," I replied, the determination in my voice surprising even me. "But you have to promise me one thing."

"What's that?" he asked, his tone curious, as though he were afraid of the answer.

"Promise me you won't shut me out anymore. Whatever you're involved in, I want to face it with you. Together," I insisted, pulling back just enough to meet his gaze, searching his eyes for any hint of reluctance.

He hesitated, a flicker of doubt crossing his features. "Annie, it's not just about the business deals or the money. There are people who don't take kindly to threats. If they think you're a liability—"

"Then I'll make sure I'm not," I interrupted, my voice steady. "I'm not about to hide in the shadows. We can't keep pretending everything is fine when it's not."

Caden's jaw tightened, and I could see the struggle within him, the part of him that wanted to protect me clashing with the undeniable bond we shared. "You don't know what you're asking for," he said, his voice low and gravelly. "You might think you're ready for this, but I don't want to see you get hurt."

"Hurt is a part of life," I countered, my heart racing. "But being left in the dark is worse. Trust me, Caden. Let me in."

He searched my face, and for a moment, I thought I might have cracked the armor he wore like a second skin. Finally, he nodded, albeit reluctantly. "Alright. I'll tell you everything."

The weight of his words hung between us, heavy yet liberating. I felt a surge of adrenaline at the thought of finally understanding the complexities of his life. "Let's start with the people you work with," I prompted, leaning in, eager to unravel the threads of his past.

"Fine," he said, releasing a breath he seemed to have been holding. "There's a group I'm involved with—business associates who operate in the gray areas. They're not just in it for the money; they have power, connections. They expect loyalty, and failing to deliver has consequences."

I could feel the tension in the air thicken, each word he spoke pulling me deeper into a world I had only glimpsed. "Loyalty to who?" I pressed. "To the business, or to them personally?"

"Both," he replied, his eyes narrowing. "These are not people you want to cross. I've seen what they can do to those who betray them. They have eyes everywhere, and if they sense even a hint of weakness... well, let's just say it's not a pretty picture."

"What do you mean?" My pulse quickened, a knot forming in my stomach. "Are you saying they're dangerous?"

Caden looked away, his gaze drifting to the city below, where the lights twinkled like stars against the inky black sky. "Dangerous doesn't even begin to cover it. They don't play by the rules, and anyone who gets in their way is dealt with harshly. I've been trying to find a way out of this for years, but every time I think I have a plan, they pull me back in."

"And you think it's safer to keep me in the dark?" I asked, my voice rising slightly, the frustration bubbling to the surface. "You're making decisions for me, and I won't have it!"

"Maybe it's better this way," he shot back, the heat of our argument simmering just beneath the surface. "I don't want you to get dragged into something you can't handle. I would never forgive myself if something happened to you."

My heart pounded as I searched his eyes for the vulnerability that had been there moments ago. "You're not giving me enough credit, Caden. I can handle my own life. If we're going to make this work, you have to let me in completely. I need to know what we're up against."

"Fine," he said, exasperation etched across his features. "There's a particular associate—his name is Victor. He's ruthless, calculating, and he doesn't take kindly to anyone who questions his authority. He's made it clear that he doesn't like me stepping out of line. If I don't stay loyal, I risk everything."

"What do you mean by stepping out of line?" I pressed, my heart racing as I imagined the depths of his troubles.

"He has this hold over me," Caden admitted, his voice dropping to a near whisper. "I owe him money, and he's been leveraging that against me, making demands that I can't ignore. I've done things for him that I'm not proud of, things that haunt me."

"What kind of things?" My heart sank at the weight of his words, the shadows creeping back into the corners of my mind.

He hesitated, his gaze slipping away from mine as he grappled with the ghosts of his past. "I've helped him move product, negotiate deals—things that put me in compromising positions. I thought I could handle it, keep it all under control, but I was wrong. It's spiraled out of my grasp."

"Caden, you can't keep carrying this alone," I said, stepping closer, the urgency of the situation pressing against us like an unwelcome force. "You need to cut ties with him. Find a way to break free."

His eyes flashed with a mixture of hope and despair. "I've been trying. But every time I think I'm close, he pulls me back in, reminding me of what I owe. I don't know how much longer I can play this game without losing everything—especially you."

The words hung heavy in the air, each syllable a reminder of the stakes we faced. Just then, a low rumble echoed through the night, a sound that wasn't quite thunder, sending a jolt of unease racing through me. Caden stiffened, his instincts sharpening. "Did you hear that?"

Before I could respond, a flash of headlights broke through the darkness, illuminating the alley below. Caden's body tensed beside me, his focus sharpening as the car pulled to a halt. "Stay here," he warned, moving toward the edge of the balcony, peering down.

"Caden, wait!" I called, panic rising in my throat. "What's happening?"

He turned back to me, his expression serious. "I think it's Victor. I can't let him see you."

"What? You're not leaving me up here!" I protested, my heart racing as I rushed to catch up with him, the gravity of our situation sinking in. "Caden, if this is about him, then I need to be there. You can't handle this alone!"

"Annie—"

But before he could finish, a figure emerged from the shadows, tall and imposing, an aura of menace radiating from him. My blood ran cold as I recognized the man from the brief, chilling glimpses Caden had shared—a man whose mere presence sent a wave of dread crashing over me.

"Caden," the man called out, his voice smooth yet edged with danger. "We need to talk."

The world around me blurred, the air thick with anticipation as I stood frozen, caught between the desire to protect Caden and the instinct to flee. In that moment, the danger was palpable, and I knew that whatever came next could change everything.

Chapter 6: A Dangerous Proposition

The clatter of heels echoed against the polished marble floor, each step punctuating the tension in the air. The sun poured through the floor-to-ceiling windows of Caden's penthouse, casting long shadows that danced like specters across the sleek furniture. I glanced at my reflection in the glass—a wild mane of dark curls framing a face that screamed ambition, yet my heart thudded with apprehension. I was standing on the precipice of something monumental, and the man who had ignited this flame was the very embodiment of danger.

Caden lounged at his desk, an artful display of confidence draped in tailored elegance. His presence was magnetic, pulling at the threads of my resolve. The way he leaned back, fingers steepled under his chin, made me wonder what secrets were buried behind his steel-gray eyes. I had always known there was more to him than the charming smile and seductive wit. The fashion world revered him, but beneath the glitz, I had seen whispers of shadows, glimpses of a man who played a game far too perilous for someone like me.

"Imagine it," he said, his voice smooth as silk, "your designs, my resources. We could redefine fashion together."

The idea settled into my mind like a bead of honey, sweet yet thick with consequence. I had spent years in the trenches of design, sketching dreams that danced just out of reach, and here was Caden, offering me the golden ticket. But that golden ticket came with a trapdoor.

"I don't know, Caden." I tried to keep my tone light, though my heart raced at the mere thought of stepping into his world. "Working for you would be... risky."

"Risky is my middle name," he quipped, a lopsided grin lighting up his face, but the humor faded quickly, replaced by an intensity that drew me in closer. "This isn't just a business proposition. It's a chance to leave a mark on the industry, to create something that resonates."

"Resonates? Or disrupts?" I challenged, crossing my arms, though I couldn't shake the excitement bubbling in my chest. "You know how volatile this industry can be. It's not just about the designs; it's about the players behind them."

"True," he conceded, his expression serious. "But sometimes you have to embrace the chaos to find beauty within it."

As I looked into those stormy eyes, I could feel my defenses wavering. The allure of his world—brimming with power, prestige, and the promise of revolutionizing the runway—was almost intoxicating. But I couldn't ignore the nagging feeling that Caden's world came with its own set of hazards. It was as if I were a moth, drawn to a flame, fully aware that the fire could singe my wings.

"What's the catch?" I asked, straightening my posture, trying to inject some formality into our conversation. "Nothing comes without strings attached when it comes to you."

Caden chuckled softly, a sound that sent a shiver down my spine. "You're sharper than I remember. I like that." He leaned forward, elbows resting on the desk, his gaze unwavering. "The catch is that I need you to be all in. This isn't just a nine-to-five gig. I need someone who can navigate the high stakes, someone who won't flinch when the pressure mounts."

"And if I say no?" The question hung heavy in the air, each syllable a weight that threatened to drag me down.

"Then you'll always wonder what could have been," he replied, a mischievous glint in his eyes. "I can see it in your face. You want this, but you're terrified."

"Terrified is an understatement," I muttered, pacing the length of the room, my mind a whirlwind of thoughts. "But why me? There are countless designers out there who would kill for this opportunity."

"Because you have something they don't," he said, his voice low and persuasive. "You have heart. You create pieces that speak, that evoke emotion. That's what I want for my brand."

His words wrapped around me like a silken scarf, warm and inviting yet suffocating. The thrill of the opportunity danced with the fear of entanglement. I could feel my mind racing, weighing the pros and cons like a seasoned diplomat. On one hand, this was my dream—the chance to see my visions come to life on the most prestigious runways. On the other, I was about to dive headfirst into a maelstrom with a man whose shadows threatened to swallow me whole.

"Fine," I finally blurted out, the word slipping from my lips before I could stop it. "I'll do it."

Caden's eyes lit up, a triumphant spark igniting within them. "You won't regret this," he promised, but there was an undertone, a whisper of warning that sent a chill down my spine.

As the reality of my decision settled in, a shiver of uncertainty raced through me. I was stepping into a realm of glamour and grit, where every decision could have consequences I couldn't begin to fathom. I could almost feel the air shifting, thickening with possibilities and peril. The very idea of Caden—so close, yet shrouded in enigma—made my heart race, stirring something deep within me, something I was not entirely ready to confront.

"We'll start tomorrow," he said, his voice a low rumble that echoed through the vast space. "I'll have my assistant set up everything you need."

And just like that, I was no longer a mere spectator in this dazzling world. I was a player, and Caden was my enigmatic partner in this dangerous dance. The stakes had never been higher, and as I looked out over the city, sprawling and full of life, I realized that I was teetering on the edge of a new beginning, one that could either lift me to unimaginable heights or plunge me into unfathomable depths.

The next morning arrived with a tangle of nerves and excitement twisting in my stomach. I threw on a simple yet elegant black dress, its fabric soft against my skin, a gentle reminder that even in the chaos of high fashion, comfort was key. I could still feel the weight of Caden's proposition from the day before; it hovered like a specter, always just at the edge of my thoughts. I checked the mirror, adjusting my hair, and though I appeared put together, my mind was a whirlwind of possibilities and dread.

Stepping into Caden's world was like entering a parallel universe, where every detail screamed sophistication and ambition. His penthouse, with its panoramic view of the city skyline, was breathtaking. Yet, as I moved through the vast space, I couldn't shake the feeling that I was walking into a lion's den, ready to serve as the main course.

When I arrived, Caden was already there, poring over sketches that lay strewn across his pristine conference table like fallen leaves. He glanced up as I entered, and the warmth of his smile momentarily disarmed me.

"Look who decided to join the fray," he said, his voice laced with mock reproach. "I thought I'd have to send a search party."

"Believe me, I was half tempted to hide under my duvet," I retorted, trying to maintain a lighthearted demeanor despite the anxiety bubbling beneath. "This whole 'working for you' thing is still surreal."

Caden laughed, a rich sound that reverberated through the room, filling the space with a comfort that was both inviting and dangerous. "Embrace the surreal. That's where the magic happens." He gestured for me to join him, and as I settled into the plush chair opposite him, I felt like a moth drawn to a flame—thrilled by the brightness but all too aware of the potential for burning.

"So, what's on the agenda for our little design revolution?" I asked, scanning the sketches laid out before me. They were bold, experimental, and utterly captivating. Each design spoke of innovation and daring, a stark contrast to the safe choices I had often made in my previous work.

"Everything." Caden leaned back in his chair, a glint of mischief in his eye. "We're going to break the mold, push boundaries. I want to see what you can do when you're untethered."

"Untethered? Is that your euphemism for chaos?" I raised an eyebrow, skepticism creeping in. "Because that's a dangerous game, Caden. We might just end up in the headlines for all the wrong reasons."

"Or the right ones," he countered, his tone playful. "This is fashion. We're supposed to shock, to inspire. Don't play it safe; it's dull. We're about to rattle some cages."

His enthusiasm was infectious, and for a moment, I forgot about the dark clouds lurking at the edges of our collaboration. Instead, I let myself dream, to envision my designs gracing runways, to feel the fabric glide through my fingers, the texture of innovation against my skin.

As we delved deeper into the designs, the conversation flowed easily, each idea sparking another. I felt the weight of my earlier trepidation begin to lift. It was exhilarating, like riding a roller coaster at full speed. Caden's energy ignited a fire within me, and I could feel the passion I had nearly forgotten flicker to life.

But just as I began to settle into this new rhythm, the atmosphere shifted. A tension crept in, uninvited and cold, as Caden's phone buzzed insistently on the table. He glanced at the screen, his expression darkening.

"Excuse me for a moment," he said, his voice clipped.

I watched as he stood, the ease of our earlier banter evaporating like morning mist. He stepped away, his back turned to me, and

I couldn't help but feel the sudden weight of uncertainty pressing down on the room. Something wasn't right. The way he held his phone, the tightness in his shoulders—it was as if the walls were closing in.

The minutes dragged on, each tick of the clock amplifying the unease. I rifled through the sketches again, but my mind was too scattered to focus. I felt like a child left alone in a darkened room, and I couldn't shake the instinctual fear that something beyond our design dreams was at play.

When Caden finally returned, his face was a mask of control, but the tension in his jaw betrayed him. "Sorry about that," he said, his tone light but his eyes were shadowed. "Just some... business."

"Business that involves shadows and whispered conversations?" I asked, trying to keep my voice steady.

He shot me a quick, assessing glance before his lips curled into a half-smile. "You're reading too much into it. This industry is rife with intrigue. Just keep your focus on our designs."

"Easy for you to say," I muttered, "you're the king of this realm. I'm just a peasant hoping not to get eaten by the dragons."

Caden laughed again, but it was strained. "Then I'll make sure to have my knights at the ready."

The banter eased some of the tension, but as the day wore on, I couldn't shake the feeling that beneath the surface, there were currents swirling that could easily pull me under. My excitement for the project was tempered by an unsettling awareness that Caden's world was as much about survival as it was about creativity. I was being drawn into a vortex where ambition and danger intertwined, and the thought both thrilled and terrified me.

As we continued to brainstorm ideas, the line between professional and personal blurred dangerously. Caden's smile lingered in my thoughts, and when his fingers brushed against mine while handing me a sketch, a jolt of electricity surged between us, igniting something I had tried to keep buried. I pulled back, a wave of embarrassment washing over me.

"Sorry," he said, a hint of amusement dancing in his eyes. "Didn't mean to shock you."

"Just... startled," I replied, trying to maintain some semblance of composure. "This whole 'creative collaboration' thing is new for me."

"Let's make it unforgettable then." His voice dropped to a husky whisper, and the air thickened with an unspoken promise.

We worked into the evening, the city lights flickering to life outside the glass walls, a reminder of the world spinning just beyond our cocoon. Each moment spent with Caden felt like walking a tightrope, thrilling yet precarious. The fabric of our collaboration was woven with threads of danger and desire, and as I stared at the sketches, I couldn't help but wonder how long I could maintain my balance before it all came crashing down.

The weeks that followed unfolded like a fabric unspooling, revealing threads of creativity intertwined with tension. Each day at Caden's penthouse felt like a balancing act on a high wire, where the stakes were both exhilarating and terrifying. I threw myself into our project, pouring my heart into sketches and fabrics, but there was always a current running beneath the surface, an undercurrent that suggested this wasn't just a partnership. It was a dance with danger.

Caden was relentless in his pursuit of excellence. He pushed me to explore designs that defied convention, urging me to unleash the wildest corners of my imagination. With every late-night brainstorming session, I felt myself getting pulled deeper into his orbit, where ambition and allure blurred together. We worked long hours, surrounded by swatches of bold colors and sketches that captured daring silhouettes, and somehow, through it all, we wove a camaraderie that felt electric.

One evening, as I stood over a particularly intricate design—one that I hoped would steal the show at the upcoming fashion gala—Caden leaned against the doorframe, arms crossed, a playful smirk dancing on his lips. "Are you sure this isn't too much? I mean, a bodice made of silver sequins and feathers? It might cause a small riot."

I shot him a look over my shoulder, feigning indignation. "Riot? This is the kind of thing that stops traffic, Caden! If you're not prepared to have people scream in awe, maybe you should rethink this whole venture."

He chuckled, pushing away from the door and stepping into the room. "You know I love a good spectacle. Just making sure you're prepared for the chaos that comes with it."

"Chaos? Please," I said, waving a hand dismissively. "I've been living in chaos for years. This feels like home."

Caden's laughter echoed in the air, lightening the tension that had been creeping in like shadows. But just as easily, the mirth vanished when his phone buzzed on the table, its screen lighting up with an incoming call. He picked it up, glancing at the name flashing on the screen, and his expression darkened.

"Can we take a break?" he asked, the lightness gone from his voice.

"Of course," I replied, sensing the shift. I turned back to my sketches, but curiosity gnawed at me. Who could possibly demand his attention this late at night? I caught snippets of his conversation—intense, sharp whispers that spoke of deals and deadlines, the kind of language that danced dangerously close to threats. My heart raced as I concentrated, trying to catch more of the words slipping from his lips, but they were too muffled.

When he returned, the air felt thick with unspoken tension, and I suddenly felt like an intruder in a world I had only just begun to explore. "Everything okay?" I ventured, keeping my tone casual.

"Just business," he replied, but the hesitation in his voice was palpable. "Let's focus on what matters."

Yet, I couldn't shake the feeling that there was more at play. Each smile and witty retort began to feel like a carefully constructed facade, and I wondered if I had unknowingly stepped into a narrative that had long been in motion before I arrived.

Days turned into weeks, and as the gala approached, our collaboration deepened. I poured everything into my work, each stitch woven with dreams of success, yet anxiety curled around my thoughts like a vine, tightening with each passing moment. I often caught Caden staring out the window, his brow furrowed, as if he was weighing the world on his shoulders. I yearned to pull him out of whatever shadow lingered over him, but I didn't know how.

Then came the night of the gala, the culmination of our efforts—a showcase where dreams were stitched into reality. The venue was a lavish ballroom, a symphony of gold and crystal, where laughter mingled with the clinking of glasses. I stepped into the room, my heart pounding, the sheer vibrancy of it all stealing my breath away.

Caden arrived soon after, looking every bit the part of a king in a tailored black suit that molded to his physique like a second skin. "You look incredible," he murmured, his gaze raking over my deep emerald gown, which shimmered under the twinkling lights. The fabric hugged my curves in all the right places, and I felt a rush of confidence. "Like you belong on this stage."

"Just wait until you see the designs," I replied, a mixture of excitement and anxiety bubbling within me.

As the night progressed, guests milled around, whispering and pointing, eyes glimmering with curiosity. Our collection, displayed like jewels on mannequins, drew attention and admiration. I felt a swell of pride every time someone stopped to marvel at the intricate details, the audacity of color combinations that screamed for attention.

Yet, amidst the applause and excitement, I couldn't ignore the growing disquiet. I caught Caden's gaze wandering again, as if he were searching for something—or someone.

"Is everything all right?" I asked as we stood near the main exhibit, the ebb and flow of guests washing over us.

His smile was charming, but the shadows returned to his eyes. "Just keeping an eye out. It's a crowded room, and there are... influential people here."

"Influential? Or dangerous?" I probed, unable to shake the unease that had settled deep within me.

He opened his mouth to respond when a loud commotion erupted across the room, drawing our attention. A group of men in dark suits, their faces serious and impassive, were pushing through the crowd, creating a path toward us. The air shifted, charged with a tension that had nothing to do with the gala's festivities.

"What the hell is going on?" I whispered, turning to Caden.

He stepped closer, his expression a mask of calm that barely concealed the worry beneath. "Stay close to me."

Before I could process his warning, the men reached us, their leader—a tall figure with slicked-back hair and piercing blue eyes—fixing his gaze on Caden. "We need to talk. Now."

My heart raced. The world around me dimmed as the reality of Caden's life crashed in, overshadowing the glamorous façade of the evening. I could see the tension in Caden's shoulders, the way his jaw clenched as if he were preparing for a fight.

"Can't it wait?" Caden replied, his voice steady yet filled with an urgency that made my skin prickle.

"No," the man snapped, an edge of menace slicing through his tone. "This can't wait any longer."

I could feel the weight of their eyes upon me, and suddenly, I was acutely aware of how out of place I was in this glittering world of privilege and peril. As Caden squared his shoulders, a flicker of fear coursed through me. I had stepped into his life, drawn by ambition and desire, but now, the depth of the danger he faced crashed over me like a cold wave.

"What do they want?" I managed to ask, but Caden's focus remained fixed on the men, his expression unreadable.

He leaned closer, his breath warm against my ear. "Just stay calm. Whatever happens, don't panic."

But the moment hung heavy, a taut thread ready to snap, and I realized that I was about to plunge deeper into a world where the lines between loyalty and betrayal were blurred. And in that instant, with tension crackling like electricity around us, I knew I was in over my head, standing on the edge of a cliff with no promise of safe landing.

As Caden's demeanor shifted, preparing to confront the men, I braced myself, knowing that whatever came next would unravel the fabric of my reality, and there would be no turning back.

Chapter 7: The Unraveling

The late afternoon sun draped itself over the city like a warm blanket, igniting the sky with hues of orange and pink that spilled over the rooftops. I leaned against the cold, smooth surface of the kitchen counter, a cup of lukewarm coffee forgotten in my hand, the bitter taste lingering on my tongue like an uninvited guest. Caden had been acting different—his laughter didn't carry the same lightness, and the shadows beneath his eyes seemed to deepen with each passing day. I told myself I was being paranoid, that my imagination was running wild, yet a gnawing feeling in the pit of my stomach whispered that something was off.

The moment came abruptly, as if the universe had decided I needed a swift kick to the gut. I stumbled upon a tattered notebook tucked behind the bookshelf, wedged between two old novels that had seen better days. It was weathered and worn, the cover fraying like a forgotten memory. Curiosity piqued, I flipped it open, and my heart dropped. The pages were filled with Caden's neat handwriting, but the words were anything but innocuous. They detailed a string of events that were dark and twisted, recounting a life I had never known. A life entwined with deceit and danger. A life connected to a crime so heinous it sent chills racing down my spine.

I couldn't breathe. The air felt thick and heavy, each inhalation a struggle. I stood frozen, the implications of what I was reading echoing in my mind. It painted a picture of Caden that I had never fathomed—a side of him that felt like a betrayal. I stumbled back, clutching the notebook as if it were a lifeline, my heart racing with disbelief. Memories of our quiet evenings together—him laughing, us cooking, dancing in the living room—flashed before me, starkly contrasting with the chaos I had just unearthed.

I had to confront him. The thought hit me like a bolt of lightning. What good would it do to keep this secret to myself? I was ready to storm into the living room where he sat, presumably lost in thought, but instead, I found myself standing at the threshold of a chasm that threatened to swallow me whole. I paced, wrestling with the pages, feeling the weight of his silence wrapped around me like an iron shroud.

"Caden," I finally called out, my voice trembling slightly as I stepped into the living room, notebook clutched tightly against my chest. The sunlight spilled in through the window, illuminating the space in a golden glow, but the warmth felt deceptive, masking the cold dread twisting inside me.

He turned, his expression shifting from relaxation to tension in a heartbeat. "What's wrong?" he asked, his brow furrowing as he leaned forward, concern etched on his features.

I took a breath, steeling myself for the confrontation that loomed before us like a storm on the horizon. "I found something," I began, my voice steadier than I felt. "Something you should have told me." I held out the notebook, my hand trembling as I fought to keep my composure. The words hung in the air, heavy and fraught with meaning.

His gaze flickered to the notebook, and for a brief moment, I could see the walls around him harden, the familiar warmth of his eyes flickering into something darker, more guarded. "Where did you find that?" he asked, his voice low, measured, as if every syllable was a calculated step across a minefield.

"In the bookshelf. It was hidden." My throat tightened as I tried to gauge his reaction. "Why didn't you tell me about this, Caden? What is all of this?"

He ran a hand through his hair, the action revealing the strain that lay beneath his calm facade. "It's... complicated," he admitted, his eyes drifting away from mine, avoiding the heat of my stare as if it were a direct challenge. "It's not something I wanted to burden you with."

"Burden me?" The word tasted bitter on my tongue. "I think I deserve to know if the person I'm falling for is connected to something like this. It's not just a burden; it's a truth."

Silence stretched between us, a taut wire ready to snap. Caden finally looked back at me, his gaze fierce yet vulnerable. "You don't understand what you're asking. This isn't just about me. It's about survival, choices that were made long before you came into my life."

I took a step closer, the notebook trembling in my grasp as my heart raced. "Then tell me. Make me understand. Because right now, I feel like I'm standing on the edge of a cliff, and you're asking me to jump without knowing if there's a net below."

He hesitated, his expression shifting as if the weight of his past was slowly unfolding before us. "There are parts of my life that I've tried to bury. Things I regret deeply. I thought I could leave it all behind, but it seems like it's catching up to me."

The tension in the air crackled, every word a jagged edge that threatened to cut through the fragile threads of our relationship. "What do you mean?" I pressed, urgency creeping into my voice. "What are you running from?"

The answer came slowly, like the dawn breaking over a dark horizon. "There are people who don't forget easily, who don't forgive. I thought I could keep you safe by keeping you in the dark."

"Safe?" I echoed, disbelief flooding my senses. "By lying to me? By hiding who you really are? This isn't safety, Caden. It feels like a betrayal."

His gaze softened, desperation flickering in his eyes. "I never meant to hurt you. I wanted to protect you, to give you a chance to walk away from this mess. But I can't let you go. Not now, not when..."

"Not when what?" The words fell from my lips, hanging between us like an unspoken promise. I felt a strange mix of anger and affection, swirling like a tempest in my chest. "What are you trying to say?"

He stepped forward, closing the distance, and for a fleeting moment, I was lost in the depths of his gaze. "Not when I can't stop loving you. Even knowing what I do, I can't let you go. It's the most dangerous thing of all."

My heart raced, caught in a dance of desire and fear, each beat echoing the weight of the truth. I felt exposed, laid bare beneath the weight of his confession, caught in the riptide of emotion and uncertainty.

"So, what now?" I asked, my voice barely above a whisper, the notebook still clutched tightly in my hands, a reminder of the darkness lurking just beyond our fragile sanctuary.

His admission hung between us like a fragile thread, taut and vibrating with unspoken emotions. The air felt thick, and I could hear the faint hum of the city outside, a world blissfully unaware of the turmoil brewing in our little sanctuary. Caden's gaze bore into mine, searching for something, perhaps an acknowledgment, perhaps forgiveness. I had only ever known him as the man who filled my life with laughter, the one who danced barefoot across the kitchen tiles, the one who made mundane grocery runs feel like an adventure. This revelation, however, altered everything, twisting my perception like a cruel trick of fate.

"What does that even mean?" I managed, my voice shaking slightly, betraying the maelstrom of thoughts colliding within my mind. "You can't just throw those words out and expect me to understand."

His lips pressed into a thin line, frustration evident as he stepped back, rubbing the back of his neck in that familiar way that screamed he was grappling with something much larger than either of us could comprehend. "I mean that I care about you more than anything, and knowing this—knowing my past—puts you in danger. You deserve to be safe, not dragged into my mess."

"And I suppose you think that hiding it is protecting me?" I shot back, irritation bubbling beneath the surface. "What if keeping it from me is what puts me in danger? I have a right to know the truth."

He took a deep breath, his eyes momentarily flickering with something akin to regret. "I thought I was protecting you, but I see now that it only creates more distance between us."

"Distance?" The word sliced through me, sharp as glass. "You're the one building walls, Caden, not me. It feels like I'm standing outside, banging on the door, and you're just watching me."

He opened his mouth to respond, but the sound of a phone vibrating on the coffee table interrupted us. Both of us glanced at it, a tension-filled silence stretching as we waited for the call to end. It felt like an unwelcome intruder, stealing our moment. Caden's brow furrowed, and I could see his reluctance to look away, but the buzzing continued, relentless. Finally, he reached for it, the momentary distraction allowing us both a breather.

"Excuse me," he murmured, his voice distant as he stepped into the hallway, leaving me alone with my spiraling thoughts. I turned the notebook over in my hands, tracing the fraying edges with my fingertips, the weight of its contents sinking deeper into my chest. I couldn't help but wonder how this twisted narrative had woven its way into the fabric of Caden's life, a tale of survival that came at such a steep price.

When he returned, his expression had shifted, a shadow lingering beneath the surface. "That was my brother," he said, running a hand through his hair again, a gesture that I now recognized as a telltale sign of his anxiety. "He's in town. He wants to see me."

"Oh, good. Nothing like family to add to the chaos," I remarked, trying to lighten the mood despite the knot tightening in my stomach. "Does he have any idea what's going on? You know, aside from the fact that you've been hiding a notebook of horrors in our living room?"

Caden's lips quirked at the corners, but the smile didn't reach his eyes. "He doesn't know. I haven't talked to him about... any of this."

"Right, because that's how families work—totally open and honest," I replied, sarcasm draping my words like a cozy blanket. "So, are you going to invite him over for dinner or something? Maybe we can clear the air over a lovely meal, discuss the thrilling adventures of your dark past while I pretend to chew my food."

His eyes softened, the tension in his shoulders easing slightly. "You know I wish it could be that simple. He's not just my brother; he's... he's involved."

"Involved how? In whatever this is?" I gestured at the notebook, a surge of frustration bubbling up. "Does he know about the crimes, about your past?"

Caden hesitated, the weight of his words palpable. "Yes. He was part of it, too. It was a long time ago, but he's never really let go of that life. I thought I had escaped it, but now I see it's like a shadow that follows me."

The air grew heavy again, and I stepped back, my heart racing with the implications. "So he's coming here? To see you? After everything?"

"He wants to talk. I think he believes he can help me, help us," Caden replied, his voice thick with uncertainty.

I shook my head, incredulous. "Help us? Help you return to whatever this is? Caden, this isn't just about you anymore. It's about me, too. I can't be part of this."

The sharpness of my words sliced through the space between us, and for a moment, we stood in silence, the air thick with unresolved tension. Caden's gaze was piercing, as if he were trying to unearth my thoughts, my fears, with nothing but the intensity of his stare.

"I can't walk away from this. Not from you," he finally said, stepping closer again, his presence a warm comfort against the chill that had settled around us. "But I need you to trust me. Trust that I won't let anything happen to you."

Trust. The word hung in the air like a fragile promise. "Trust is earned, Caden. You can't expect me to hand it over just because you say so."

"I know." His voice was barely above a whisper, heavy with the weight of his past and the uncertain future that loomed ahead. "But I'm asking for it, anyway."

Just then, the doorbell rang, cutting through the thick tension. My heart raced, uncertainty flooding my veins. Caden glanced at the door, his expression shifting from concern to something darker. "That must be him."

"Perfect timing," I muttered under my breath, my stomach churning with a mix of anticipation and dread. "I suppose I should put on my best 'welcome to my chaotic life' face."

Caden stepped toward the door, and as he turned the knob, a rush of cool air swept into the room, carrying with it the weight of the past that neither of us could shake off. When the door swung open, a tall figure stood silhouetted in the fading light, exuding an aura that was both familiar and foreboding.

"Caden," the newcomer said, his voice smooth yet layered with a tension that suggested years of unsaid words. As he stepped inside, I could see the resemblance—same sharp jawline, same stormy eyes—but there was something more in the way he carried himself, a weight that seemed to anchor him in shadows.

"Luke," Caden replied, a note of hesitance creeping into his tone. "You're here."

"Of course, I am. We need to talk," Luke said, his gaze flickering to me before returning to Caden, the air between them thick with unspoken history.

I stood there, caught in the whirlwind of their reunion, my heart pounding in sync with the uncertainty that loomed overhead like an ominous storm cloud. I had been swept into a world I barely understood, where trust felt like a tightrope, and I was teetering on the edge.

The tension in the room crackled like electricity, thickening the air as Luke stepped inside, his presence an unwelcome shadow in the sanctuary I had thought was ours. Caden's posture shifted, rigid and defensive, as if Luke's arrival had pulled the strings of some long-dormant puppet show, with hidden narratives and unresolved conflicts springing to life in the flickering light. I felt like an outsider in my own home, an unwitting audience to a performance I had never signed up for.

"Thanks for coming," Caden said, his voice steady but tinged with an underlying strain. He motioned for Luke to enter fully, a forced politeness clashing with the tension radiating from him.

Luke stepped inside, the light illuminating sharp features that seemed to have been carved from the same stone as Caden's but were etched with an edge of danger. "I didn't come all this way to exchange pleasantries," he said, his tone cool and direct. He turned his gaze to me, assessing, weighing the variables of this unforeseen equation. "And who is this?"

"Just someone I care about," Caden replied, his voice firm yet defensive, an unexpected heat rising in his tone. I had expected him to brush me aside, as if I were a passing moment in his turbulent history, but instead, he anchored me, grounding us both against the rising tide of uncertainty.

"Care about?" Luke echoed, skepticism draping his words like a heavy cloak. "Does she know what she's getting into?"

The insinuation sent a rush of heat to my cheeks, indignation flaring within me. "I'm perfectly capable of making my own decisions, thanks," I interjected, crossing my arms defiantly. "I didn't realize that my presence needed your approval."

Luke studied me with an intensity that felt almost predatory. "You really have no idea what you're tangled up in, do you?" His words cut through the air, sharp and deliberate. "Caden's past isn't just a chapter in a book—it's a living nightmare. He thinks he's protected you by hiding it, but it will consume you both if you let it."

I shot a glance at Caden, whose expression had darkened, clouds of conflict gathering in his eyes. "Luke, don't. She deserves the truth, not your dramatics," he warned, but there was an underlying tension in his voice, a hesitation that suggested he was still grappling with the ghosts of his choices.

"Dramatics?" Luke's voice rose, laced with disbelief. "You think this is a game? I've seen what happens when people get too close. This isn't a fairytale, Caden. You're playing with fire."

"Enough!" I exclaimed, my patience fraying at the edges. "You both act as if I'm some delicate flower that needs protection. I'm here, and I want to understand. So, if you think you can scare me off with vague threats, you're sorely mistaken."

Luke's gaze turned to me, a flicker of respect mingling with caution. "It's not about scaring you; it's about survival. You have no idea how dangerous the past can be, especially for someone like Caden."

Caden's jaw clenched, the muscles in his face tightening as if he were fighting against an invisible force. "My past is mine to own, and I won't let it dictate my future. I won't let it touch you."

"Touch me?" I shot back, the heat of anger flaring within me. "You're already letting it touch me by keeping me in the dark. You think I can just ignore the fact that I found a notebook filled with your darkest secrets? That I'm supposed to just pretend it doesn't exist?"

The tension in the room swelled, a tempest building, and I could feel the unspoken words crackling like a live wire. Luke stepped closer to Caden, their proximity igniting the air with unbridled energy. "You think you can just walk away? The things you've done will always be there, lurking in the shadows, waiting for the moment to pounce. I can help you, but you have to be willing to face it."

Caden shook his head, the lines of his face hardening. "I don't need help. Not from you. I've made my choices, and I'm dealing with them."

"And what about her?" Luke shot back, his voice a fierce whisper, tension crackling like a fire about to engulf the room. "You're dragging her into a storm she didn't ask for. You think you're protecting her by pushing her away, but that's not how it works."

Caden turned to me, his eyes dark with frustration. "You don't have to be part of this, you know. You can walk away."

"Is that really what you want?" I asked, feeling the tremor in my voice, the vulnerability spilling over. "For me to just walk away? Because I don't think I can. Not anymore."

The silence that followed was charged, a moment of realization dawning like a hesitant sunrise. "You don't get to make that choice for me, Caden," I continued, taking a step forward, bridging the gap between our conflicting emotions. "You think that you're the only one affected by this? You're wrong. I care about you, and that means facing whatever this is together."

Luke's expression shifted slightly, a flicker of understanding in his eyes. "You're braver than you look," he conceded, surprising me with the compliment. "But bravery doesn't equal safety. You both need to understand the depth of what you're dealing with."

Caden's gaze was fierce, a blend of determination and desperation. "I won't let you take her away from me, Luke. I won't let you scare her into submission."

"I'm not trying to scare her," Luke insisted, his voice dropping an octave. "But you can't ignore the reality of your situation. There are people who won't let you go so easily. If they find out you're involved with her, it could endanger her life."

The weight of those words sank into me like a stone thrown into still water, sending ripples of fear coursing through my veins. I could feel the color draining from my face as the reality of Caden's past collided with my present. "What do you mean? Who are these people?"

Luke's jaw clenched, and for a moment, I thought he might refuse to answer, but then he spoke, his voice low and grave. "They're the ones who don't forgive. They've been watching Caden, waiting for him to slip. And if they realize he's gotten close to someone..."

I swallowed hard, a chill settling over me. "So, I'm just a target now? A pawn in this game?"

"It's not a game," Caden snapped, the urgency in his tone rising. "You're not a pawn; you're a part of my life. But my past... it could destroy everything we've built."

I stepped back, the reality of the situation crashing over me like a relentless wave. "So what do we do? Just wait for them to show up on our doorstep? Hope they don't notice I'm here?"

Luke's eyes darkened with determination. "We prepare. We have to face this head-on. There's no running from it."

Caden took a deep breath, the tension in his shoulders easing slightly as he met my gaze. "I'll protect you. Whatever it takes."

"And how do you plan to do that?" I asked, skepticism creeping into my voice. "By pushing me further away? Because that's not going to work."

He reached for my hand, the warmth of his touch igniting a flicker of hope amid the uncertainty. "No more hiding. No more secrets. Together, we'll confront this."

Just as I was about to respond, a loud crash echoed from outside, a sound that rattled the windows and sent a jolt of panic racing through me. Caden's grip tightened around my hand, and Luke's expression shifted to one of immediate alarm.

"What was that?" I gasped, my heart racing as the reality of our situation collided with the urgency of the moment.

"It's them," Luke breathed, his eyes narrowing as he moved to the window, peering out into the gathering twilight. "They're here."

A rush of adrenaline surged through me, and I felt my breath quickening, the weight of fear anchoring me in place. Caden's eyes locked onto mine, a storm of emotions swirling within them—fear, determination, love—but more than anything, I saw a flicker of desperation.

"Stay behind me," he said, his voice low and fierce.

As I shifted closer to him, my heart raced, every instinct screaming that this was just the beginning. The door rattled, a hard knock reverberating through the house, and I knew that whatever lay beyond that door would alter our lives forever.

Chapter 8: Lies Between Us

The sun hung low in the sky, casting a golden hue over the bustling city as I sat in the corner of our favorite café. The aroma of freshly brewed coffee mingled with the sweetness of pastries, a comforting scent that had once been a balm for my restless soul. Now, it merely served as a reminder of how tangled our lives had become. Caden was supposed to meet me here, our usual spot where laughter and shared dreams used to echo. Instead, I found myself staring into the depths of my latte, swirling the foam as if it could reveal the answers I desperately sought.

I could hear the laughter of a nearby couple, their easy banter a painful contrast to the silence that had settled between Caden and me. Our conversations felt strained, the words heavy with unspoken accusations and lingering doubts. I could almost see the cracks in our foundation, spiderwebbing beneath the surface of our relationship. It was as if we were playing a game of chess, each move calculated and fraught with tension. I wanted to believe in him, in us, but the truth of his confession echoed in my mind like a haunting melody I couldn't shake.

"Hey," a familiar voice broke through my thoughts, pulling me back to reality. I looked up to see Caden standing before me, his expression a mix of vulnerability and determination. His hair, tousled from the wind, framed his face in a way that made my heart clench despite the turmoil brewing inside. I gestured to the seat across from me, my heart racing at the thought of what might unfold.

"Can we talk?" His voice was soft, almost a whisper, but the weight of it was undeniable.

I nodded, trying to ignore the flicker of doubt that flared within me. The way he looked at me, with those deep, searching eyes, reminded me of the man I had fallen for—before the lies, before the revelation that had turned our world upside down. But could I trust that look? Was it genuine, or was it simply another mask he wore to hide the truth?

"I've been thinking..." I began, my voice steady despite the storm inside me. "About what you said. About the secrets. They don't just disappear, Caden. They linger, tainting everything."

He rubbed the back of his neck, a gesture I recognized as his way of grappling with his own guilt. "I know I messed up. I didn't want to hurt you. I thought keeping it from you would—"

"Would what? Protect me?" I interrupted, a bitter edge creeping into my tone. "All it did was shatter whatever trust we had left. It's like you took a wrecking ball to my heart and expected me to just rebuild it."

Silence hung heavy between us, filled only by the distant clinking of cups and the hum of conversations around us. I could see the struggle in his eyes, the way he wrestled with the consequences of his choices.

"Do you really think I wanted this?" His voice was strained, frustration coloring his words. "I thought I was doing the right thing, that you wouldn't understand. I was trying to protect you, to shield you from my world—"

"Your world?" I shot back, incredulous. "You mean the one that's filled with deceit and manipulation? You think I don't want to be part of that? To understand? I've always been on your side, Caden! But you pushed me away, wrapped me in lies instead of letting me in."

His jaw clenched, and for a moment, I saw the walls he had built around himself. But then, the softness returned, and he reached across the table, his hand hovering above mine, hesitating. "I'm sorry. I never meant to hurt you. I thought if I kept you out of it, I'd keep you safe."

Safe. The word hung in the air like a ghost, reminding me of the truth I couldn't escape. The pressure of my career loomed over me, Valleria demanding results while Caden's business partners scrutinized every design I presented, their opinions suffocating my creative spirit. It felt as if I was being pulled apart, every thread of my life fraying at the edges.

"I'm drowning, Caden," I confessed, the words spilling out before I could catch them. "Between Valleria's expectations and your tangled web of secrets, I don't know how much longer I can hold everything together. I'm afraid I'll lose myself in all of this."

His gaze softened, and he finally took my hand, his warmth igniting a flicker of hope within me. "We can figure this out. Together. I promise, no more secrets. I'll lay everything bare if that's what it takes to earn your trust back."

"But can you?" I challenged, my heart pounding at the vulnerability we were both tiptoeing around. "Can you really be that honest with me? Can you share your world without the fear of dragging me into the darkness?"

"I have to try," he replied, determination etched across his features. "You deserve that much. You deserve to know everything, even the parts that make me uncomfortable."

Just then, the café door swung open, the bell chiming softly as a gust of wind brought in the crisp autumn air. My gaze drifted past Caden, landing on a figure standing just inside the threshold. The world outside seemed to pause, the laughter and chatter fading into a dull hum as recognition washed over me like a cold wave.

It was Lena, Caden's business partner, her sharp eyes scanning the room until they locked onto ours. The tension in the air shifted, thickening like fog as she advanced toward our table, her presence unsettling. I exchanged a glance with Caden, the unspoken words hanging between us. Whatever moment of clarity we had found was about to be interrupted, and the intricate web of lies and truths we were attempting to navigate threatened to unravel completely.

The moment Lena strode over, her presence eclipsed the gentle buzz of the café. Her tailored suit hugged her form with the precision of a surgeon's scalpel, and her sharp features seemed chiseled from marble—imposing and cold. She exuded an aura of authority that made the hairs on the back of my neck stand on end. I hadn't seen her in a while, but I had a sinking feeling that her sudden appearance was anything but coincidental.

"Caden," she greeted, her voice dripping with the kind of sweetness that only a predator can muster when approaching its prey. She flicked her gaze to me, and for a heartbeat, the air felt charged. "I didn't expect to find you here, especially not with... her."

"Lena," he replied, his tone more guarded than I'd ever heard. "What brings you by?"

"I wanted to discuss the upcoming presentation," she said, her eyes narrowing slightly, as if trying to assess the nature of my relationship with Caden through a microscope. "I heard we're incorporating some of our new projects. I thought you might want to—" she glanced at me again, "—get my input."

"Right," I said, unable to help the irritation that slipped into my voice. "Because I'm sure your vision of our designs is perfectly aligned with the creative direction we've been aiming for."

Lena raised an eyebrow, her lips curling into a smile that was anything but friendly. "Well, we all know how... subjective creativity can be, don't we? I'm just here to ensure our clients get what they pay for."

I could feel Caden's tension radiating across the table, and I wondered if he was thinking the same thing I was: that our clients' interests seemed to always align with Lena's agenda. I had hoped, naïvely, that she had merely been a distant shadow in our projects, but now, she was becoming an unwelcome guest in our fragile truce.

"Actually, I'd prefer to handle this alone," I said, my resolve hardening. "I've got a pretty clear vision, and I don't need any outside influence right now."

Lena's smile faltered, her polished exterior momentarily cracking. "Is that so? Well, you certainly have a way of making things... interesting." She leaned in slightly, lowering her voice as if sharing a secret meant just for us. "Just remember, the stakes are high, and we all know how unforgiving this industry can be."

My heart raced at her veiled threat, but before I could respond, Caden interjected, his voice steady. "I think we should stick to the original plan. Julia is more than capable of delivering exactly what we need without any additional input."

Lena straightened, her eyes darting between us, a fleeting look of surprise etched across her features. "Well, I won't keep you. Just remember, I'll be watching. Good luck." With that, she turned and strode away, leaving a chilling silence in her wake.

"Wow," I breathed out, my heart still racing from our encounter. "Is she always that... delightful?"

Caden chuckled, but it was strained, almost painful. "She has her moments."

"Moments? That was an Olympic-level display of passive aggression," I shot back, half-laughing and half-trying to ease the tension. "Are you sure you want to work with her?"

"Believe me, I've questioned it more than once," he admitted, rubbing his temples as if trying to relieve the pressure that seemed to hang around us like an unwelcome fog. "But she's got connections, and in this business, it's all about who you know. It's frustrating, but I can't just cut her loose."

"Fine," I said, my frustration simmering beneath the surface. "But I refuse to let her derail what I've been working on. I need this to be my project, not a playground for her ego."

He nodded, his gaze steady. "I want that for you, too. Just... let's keep the lines of communication open, alright? We need to be on the same page."

"Communication," I echoed, my voice laced with irony. "That's a funny word between us right now."

He flinched, and the tension crackled again. I could almost see the walls he'd built around himself, fortified with layers of uncertainty. But I also recognized the flicker of determination in his eyes—the same fire that had drawn me to him in the first place.

"I know I messed up," he said, his voice barely above a whisper. "But I'm trying to be better. I don't want to lose you."

My heart swelled at his words, but the shadows of doubt still loomed large. "You're saying that now, but how can I trust you when I still don't know everything?"

"I'll tell you," he replied, his expression earnest. "I promise to share what I can, when I can. But it's not always easy—my past... it's complicated."

"Complicated seems to be an understatement," I replied, crossing my arms over my chest. "You've built a fortress, Caden. I can see it, and it's starting to feel like I'm the one who's trapped inside it."

"Then let me tear down those walls," he said, his voice suddenly fervent. "I want to be honest with you. I want you to see all of me, even the ugly parts."

The sincerity in his eyes sent my pulse racing, and for a moment, I considered the possibility that maybe, just maybe, he was sincere. The warm flicker of hope ignited within me, but it was quickly snuffed out by the memory of Lena's icy stare and the pressure mounting from Valleria. I took a breath, steadying myself against the whirlwind of emotions threatening to consume me.

"I need to think," I finally said, my voice steady despite the chaos within. "We both do. We're not just navigating our relationship; we're trying to survive this entire situation with your business partners breathing down our necks. And if I'm honest, I'm feeling suffocated."

Caden's expression softened, and he squeezed my hand, grounding me in the moment. "Let's take it one step at a time. We'll figure this out together, I swear."

But as I looked into his eyes, I couldn't shake the feeling that there were still pieces of the puzzle he wasn't ready to share. Just then, the café door swung open again, and a familiar face walked in—Valleria. Her presence was like a tempest, and I could feel the tension ramping up. She was here for business, and I was already bracing myself for another confrontation.

As Valleria entered the café, her presence was akin to a sudden thunderstorm crashing into a tranquil afternoon. The vibrant chatter muted, and I could almost hear the collective intake of breath from the other patrons as she swept in, her designer heels clicking on the hardwood floor with the authority of a seasoned general. Dressed in a tailored blazer that fit her like a second skin, she radiated a power that was both alluring and intimidating. I could sense the air shift, thickening with the weight of expectations as she locked her gaze onto our table.

"Caden," she called, her voice smooth as silk but edged with steel. "I see you're keeping... interesting company."

"Valleria," he replied, his voice taut. The warmth of our earlier conversation evaporated like mist under the sun. "I thought we had a meeting scheduled for later."

"I wanted to discuss a few things now," she said, gliding over to us with an effortless grace that spoke volumes about her confidence. "Especially since it appears we have a new stakeholder in our projects." She turned her gaze to me, and I fought the urge to squirm under her scrutiny. "Julia, darling, how lovely to see you. I hope you're keeping Caden on track. He tends to get... distracted."

"Is that a polite way of saying he has commitment issues?" I shot back, unable to resist the barb. The tension in the air crackled, and Caden's eyes widened in surprise, though a ghost of a smile tugged at the corner of his lips.

"Oh, sweetie," she replied with a saccharine smile that could have melted ice, "it's not his commitment I'm worried about. It's your ability to navigate this industry without getting swept away."

"Thanks for your concern," I retorted, trying to maintain my composure while internally battling the urge to retreat. "I'm perfectly capable of holding my own."

"Capable? Of course, you are. But the question is, are you ready for the pressure?" Valleria leaned in slightly, her tone shifting to something softer, almost conspiratorial. "Because this isn't just about you anymore, Julia. It's about the reputation we're building—and tearing down. You do understand that, don't you?"

A ripple of uncertainty coursed through me. I had felt the pressure mounting, but hearing it articulated so bluntly made the weight of it settle on my shoulders like a heavy cloak. Caden's hand tightened around mine, grounding me in this moment, but I could feel his tension alongside my own.

"Look, Valleria," Caden said, his voice firm but edged with restraint, "Julia has the vision we need. She's been pivotal in bringing fresh ideas to the table. I believe in her."

"Ah, but belief isn't enough, darling," Valleria replied, her voice dipping into that seductive tone she reserved for persuasive moments. "Results are what matter. You two can engage in this little romantic subplot all you want, but when it comes to business, feelings don't pay the bills."

The barb stung, and I could feel my cheeks flush with indignation. I opened my mouth to retort, to defend the work I had poured my heart into, but Caden beat me to it.

"Why don't we focus on what's actually important?" he snapped, his frustration bubbling to the surface. "We have a presentation in two days, and Julia's designs are critical to our pitch. We should be supporting her, not throwing her off her game."

"Supporting her? Oh, honey, this isn't a cheerleading squad," Valleria shot back, her smile hardening into a mask of professionalism. "This is business, and if you're not prepared to play the game, you might find yourself on the sidelines—if you're lucky."

"Valleria, we're not sideline players. We're in this together, all of us," I asserted, matching her intensity. "I know what's at stake, and I'm not going to let you undermine my efforts."

A flicker of surprise crossed her face, but it quickly morphed into something more calculating. "Spunk. I like it. But I hope you can back it up with substance, because if this presentation fails, it's not just your career at stake—it's all of ours."

With that, she turned on her heel, striding away with an air of authority that left us both reeling. The café was alive again, the previous hush lifting like fog retreating at dawn, but the tension lingered between us like a taut string ready to snap.

"Wow," I breathed, letting out a nervous laugh. "She really knows how to lighten the mood, doesn't she?"

"More like she knows how to make you question every choice you've made," Caden replied, running a hand through his hair in frustration. "I'm sorry about that. I didn't realize she'd come here."

"It's not your fault," I said, trying to shake off the unease that had settled in my stomach. "But you've got to admit, she knows how to get under your skin."

"Trust me, I'm well aware," he said, a hint of wry humor creeping into his voice. "But I want to protect you from her influence. You deserve to shine on your own terms."

The sincerity in his words ignited a spark of warmth within me, but it was quickly overshadowed by the looming reality of our impending presentation. "I just need to focus on my work," I murmured, my thoughts swirling around the designs that had consumed my nights and dreams. "But with her breathing down my neck, I don't know how I'll manage."

"Together," he insisted, leaning forward, his eyes locking onto mine. "We'll figure this out. You're not alone in this."

But just as I opened my mouth to reply, the café door swung open again, and this time, it was a figure I never expected to see: my estranged sister, Sophia, who I hadn't spoken to in years. Her entrance felt like a jolt of electricity, and my heart plummeted into my stomach. Dressed in a flowing bohemian dress that seemed to dance around her as she walked, she looked both ethereal and out of place amidst the coffee-sipping crowd. Our eyes met, and in that instant, I felt every unspoken word and past grievance surge to the surface.

"What is she doing here?" I whispered, my pulse quickening, fear and disbelief mingling in a cocktail of emotion.

Caden's brows furrowed, confusion etched across his features. "Julia, who—"

But I was already on my feet, my chair scraping against the floor as I moved towards her. The air thickened with tension, my heart pounding in my chest as I prepared to confront the ghost of my past. I could feel Caden's eyes on me, a mix of support and concern, but Sophia's presence demanded my attention like a magnet.

"Why now?" I called out, my voice quavering slightly, betraying the years of hurt that lay buried beneath the surface.

She met my gaze, and for a moment, it felt like the world had narrowed to just the two of us. "I came to talk," she replied, her voice softer than I remembered, yet it echoed with a timbre of uncertainty.

I hesitated, caught between the years of estrangement and the desire to know what had brought her here. "Talk? After all this time? What could you possibly want to say?"

Her lips parted, and just as she opened her mouth to respond, a commotion erupted behind her—a group of men in sharp suits entered, their laughter filling the café with an undercurrent of tension. Among them was a familiar face, someone I'd only seen in Caden's company. My heart raced as I realized they were Caden's business partners, the very people whose expectations hung over us like a dark cloud.

"Caden! Julia!" one of them called, their voices cutting through the air. "We need to discuss the presentation. Now."

Panic surged within me as I stood frozen, the past colliding with the present in an explosion of uncertainty. Sophia, Caden, the looming presentation—it was all spiraling out of control. Just when I thought I could finally grasp the situation, it slipped through my fingers like sand, leaving me standing at the crossroads of decisions I never wanted to face.

Chapter 9: The Line We Crossed

The city sprawled beneath us, a glittering tapestry of lights and shadows, its heartbeat pulsing through the window like a relentless drum. I leaned against the cold glass of Caden's penthouse, staring out at the skyline, the air thick with tension and unspoken words. I could feel the warmth of the room pressing against me, almost suffocating in its intensity. The faint hum of traffic below was a distant reminder of a world outside this bubble we had created, a world that felt increasingly alien to me.

"Why can't you just say it?" I snapped, my voice sharper than intended, slicing through the silence that had draped itself around us. The way Caden stood there, arms crossed, his jaw clenched, sent a shiver of both anger and longing through me. His eyes—dark and stormy—were fixated on me, but they held secrets I was no longer sure I wanted to uncover.

He shifted slightly, the fabric of his crisp white shirt catching the light, illuminating the contours of his chest. "Because it's complicated," he replied, his voice low and gravelly, a sound I used to find comforting but now felt like a warning bell. Complicated. It was a word that had lost its meaning in the endless cycles of our late-night conversations. It had become a catchall for everything he refused to admit.

"Complicated?" I scoffed, rolling my eyes. "That's rich coming from you. You've built this fortress around your feelings, and I'm standing here with a sledgehammer trying to break through. If you think keeping secrets will make this any easier, you're wrong." I gestured wildly, my hands expressing the frustration I could no longer contain. "This isn't just about you anymore, Caden. It's about us."

He stepped closer, his eyes narrowing. "You think I want to keep secrets? You think I want this distance between us?" The intensity of his gaze was almost enough to make me falter, but I held my ground, heart racing. The distance had become a chasm, and every day felt like another brick added to the wall.

"You've done a fantastic job of keeping me at arm's length," I countered, my voice rising. "Every time I think we're moving forward, you pull back. I can't keep playing this game, Caden. It's exhausting."

With a heavy sigh, he ran a hand through his tousled hair, the golden strands catching the light as he looked away, as if searching for an answer in the sprawling city beyond us. "You don't understand," he murmured, almost to himself. "You don't know what I've done."

And just like that, the air shifted. I felt a chill creep up my spine, a sense of foreboding tightening around my chest. "What do you mean?" My voice trembled, and for the first time, I saw a flicker of vulnerability cross his features. It was fleeting, but it was there—an unguarded moment that felt almost surreal.

He turned back to me, the weight of something heavy in his eyes. "I've hurt people. People who trusted me. I thought I could keep it all separate—my work, my life, my feelings for you—but it's all tangled together. I don't know how to unwind it without destroying everything."

"Destroying everything?" I echoed, incredulous. "What does that even mean? Caden, you can't just drop that on me and expect me to understand."

"I was involved in something... I didn't think it would go this far. I didn't think it would affect you." His voice cracked, and I could see the battle within him, the conflict between wanting to protect me and the desperation to be honest.

"Just tell me!" I shouted, frustration boiling over. "Whatever it is, I can handle it. You can't keep hiding behind your walls." My heart pounded, an erratic rhythm echoing the chaos in my mind.

He took a deep breath, as if summoning the courage to reveal the truth that had been festering between us like an open wound. "I've been involved with some people who aren't what they seem. I thought I was making smart choices, but now... now I'm not so sure." His words fell like stones into the silence, each one sinking deeper into the reality we'd built around us.

"What kind of people?" I pressed, feeling the ground beneath me shift dangerously. "Caden, you're scaring me." The intimacy of his space suddenly felt suffocating, and I took a small step back, needing to create some distance between his revelation and my racing heart.

"People who..." he hesitated, searching for the right words. "People who play with lives and fortunes, who see the world as a chessboard and everyone else as mere pawns." The admission hung in the air, thick with the weight of unspoken fears and unfulfilled desires.

I stared at him, my heart racing and my mind whirling with the implications. "You got involved with them?" The accusation tasted bitter on my tongue, mingling with the hope that maybe there was an explanation that would make it all okay.

"I didn't mean to. I thought I could control it, but it spiraled out of my hands. I've tried to keep you out of it, but... I don't know if I can anymore." His voice broke, vulnerability exposing a side of him I had never seen.

"And now you're telling me this? After everything we've built? Caden, you're not just putting yourself at risk. You're putting me at risk too." The realization slammed into me, a cold wave that washed over my anger, leaving only fear in its wake.

"I know," he said softly, his gaze never wavering. "And that's why I have to be honest with you now. No more secrets, no more lies." The sincerity in his voice was both a balm and a dagger, soothing the ache in my heart while plunging deeper into the raw wound he'd just opened.

"What do we do now?" I whispered, feeling utterly lost as the walls around my heart trembled under the weight of his revelations. "Is there even a way back from this?"

The silence stretched between us, heavy and suffocating, as we faced the harsh reality of the line we had crossed. There was no turning back, no escaping the truth that had now changed everything. And as I looked into his eyes, I realized that whatever happened next, it would either forge us into something stronger or tear us apart forever.

The silence between us was deafening, broken only by the distant murmur of the city. I could still feel the heat of his confession hanging in the air like smoke, wrapping around me, suffocating in its intensity. Caden stood before me, his shoulders tense, every inch of him radiating a mixture of defiance and vulnerability that only complicated my feelings further. I didn't know whether to yell at him or to throw my arms around him and cling tightly, hoping to weave our frayed threads back together.

"How could you think keeping this from me would protect me?" I finally managed, my voice trembling with the weight of his admission. "You've made me part of this world you were so desperate to hide. You've put me in danger without even telling me." I could hear the sharpness in my tone, but it felt justified, a necessary blade to cut through the haze of confusion and hurt.

"Trust me, that was never my intention," he replied, his tone earnest, yet his eyes flickered with something I couldn't quite place—regret, perhaps, or a realization of the mess he'd made. "I thought I could handle it. That I could keep you out of it. I didn't want to drag you into my chaos."

"And yet here we are," I shot back, crossing my arms, mirroring his stance, both of us caught in a silent standoff. "It seems like your chaos is now my chaos too. So, what happens next, Caden? Do we just sweep it under the rug and pretend everything is fine?"

He took a step closer, lowering his voice as if afraid the very walls would hear his secrets. "No, I want to fix this. I want to fix us." The earnestness in his eyes sparked a flicker of hope within me, yet it was tethered to a thousand doubts, each one wrapping itself around my heart like a chain.

"Fix us?" I echoed, skepticism lacing my tone. "How do you even propose to do that? Just wave a magic wand and pretend this mess doesn't exist?"

He exhaled sharply, running his hand through his hair again, a gesture that spoke of frustration and a hint of vulnerability that only served to deepen my confusion. "I'm not asking for a miracle. I just want to be honest with you. There's a lot I haven't told you, and it's time you knew everything."

The way he spoke, with that edge of urgency, made my stomach twist. There was a part of me that craved that honesty, that wanted to peel back the layers of the man standing before me, while another part screamed to run away as far as I could. "Fine," I said, forcing my voice steady. "Tell me everything. If we're going to do this, let's do it right."

Caden nodded, taking a deep breath that seemed to draw in the very essence of the room, the tension thickening with every passing moment. "You remember when I told you I was working late a lot? That I had some 'business deals' to manage?"

I nodded, my heart pounding as the memories flashed through my mind. "Yeah, you never really elaborated on those."

His jaw tightened, and I could see him weighing the consequences of his next words. "Those deals weren't just about investments. I got involved with some people who have... questionable ethics. I didn't realize how deep I was in until it was too late."

I held my breath, feeling the world tilt slightly beneath my feet. "And these people? What are they doing that's so dangerous?"

"They're involved in operations that... let's just say, cross lines. Lines I never wanted to cross." His gaze turned distant, as if he was peering into a past that haunted him. "At first, it was just business. I thought I could keep it separate, but soon enough, I was too entangled. And the longer I stayed, the harder it became to get out."

"Is that why you've been acting so distant?" I probed, a swell of emotions crashing within me. "Because you didn't want me to see who you really are?"

He met my gaze, the weight of his secrets pressing heavily between us. "Partly. But it's more than that. I didn't want to drag you into this world. I thought if I kept you away from the darkness, you'd be safe."

"Safe? Is that what you call it? You think you're protecting me by keeping me in the dark?" My heart raced with anger and fear. "What if these people come after you? After me? You can't just decide what's best for me, Caden."

"I know that now," he said, his voice strained. "I was scared. Scared of what they'd do if they found out about you. And scared of what I might have to do to protect you. It's all spiraled so out of control."

"Have you ever thought that maybe I could handle the truth?" My words poured out, charged with emotions I could barely articulate. "Maybe if you'd trusted me enough to share your burdens, we wouldn't be in this mess."

He took a step back, visibly shaken by my words. "You're right. I didn't give you enough credit. I thought I could shield you from everything, but I was wrong."

For a moment, we were both silent, the weight of his confession pressing down like a heavy fog. The city below continued its rhythmic pulse, unaware of the turmoil raging above. I felt caught in the crossfire of conflicting emotions—a strange mix of anger, concern, and an unexpected surge of love that refused to be extinguished.

"What do we do now?" I finally asked, my voice softer, tinged with uncertainty. "Can we really move forward after this?"

Caden stepped closer, his expression shifting from tension to desperation. "I want to try. I want to prove to you that I can be better, that we can be better together. I'll do whatever it takes."

The sincerity in his voice struck a chord deep within me, and for the first time that night, I felt a glimmer of hope pierce through the heavy fog of confusion. "And what if it isn't enough? What if your past catches up with you, with us?"

He reached for my hand, his touch sending a jolt of warmth through me, grounding me in the chaos. "Then we face it together. I won't let you go through this alone. I promise."

I wanted to believe him. I wanted to think that our love was strong enough to withstand the storms brewing around us, but the reality was heavy, and the stakes were higher than ever. "Okay," I whispered, squeezing his hand. "We'll figure it out together. But I need you to be all in. No more secrets."

His gaze locked onto mine, and in that moment, I saw a flicker of determination that made my heart skip a beat. "No more secrets," he vowed, and for the first time that night, the weight of our truths felt a little lighter.

But as we stood there, intertwined in a delicate promise, I couldn't shake the feeling that the real battle was still ahead of us, lurking in the shadows, waiting for the moment we least expected.

The air between us hung thick with unspoken promises and hidden fears, a fragile balance precariously teetering on the edge. I could feel the weight of Caden's hand in mine, a tether anchoring me to the moment even as the world around us swirled in chaos. The neon lights of the city flickered through the window, illuminating the tumultuous shadows that danced across his face, each flash of color revealing another layer of his complicated soul.

"I can't keep doing this, Caden," I said, my voice a whisper, as if raising it would shatter the delicate truce we had forged. "I need to know you're serious about this. You need to show me you're committed to making things right."

"I'm all in, I promise," he replied, his gaze intense and unwavering. "But I need your trust. I need you to believe that I can change."

"Trust?" I echoed, my heart battling between the urge to believe him and the instinct to run. "Trust is a fragile thing, Caden. It takes time to rebuild, especially after it's been shattered."

He squeezed my hand, his warmth a grounding force against the chill creeping into my thoughts. "Then let's take it one step at a time. We can start right here, right now. I'll tell you everything. No more holding back."

I nodded, heart racing, feeling like we were both teetering on the brink of something monumental. "Okay, then tell me everything. No omissions, no white lies. If we're going to do this, we're going to do it right."

Caden took a deep breath, his eyes flickering with emotions that danced just out of reach. "You deserve the whole truth, and it's ugly. I got involved with a group that deals with some very dangerous people. They think they own me now."

"Own you?" I repeated, incredulous. "You're not some toy to be owned. You're a person with choices."

His eyes darkened, and the vulnerability I had seen moments before morphed into something more guarded. "Not when you're in too deep. They don't let you walk away. I thought I could manage it, control it, but I was wrong. Now, if I try to cut ties, they could come after me—and you."

A cold chill slithered down my spine at the mention of danger. "And what exactly does that mean for us?" I asked, each word laced with anxiety. "Do I need to be worried about my safety?"

"Not if I can help it," he said, his voice low and fierce. "But I can't promise you complete safety. I just need you to trust me while I find a way out of this mess. I need you to stay by my side."

"What if staying by your side puts me in more danger?" I challenged, my heart pounding against my ribcage. The thought of being swept into his chaotic world sent my pulse racing. "What if it's not just you they're after?"

"I'll protect you," he insisted, desperation creeping into his tone. "That's why I pushed you away in the first place. I didn't want to involve you in my life, and now that I've let you in, I realize how foolish that was."

"You can't just decide what's best for me," I said, frustration bubbling up. "I want to be in this with you, but it's hard to stand by someone when every choice they've made has led us here. You need to help me understand the gravity of the situation, Caden. What are we really up against?"

He glanced out the window, his jaw tightening as he seemed to wrestle with his thoughts. "There are people who won't hesitate to hurt those around me to make a point. I've seen it. They have eyes everywhere, and they know how to get to me through the ones I care about."

"I refuse to be a pawn in this game," I replied, crossing my arms, feeling the heat of anger flush through me. "I don't want to be in the dark while you fight your battles. You need to let me in, Caden."

He turned to me, his expression pained, almost haunted. "I'm trying. I really am. But you have to understand, this is bigger than just us. I need to find a way to get out of this, but it's complicated. The people I'm involved with—"

"Complicated? That's one word for it." I rolled my eyes, frustration surfacing again. "How can we possibly move forward if you won't be straight with me? What are their plans? What do they want from you?"

"I don't know exactly," he admitted, his voice lowering. "But I know they're not just going to let me walk away. They're invested in me, and they have ways of making people disappear if they think you're a liability."

The gravity of his words settled heavily in the pit of my stomach. "Caden, I need you to promise me one thing."

"Anything," he said, his eyes fierce, a promise reflected in their depths.

"If it ever gets too dangerous, if you see a chance to escape, you have to take it. You can't put my safety on the line for some misguided loyalty."

His expression darkened, and for a moment, I felt a pang of guilt for what I had just said. "I can't leave you behind," he said, his voice a low growl. "You're everything to me."

"And you're everything to me," I countered, my heart racing at the truth of my words. "But love can't flourish in a shadow. I won't let myself be consumed by your past."

"Then we need to figure this out together," he replied, determination etched into his features. "We can't let fear dictate our choices. I will do everything I can to protect you, to keep you out of harm's way."

"I want that too," I whispered, my heart aching with the tension between us. "But it won't be easy. We need to stay alert. We need to have a plan."

Caden nodded, a spark of something fierce igniting in his gaze. "Then let's start tonight. I have some contacts who can help us. We can't waste any time."

The urgency in his voice pulled me back to reality, and the city outside continued its vibrant pulse, a stark contrast to the uncertainty swirling within the walls of the penthouse. "Okay," I agreed, feeling a surge of adrenaline. "Let's do it."

Just then, a loud crash echoed through the air, rattling the windows as if the city itself were shattering into pieces. My heart dropped, and I turned to Caden, fear etched across my face. "What was that?"

He stiffened, his instincts kicking in as he moved closer, scanning the room with a practiced vigilance. "Stay behind me," he commanded, and I could see the shift in him, the fierce protector emerging as he stepped forward.

As I clung to his arm, a creeping dread settled in the pit of my stomach. Just outside the door, heavy footsteps echoed ominously, approaching quickly. "Caden, what's happening?" I breathed, my voice barely above a whisper.

"Whatever it is, it's not good," he replied, his face set in grim determination. The door rattled, and for a moment, everything stood still, suspended in the air as if the world was holding its breath.

Then, the door burst open, and shadows spilled into the room, menacing figures that filled the doorway. My heart raced as I realized that whatever had been lurking in the darkness was now crashing into our fragile world, shattering our hopes of safety and leaving us teetering on the edge of an unimaginable abyss.

Chapter 10: The Price of Love

The air hangs thick with tension, a tangible force pressing down on my chest, almost choking me as I steal a glance at Caden. His dark hair falls in tousled waves, framing a face that is achingly handsome yet shadowed by secrets I can't begin to comprehend. The city sprawls out behind him, a shimmering backdrop that seems to pulse with its own heartbeat, indifferent to the storm brewing between us. I could lose myself in the twinkling lights, but my eyes are magnetized to him—his expression caught somewhere between desperation and defiance.

"Why didn't you tell me sooner?" I finally manage to utter, my voice barely above a whisper. The question hangs in the air like a dare, and I immediately regret it, the weight of it almost suffocating. I can see the muscles in his jaw tense, and it feels as though I've drawn a line in the sand.

Caden's gaze shifts away, out toward the horizon where the sun has dipped low, casting everything in a golden hue that feels like a cruel contrast to our dark reality. "I was trying to protect you," he replies, his voice low and gravelly. It sends a shiver down my spine, the combination of the truth and the lie wrapped in that sentence. Protect me? Or shield himself?

The penthouse is an extension of him—lavish but eerily sterile, like a museum dedicated to a man who had everything but the one thing he truly wanted: honesty. I can almost hear the ghosts of all his secrets echoing off the marble floors, whispering about the danger that lurks just beyond the city lights. My fingers trail along the edge of the sleek glass coffee table, feeling the chill of its surface beneath my touch. "Protect me from what?"

His eyes finally meet mine, a storm brewing within their depths. "From the truth."

I swallow hard, the lump in my throat growing larger. "What truth? That you've lied to me since the beginning?" I can hear the bitterness in my own voice, the accusation like a weapon. It's as if I've been standing on the edge of a precipice, peering into an abyss that's suddenly widened, threatening to swallow me whole.

He looks at me as though I've struck him, and for a brief moment, I see a flicker of vulnerability cross his features. "Everything I did was for you, for us," he insists, though the conviction in his voice falters. "You deserve to know the truth about my past. It's just... it's complicated."

"Complicated?" I scoff, the sound bitter on my tongue. "You mean it's messy and dangerous and completely outside the realm of what I signed up for." My heart races, not just from fear but from the realization that I've been living in a fairytale, unaware of the dark magic lurking just out of sight.

Caden takes a step closer, the distance between us shrinking as he reaches for my hand. His touch is electric, but there's an edge to it that makes me pull back instinctively. "I know I've made mistakes, but you have to trust me," he says, the earnestness in his voice causing my heart to flutter despite the storm raging in my mind. "I never meant for you to get involved in any of this."

"Then why did you let me?" I counter, my voice rising with the urgency of the moment. "You could have pushed me away, but you didn't. You chose to let me in."

A sigh escapes him, heavy with the weight of all that remains unspoken. "I wanted you too much," he admits, his eyes boring into mine with a sincerity that makes my heart stutter. "And now I can't stand the thought of losing you."

The honesty in his words makes my insides twist, the ache of longing intertwined with the fear of the unknown. I can't ignore the pull between us, the undeniable chemistry that crackles in the air like static electricity. But at what cost?

"Caden," I start, but he interrupts me, his voice urgent, almost desperate.

"I can fix this. I'll do whatever it takes to make you safe. Just give me a chance."

"What does that even mean?" My tone is sharp, a defense mechanism against the chaos swirling in my chest. "What are you planning?"

He hesitates, and in that moment, I can see the shadows flickering behind his facade—the battles he's fought, the people he's lost, and the consequences of a life lived in the shadows. "There are things you don't understand, things I can't explain without putting you at risk."

"Risk? I'm already at risk, Caden! You've put me in danger just by being here." My pulse quickens, the realization dawning that I'm standing on a precipice, and one misstep could send me spiraling into the unknown.

"I can't lose you," he says again, his voice a low rumble, filled with raw emotion. "Let me prove to you that I'm not the monster you think I am."

"Prove it?" I echo, disbelief flooding my veins. "You expect me to just take your word for it? You've kept so much from me. How am I supposed to trust anything you say now?"

"Because I love you," he replies, the words tumbling from his lips with the weight of all his unspoken fears.

The admission hangs in the air, electrifying and terrifying all at once. My heart thuds in my chest, caught between disbelief and the ache of longing that has grown between us like a vine, entwining itself around my heart. I want to believe him, to succumb to the magic we've woven together. But the shadows linger, haunting me with the price that love demands.

In that moment, everything I thought I knew about love, trust, and loyalty unravels like a thread pulled from the fabric of my reality.

Caden's confession echoes in my mind, a siren call I can't ignore. But what does it mean for us, for the life I thought I was building? The truth is, I'm not sure I can afford to find out.

The silence stretches between us, thick and palpable, like the fog rolling off the East River on a cold autumn morning. I can feel the weight of his words settling in the pit of my stomach, heavy and unyielding. Love is supposed to uplift, to set your heart soaring, yet here I am, grounded by the reality of Caden's past, unsure if I'm anchored or trapped.

"What do you expect me to say to that?" I ask, my voice steadier than I feel. I'm grasping for clarity, but my fingers keep slipping through the threads of this tangled web.

Caden runs a hand through his hair, a gesture that makes him look boyish and vulnerable, so unlike the man who wields power like a sword. "I just want you to understand. There are forces at play here, things I can't control. But you—" He pauses, taking a breath that seems to gather all his courage. "You're the only thing I want to protect."

"Protect me from what? Knowing the truth?" I scoff, crossing my arms tightly over my chest, as if shielding myself from his words. I can feel my heart racing, each thump echoing the battle raging inside me. Part of me wants to believe him, wants to be wrapped up in the safety of his arms, while another part screams to run, to distance myself from this beautiful mess.

"I didn't want to burden you with my past," he says, the vulnerability in his voice washing over me like a wave. "I thought I could just be... me, for once. The man who loves you, not the man who's made choices that haunt him."

The room feels smaller, the air thicker. "But you've kept me in the dark. How can I love you if I don't even know who you really are?"

"I'm trying to show you." His frustration is palpable, a tangible thing that snaps in the air between us. "It's not easy for me, either. I'm not just some heartthrob in a penthouse. I'm—"

"Complicated?" I cut him off, a flicker of a smile breaking through the tension. "Maybe we should get matching t-shirts, then. 'Complicated' sounds like a great theme for a couple's retreat."

His lips twitch at the corners, the briefest glimmer of a smile piercing through the storm. "I'd rather we skip the retreat and figure this out ourselves."

"Right. Because nothing screams romance like unraveling a life shrouded in secrecy." My voice drips with sarcasm, but the truth is, I can't shake the feeling that the stakes are higher than I want to admit.

Caden steps closer, closing the space between us, his presence both reassuring and alarming. "What if I told you I've made arrangements? To keep you safe?"

"Arrangements?" I echo, my brows knitting together in confusion. "What does that even mean? Are we talking bodyguards, or are you enlisting the Avengers?"

He chuckles softly, the sound soothing my frayed nerves, but I can't let it distract me. "I'm serious, Lila. I've reached out to some people. I can make sure you're protected while I deal with everything."

The laughter dies in my throat. "Protected from what? Caden, this isn't a game. You can't just wave a magic wand and make your problems disappear."

"I wish I could." He runs a hand through his hair again, revealing the tension hidden behind his confident facade. "But I can't sit back and let anything happen to you. Not again."

The air shifts, charged with the gravity of his words. "Not again? What happened before?"

He hesitates, his eyes clouding over as memories flicker across his face. "It's complicated."

"Of course, it is," I mutter under my breath. "It always is."

"Lila, please." He reaches for me, his fingers brushing against my wrist, igniting a spark of warmth. "I'm asking you to trust me. I know I don't deserve it, but I'll do whatever it takes to make this right."

"Make what right? This whole situation feels like a disaster waiting to happen." My heart races as his words sink in. I want to trust him, to leap into his arms and let the world fade away, but fear is a cunning beast that creeps in, gnawing at my resolve.

"I can't stand the thought of you getting hurt because of my mistakes."

My chest tightens. "And yet, here I am, standing on the precipice of your mistakes. How does that make sense?"

He draws in a shaky breath, his eyes pleading. "I'll make it right. Just... let me show you what I can do."

"And what do you plan to do? Start a one-man army?"

His lips curl into a wry smile, and for a brief moment, I can see the lightness of who he is beneath the weight of his troubles. "If that's what it takes."

"Then what? You'll just throw yourself into danger, and I'm supposed to sit here twiddling my thumbs? I've read enough thrillers to know how this ends."

"You'll never be in danger, I promise."

"And what if that promise gets broken?" I challenge, pushing back against the tide of emotions surging within me. "What if I lose you in the process?"

"Then I'll come back and drag you into this mess with me."

"Fantastic. Because nothing says love like a good ol' fashioned mess."

As the banter flows between us, a part of me revels in this familiarity, but the stakes keep rising, threatening to unravel the thread that holds us together.

"Lila," he murmurs, his tone shifting as he moves even closer, closing the space between our hearts. "I can't lose you. Not when I've finally found something worth fighting for."

My heart aches with the weight of his words, a truth that resonates deep within me. "Caden..."

He takes a step back, shaking his head as if shaking off the gravity of the moment. "You deserve to know the truth. I'll tell you everything. Just give me time."

I nod slowly, the unspoken pact hanging in the air like the city skyline beyond the window—a beauty tinged with danger.

"Time," I whisper, the word echoing in the silence that follows. But deep down, I can't help but wonder if time is something we can afford.

Suddenly, the intercom buzzes, breaking the moment like glass shattering against concrete. We both jump, and I can feel my heart stutter as Caden's expression shifts, instantly alert.

"Who is it?" he asks, tension wrapping around his words.

"Delivery for Mr. Shaw," a voice crackles through the speaker.

"Now?" Caden's irritation is palpable, his hand balling into a fist at his side. "What delivery?"

"Maybe it's a peace offering for your tortured soul," I quip, trying to lighten the mood, but my heart races at the uncertainty swirling in the air.

"Just stay here," he says, tension lacing his words as he moves toward the door. "I'll be right back."

I nod, trying to keep my composure, but the unease coils around me like a snake. Something about this feels wrong, an impending storm lurking just out of sight.

As he disappears into the hallway, I take a moment to collect my thoughts, the ache in my heart growing heavier with each passing second. Trust is a fragile thing, and the cost of love may be more than I can bear. The flicker of danger is like a candle in the dark—illuminating, yet casting long shadows that whisper secrets I'm not ready to face.

The intercom buzzes again, shattering the fraught silence like a firework against a midnight sky. My heart skips a beat, and I can hear Caden's footsteps retreating down the hallway, the sound echoing through the lavish penthouse. I should be grateful for the distraction, but the way he'd tightened his jaw before leaving tells me something more sinister lurks beneath the surface.

I look around the penthouse, at the modern art that decorates the walls and the sleek furniture that looks as if it had never been sat upon. This place feels more like a fortress than a home, a sterile prison where secrets are kept in hidden corners. The city outside continues to pulse with life, its vibrant energy contrasting sharply with the growing unease inside me.

"Delivery for Mr. Shaw!" the voice calls again, more insistent this time.

I can't shake the feeling that the delivery man is merely a messenger of chaos, heralding whatever dark storm Caden has been trying to shield me from. I stand, pacing the marble floor, my mind a jumble of questions and fears. What if it's something that puts us both in danger? What if this is the beginning of something terrible, an unraveling of everything we've built?

When Caden returns, his expression is a mixture of irritation and concern, eyes flaring with a protective fire that makes my breath catch. "It's just a package," he says, attempting to ease my tension with a reassuring smile, though I can see the anxiety lurking just beneath the surface. "Nothing to worry about."

"Is that what you tell yourself?" I can't help but shoot back, the sarcasm slipping out before I can rein it in. "Just a little package, no big deal."

"Lila," he warns, stepping closer, his voice low and steady. "I mean it. I don't want you getting caught up in my mess."

"Caught up? You already dragged me in without asking. At this point, I'm the unwilling lead in your thriller novel."

Caden's lips twitch at the corners, but his eyes remain serious. "You're more than that to me. You're everything."

"Everything? Even more than the package?" I tease, but the joke feels thin, a fragile layer of humor draped over a chasm of uncertainty.

"Funny," he mutters, but the tension in his shoulders tells me he's not laughing. "Let's just open it."

As he tears into the package, I take a step back, curiosity battling my unease. It's wrapped in unassuming brown paper, but the way he handles it is cautious, as if he's expecting something to jump out at him. I watch as he lifts out a sleek black box, his brow furrowing deeper with each passing second.

"What is it?" I ask, the question tumbling from my lips, laced with concern.

"It's... complicated," he replies, echoing his earlier refrain, his fingers brushing over the surface of the box as if it holds the secrets to his soul.

"Does it come with a warning label?"

His eyes meet mine, a flicker of fear breaking through the bravado. "Something like that."

"Caden, you're killing me here. Just open it!"

With a resigned sigh, he pops open the box, revealing an assortment of gadgets and devices that look like they belong in a spy movie rather than his high-rise abode. I lean in closer, curiosity piqued, and as I study the contents, a chill runs down my spine.

"Why do you have surveillance equipment?" I ask, my voice barely above a whisper.

"It's not what it looks like," he says, his voice low but strained. "This is for my safety... and yours."

I take a step back, the reality of the situation crashing over me like a wave. "What are you involved in, Caden? You can't just keep dropping these bombs and expecting me to stay calm."

"I'll explain everything," he insists, his voice earnest, yet I can see the tension tightening his features. "But first, I need you to promise me one thing."

"What's that?"

"Promise me you'll stay here. Don't leave, no matter what."

"Now you're really pushing it," I shoot back, the anxiety clawing at my chest. "I'm not some damsel waiting for a knight to rescue me from the tower. I can handle myself."

"And that's exactly why I need you to stay put. You're stronger than you know, but right now, I can't risk you being out there while I deal with this."

The gravity of his words weighs heavily on my shoulders, and for a brief moment, I feel a flicker of panic. "Deal with what?"

Caden runs a hand through his hair, frustration etched on his face. "Let's just say I have some people who aren't too happy with me right now."

"People? Like in the mafia? Because I'm not exactly dressed for a turf war."

His lips curl into a half-smile, but the humor doesn't quite reach his eyes. "Not exactly, but let's just say they play rough."

"I don't like where this is going," I murmur, my heart racing.

Before he can respond, there's a sudden knock at the door, sharp and demanding. Both of us freeze, and I can feel the air thicken with tension. "Caden?"

"Stay here," he hisses, moving toward the door, his expression shifting into something unreadable.

I want to protest, to demand he explain what's happening, but the weight of his concern grips me, rooting me to the spot. As he inches closer to the door, my breath quickens, anxiety coursing through me.

Caden glances back at me, eyes fierce and determined. "I mean it. Don't come out."

"Like that's going to happen," I retort, but my heart races as he slowly turns the doorknob.

The door creaks open, revealing a tall figure shrouded in shadows, the hallway lights flickering ominously around them. I strain to hear their voice, low and threatening, and I can't help but inch closer, desperate to understand the danger that's knocking on our door.

"Caden Shaw," the figure drawls, a hint of malice lacing their tone. "We need to talk."

I can feel my pulse quickening as the tension crackles in the air, and a sickening feeling settles in my stomach. My instincts scream for me to flee, but I'm rooted in place, caught in a web of fear and uncertainty.

"Who are you?" Caden's voice is steady, but I can see the muscle in his jaw clenching as he tries to keep his composure.

"We know about her," the figure says, their eyes glinting with something dark and predatory.

Panic surges within me, a wave of adrenaline flooding my veins. I've stepped into a world I never wanted to be a part of, and the stakes have never felt higher. I'm about to say something—anything—when the figure's lips curl into a smirk, a predatory smile that sends a chill racing down my spine.

"Time's up, Caden."

My heart drops, the weight of their words crashing down on me like a falling sky. The future I thought I could hold onto slips through my fingers, and as the door swings wider, the shadows spill into the light, bringing with them an unsettling sense of dread that wraps around me like a vice.

I realize, with dawning horror, that this is only the beginning of a battle I never signed up for, and as the door closes behind Caden, I know that whatever happens next will change everything.

Chapter 11: Tangled in Secrets

Caden's office buzzed with the kind of energy that made the air feel charged, like static before a storm. Sunlight streamed through the tall windows, illuminating the sharp lines of his minimalist desk, yet the warmth of the golden rays did little to ease the chill creeping up my spine. I perched on the edge of my seat, my hands cradling a sketchbook filled with ideas for the upcoming collection. Every brushstroke on the page felt like a piece of my heart laid bare, and yet, an unsettling weight pressed down on me.

The faint click of heels echoed outside, a sound so familiar yet jarring now that it turned my attention away from the designs. A hushed murmur fluttered through the room like a secret caught in the wind. I glanced up, meeting the gaze of a tall woman with perfectly coiffed hair and an immaculate suit that screamed authority. She wasn't just here to deliver bad news; she was here to remind me of my place. As the co-owner of the fashion line, she wielded power that coiled tighter around me with each passing day.

"Is that another one of your whimsical creations?" she asked, her voice dripping with a saccharine sweetness that barely concealed her disdain. "Perhaps a bit too...vintage for our target audience?"

I held back a sharp retort, the kind I'd practiced in the mirror at home, where no one could judge me. Instead, I flashed a tight smile, pretending it didn't hurt that someone could dismiss hours of painstaking work with a mere flick of her wrist. "It's an homage to the '90s," I replied, my voice steady despite the acid burning in my stomach. "Fashion always cycles back, doesn't it?"

She pursed her lips, as if considering whether my comment was worth her time. "Cycles are fine, but we need to move forward. We can't afford to linger in the past." The message hung heavy in the air, a dagger cloaked in silk.

Just then, Caden walked in, his tall frame a beacon of charisma amid the tightening tension. His presence wrapped around me like a safety net, yet it felt increasingly fragile. I caught his eye, hoping for the connection we used to share—a look, a smirk, a silent promise that we were in this together. But today, his gaze flicked away too quickly, landing on the woman whose words had just pierced my defenses.

"Lydia, good to see you," Caden said, his tone polite but strained. It was the kind of politeness that raised red flags, and a sinking feeling twisted in my chest. He turned to me, his smile fading into something more unreadable. "Have you finalized those sketches?"

The room crackled with an unspoken urgency, and I could feel the weight of the unrelenting scrutiny as the other partners observed from their desks, their eyes hawkish and unyielding. "Almost," I managed, fighting the tremor in my voice. "Just a few tweaks."

Caden nodded, but there was a shadow behind his eyes, a flicker of something that made my heart race in a different way. "Good. Let's get them ready for the meeting next week."

As he said this, the partners exchanged glances, each one seemingly weighing my worth in the grand scheme of their twisted game. They were wolves in designer suits, circling closer to the prey they sensed was vulnerable, and I was that prey. It was becoming harder to ignore the whispers, the cautious glances exchanged among them when they thought I wasn't looking.

After the meeting, I retreated to my studio, hoping to drown out the world with a surge of creativity. But instead, a sense of unease wrapped around me like a heavy blanket. I flipped through my sketches, vibrant illustrations of flowing fabrics and bold patterns, yet even the colors seemed dull against the backdrop of my spiraling thoughts. What had begun as a dream of fashion and art was morphing into a nightmare where my every move felt orchestrated, monitored by eyes I couldn't quite see.

I needed a distraction. I reached for my phone, fingers hovering over the contact list until they landed on Caden's name. A simple text would suffice—just a line about our designs, a request for reassurance, something to remind me that we were still a team. But when I pressed send, doubt gnawed at me. Would he read it? Would he care?

As the minutes dragged on, my phone remained stubbornly silent. The vibrant sketches mocked me from the table, their colors losing their brilliance in the dim light of my studio. The soft rustle of fabric filled the air, a reminder of what was at stake. Each piece I designed was a fragment of my soul, woven into the fabric of Caden's collection, yet now they felt tainted by shadows of doubt.

Just as I was about to push the feelings aside, the door swung open, and in walked Caden, his expression a mix of determination and apprehension. "Can we talk?"

I nodded, surprised to feel a flicker of hope. Maybe I could still reach him, peel back the layers of tension and distance that had begun to smother our connection. He stepped inside, shutting the door behind him as if sealing us off from the world outside.

"Something's not right," he said, his voice low, eyes searching mine. "I can feel it. You're not yourself."

"I don't know how to be myself when I'm constantly under the microscope," I admitted, frustration creeping into my voice. "It's like I'm drowning in expectations that have nothing to do with my designs."

His brow furrowed, a storm brewing in those deep blue depths I had come to rely on. "I'll handle it," he promised, yet the way his jaw tightened suggested he was grappling with demons of his own.

"Handle what? The partners? They're not just business associates, Caden; they're sharks circling for blood. I don't know how to navigate this." The words spilled out, raw and unfiltered, and in that moment, I could almost see the weight of my fear reflected in his eyes.

"I thought I could keep you safe from this," he said softly, stepping closer, the tension between us thickening like the fabric we worked with. "But it's complicated. They've invested too much, and they don't see you the way I do."

"Then how do you see me?" I asked, my heart pounding, a tremor of hope threading through my vulnerability.

He hesitated, and in that breath, time seemed to stretch, leaving us suspended in a moment that felt both terrifying and electric. "I see you as the heart of this collection, the one who breathes life into every piece. But they're not just watching your designs; they're watching you. And I can't lose you to this."

The gravity of his words settled around us, grounding me in a reality I had tried to ignore. Suddenly, I was acutely aware of the tangled web of secrets and lies we were both caught in, threatening to ensnare us at any moment. In that charged silence, it became evident that our fight wasn't just for a collection; it was for something much deeper, much more fragile. It was a fight for trust in a world where trust felt increasingly elusive.

And as we stood there, hearts racing in tandem, I knew that whatever happened next would determine the fate of not just our designs, but the very fabric of our lives intertwined.

The air crackled with an electric tension that felt as tangible as the fabric draped around us. Caden stood so close that I could see the tiny flecks of concern in his eyes, a storm brewing beneath the surface. I had always found solace in his presence, a warm glow that seemed to wrap around me like a soft cashmere sweater, but today it felt more like an interrogation room, the stakes too high and the consequences too real.

"I can't let them dictate what I do or how I create," I said, my voice barely above a whisper. The passion bubbled just below my skin, but I tempered it, knowing that too much fire could burn us both. "Every stitch, every seam, it's my expression, Caden. If they take that from me, what's left?"

His gaze softened, but the undercurrent of worry remained. "We'll find a way to navigate this. I promise," he said, his tone resolute, but the unspoken words hung heavy between us. I wanted to believe him, to cling to the hope that he could shield me from the prying eyes of his partners, but doubt gnawed at my confidence.

The conversation shifted abruptly as Caden's phone buzzed on the desk, shattering the moment like glass. He glanced at the screen, and the color drained from his face. I couldn't help but notice how the joy that often sparkled in his eyes dimmed under the weight of whatever message had just appeared. "I need to take this," he said, a touch of urgency creeping into his voice.

"Of course," I replied, though a knot tightened in my stomach. As he stepped away, I couldn't shake the feeling that I was being left behind in a world that was spiraling out of control. I turned back to my sketches, desperate for distraction. Each drawing, vibrant and full of life, felt like a lifeline—a tether to the creativity that had once flowed so freely. But the colors began to blur, the edges softening until they merged into an indistinct haze.

I caught snippets of Caden's conversation, a low murmur that sent waves of unease crashing over me. "No, I can't... It's not right... I'll talk to her," he said, each word a jagged edge, cutting through the fabric of my composure.

My heart raced, each beat drumming out a rhythm of anxiety as I paced the small space of my studio. I stopped at the large window overlooking the bustling street below. The world outside moved with an effortless grace—strangers darting past, each one absorbed in their own life, their own story. A sense of longing washed over me. I craved that kind of freedom, the ability to be simply a part of the world instead of a pawn in a dangerous game I had never intended to join.

Caden returned, his expression unreadable. "We need to talk," he said, a firm resolve in his voice. I nodded, but the tightness in my chest returned, a warning bell echoing in my mind.

"Is it about the partners?" I asked, bracing myself for whatever storm was about to break. "What did they want?"

He leaned against the desk, arms crossed as he regarded me, his brow furrowing. "They want to push the collection forward, and they're considering bringing in an outside consultant."

The words hit me like a slap. "An outside consultant? For what? To take over my designs?"

"It's not like that," he rushed to explain, though the urgency in his voice only amplified my fears. "They think it'll help elevate the brand, but I know they're just trying to regain control."

"Control. That seems to be their favorite word." I crossed my arms, feeling a wave of defensiveness wash over me. "And what about me, Caden? Where do I fit into this? Am I just a means to an end?"

"You're not just anything. You're the heart of this collection," he insisted, his voice rising, frustration etching lines on his forehead. "But they don't see that. They see numbers, profit margins, bottom lines. I don't want you to feel pressured, and I want to protect your vision."

"Protect it from whom? From your partners? From me?" The hurt seeped into my words, bitterness staining the air between us.

Caden took a step closer, the intensity of his gaze piercing through my defenses. "From everyone, including yourself. You can't let them shake your confidence. You're brilliant, and you deserve to be recognized for that."

A silence enveloped us, a moment stretching out, taut like the fabric of the gowns I designed. "But what if I'm not good enough?" I whispered, the vulnerability spilling out before I could catch it.

"What if everything I create is just... a fleeting whim, like a spark that fades too quickly?"

He took a deep breath, his shoulders relaxing slightly. "That's part of the process. Every artist doubts themselves. But you have something special, something real. Don't let them take that away."

Just then, the door swung open, and Lydia entered, her perfectly manicured nails tapping impatiently against her phone. "Caden, we need to discuss the meeting—"

Her words trailed off as her gaze flitted between us, a predator sizing up its prey. "Oh, sorry to interrupt. I didn't realize you were busy." The undertone dripped with sarcasm, and I felt a familiar prickle of resentment.

"We were just wrapping up," Caden replied, the protective edge creeping back into his voice. "What's on your mind?"

Lydia's gaze slid to me, her lips curving into a smile that didn't reach her eyes. "Just a few adjustments to the presentation. I hope you're ready for it. I wouldn't want any surprises."

My heart raced at the suggestion that my designs, my identity, were now part of a presentation I wasn't in control of. "What kind of adjustments?" I interjected, unwilling to be a silent participant in this unfolding drama.

"Oh, just the usual tweaks to make it more appealing to the investors," Lydia replied, her tone saccharine yet sharp. "We want to highlight the parts that really sell, not just what tugs at the heartstrings."

Caden shifted uncomfortably, his fingers tapping against the desk. "You can't just strip it down to what sells. It's about the artistry too."

"But artistry doesn't pay the bills, does it?" she shot back, her voice clipped. "This is a business, and we have to think practically. If you want to impress the investors, we need to show them numbers, not daydreams."

My pulse quickened as I took in the tension. "Daydreams are what make this collection unique. If we compromise that, what's left?"

Lydia's eyes narrowed slightly. "Perhaps you're too emotionally attached to your creations. It might be worth considering how you present them to those who can truly appreciate their value."

I felt Caden's frustration radiate beside me, a palpable heat that both comforted and alarmed me. "Lydia, we can't sacrifice the essence of the collection for marketability," he said, his voice steady but tinged with urgency.

She rolled her eyes. "We'll see about that. The meeting is tomorrow. Just be ready." With that, she turned on her heel, strutting out like a queen whose crown was slightly askew, leaving us in her wake.

Once the door clicked shut, the air felt heavier, laden with unspoken words and unmet expectations. "This isn't just about the designs anymore, is it?" I murmured, more to myself than to him. "It's about power, control, and who gets to decide the narrative."

Caden took a step closer, his presence a shield against the turmoil outside. "And we need to reclaim that narrative before it's rewritten without us. We can't let them dictate our vision."

The determination in his voice ignited a spark within me, and for the first time since this whirlwind had begun, I felt a glimmer of hope. "Then let's fight back," I said, a fire lighting in my chest. "Let's make sure they see the true heart of this collection and what it stands for. I won't let them take my designs without a battle."

The path ahead was still fraught with uncertainty, but standing together, I felt ready to face the chaos swirling around us. With our combined resolve, we could push back against the shadows threatening to engulf us, reclaiming our narrative one stitch at a time.

The next day, a haze of determination enveloped me as I returned to the studio, the morning sun casting a golden hue over my sketches.

I had vowed not to let Lydia's dismissive words derail my vision. If anything, they fueled my fire. I would show them what passion and creativity could achieve when combined with hard work. I grabbed my favorite pencil, the one that felt like an extension of my hand, and began to sketch anew, channeling my frustration into every line and curve.

Each stroke on the paper whispered stories of the designs that danced in my head, the vibrant hues of fabric calling out like old friends. I lost myself in the rhythm of creation, blocking out the concerns that lurked at the edges of my mind. But then came the familiar sound of Caden's footsteps, his presence a comforting balm against the day's challenges.

"Morning," he said, leaning against the doorframe, arms crossed, a hint of a smile breaking through his earlier tension. "How's the creative genius this fine day?"

"Ready to fight the good fight," I replied, raising my chin defiantly. "I've got a new vision for the collection that will knock their socks off. They'll have no choice but to recognize the artistry."

"Now that's the spirit!" Caden stepped inside, his demeanor shifting from caution to encouragement. "What do you have in mind?"

As I spread my sketches across the table, I explained my ideas, the colors and textures flowing from my lips like a symphony. "This piece here," I said, tapping a design with a high neckline and cascading sleeves, "is inspired by the fluidity of water, capturing movement in every stitch. I want it to be a celebration of strength and grace."

Caden leaned closer, his eyes sparkling with admiration. "You've truly outdone yourself this time. It's powerful and beautiful—just like you."

A warmth bloomed in my chest, but the compliment held a bittersweet tinge. The thought of the partners tearing my passion apart loomed over me, casting a shadow on our shared enthusiasm.

Before I could voice my concerns, Caden's phone buzzed again, pulling him back to reality. "Excuse me," he said, and stepped outside to take the call. I turned back to my sketches, the momentary distraction sharpening my focus. I needed to finalize my designs before the meeting, to ensure I was ready to present my case with confidence.

Time slipped away like sand through my fingers as I worked, absorbed in the world I was building, until Caden reentered, his expression more serious than before. "We need to talk about the meeting," he said, his voice low, tension etched into his features.

"What did they say?" I asked, my heart pounding in my chest.

"They're not just interested in numbers; they're also eyeing the direction of the collection," he explained, his jaw clenched. "Lydia thinks it needs a complete overhaul, and she's pushing for some radical changes. They want to shift the focus to what will sell, not what resonates."

I felt the blood drain from my face. "Are they really willing to risk everything for a quick buck? They can't do this!"

"They think they're making a smart business move. But it's not just about profit margins; it's about the heart of what we're creating." His voice dropped, urgency threading through his words. "They don't see the potential like we do. They want to cut corners to make it marketable, and that's not what this collection is about."

"Then we need to stand our ground," I insisted, anger boiling beneath the surface. "I refuse to let them compromise our vision. We can't let them erase what makes this collection unique."

Caden nodded, his gaze steady, but uncertainty flickered in his eyes. "We'll need a solid strategy, and we have to be prepared for their pushback. They won't give in easily."

"Then let's give them a reason to listen," I declared, a spark igniting within me. "We'll present our designs with conviction, show them the artistry, the story behind each piece. I'll make them see what they're missing."

A fire ignited between us, and for a brief moment, it felt like we could take on the world together. But as quickly as it kindled, the doubts returned, settling like a dense fog. The realization that we were standing on the precipice of a battle against powerful adversaries weighed heavily on my heart.

The morning faded into afternoon, and the atmosphere in the studio grew heavier as the hour of the meeting approached. The once-inviting light seemed to dim, shadows creeping along the walls. I paced the room, my mind racing as I reviewed my sketches one last time. Each design was a piece of my soul, yet the thought of presenting them in front of Caden's partners made my palms sweat.

"Are you ready?" Caden's voice cut through the haze of anxiety, and I turned to face him.

"As ready as I'll ever be," I replied, forcing a smile despite the knot in my stomach.

We entered the conference room, where the partners were already gathered. The air was thick with expectation, their expressions a mix of impatience and intrigue. I felt their eyes on me, assessing, calculating. This was more than just a meeting; it was a trial, and I was the one on the stand.

"Thank you for joining us today," Caden began, his voice steady, but I could hear the subtle edge of tension. "We have some exciting developments regarding the collection."

Lydia interjected, her tone sharp as she folded her arms. "Exciting? I hope you're not referring to those... whimsical sketches again."

I took a breath, ready to defend my work. "Whimsical can be powerful," I said, feeling my voice grow stronger. "Art isn't merely a commodity; it tells a story, connects with people. My designs are an expression of that connection, not just items to be sold."

Lydia rolled her eyes, but I pressed on, determined to make my point. I showcased my sketches one by one, describing the inspiration behind each piece, weaving in the themes of empowerment and individuality. "This collection isn't about quick sales; it's about making a statement in the fashion world, a statement that will resonate beyond just this season."

As I spoke, I could see some of the partners leaning in, intrigued despite their initial skepticism. A flicker of hope ignited within me, and I pushed forward, passionately describing the essence of each design. But as I neared the end of my presentation, the atmosphere shifted. The tension thickened, and I could feel the room's energy change.

Just as I finished, one of the partners leaned forward, his voice dripping with condescension. "That's all very poetic, but we need numbers. Show us how this will translate into profits."

Caden's expression hardened, frustration evident as he clenched his fists. "This is not about numbers; it's about the brand identity we're building. If we chase profits at the cost of creativity, we lose our essence."

"Essence doesn't pay the bills, Caden," Lydia snapped, her tone biting. "We have a responsibility to our investors."

With each word exchanged, I felt the walls closing in, the ground beneath me shifting. I glanced at Caden, his eyes reflecting the same storm of emotion swirling within me. "But if we compromise our vision, what are we left with? A hollow shell that doesn't represent who we are as artists or as a brand."

The partner narrowed his eyes, a predatory gleam settling in his expression. "You need to understand something, both of you. This is not your playground. This is business. If you want to play, you must follow the rules we set."

A chill ran down my spine, each word dripping with menace. I looked at Caden, who seemed to be holding back a storm of emotions, a flicker of anger flashing across his face. "We're not going to give up our integrity for short-term gains," he stated, voice steady yet defiant. "We'll find a way to make this work without sacrificing what matters."

Just as I opened my mouth to add my agreement, the door swung open, and a tall figure stepped in. The atmosphere shifted immediately, the air thick with an unspoken tension.

"Gentlemen, and lady," he said, his voice low and gravelly. "I couldn't help but overhear your conversation." The eyes of every partner snapped to him, a mix of surprise and wariness. "I'm here to offer a different perspective."

Caden and I exchanged glances, confusion washing over us. Who was this man? And how could he possibly tip the scales in our favor?

"Who are you?" Lydia demanded, her composure faltering slightly.

He smiled, but there was an edge to it, as if he reveled in the chaos he was about to unleash. "Let's just say I have a vested interest in this collection and an idea that could change everything."

A hush fell over the room, the tension palpable as we awaited his next move. It felt like the air had turned to ice, a fragile silence pregnant with possibilities.

"Perhaps I can help you all find common ground," he continued, his gaze sweeping over the table, lingering on me. "But first, I need to know how far you're willing to go to protect your vision."

I felt my heart race as I stared into his eyes, searching for an answer in the depths of his inscrutable expression. This was a crossroads, and I was acutely aware that whatever path we chose next could change everything—our designs, our future, and perhaps even the very fabric of who we were.

Chapter 12: Breaking Point

A gust of wind rushed through the cracked window of my tiny apartment, carrying the bitter scent of rain-soaked pavement. The hum of the city played like a dissonant symphony outside—a cacophony of distant sirens, the soft thud of feet on the pavement, and the incessant chatter of life unspooling in a million directions. My heart raced as I stared at the flickering screen, the words of that anonymous email searing into my mind like a brand.

Caden. Underground. Crime.

Three words strung together with a sinister grace that sent shivers skittering down my spine. I didn't want to believe it. The man I loved, the one who'd held my hand through late-night movies and spontaneous road trips, could never be involved in something so sordid, so dangerous. But the nagging doubt burrowed into my chest, twisting like a vine, choking off the air.

"Hey, you okay in there?" Mia's voice drifted in from the living room, a soft lull in the chaos swirling in my head.

"Yeah, just... working on something," I called back, forcing a casualness into my tone that felt like trying to slip into a dress two sizes too small.

She appeared in the doorway, her brow furrowed with concern. "You sure? Because you look like you've just seen a ghost. Or worse, the last episode of that terrible reality show you insist on watching."

A weak laugh escaped me, but the flutter in my stomach remained. The question gnawed at me: How could I face Caden when I had this dark cloud hovering over us? "Just a lot on my mind. You know how it is."

Mia, with her thick curls bouncing around her shoulders like a spring of laughter, stepped closer, her intuition often sharper than the knives in my kitchen. "You can talk to me, you know. I'm always here, even when you're being all moody and cryptic."

"Thanks, I appreciate it," I replied, waving her off as if she were an insistent fly. I needed to process this alone, to wrap my mind around the implications of what I'd discovered.

The faint sound of rain pattering against the window matched the erratic beat of my heart. I returned to the email, the text glowing ominously. The sender had slipped through the cracks of my life, someone who knew enough to rattle me but remained an elusive phantom. I scanned the words again, looking for some glimmer of deception, a thread of hope that would weave itself into a story of innocence.

"Caden's in deep," it read. "He's involved with the Red Syndicate. You need to get out before it's too late."

My mind flipped through memories of Caden—his easy smile, the way his laughter echoed in the quiet corners of my mind. He was everything that felt right in a world that often made no sense. But had I been blind? Had I overlooked the signs, too lost in the romance of it all to notice the cracks forming in the facade?

With a deep breath, I steeled myself and grabbed my coat. Confrontation was necessary. I couldn't hide from this, no matter how terrifying it felt.

Caden's apartment was a short drive away, a sleek space that reflected his ambition and taste. I drove through the streets, each red light a momentary pause in my racing thoughts. Would he deny it? Would he throw me out, his face morphing into that of a stranger I no longer recognized?

As I arrived and parked, I felt the weight of the world settle on my shoulders. I climbed the stairs to his door, each step heavy with anticipation. Knocking felt like a formality; it was already clear that whatever I was about to say could change everything.

He opened the door, his expression shifting from surprise to concern. "Hey, I wasn't expecting you."

"Can I come in?" I didn't wait for an invitation, stepping past him into the cozy space that had once felt like a sanctuary.

"What's going on? You look like you've seen a ghost," he echoed Mia's words, his eyes scanning me, searching for clues.

"I received an email." The words came tumbling out, each one sharper than the last. "It said you're involved with the Red Syndicate."

His face went momentarily blank, the lightness in his eyes dimming to something far more serious. "I can explain—"

"Explain?" I interrupted, my voice trembling with a mix of anger and hurt. "You can explain why you've been lying to me? Why I found out about this from some anonymous tip instead of you?"

He ran a hand through his hair, a gesture I had always found endearing. "It's not what you think."

"Then what is it, Caden?" I crossed my arms, feeling the chill of betrayal seep into my bones.

"It's complicated. I got involved with some people—"

"Some people?" I echoed, disbelief twisting in my gut. "You mean criminals. You're in over your head."

He stepped closer, frustration etching lines around his mouth. "I didn't choose this. It's about business, and it spiraled out of control."

"Business? You're playing with fire, and I don't want to get burned."

He took a step back, the distance between us suddenly feeling like an insurmountable chasm. "I thought I could handle it, but now—"

"Now what? You're caught in something you can't escape from? What happened to the man who promised he'd protect me?" My heart was thundering in my chest, a storm of conflicting emotions swirling within.

He looked at me, a mixture of regret and resolve dancing in his eyes. "I still want to protect you. That's why I didn't tell you. I wanted to keep you safe."

"Safe?" I laughed, a harsh sound that felt foreign in the air between us. "You're putting me in danger by keeping me in the dark!"

The silence that followed was heavy, filled with the weight of unspoken words and shattered trust. I wanted to reach out, to bridge that gap, but the fear of what lay beneath the surface held me back. This wasn't the Caden I knew; this was a man backed into a corner, one I didn't recognize.

"Tell me the truth," I demanded, my voice barely above a whisper. "Are you in this for the money? The power? Or is it something darker?"

"I can't walk away from it now. But I promise I'll keep you out of it."

The hollow promise hung in the air, echoing like a distant bell. I wanted to believe him, to wrap myself in the warmth of our love and shield it from the cold reality outside. But as I looked into his eyes, I knew I was standing on the precipice of something far more dangerous than I could have ever imagined.

Every moment stretched like taffy, thick and gooey with tension, as I stood in Caden's living room, the air between us crackling with unspoken words. The walls, usually adorned with photographs of us—smiling, carefree, wrapped in the cocoon of our love—now felt like a prison, each frame a reminder of what was slipping away. I couldn't shake the feeling that I was watching a stranger transform before my eyes, the man I adored morphing into something I feared.

His silence hung heavily, each second ticking by like a slow countdown to something I dreaded. "You can't keep me out of this, Caden," I pressed, my voice firm yet trembling at the edges. "You're my life, and whatever you're involved in... it affects me."

"Stay out of it, please," he replied, running a hand over his jaw, frustration evident in the tight lines of his face. "I'm trying to protect you. You don't understand what's at stake."

"What's at stake?" I shot back, my hands clenching into fists. "Your freedom? My safety? Or is it the integrity of your precious business? Because I can't tell anymore."

His gaze flickered, betraying a glimmer of something beneath the bravado—fear, perhaps? The raw truth of his predicament? I desperately wanted to reach through the fog of his defenses and pull him back into the light.

"I need time," he finally said, his voice quiet yet commanding. "Let me handle this."

"Handle it?" I laughed, a bitter sound that echoed in the confined space. "Is that what you call it? Because it looks to me like you're spiraling into a pit of your own making, and I'm standing here at the edge, peering in. Do you really think I can just turn my back and walk away?"

With each word, I felt the wall I had built around my heart begin to crack. Caden's eyes softened, the steel hardening them slipping away for a moment. "You're stronger than you realize, you know? I thought I could shield you from this. But you're right—I should have trusted you more."

My breath caught. It was a small victory, but one I clung to fiercely. "I'm not asking for protection; I'm asking for honesty. I can't fight battles I don't know about."

He stepped forward, closing the distance between us. "I don't want you in the line of fire. You mean too much to me."

"And you mean everything to me," I replied, my voice low but fierce. "But how can we face this together if you keep the truth from me?"

The vulnerability in his gaze mirrored my own fears, and for a fleeting moment, the world around us faded. But reality crashed back in, reminding me of the urgency of our situation.

"I need to know if you're involved with them," I urged. "If there's a choice to be made, I want you to make it now. I'm not waiting around while you dance with danger."

His expression hardened again, the walls he had built re-erecting themselves. "You're asking me to choose between you and my life. It's not that simple."

"Then help me understand," I insisted, frustration bubbling beneath the surface. "I don't want to lose you to whatever darkness you've stepped into. We can fight this together."

The silence that followed was deafening. Caden's eyes searched mine, a tempest of emotions swirling within. "You don't know what you're asking," he finally said, the weight of his words pressing down on both of us.

"Then make me understand," I replied, my heart racing as the words poured out like a flood. "Tell me what you're involved in, and I'll decide if I'm willing to stand by your side or run far away."

He took a deep breath, his shoulders slumping as if the weight of the world had settled upon them. "Okay. But promise me you won't react until I finish."

"I promise." My heart raced, the anticipation thick in the air.

"I got involved with some investors for a business deal," he started, his voice steadier now. "At first, it seemed legitimate. They wanted to fund a startup I've been working on—a new tech venture that could really take off."

"Sounds great so far," I said, trying to remain calm, though my gut twisted with unease. "But...?"

"But then I discovered they weren't exactly who they claimed to be. The deeper I got into the negotiations, the clearer it became that they had ties to something... shady. I should have walked away, but it was too late. I was in too deep."

"Why didn't you tell me?" I pressed, incredulous. "You could have asked for help."

"I thought I could fix it myself," he admitted, frustration mingling with regret. "But it's more complicated than I realized. Now they want their money, and they're not going to wait patiently for me to sort it out."

The implications sank in like a stone in water, rippling outwards. "Are they threatening you?"

"Not yet," he said, eyes narrowing. "But I can feel the noose tightening. I don't know how much longer I can keep them at bay."

"Caden, this isn't a game. You need to cut ties," I urged, my heart racing as the urgency of the situation washed over me. "Get out before it's too late."

He shook his head, determination etched into his features. "I can't just abandon everything I've worked for. I won't let them win."

"Do you even hear yourself? They already are!" The frustration bubbled over, the fear of losing him clawing at my insides. "You're playing with fire, and you're going to get burned. You need to find a way out, now."

"Maybe I can negotiate. If I can just stall them—"

"No," I cut him off, my heart racing. "You need to go to the police."

"The police?" His laugh was incredulous, a bitter sound that echoed off the walls. "You think they'll help? They're part of the problem, not the solution."

My stomach dropped, the reality of his words sinking in like an anchor dragging me down. "Then what? You think you can handle this alone?"

"Maybe." The way he said it made me want to scream.

"Caden, this isn't just your fight anymore. You have to realize that." I stepped closer, my voice low and steady. "You're risking everything. We're risking everything."

He looked at me, and for a brief moment, the walls around his heart cracked again, revealing the turmoil inside. "I never wanted to drag you into this."

"I know," I whispered, feeling the weight of his gaze on me. "But I'm here now, whether you want me to be or not. So let's figure this out together."

He sighed heavily, the resolve in his eyes wavering as the enormity of our situation sank in. "I don't know if I can protect you," he murmured, his voice barely above a whisper.

"Then let me protect you," I offered, my heart racing as I stepped closer, our worlds colliding in a whirlwind of emotions. "Together, we can find a way out."

For a moment, it felt as if the universe held its breath, the chaos outside fading into a distant hum. I could see the struggle on his face, the fight between love and the fear that clawed at him, threatening to pull him under. In that instant, I realized that while the truth had shattered the illusion of our perfect love, it had also opened a door—one that led us back to each other, back to the possibility of fighting for what we had.

"Okay," he finally breathed, his voice steadying. "We'll figure it out together."

And in that moment, amidst the chaos, I felt a flicker of hope ignite between us, a spark that dared to believe that love could triumph over the darkness closing in.

Caden's gaze softened, the storm swirling in his eyes transforming into a fleeting calm. It was an expression I hadn't seen in a while—vulnerable and open, yet still wrapped in layers of apprehension. "Together," he echoed, the word hanging in the air like a lifeline. "That's what you want?"

"Yes," I replied, feeling a surge of warmth despite the turmoil surrounding us. "But it means you have to trust me. We need to figure out your next steps. And quickly."

He nodded, his posture shifting as if a weight had been lifted. "I'll tell you everything. I promise."

"Good," I breathed, allowing a flicker of hope to kindle in my chest. "But we need a plan. One that doesn't involve you going it alone."

"Let's start with who I'm dealing with," he said, moving to the coffee table littered with papers and a laptop. He opened the lid, and the glow illuminated his determined expression. "The Red Syndicate has their hands in everything—money laundering, trafficking, the works. I got pulled into it because of the investors. They were too charming, too persuasive. And now I owe them. I thought I could charm my way out, but it's not that simple."

"Charming your way out?" I smirked, trying to lighten the mood. "Last time I checked, charm doesn't work well with criminals. They tend to prefer muscle over charisma."

He shot me a half-hearted smile, a glimmer of the man I loved breaking through the tension. "Point taken. So, what do we do? Go in guns blazing?"

"Not exactly," I replied, crossing my arms. "We need information first. If they're as dangerous as you say, we can't just waltz in and demand answers. We need to outsmart them."

"Smart is good," he said, tapping his fingers against the table. "But how do we gather intel without putting you in danger?"

"Let me worry about that," I replied, feeling a surge of adrenaline course through me. "I can poke around, talk to a few people. I know my way around this city, and I have connections."

"Are you sure about this?" he asked, concern knitting his brows together. "I can't stand the idea of you getting mixed up in this mess."

"You've dragged me into it already, Caden," I said, my voice steady. "I'm not going to sit back and watch while you dive headfirst into trouble. We're in this together now."

With a resigned sigh, he leaned back in his chair, running a hand through his hair in that familiar, frustrated way. "Fine. But if you get into trouble, I swear—"

"What? You'll swoop in to save me?" I quipped, raising an eyebrow. "Oh, please. This isn't a movie."

A half-smile broke through his frown. "Not even a romantic comedy? Because I could work on my timing."

"Sweet talk won't get us out of this," I retorted, but the banter eased some of the tension. It reminded me of who we were before all of this—two people in love, making jokes and stealing kisses in the rain.

As we strategized, Caden pulled out his phone and opened a contact list. "I have some contacts who might know more about the syndicate. I'll reach out to them. But I want you to promise me something."

"Anything," I replied, my heart racing.

"If anything feels off, you call me. You don't engage without backup."

"I promise."

"Good. I'd rather have you safe than brave," he said, his eyes locking onto mine with an intensity that made my stomach flutter.

"Safe and brave can coexist, you know," I replied, meeting his gaze.

"Just don't be reckless," he said, his tone softening. "I can't bear the thought of you getting hurt."

I nodded, the gravity of our situation pressing down on me. But beneath the weight of it all, an ember of determination ignited. I would protect what was ours, no matter what it took.

As we finalized our plan, I couldn't shake the feeling that we were dancing on the edge of a precipice, the abyss yawning below us. Caden began making calls, his voice steady and low, each conversation thick with urgency. I busied myself with gathering supplies—phones, a laptop, anything that could help us delve deeper into the shadows of his dealings.

Hours passed in a blur, and by the time we stepped outside, the sun had dipped below the horizon, casting the city in a cloak of twilight. The streets were alive with the buzz of nightlife, the glow of neon signs illuminating faces filled with laughter and purpose. But for us, the world felt different, the laughter masking the danger lurking in the corners.

"Let's grab something to eat before we start," Caden suggested, his eyes scanning the street as we walked. "You know, something that doesn't involve crime syndicates."

"Best idea you've had all day," I said, feeling a bit of normalcy seep into the chaos. We found a small, bustling café, the aroma of coffee and freshly baked pastries wafting through the air.

Sitting across from each other, we shared bites of food, laughter, and stolen glances that spoke volumes. The tension ebbed and flowed, a comforting rhythm amid the uncertainty that loomed over us.

"What if this all blows up in our faces?" Caden asked suddenly, his eyes serious. "What if they come after us?"

"Then we deal with it," I replied, meeting his gaze head-on. "Together. We won't let fear dictate our actions."

"Right. Together," he echoed, though the worry still lingered in his expression.

Just as the words settled between us, a figure stepped into the café. My heart dropped as I recognized the sharp, suited silhouette—Evelyn, one of Caden's investors. She was the kind of woman who could command a room with a single glance, and right now, that glance was fixed on us.

"Caden," she purred, her voice dripping with false sweetness as she approached our table. "Fancy seeing you here."

"What are you doing here, Evelyn?" Caden's voice was clipped, and I could feel the tension crackling in the air.

"Just came to discuss business, of course," she said, her gaze drifting to me. "And it seems you're entertaining the competition. How quaint."

I held her stare, defiance bubbling beneath the surface. "I didn't realize you were so interested in Caden's social life."

Evelyn's lips curled into a smirk. "Oh, darling, I'm interested in much more than that."

Caden shifted, his body tense, as if he were preparing for a fight. "We're not discussing anything with you."

"Really?" She leaned in closer, her voice dropping to a conspiratorial whisper. "Because I think we have a lot to talk about. After all, I heard you've been getting a bit too close to the Red Syndicate."

The air thickened, and my heart raced as a chill shot down my spine. How did she know?

"What do you mean?" Caden asked, his voice steadier than I felt.

"Oh, I'm just saying that your little endeavor might not stay under the radar for long," she replied, her eyes glittering with malicious intent. "You're playing a dangerous game, and I think you'll find it's not so easy to win."

The implications hung in the air, heavy and suffocating. I felt Caden tense beside me, the gravity of her words crashing down around us.

"And I'd hate for something unfortunate to happen," she continued, her smile unyielding. "Especially to someone so... charming."

Caden's jaw clenched, and I could see the wheels turning in his mind. "What do you want?"

"Let's just say, I can help you navigate this mess. But it comes at a price."

"What kind of price?" I interjected, my voice stronger than I felt.

Evelyn turned her gaze back to me, amusement dancing in her eyes. "Oh, sweetheart, you wouldn't want to know."

As I exchanged glances with Caden, the walls began to close in around us, the weight of the situation pressing heavily on my chest. I could feel the threat lurking in her words, a specter of danger that promised to haunt us if we didn't tread carefully.

But before I could react, a loud crash echoed from outside, followed by shouts that shattered the fragile tension we'd built. Caden and I exchanged panicked looks, the realization dawning on us that whatever danger had been lurking was now bursting through the door.

"Stay close," he commanded, his tone turning steely as he slid his chair back.

But before we could move, the café door swung open, and a group of men stepped in, faces obscured by the shadows. The air was thick with the promise of chaos, and I felt the ground shift beneath my feet as fear clutched at my heart.

Evelyn's smile widened, satisfaction gleaming in her eyes as she stepped back, watching the unfolding scene with a predatory glint.

"Looks like you have company," she said sweetly, the words curling like smoke.

And as the men advanced, I realized we were standing on the precipice of something far more dangerous than I had anticipated—caught in a web of lies, betrayal, and darkness that threatened to swallow us whole

Chapter 13: The Betrayal

The room felt colder without Caden, a chill that seemed to seep into my bones, wrapping around me like an unwelcome shawl. I sat alone in my studio, surrounded by swatches of fabric that had once sparked joy and creativity. Each bolt of silk, every roll of chiffon whispered of dreams we had woven together, of collections that were supposed to launch us into the limelight. Now, they lay scattered around me, silent witnesses to my unraveling trust.

The day had started like any other, the sun streaming through the tall windows, casting a warm glow on the chaos of my workspace. I had a sketch pinned to the wall—a daring design with bold lines and an explosion of colors that felt more like a lifeline than a mere garment. It represented hope, a vision of what I could achieve in a world where Caden's shadow no longer loomed over me. But that hope felt tarnished, smudged like charcoal on an artist's canvas. Just as I thought I could put my faith in something tangible, Victor's intrusion shattered the fragile veneer of my reality.

His presence had a way of creeping into a room like a dark cloud, suffocating and ominous. When he approached me that day, I felt my stomach twist. Victor had always struck me as charming in a disarming way, but his smile held too many secrets. He leaned against my doorway, arms crossed, an air of confidence that masked the underlying menace. "We need to talk," he said, his voice smooth like silk yet laced with a sharpness that sent chills down my spine.

"Is Caden with you?" I asked, the knot in my stomach tightening. The empty space beside me felt like an aching void. I had gotten so used to his laughter echoing off these walls, his energy weaving through my creative chaos, that the absence was deafening.

"He's... occupied," Victor replied, dismissing my concern with a wave of his hand. "But I have something far more important to discuss." The way he said it made my skin crawl.

He stepped inside, closing the door behind him as if to seal me in a confining chamber of secrets. The sunlight, once bathing me in warmth, seemed to dim as Victor's words cast a shadow over my heart. "You're not just a designer, you're part of something bigger. Something Caden never told you about."

I folded my arms, defensive. "I don't know what you're talking about." But the tremor in my voice betrayed me. My mind raced, recalling all the late nights spent sketching, the conversations that had turned into arguments, and the moments where trust had flickered like a candle about to extinguish.

Victor produced a folder from under his arm, opening it with a flourish that suggested he relished the impending revelation. "I believe you deserve to know the truth." He slid the documents across my desk, the sound crisp and final.

The first photo caught my eye: Caden with a group of men, their faces obscured but the atmosphere thick with tension. They were gathered around a table laden with sketches—my sketches. The room was dim, filled with shadows, but the glow of the lamps illuminated their intent expressions. I felt bile rise in my throat. "What is this?" I croaked.

"Evidence," Victor replied, his tone dripping with satisfaction. "Caden has been using your designs to mask his true dealings—deals that are, let's say, less than legal."

Each word he spoke felt like a jagged knife carving deeper into my gut. I scanned the documents, the betrayal seeping into my consciousness like a dark stain. There were receipts, bank transfers, emails that outlined a web of deceit, one I had naively stepped into.

"Lies," I whispered, shaking my head as disbelief churned within me. "You're lying. Caden wouldn't..." But even as I spoke, the foundation of my faith began to crumble. The evidence was damning, a Pandora's box of treachery that I never wanted to open.

Victor leaned in closer, his breath warm against my cheek. "Oh, he would. You've been nothing but a pawn in his grand scheme to climb to the top of the fashion industry. He needed someone with your talent to distract from his dealings. And you fell for it."

A stifled gasp escaped my lips as the weight of his words crushed me. The room spun, colors swirling into a vortex of confusion and betrayal. I had poured my heart into my work, believed in our partnership, in our future. How could I have been so blind? Caden, the man who had held me close, who had whispered dreams into my ear, had used those dreams to cloak his ambitions.

"What do you want from me?" I managed, my voice barely above a whisper.

Victor straightened, a predatory gleam in his eyes. "I want you to understand your position. You can either continue to be Caden's unwitting accomplice or choose to walk away from this mess. I can help you. Together, we could expose him, take back the power he stole from you."

The suggestion hung in the air, thick and charged with potential, yet I felt as if I were standing on the precipice of a cliff, the ground beneath me crumbling. "Why would you want to help me?" I asked, suspicion lacing my words.

"Because, dear, the truth can be a powerful ally," he said, his smile a calculated curve. "And I believe in your talent. You deserve better than being a footnote in Caden's story."

In that moment, I faced a fork in the road, two paths diverging before me. One led back to Caden, to the warmth of our shared dreams and the promise of love, even if it was now tainted by betrayal. The other beckoned with the thrill of uncovering the truth, the chance to reclaim my narrative. My heart raced as I weighed my options, but deep down, I knew that the choice I made today would shape my tomorrow. The vibrant world I once cherished felt like a distant memory, but I could still choose to paint it anew.

The air in my studio thickened with tension, each breath feeling labored, as if the walls themselves conspired to crush me under the weight of Victor's revelations. My heart thudded heavily in my chest, a relentless drumbeat that echoed my racing thoughts. With every piece of evidence he laid before me, I felt the distance between Caden and me stretch into an abyss, dark and daunting.

Victor leaned back, a satisfied smile creeping onto his lips. It was the kind of grin that hinted at secrets shared and pleasures taken in the misfortunes of others. "You see," he continued, his tone lilting with condescension, "Caden thinks he's untouchable. But you, you hold the key to unmasking him."

"Why would I want to betray him?" The words escaped my lips before I could think, tinged with a desperation that made me sound weaker than I intended. Caden's laughter still echoed in my mind, that deep, comforting sound that wrapped around me like a warm blanket. How could the same man be the architect of such betrayal?

"Betrayal?" Victor chuckled softly, shaking his head. "What you're feeling is not betrayal; it's liberation. Caden has built a facade, and you're standing at the edge of it. All you need to do is push." His voice dripped with false sincerity, and the sinister undertone sent chills down my spine.

I turned my gaze to the sketches spread across my desk, lines and colors that once pulsed with life now felt tainted by deceit. I could almost hear the fabric whispering my name, the dreams of vibrant runways and applause fading into a dissonant hum. "You're asking me to choose," I said, my voice steadier than I felt. "Choose between the man I love and the truth you're trying to sell me."

He shrugged, feigning indifference, but his eyes glinted with the thrill of manipulation. "Love doesn't shield you from lies, darling. Caden has turned you into his cover, and you're too talented to be relegated to the shadows. You have the power to expose him, to reclaim your story."

I wanted to scream that I didn't want any part of this tangled web he spun, yet the tantalizing pull of freedom gnawed at me. If I could unravel Caden's plans, what would that mean for me? The thoughts danced like moths around a flame, each flickering light illuminating a path I had never imagined walking.

"Caden and I are partners," I insisted, but the conviction in my voice felt thin, like the delicate fabric I so often worked with, fragile and easily torn. "We have dreams together."

"Do you really?" Victor pressed, leaning closer, his intensity palpable. "Or are those dreams merely his, using you as a canvas while he paints a masterpiece of his own design?"

For a moment, I was lost in my memories of Caden—his hands guiding mine as we sketched late into the night, the way he had looked at me when I revealed my first collection. Was it all a ruse? Had I been a mere tool in his game? The very thought sent a shudder through me.

Victor cleared his throat, bringing me back to the present, and I felt the weight of his gaze. "Think about it. What do you want? Do you want to be remembered as Caden's forgotten muse, or do you want to stand tall, owning your designs, your destiny?"

As if compelled by a force greater than my own resolve, I picked up one of the photographs, my hands trembling as I studied it closely. Caden's face was a mask of confidence, surrounded by men whose intentions looked as murky as the waters of a darkened sea. The pieces began to shift in my mind like a jigsaw puzzle revealing a picture I had never wanted to see.

"I need time," I finally said, the words heavy but necessary. "I can't just decide on a whim."

Victor's smile turned almost paternal, and I could sense the satisfaction brimming beneath his calm facade. "Take all the time you need. Just remember, every second you spend hesitating is a second Caden continues his deception."

With that, he turned to leave, the door creaking ominously behind him. I watched him go, a wave of confusion crashing over me, flooding my senses. Alone again, I sunk into my chair, the fabric of my once-safe haven now feeling like a noose tightening around my throat.

Days turned into a blur of sketches and sleepless nights, with every stroke of my pencil reminiscent of Caden's laughter and the warmth of his embrace. I wanted to believe in him, in the love we had shared, but shadows loomed larger with every passing hour. I needed clarity, a way to separate the love I had for him from the treachery threatening to engulf me.

So I dove into my work, crafting designs that told stories of resilience, of independence. Each piece was a rebellion against the fear gnawing at my heart, a silent protest against the betrayal that threatened to suffocate me. I turned to the fabrics that had once sparked joy and hope, pouring my anguish into every stitch, every seam.

It was late one night when I heard the familiar sound of the door opening. I glanced up, my heart racing at the thought it might be Caden. Instead, it was Sarah, my closest friend and confidante. She stepped into the room, her expression a mixture of concern and curiosity.

"Hey, I brought coffee," she said, waving a to-go cup in my direction. "You look like you could use some caffeine and a break from whatever secret project you've been locked away working on."

I accepted the cup, grateful for the warmth it provided. "You have no idea," I muttered, taking a sip as I steeled myself to confide in her.

"Talk to me," she urged, settling onto a stool, her eyes scanning the sketches scattered across my desk. "You've been in a funk lately. What's going on?"

With a heavy heart, I recounted Victor's visit, the chilling evidence he presented, and the darkness that had seeped into my relationship with Caden. Each word felt like a weight lifted, yet I was left raw and exposed under the bright lights of honesty.

Sarah listened, her brow furrowing in concentration. "That sounds like a nightmare, but have you talked to Caden about it? I mean, really talked?"

"Would you believe anything he says after what I've seen?" The frustration bubbled up within me, a tight coil of emotion that threatened to unravel. "How can I trust him when it feels like everything has been a lie?"

She reached across the table, squeezing my hand. "You can't make a decision based on half-truths. You need to confront him, Julia. You deserve to hear his side."

The thought of facing Caden, of confronting the man I had loved so fiercely, sent another wave of uncertainty crashing over me. But Sarah was right; I couldn't live in this limbo any longer. It was time to either solidify my faith in him or to reclaim my narrative.

I didn't know how long I sat in that swirling haze of despair, my thoughts racing like wild horses on a precipice, almost daring me to leap. Sarah's words echoed in my mind, urging me to confront Caden, but fear coiled around my heart like a serpent, squeezing tighter with each beat. The comfort of ignorance had felt like a blanket, but now, it was suffocating me, the truth just out of reach yet burning hotter than the sun.

The next few days blurred into a storm of sketches and coffee runs, the rhythmic clattering of my sewing machine mingling with the chaotic thrum of my thoughts. Every piece I created felt imbued with the urgency of my predicament, the urgency to make a decision that weighed heavier than the fabric I draped around my shoulders. The walls of my studio, once a sanctuary of creativity, now felt like a cage, enclosing me in a labyrinth of doubt.

It was a Friday evening when I finally mustered the courage to call Caden. The air outside was crisp, the kind of cool that hinted at autumn's arrival, where the leaves would soon dance in hues of orange and gold, and I couldn't shake the sense that my life was about to change in a way I couldn't fully anticipate. I dialed his number, each ring a drumroll for the impending confrontation, my heart thrumming in sync.

"Hey, Julia," he answered, his voice warm, the familiar timbre wrapping around me like a comfortable blanket. It was maddening how easily he could still make my heart flutter despite everything swirling around us. "What's up?"

I hesitated, the words hovering on the tip of my tongue. How could I begin? "We need to talk. Can you come over?"

"Of course. I'll be there in ten," he said, and I could hear the smile in his voice. It felt like a knife twisting in my gut.

The anticipation of his arrival turned my studio into a battleground, each moment stretching like the fabric I worked with. I paced, the sound of my footsteps a frantic tempo against the hardwood floor. My sketches stared back at me, vibrant and alive, a testament to the visions I had shared with Caden. Each line seemed to mock me, whispering secrets I was too scared to uncover.

When Caden finally walked through the door, the familiar scent of his cologne mixed with the floral notes of my studio. He was disarmingly handsome, a vision in a tailored jacket that hugged his frame perfectly. For a brief moment, I was overwhelmed by nostalgia, the pull of our shared laughter and whispered dreams threatening to drag me under.

"Hey," he said, his eyes lighting up, but the warmth in them faded as he took in my serious demeanor. "What's going on?"

I gestured for him to sit, my heart pounding as I gathered the courage to speak. "I met with Victor."

His expression shifted, a cloud passing over the sun. "Victor? What did he want?"

"I think you know." My voice wavered, the weight of the evidence I'd seen pressing heavily on my chest. "He told me things, Caden. Terrible things about you. About us."

"What things?" He leaned forward, concern etching lines across his brow, and I almost faltered. But I forced myself to continue, the truth bursting forth like a dam breaking. "About how you've been lying to me. Using my designs for... for something illegal."

The silence that followed was palpable, thick with unspoken words. Caden's face turned pale, and for a moment, I could see the churning storm of emotions in his eyes—fear, anger, and something that looked a lot like guilt.

"Julia, I can explain—" he started, but I cut him off, needing to assert my voice against the tempest of confusion swirling around us.

"No! I need to hear the truth. I deserve that much," I said, rising from my chair as the adrenaline surged through my veins, forcing me to stand tall. "I need to know why I should trust you."

He opened his mouth, his features tightening as he searched for the right words. "You have to understand, I was trying to protect you."

"Protect me? From what? The truth?" My pulse raced, a mix of anger and hurt igniting inside me. "It doesn't feel like protection when you're hiding things from me!"

"I didn't want you to get involved in my business," he said, frustration lacing his words. "Victor is a loose cannon, and the things I've been involved in... it's dangerous."

"Dangerous? Caden, it sounds like you've been running a criminal operation! And I'm just supposed to sit back and take it?" I could feel the tears threatening to spill over, but I wouldn't let them. Not now.

"It's not like that! I never intended for it to go this far," he pleaded, rising to stand before me, desperation etched into every line of his face. "I thought I could control it. I thought I could keep you safe."

"By lying to me?" I shook my head, anger battling with the flicker of affection that refused to die. "You've put me in a position I never asked for. I'm not a pawn in your game, Caden."

His expression softened, and for a moment, the world around us faded as I searched his eyes for the truth. "I wanted to keep you out of it, but I made mistakes. I thought I could get out clean without dragging you into it."

I wanted to believe him. My heart ached for the man who had once whispered sweet promises in my ear. "Then tell me how you plan to get out of this mess without dragging me down with you."

His gaze hardened, and I saw a flicker of something cold pass through him, a shadow of the man I had thought I knew. "I'm not sure I can. There are things about Victor you don't understand, and if he knows I'm talking to you..."

The weight of his words hit me like a punch to the gut. "What are you saying?"

"I'm saying that my choices have consequences, and now those consequences are threatening you," he said, his voice low and urgent. "I never wanted this for you."

"What do you mean?" My voice barely rose above a whisper, a tremor of fear threading through it.

Before he could respond, the door swung open again, and in strode Victor, a smug grin plastered across his face. "Well, well, what do we have here? A little family reunion?"

Caden's eyes widened in horror, and my heart dropped, an icy knot forming in my stomach. "Victor, what are you doing here?"

"I couldn't resist the urge to see how our little designer was handling the truth," he said, eyes gleaming with malicious delight. "And it seems, Caden, that you're in quite a bind."

The tension crackled in the air, the two men locked in a silent battle of wills, and I stood frozen, caught in the crossfire of betrayal and deceit. Caden's jaw tightened as he turned to me, a silent plea etched across his face. The weight of the decision I had to make pressed down on me, a chasm of uncertainty yawning wide beneath my feet.

Victor stepped forward, the predatory glint in his eyes unmistakable. "You should choose wisely, Julia. You don't want to end up like Caden—lost in a game he can't win."

And just like that, I stood on the precipice of my future, the choices I made hanging precariously in the balance, as the world around me spun into chaos.

Chapter 14: Running Away

The rain fell steadily against the window, a rhythmic tap that matched the dull thrum of my heart. Each droplet seemed to echo my sense of loss, pooling in tiny rivers that trickled down the glass. I sat on the edge of the bed, my suitcase still open and half-packed, remnants of my old life spilling out like a confession. A red silk blouse, a pair of heels that once made me feel invincible, and a worn sketchbook, its pages filled with dreams that now felt utterly out of reach.

I had walked away from the penthouse, from Caden, and from the image I had carefully constructed of us. The view from his apartment had once felt like the pinnacle of my ambition: a skyline that sparkled with promise. Now, it felt like a mirage, a cruel reminder of everything I thought I had. Was I really so naive to believe in a future that had been built on illusions?

As I stared at the crumpled sketches, ideas that once danced through my mind with vibrant clarity now lay dormant, buried beneath layers of uncertainty. My work was my lifeblood, a world I had sculpted with my own hands, yet every line I attempted to draw now felt heavy with doubt. I had prided myself on my ability to create, to channel the chaos around me into something tangible, but now? Now, it felt as though I was trying to paint with watercolors on a canvas made of glass, every stroke slipping away before it could dry.

With a huff, I tossed the sketchbook back into the suitcase. It landed with a soft thud, like a reminder of a life I wasn't ready to reclaim. Maybe I should just close it up, put it away, and let the silence wrap around me like a thick fog. I was tired of pretending everything was fine, tired of forcing a smile that no longer felt genuine.

I pulled my phone from the pocket of my jeans, staring at the screen as though it held the answers I sought. My thumb hovered over Caden's name, a temptation laced with the sweet poison of longing. I could message him, ask him why he had betrayed me, demand an explanation. But deep down, I knew the truth: there would be no satisfactory answer. He was a man who thrived in shadows, whose charm was a well-practiced mask that he wore like armor. I had stepped into his world, believing I could change it, but all I had done was expose my own vulnerability.

Pushing the thought aside, I decided to venture out, to lose myself in the pulse of the city. I wrapped a scarf around my neck, a soft woolen embrace against the chill that clung to the air, and stepped into the cool embrace of a rainy evening. The streets shimmered with reflections of neon lights, the vibrant energy of Manhattan still alive despite the downpour. I walked, my boots splashing through puddles, lost in the rhythm of my own thoughts, the city around me a blur of color and sound.

As I turned a corner, I stumbled upon a little café tucked between two towering buildings. Its windows glowed warmly, the scent of freshly brewed coffee beckoning me inside like a siren's call. I hesitated for a moment, but the need for a refuge overpowered my reluctance. I pushed open the door, the bell chiming softly above me, and stepped into the inviting warmth.

The café was a cozy labyrinth of mismatched furniture and eclectic decor, the walls lined with shelves of books and art. I found a corner table, tucked away from the bustle, and settled in, pulling out my sketchbook once more. This time, I couldn't resist the urge to doodle. I needed to feel something—anything—other than the heaviness in my chest.

I sketched aimlessly, letting my hand move across the page, tracing lines that felt familiar yet foreign. Suddenly, the door swung open with a gust of wind, bringing with it a jolt of energy that sent shivers down my spine. I looked up, momentarily distracted from my drawing, and my heart nearly stopped.

Caden stood there, drenched from the rain, his dark hair plastered against his forehead. His eyes, usually so cool and calculating, were filled with something I couldn't quite decipher—was it regret? Hope? Before I could process what was happening, he spotted me, his expression shifting from surprise to something more intense.

I froze, caught in a moment that felt like a movie playing in slow motion. The world around us faded, the sounds of clinking cups and chatter dimming to a dull roar. He approached, water droplets still clinging to his skin, and every step felt like a tug on my heartstrings.

"What are you doing here?" I managed to ask, my voice barely rising above a whisper.

"I was looking for you," he said, his voice low and edged with urgency. "Can we talk?"

The words hung between us, heavy with meaning. I felt a spark of anger flare within me, battling against the ache of longing. He had shattered my world, left me questioning everything, yet here he was, standing in front of me like he had a right to explain himself. I had walked away, hadn't I? So why did the sight of him ignite a wildfire of emotion?

"I don't think there's anything left to say," I replied, my tone sharper than I intended. The heat of my frustration mingled with the cool air of the café, creating an atmosphere thick with tension.

"Please," he pressed, taking another step closer. "I know I messed up, but I need you to hear me out."

I looked into his eyes, searching for the truth hidden beneath layers of charm and deceit. Did I dare allow him to unravel the knot in my heart, or would it only lead to further chaos? The decision felt monumental, as if I were standing at the edge of a cliff, peering into the depths below. Would I leap into the unknown, or would I turn away and protect what little was left of my shattered self?

The silence of the café wrapped around us like a warm blanket, but the tension crackled in the air, making every breath feel charged. Caden stood there, soaked to the skin, an oddly handsome mess, his shirt clinging to his chest in a way that would have been charming under different circumstances. "Can we talk?" he repeated, each word heavy with unspoken apologies.

"I'm not sure what's left to discuss," I said, my voice trembling slightly as I tried to maintain my composure. The heat radiating off his body made me acutely aware of how cold I felt, despite the warmth of the café. His presence stirred a mix of emotions—anger, longing, confusion. I could almost taste the bitter sweetness of nostalgia on my tongue, a reminder of what had been.

"I get it. You have every right to be angry," he said, and for a moment, I saw vulnerability flash in his eyes, raw and unfiltered. "But I can't just let you walk away without at least trying to explain."

My heart raced, battling between the urge to tell him off and the undeniable pull that he still had over me. "Explain what? How you managed to charm me into believing we were something real? Or how you turned my life into a plot twist I didn't ask for?" The words slipped from my lips sharper than I intended, but I had long since run out of patience.

"I never meant for any of this to happen," he replied, his voice earnest, almost pleading. "You have to believe me. I was caught up in things that... that spiraled out of control."

"Caught up in what, exactly?" I demanded, my curiosity warring with my better judgment. Part of me wanted to know the depths of his deception; another part craved the peace of letting it all go. "Was it your job? Or was it just another game for you to play?"

He raked a hand through his damp hair, frustration and desperation mingling in his expression. "It was a mistake. A misunderstanding, really. I thought I could keep everything separate—my life, my work, and you. But the lines blurred, and I got lost in it. I didn't know how to pull back without hurting you."

"Maybe you should have thought about that before you tangled me up in your web," I snapped, my voice barely above a whisper but sharp enough to cut through the humid air.

He looked pained, and for a fleeting moment, I felt a flicker of sympathy. But then the memory of how he had made me feel—like a prize to be won rather than a partner—surged back, fueling my anger.

"I was afraid," he said quietly, leaning closer. "Afraid of what you would think if you knew everything. I thought I could protect you from it, but I see now that I only pushed you away."

"Protect me?" I laughed bitterly, the sound echoing in the intimate space between us. "You think lying and manipulating were ways to protect me?"

The café felt stifling, the walls closing in as the atmosphere shifted around us. Patrons began to look our way, their glances filled with a mix of curiosity and concern. I could feel heat creeping up my cheeks, a mix of embarrassment and rage.

"Let's step outside," he suggested, a hint of urgency creeping into his voice. "We're drawing too much attention."

Before I could protest, he reached for my hand, his fingers brushing against mine, igniting a familiar spark that made my heart race despite myself. I recoiled slightly, half-tempted to yank my hand away, but the moment was already in motion, and he was leading me toward the door.

The rain had lightened, but the air was thick with humidity, the scent of wet concrete and blossoming city life swirling around us. I took a deep breath, filling my lungs with the intoxicating smell of rain-soaked asphalt mixed with the sweet aroma of street food wafting nearby. We stepped onto the sidewalk, the noise of the café fading behind us, and I felt an unsettling mix of anxiety and anticipation settle in the pit of my stomach.

"Look, I know I don't deserve it, but please just hear me out," Caden urged, his voice low and sincere. "I'll answer anything you want to know. No more secrets, I promise."

"Why now? Why not when it mattered?" I challenged, my heart pounding in my chest, caught between wanting to hear him out and the instinct to run.

"Because I didn't realize how much you meant to me until I felt you slipping away," he admitted, his gaze unwavering. "I was too wrapped up in my own issues to see the damage I was causing. It took losing you to understand just how real this was for me."

"Real?" I echoed incredulously. "You think a few heartfelt words can erase the mess you made?"

"I don't expect forgiveness. I don't even expect you to trust me again. But I can't walk away without at least trying to make things right."

Something about his tone, the raw vulnerability in his voice, caught me off guard. There was a sincerity that was hard to ignore, a flicker of the man I had fallen for in the first place. Yet, I couldn't help but feel the weight of his past hanging between us like a dark cloud, threatening to rain on whatever fragile bond we still had.

"Caden," I started, my voice wavering, unsure of how to articulate the whirlwind of emotions swirling within me. "You hurt me. Deeply. I'm not sure I can just brush that aside."

"I know," he said softly, stepping closer, his eyes searching mine for something I wasn't ready to give. "But if you let me, I'd like to show you that I can be better. That I can be the man you thought I was."

I felt a rush of warmth at his words, a part of me yearning to believe in the possibility of redemption. But skepticism clawed at my insides, reminding me of the illusions he had crafted so expertly. "What if you're just saying what I want to hear?"

"Then you'll walk away knowing that I tried. But I'm not that man anymore," he insisted, his voice firm and resolute. "I've had time to think, and I want to prove to you that I'm worth another chance."

An unexpected wave of emotion washed over me, catching me off guard. The air crackled with unspoken possibilities, yet doubt lingered like a persistent shadow. Could I trust him again? Could I allow myself to be vulnerable, to risk everything once more?

As the drizzle picked up again, I glanced at the sky, the clouds heavy and pregnant with rain, mirroring the turmoil brewing inside me. Maybe, just maybe, there was a chance for a different outcome—a new beginning buried beneath the wreckage of the past. Or perhaps I was setting myself up for heartbreak all over again. But in that moment, under the dim glow of the streetlights, I stood at a crossroads, caught between the desire for safety and the intoxicating lure of possibility.

The rain had eased to a gentle mist, cloaking the city in a surreal veil as Caden stood before me, the world around us fading to a distant hum. I could feel the weight of his gaze, a gravity that pulled at me, coaxing me to remember the warmth of his laughter, the way his smile could ignite a room. But could I separate the man I knew from the shadow of betrayal that hung over him like a storm cloud?

"I don't want to waste this moment," he said, breaking through the turmoil in my mind. "Please, just listen."

I crossed my arms, a defensive stance I hoped would shield me from the uncertainty brewing in my heart. "Listening is one thing. Trusting is another."

"Fair enough," he replied, a hint of amusement sparking in his eyes despite the tension. "But if we're going to start over, we might as well do it without the fog of mistrust."

A chuckle escaped me, surprising both of us. "And how exactly do you propose we do that? Trust falls? A scavenger hunt?"

"Honestly? I was thinking more like a cup of coffee," he shot back, the corners of his mouth quirking up in that infuriatingly charming way I remembered too well. "But if you prefer scavenger hunts, I can work with that."

I let the humor linger for a moment, but my heart still thrummed with doubt. "Caden, this isn't a game for me. I need to know if you're serious."

"I am," he replied, his voice earnest, the air around us growing thick with anticipation. "I want to be a part of your life again. Not as a player in a game but as someone who values what we had."

I felt the stirrings of hope fight against the tendrils of fear coiling around my heart. His sincerity was palpable, but the scars from our past felt too fresh, too raw. "And what if you mess up again?"

"Then I'll let you throw coffee in my face," he said, a smirk forming as he shifted closer, his gaze never leaving mine. "But you have to admit, it would be pretty satisfying."

"I'll consider it," I said, trying to maintain a semblance of control as laughter bubbled up unexpectedly, momentarily easing the tension. But as quickly as the laughter came, it faded, replaced by the reality of our situation.

"Let's at least start with coffee, yeah?" he asked, his tone shifting to something softer, more genuine. "My treat."

"Your treat?" I raised an eyebrow, a playful smile threatening to break through my façade. "Do you plan on using it as a bribe?"

"Only if it works," he quipped, his eyes sparkling with mischief. "So, what do you say? Let's take this to a place that doesn't feel like the backdrop for a soap opera."

Against my better judgment, I found myself nodding, curiosity creeping in where doubt had resided. The faintest flicker of excitement sparked within me. "Fine, but if you start with the excuses, I'm out."

He laughed, relief washing over his features as he stepped back, gesturing toward a nearby coffee shop that seemed to radiate warmth through the mist. "Deal. But first, let me grab my jacket. I don't want to catch a cold and ruin the moment."

As we walked together, side by side, the streetlights glowed like fireflies, casting a golden hue over the pavement. The world around us seemed to fade, leaving just the two of us suspended in a bubble of possibilities. I could feel my heart hesitating, caught between hope and fear, but I let myself indulge in the moment, the air buzzing with something almost electric.

Inside the café, the aroma of fresh coffee enveloped me, rich and comforting. I ordered a simple cappuccino, and as I turned to find a table, I caught Caden watching me, his expression a mix of admiration and something deeper. The air was filled with the low murmur of conversations, the clinking of cups, and the hiss of the espresso machine, creating a cozy backdrop to our tentative reunion.

"Here's to new beginnings," he said, raising his cup in a toast as we settled into a corner booth.

"To new beginnings," I echoed, tapping my cup against his with a touch of caution. As we sipped, the warmth of the coffee spread through me, an inviting contrast to the swirling emotions still churning within.

"So," Caden began, his voice steady, "let's start with the basics. I want you to tell me everything you've been up to since... well, since everything."

I hesitated, memories flooding back—designs half-finished, ideas abandoned, the quiet ache of solitude that had become my constant companion. "I've been working a lot. Trying to find my footing again," I said slowly. "But the truth is, everything feels different now. I'm not sure how to move forward."

"I get that," he replied, his gaze unwavering. "But you're not alone. You have me."

"Do I?" I challenged, leaning forward slightly. "Because I'm not sure I can trust that after everything."

"I'm asking for a chance," he said, a hint of vulnerability creeping into his voice. "Just one chance to show you that I can be more than the man who hurt you."

A heavy silence settled between us, charged with the weight of our shared history and the uncertainty of the future. I could see the sincerity in his eyes, a flicker of the man I had once fallen for, and it stirred something deep within me. Yet, I still felt a nagging sense of caution.

"I want to believe you," I admitted, my voice barely above a whisper. "But how do I know this isn't just another game for you?"

"Because I'm here, aren't I? No distractions, no secrets. Just me and the truth."

As we spoke, the café seemed to fade away, our surroundings blurring into the background. I could almost forget the world outside, the rain pattering against the windows like a gentle reminder of my own fragility. But with every moment I spent with him, the walls I had built around my heart began to tremble, cracking under the weight of possibility.

And just as I felt the edges of my resolve soften, the door swung open, a rush of cold air gusting into the café. A tall figure stepped inside, shaking off droplets of rain, and my stomach dropped. The moment our eyes met, recognition ignited between us, a chilling reminder of the past I had tried to escape.

It was Jessica, Caden's ex-girlfriend—the one who had stirred up the chaos that led to our fallout. Her gaze flicked toward us, surprise widening her eyes as she took in the scene. The atmosphere shifted instantly, tension crackling in the air as if a storm had just broken overhead.

Caden's expression hardened, his relaxed demeanor vanishing like mist in the wind. "What is she doing here?" he muttered under his breath, an edge of urgency creeping into his voice.

Before I could respond, Jessica approached our table, an unsettling smile plastered on her face, her presence a sudden storm cloud looming over the fragile hope that had just begun to blossom between Caden and me.

"Fancy running into you two here," she said, her voice dripping with feigned sweetness. "Didn't think you'd be back in the game so soon, Caden."

"Jessica," he replied, his tone flat, tension radiating from him as he clenched his jaw.

I felt the color drain from my face, the fragile atmosphere of our reunion crumbling beneath the weight of her presence. The last thing I wanted was a confrontation, but the look in her eyes told me she wasn't here to reminisce.

"Just when I thought you'd moved on," she continued, her eyes flicking to me, assessing, judging. "Guess I underestimated you, huh?"

I held my breath, uncertainty and anger boiling beneath the surface. Caden's expression shifted, the protective barrier around him snapping back into place. "What do you want, Jessica?"

Her smile widened, and I could sense the underlying venom. "Oh, nothing much. Just came to see how you were doing, you know?"

"Right," he replied, his voice tight. "Because you care."

"Always." She leaned in slightly, her gaze piercing. "But I'm really curious to see how this little reunion is going to unfold. You know how relationships can be... fragile."

My heart raced, adrenaline surging through me as I realized I was caught in a web far more complicated than I had anticipated. Jessica's presence felt like an unwelcome omen, a reminder that the past could claw its way back into the present at any moment, threatening to shatter everything I was just beginning to rebuild.

"What's that supposed to mean?" I asked, my voice steadier than I felt.

"Oh, just that Caden and I have history," she replied casually, but her eyes danced with a dangerous glint. "And history tends to have a way of repeating itself."

As her words hung in the air, I felt the weight of uncertainty crash down around us, my pulse quickening as I glanced at Caden. He looked torn between anger and regret, his eyes flickering between me and Jessica.

I realized then that our fragile connection hung by a thread, and that thread was about to be tested in ways I had never anticipated. The tension crackled like electricity, and I could sense that everything was about to change.

Chapter 15: A Fragile Alliance

The sun hung low in the sky, casting a golden hue across the city, wrapping everything in a soft, dreamy light. I stood at the edge of the rooftop terrace, a glass of merlot cradled in my palm, the wine glistening like rubies against the fading daylight. The air was crisp, a whisper of autumn threading through the vibrant landscape of concrete and glass. Below me, the world pulsed with life, an ebb and flow of hurried footsteps and laughter that wafted up, mingling with the faint strains of music from a nearby café.

Yet, the rhythm of the city felt dissonant to me, each note sharp and discordant. Victor's presence loomed over me, heavy and suffocating. Just hours earlier, he had appeared at my door, his face carved in shadows, eyes glinting with the promise of danger. I had thought I'd seen the last of him, that our dance through deceit and betrayal had come to an end. Yet here he was, like a bad penny, turning my world upside down again.

"Cora," he had said, the name sliding off his tongue like poison, "we need to talk."

With a heart that threatened to leap from my chest, I had invited him in, the warmth of my home a stark contrast to the chill he exuded. I braced myself for the storm, but nothing could have prepared me for his proposal. Victor had laid out a scenario so twisted, so laced with moral decay, that my insides twisted in revulsion.

He spoke with a calculated calm, weaving a web of reasons and rationalizations. "Caden is playing you, Cora," he said, his voice smooth like silk but edged with steel. "He's deep in something far darker than you can imagine. You need to use your influence in the fashion world to expose him. It's the only way to protect yourself. Help me bring him down, and I'll ensure you stay clear of this mess."

I clenched the glass in my hand, the sharp edges biting into my palm. The mere suggestion felt like a slap, a betrayal not just of Caden, but of everything I believed about love and loyalty. Yet beneath my revulsion, a flicker of fear ignited—a whisper of self-preservation that clawed at the back of my mind. If I didn't comply, Victor's shadows would stretch around me, and everything I had built, everything I cherished, could crumble to dust.

"Why should I believe you?" I shot back, my voice steadier than I felt. "You're the last person I'd trust."

Victor leaned closer, his voice a conspiratorial murmur. "Because, darling, you have more to lose than you think. Caden is not just some charming rogue; he's involved in serious criminal activities. And if you're tied to him, if he gets caught, so do you."

His words resonated like a bell tolling in a quiet church, heavy with the weight of truth. I had seen Caden's darker sides, the shadow that clung to him like a second skin, but to believe he was knee-deep in something illegal? It felt like an anchor pulling me under, into dark waters where I might drown in my own uncertainty.

I had always been drawn to the rough edges of Caden's persona, the allure of danger that shimmered in his smile. But as the pieces of Victor's puzzle fell into place, I realized how naive I had been. The late-night phone calls, the constant secrecy, the way Caden had recoiled whenever I touched on his past—each instance now loomed larger, transformed into signs I had willingly ignored.

"No," I said, the word tasting bitter on my tongue. "I won't betray him. He deserves better than this."

Victor's laughter cut through my resolve, cold and devoid of warmth. "Does he? Or does he deserve exactly what's coming? It's either him or you, Cora. Choose wisely."

With those words, he left, his figure silhouetted against the fading sun, a specter fading into the shadows. I felt hollow, a fragile shell stripped of its substance, standing alone on my terrace with the city sprawling beneath me.

Night fell swiftly, wrapping the world in darkness, and with it came a deepening dread. Caden would be home soon, unaware of the tempest brewing just beneath the surface of our lives. I sank onto the plush cushions of the terrace furniture, staring out at the twinkling lights, trying to sort through the chaos in my mind.

I loved him. I had never doubted that, not for a second. But how could I reconcile that love with the man Victor painted? My heart and my head clashed in a fierce battle, each side waging a war of emotions that left me reeling.

The sound of the door creaking open broke my reverie, and I looked up to see Caden silhouetted in the doorway, his tall frame outlined by the soft light spilling in from the hallway. His smile was bright, an incandescent glow that chased away some of my shadows. "Hey, there you are," he said, stepping outside, the warmth of his presence enveloping me like a favorite blanket. "I was hoping to find you out here."

I tried to muster a smile in return, but my heart was still heavy with Victor's ultimatum. Instead, I forced a laugh, a desperate attempt to mask the turmoil swirling within. "Just enjoying the view."

He joined me on the terrace, his fingers brushing against mine as he settled beside me, a gesture so simple yet fraught with intimacy. "This city looks good from up here, doesn't it?" he said, gazing out over the rooftops, the glimmering lights reflecting in his eyes.

"Yeah," I replied, feeling the weight of unspoken words pressing down on my chest. "It really does."

He turned to me, his gaze piercing, and I felt an urgency in his expression, a need to draw me closer, to bridge the gap between us that had begun to widen. "You okay? You look...lost."

"I'm fine," I insisted, though my voice faltered. How could I share my fears with him when I was still grappling with the reality of what Victor had proposed? I could feel the tension crackling between us, a taut wire ready to snap.

Caden leaned in, his voice low and steady. "You can tell me anything, Cora. You know that, right?"

I wanted to believe him, wanted to surrender to the safety of his words, but Victor's threat loomed large, and I could already feel the fraying threads of our relationship begin to unravel. "I know," I whispered, forcing myself to hold his gaze. "But some things are just... complicated."

He studied me, a flicker of concern darkening his eyes. "Complicated is my middle name," he said, a playful smirk tugging at his lips, attempting to lighten the heavy air between us. "Why don't you let me in? I promise I won't bite—at least not hard."

A laugh bubbled up despite my turmoil, a flicker of warmth igniting in the pit of my stomach. "You're incorrigible," I replied, grateful for the momentary reprieve from my thoughts.

"Only when I'm with you." Caden's voice softened, his expression shifting to something deeper, something that mirrored the conflict brewing inside me. In that moment, everything felt achingly perfect, yet precariously fragile. I took a breath, the weight of my decision pressing down on me like an anchor.

As the stars began to twinkle above, I felt the walls I had built around my heart start to crack. I could either protect myself and betray the man I loved or embrace the chaos of our reality, risking everything for the chance to uncover the truth. In that fleeting moment, everything hinged on the delicate balance of love and betrayal, and I found myself teetering on the edge, yearning for clarity in a world steeped in shadows.

The moon hung like a silver coin in the velvet sky, casting a soft glow over the city as I moved through the narrow streets, my heels clicking on the cobblestones with a rhythm that felt both familiar and foreign. My heart was a riot of conflicting emotions, a tempest threatening to spill over as I replayed Victor's proposal in my mind. Each step felt weighted, as if the very air around me conspired to keep me tethered to this dilemma that had landed squarely on my shoulders.

Caden's face swam before me, his easy smile and the way his laughter echoed in my thoughts. I could almost hear him whispering sweet nothings, could almost feel his hands warm against my skin. The way he looked at me made me believe I was more than just a fashion designer; I was the muse, the one who could breathe life into his darker corners. But now, that image was beginning to crack.

I rounded a corner, catching sight of a small café, its warmth spilling onto the street like an invitation. Inside, the atmosphere buzzed with chatter, the clinking of cups blending harmoniously with the sound of laughter. I pushed the door open, the bell jingling above me, and slipped inside, seeking refuge in the cozy ambiance. The barista, a bright-eyed woman with a friendly smile, took my order, and as I waited for my drink, I felt the weight of eyes upon me.

A familiar figure was seated in the corner, backlit by the glow of a table lamp. My heart skipped a beat. Caden. He was absorbed in a sketchbook, pencil dancing across the pages as if it were an extension of his very soul. I hadn't expected to see him here, not tonight, not when my mind was tangled in Victor's dark web.

"Hey," I called, forcing a smile to mask the turmoil churning within. His head snapped up, and his face broke into that dazzling smile that always made my heart race.

"Cora! I didn't know you were coming here." He gestured to the empty seat across from him. "Care to join me?"

I hesitated, caught between wanting to bury myself in his presence and the treacherous thoughts swirling like storm clouds.

But I slid into the chair, needing his warmth to ground me, even if just for a moment.

"You look busy," I said, nodding toward the sketchbook, hoping to keep the mood light, to keep him from prying too deeply.

"Just doodling," he replied, his tone playful as he flipped the pages to reveal a myriad of designs that leapt off the page with color and life. "Trying to capture the essence of the city. What do you think?"

The sketches were breathtaking, swirling with vibrancy and the kind of flair only Caden could conjure. Each stroke reflected his passion, a kaleidoscope of ideas spilling onto the paper. "They're amazing, as always," I said, genuinely impressed. "You have a gift."

His cheeks flushed with pride, and for a moment, the world faded away, leaving just the two of us wrapped in this cocoon of creativity and connection. But the nagging thought of Victor's ultimatum clung to me like a shadow.

"Are you alright?" Caden's voice cut through my reverie, his eyes narrowing with concern. "You seem a bit off tonight."

I tried to laugh it off, but it came out strained. "I'm just... processing some things. You know how it is."

He leaned back, arms crossed, an unyielding intensity in his gaze. "Processing? Or avoiding?"

Caught off guard, I opened my mouth to protest but faltered. He was right, of course. I was skirting around the truth like a coward, but how could I lay it all bare? How could I tell him that my world was tilting on its axis because of Victor's threats?

Before I could respond, my phone buzzed insistently in my bag, a shrill reminder of the chaos threatening to swallow me whole. I fished it out, heart sinking as I saw Victor's name flash across the screen.

"Are you going to answer that?" Caden asked, his brows furrowing.

"No," I replied, sliding the phone back into my bag, trying to maintain a casual air even as dread curled in my stomach. "It's just spam."

Caden's expression shifted, a flicker of doubt crossing his features. "Cora, if something's bothering you—"

"I said I'm fine!" I snapped, a little too harshly. Instantly, regret washed over me. "Sorry, I didn't mean to—"

"It's alright," he said, his voice softening. "I just want to help. I care about you."

His words wrapped around my heart, a warm embrace that both soothed and stoked the flames of my inner turmoil. But just as I was about to lean into the comfort of his affection, a flash of movement in the corner of my eye drew my attention.

A figure loomed near the entrance, the shadows twisting around him like a dark cloak. Victor stepped into the café, a wolf among the sheep. My heart raced as I recognized the predator in my midst, and all the air seemed to suck out of the room.

Caden turned, spotting him immediately, and the playful light in his eyes extinguished. "Is that—"

"Please," I whispered, gripping his hand across the table, desperate for his understanding. "Just... don't say anything."

Victor sauntered over, his smile wide but devoid of warmth. "Fancy seeing you here, Cora. And you brought company. How charming."

"What do you want, Victor?" I said, forcing my voice to remain steady, even as panic clawed at my insides.

He leaned closer, his tone dripping with false congeniality. "Just wanted to chat, that's all. You know, about your career, and how quickly things can spiral out of control."

Caden stiffened beside me, sensing the undercurrent of tension, and I could see the protective instinct flare in his eyes. "I think you should leave," he said, his voice low and commanding. "You're making her uncomfortable."

Victor chuckled, a sound like broken glass. "Oh, I wouldn't dream of it. I'm simply here to offer Cora an opportunity. After all, it would be such a shame if her talents went to waste, wouldn't it?"

Caden's eyes narrowed, a storm brewing within their depths. "Cora doesn't need anything from you. You're not welcome here."

"Ah, but you see, Caden," Victor replied, leaning back, feigning a relaxed demeanor that belied the menace in his posture. "Cora is at a crossroads. She has decisions to make, and I happen to know a few secrets that could alter her path."

The implication hung in the air like a guillotine poised to drop, and I felt Caden's grip on my hand tighten, a silent promise to protect me. "Enough games, Victor," I said, trying to assert control over the spiraling chaos. "Whatever you have to say, say it. But leave him out of it."

Victor's gaze shifted between us, and I could see the wheels turning in his mind, contemplating how best to exploit the moment. "Very well. Let's cut to the chase. You can save yourself a lot of trouble, Cora, and perhaps help a certain someone along the way."

"I'm not interested," I said, though my heart raced with fear and uncertainty.

"Really? Because the truth is, Caden's world isn't as glamorous as you might think," he continued, his tone oily and smooth, like a snake slithering through the grass. "He's knee-deep in a business that could ruin you both. I'm offering you a way out, Cora."

"Shut up!" Caden snapped, rising to his feet, his chair scraping harshly against the floor. The café had grown silent, eyes turning to us, the atmosphere thick with tension. "You're trying to intimidate her, and it's pathetic."

Victor merely smirked, a predator enjoying the hunt. "Oh, I'm not the one you should be worried about, Caden. This is bigger than you think."

I stood, urgency coursing through my veins, the urge to protect Caden swelling in my chest. "Victor, I won't listen to this. You're nothing but a bully."

He leaned closer, his expression darkening. "Watch your back, Cora. Because the moment you turn your gaze away, you might find yourself on the wrong side of everything you hold dear."

With that, he turned on his heel, striding away, his exit leaving a palpable void that seemed to echo in the silence. Caden's breathing was ragged, his expression a mixture of anger and concern.

"Are you alright?" he asked, reaching for me, his hand warm and grounding.

I looked into his eyes, and for the first time, the doubt and fear began to unravel. "I don't know what to do, Caden. I feel trapped."

"You're not trapped. We'll figure this out together," he assured me, but I could sense the tension simmering beneath the surface of his words. "We'll confront Victor. We won't let him dictate our lives."

I wanted to believe him, but the truth lingered like a specter, a reminder of how precarious our situation had become. The bond we shared felt strained, tested by the weight of secrets and the looming threat of betrayal. And as I stood there, the warmth of his presence battling the chill of Victor's words, I realized that

The aftermath of Victor's departure left the café heavy with unspoken words, a tangible tension that seemed to cling to the air like smoke. Caden's gaze bore into me, his concern palpable as the silence stretched between us, fraught with meaning. I could see the question written across his face: what had Victor said to shake me so deeply?

I swallowed hard, the knot in my throat tightening. "Caden, I—"

"Don't," he interrupted, raising a hand as if to physically block my words. "You don't have to explain anything right now. Let's just get out of here."

His protective instinct wrapped around me, a blanket of warmth that was both comforting and alarming. I nodded, grateful for his presence, yet the weight of my secret felt like an anchor dragging me down. As we stepped outside, the night air hit me, cool and bracing, sharpening my senses. The city buzzed around us, but I felt adrift, lost in a sea of uncertainty.

"Where to?" Caden asked, his voice laced with urgency. "We can go back to your place, or I can take you to mine. Just say the word."

"Let's go to mine," I replied, needing the familiar safety of my home, a place where I could think, even if I was on shaky ground. We walked side by side, but the distance between us felt insurmountable. I could sense his desire to reach out, to close the gap, but I was trapped in a whirlwind of my own making, an internal storm raging against the horizon of my heart.

Once inside, I let the door click shut behind us, the soft sound echoing in the stillness. My apartment was a sanctuary, filled with splashes of color and the faint scent of vanilla from the candles I always kept lit. It was my haven, yet now it felt like a cage, walls closing in as I struggled to find the right words.

"Cora," Caden said, stepping toward me, his eyes searching mine. "What did Victor mean? What does he know?"

I hesitated, weighing the truth like a heavy stone in my hand. "He... he thinks you're involved in something criminal," I finally admitted, the words falling from my lips like shards of glass. "He wants me to expose you."

Caden's expression hardened, his jaw clenching. "He's lying. You know that, right?"

"I don't know anything anymore!" I snapped, frustration boiling over. "Victor knows things about you, things you haven't told me. I feel like I'm walking on a tightrope, and one misstep could send me crashing down."

"I didn't want to burden you," he replied, his voice barely above a whisper, each word laced with a vulnerability that cracked my defenses. "I thought I could handle it, but it seems like it's all crashing down around us."

I turned away, pacing the small living room as thoughts collided in my mind. The shadows of the evening loomed larger than ever. "What do you mean, crashing down? What is Victor talking about?"

Caden ran a hand through his hair, frustration etched across his features. "There are things I've been involved in—business deals that skirt the edges of legality. But I'm not a criminal, Cora. I'm trying to make a name for myself in a world that doesn't play by the rules."

"Trying to make a name?" I echoed incredulously, turning to face him. "By what, getting involved with Victor? The very man who's threatening everything we have?"

"It's complicated," he insisted, stepping closer, his voice low and urgent. "I thought I could separate myself from Victor's influence. I was trying to break free, but now it feels like he's pulling me back into the dark."

A bitter laugh escaped my lips, a sound of disbelief. "Break free? Caden, it seems like you're still entangled in his web. You have to realize that he won't let you go that easily."

"What do you want me to say?" he snapped back, frustration radiating from him. "That I should have played by the rules? This is the world we live in, Cora. It's ruthless."

"But I thought you were better than that!" The words spilled out, raw and unfiltered. "I thought you were worth fighting for."

The silence hung between us, thick and suffocating. I could see the pain in his eyes, the way my words cut deeper than I intended. "You are worth fighting for," he replied finally, voice strained. "But

I'm afraid, Cora. Afraid of what Victor will do if he finds out I'm trying to get out. And now, because of me, you could be in danger."

The realization hit me like a punch to the gut. "I don't want to be a pawn in this game, Caden. I refuse to be his collateral damage."

He stepped forward, the distance between us evaporating. "Then let's take control. We need to confront Victor. Together."

The thought sent a shiver down my spine. "And what, give him more power over us? That sounds like a recipe for disaster."

"I know it's dangerous," he said, eyes fierce, "but it's the only way to end this. We can't keep running. If we want to survive, we need to face him head-on."

"I don't know if I can do that," I admitted, my voice trembling. "What if he turns on us? What if he exposes everything?"

Caden's gaze softened, a blend of determination and tenderness that made my heart ache. "We'll find a way to protect each other. I promise. You have to trust me."

Trust. The word hung between us, a fragile lifeline tethering us to one another. But with every moment that passed, I could feel the fabric of our reality fraying at the edges, and Victor's threat loomed larger than ever.

"Okay," I finally said, resolve hardening in my chest. "Let's confront him. But we need a plan, and we need to be ready for anything."

Caden nodded, the tension in his shoulders easing just a fraction. "I'll do whatever it takes. We'll figure this out, together."

But just as I was about to embrace the flicker of hope igniting within me, a sudden noise shattered the moment—a loud bang echoed from the hallway, followed by the unmistakable sound of hurried footsteps. My heart plummeted as I exchanged a terrified glance with Caden.

"What was that?" he asked, the protective instinct surging back to life.

I held my breath, fear pooling in my stomach. "I don't know, but it doesn't sound good."

Before we could process the implication, the door burst open, and Victor stepped into my apartment, his face a mask of fury and triumph. Behind him, shadows shifted, figures emerging from the dark like phantoms ready to seize what was rightfully theirs.

"Did you really think you could escape me?" Victor sneered, his eyes glinting with malice. "Let's see how long your little alliance can last when the truth comes crashing down."

And just like that, the walls of my world crumbled, a swift and merciless descent into chaos, the darkness swallowing us whole as we stood on the precipice of something we couldn't foresee.

Chapter 16: The Return

The storm outside howled like a wounded animal, rain lashing against the hotel window as if trying to gain entry into the sanctum of my turbulent thoughts. Each drop ricocheted against the glass, mirroring the chaos in my heart. I stood there, feeling as frayed as the threadbare carpet beneath my feet, waiting for clarity in the eye of my personal tempest. Decisions swirled like leaves in a whirlwind, and I was caught in the midst, unable to settle on a single one.

Just as I thought I'd found some semblance of peace in solitude, he appeared—Caden, with his wild hair and that rugged, almost otherworldly charm that had once stolen my breath. He was a figure painted against the storm, dark and mesmerizing, yet just as likely to drown me if I dove too deep. The door creaked open, and he stepped inside like a rogue breeze, brisk and unpredictable.

"Why here?" I managed, the words tumbling from my lips before I could stop them, laced with disbelief and a hint of vulnerability. My voice cracked like thunder outside, struggling to find strength in the face of his presence. I had braced myself for this moment, but now that it was here, I felt raw, exposed, and utterly unprepared.

Caden's eyes danced with an intensity that made my pulse quicken. "I didn't know where else to find you. I've been looking everywhere." He ran a hand through his tousled hair, and I could see the tension etched in the lines around his mouth. The man who had once seemed so infallible now appeared as if he had run a marathon through his own demons, panting and desperate.

"What do you want from me, Caden?" I crossed my arms, a defensive posture that felt as flimsy as the fabric of my oversized hotel robe. "You disappeared without a word. You left me to pick up the pieces, and now you want to come back as if nothing happened?"

He stepped closer, the scent of him—a mix of cedar and something faintly spicy—wrapped around me like a long-lost memory. "I came to protect you," he insisted, his voice steady but laced with urgency. "Everything I did was for us. I thought I was doing the right thing."

My heart beat an erratic rhythm, torn between the pull of his words and the weight of his silence. Protecting me? It felt like a fragile excuse wrapped in layers of deception. "Protecting me from what? Or rather, who?" I fired back, determination coloring my tone. "You can't just keep secrets and expect me to fall into your arms. You have to tell me everything."

The space between us crackled with unspoken truths. He hesitated, the raw edge of his expression revealing a man caught between fear and regret. I couldn't help but wonder what he was holding back, what shadows trailed him like ghostly whispers. The questions hung in the air like the mist outside, thick and suffocating.

"I thought I could shield you from it," he said at last, his gaze slipping from mine as if the weight of his confession was too much to bear. "But the truth is, I've been trying to protect you from my own mistakes."

His words were a dagger, sharp and precise, piercing through the haze of my emotions. I wanted to scream, to unleash the turmoil that had brewed within me during his absence. "So this was your plan? To protect me by leaving me in the dark?" My voice was a mere whisper, cracking under the strain of emotions I'd bottled up for far too long.

Caden took a deep breath, a flicker of anguish crossing his face. "It wasn't supposed to be like this. I thought I could handle it, but..." He faltered, the uncharacteristic vulnerability drawing me in against my better judgment. "I didn't want you to see the worst of me. You deserved better."

I stepped forward, closing the distance between us, my heart thudding with the rhythm of an approaching storm. "Maybe I deserved honesty instead," I shot back, feeling the heat of my own anger swirl with something else—a need to bridge the chasm that had opened between us.

For a moment, we stood there, caught in an electric moment, the world outside forgotten. I could feel the familiar spark that had always ignited our chemistry, but beneath it lay an intricate web of uncertainty. Could love truly withstand the pressure of secrets?

"I need to know what you're hiding, Caden. I can't do this if you keep pushing me away," I implored, the words tumbling from my lips like desperate confessions.

He met my gaze, and for the first time, I saw the depths of his turmoil mirrored in his eyes. "I can't lose you again," he whispered, reaching out as if afraid I would slip away.

As his fingers brushed against my arm, a rush of warmth flooded through me, igniting that undeniable connection. The battle within me raged on, torn between the longing to forgive and the necessity of truth. "Then stop hiding," I breathed, the vulnerability of the moment washing over me like the rain pounding against the window. "Show me what you're afraid of."

Caden hesitated, the uncharacteristic earnestness etched in his features. "It's not just about us, it's bigger than that. I've made choices, choices I can't undo, and I—"

Before he could finish, the hotel room trembled, a loud crash resonating from outside, interrupting our fragile exchange. The storm unleashed its fury, and for a brief moment, the outside world intruded on our fragile bubble. Fear flickered in his eyes, but it wasn't just the storm that troubled him.

"I can't let this end like it did before," he said urgently, the intensity in his voice cutting through the chaos. "I won't let you go without a fight."

Just as I felt the walls of my resolve begin to crack, the door swung open again, this time with the wind as its accomplice. A figure stood silhouetted in the doorway, drenched and breathless, shrouded in the storm's shadows. My heart sank as I realized the last thing I wanted to see now was an unwelcome witness to our unraveling.

The air crackled, thick with unspoken words and the scent of rain-soaked earth filtering through the slightly ajar window. The storm outside raged like a tempestuous lover, slamming against the hotel walls, while inside, the atmosphere shimmered with unresolved tension. I blinked at the figure in the doorway, momentarily lost in the chaos of emotions swirling between Caden and me.

The newcomer stepped into the light, shaking droplets from his hair like a startled dog, and I immediately recognized him—Tyler, my once-loyal confidant, now a rogue storm of unexpected appearances. He looked disheveled, but there was a spark in his eye that hinted at mischief, or perhaps trouble. "I thought I'd find you here, seeking shelter from your storm," he said, his grin both cheeky and disarming.

"Just when I thought this day couldn't get any more complicated," I muttered, eyeing Tyler warily. "What are you doing here?"

Tyler flashed that signature smile, one that had charmed countless baristas and taxi drivers alike. "I'd say I'm here to rescue you, but from what exactly? A brooding ex or the deluge outside? Tough choice." He glanced between us, the corners of his mouth twitching with suppressed amusement.

Caden shot him a look that could curdle milk. "This isn't a game, Tyler. You should have knocked." His voice was low, a warning that danced just above the growing tension.

"Yeah, but where's the fun in that?" Tyler retorted, taking a step further into the room, as if he had every right to invade this moment. "Besides, I always knew I'd be the one to make a grand entrance." He feigned a bow, eliciting a reluctant smile from me despite the swirling tempest of feelings.

But Caden's eyes were dark, his frustration palpable. "We were having a private conversation," he said, the words laced with an irritation that hinted at deeper issues.

"Clearly," Tyler shot back, hands raised in mock surrender. "But let's not pretend this isn't better than whatever tortured love drama you were engaged in. I thrive on chaos, and trust me, this is chaos in its finest form."

"Your timing is impeccable as always," I said, a hint of exasperation threading through my tone. The tension between Caden and me thickened, and I wasn't sure how to slice through it. "What exactly do you want, Tyler?"

He leaned back against the wall, arms crossed, a playful smirk refusing to leave his face. "You might not want to hear it, but I've got some intel. Rumor has it your 'protected future' isn't as secure as Caden seems to think."

I glanced at Caden, whose expression morphed from irritation to something more complex, the lines of his jaw tightening like a coiled spring. "What are you talking about?" he demanded, his voice low and dangerous.

Tyler shrugged, unfazed. "Word on the street is that people aren't just looking at you anymore, Caden. They're looking at your past. You know the things you thought were buried? They're surfacing like the goddamn Loch Ness Monster, and not even the best excuses can sink that."

"What does that even mean?" I asked, frustration bubbling beneath the surface. "Caden, is this true? Is there something about your past that could hurt us?"

Caden's gaze flickered away, shadows crossing his face like a cloud passing over the sun. "It's complicated," he replied, his tone tinged with resignation. "Things I thought were behind me are suddenly back in play. I didn't want you to get pulled into it."

"Oh, great," I scoffed, feeling my temper flare. "So, your brilliant plan to protect me was to keep me in the dark? Fantastic strategy."

Tyler leaned forward, his playful demeanor shifting into something more serious. "Listen, I get it. You love him, and he loves you—at least, I hope he does," he added, giving Caden a pointed look. "But you need to know the truth. No more half-measures. If there's something lurking in the shadows, it's better to confront it than let it fester."

Caden's jaw clenched as if the truth were a bitter pill lodged in his throat. "It's not that simple," he said, his voice strained. "I've spent too long trying to outrun my past. You don't know what it's like—how hard it is to keep those skeletons from rattling."

"Try me," Tyler shot back, his tone softening but still firm. "I've known you both long enough to know that if you don't face this together, it'll destroy you."

The weight of his words hung in the air, a tangible force pressing down on us, compelling us to confront the chaos swirling just beneath the surface. The tension morphed into something almost palpable, drawing me closer to Caden, while simultaneously threatening to tear us apart.

I took a deep breath, grounding myself amid the whirlwind. "Caden, I can't navigate this blind. If there's something out there, I need to know. I deserve to know."

He hesitated, the moment stretching between us like an elastic band, ready to snap. "You're right," he admitted finally, a glimmer of vulnerability breaking through his stormy exterior. "I should have told you sooner."

Just as he seemed on the verge of revealing whatever dark secret haunted him, a loud bang resounded outside, jolting us. The hotel shook, and the lights flickered ominously. Tyler raised an eyebrow, the grin returning to his face. "Is that part of your dramatic reveal, or are we in a horror movie now?"

"Not helping," I snapped, feeling my heart race. Caden remained silent, his focus shifting toward the window where the rain pounded relentlessly, obscuring the view.

"I need to get to the bottom of this," I murmured, feeling the weight of my resolve deepen. "If something is coming, we have to face it head-on. Together."

Caden met my gaze, the intensity in his eyes revealing a mixture of fear and admiration. "Together," he echoed, his voice steady, though I could sense the storm brewing inside him.

"Now, can we please focus?" Tyler interjected, his tone lightening the moment as he rubbed his hands together. "I'm not keen on being the comic relief while you two play a high-stakes game of emotional chess. Let's untangle this before it blows up in our faces."

Before we could respond, another loud crash echoed from outside, followed by a blaring horn. I turned to the window, my heart racing, the reality of our circumstances hitting harder than the relentless rain. Whatever had been lurking in the shadows was now uncomfortably close, and I had a feeling the storm wasn't just outside—it was brewing within us, too.

The wind howled outside, a ghostly wail that intertwined with the sound of rain hammering against the hotel window. I could feel my heart thrumming in my chest as the tension wrapped around us like a tight band, ready to snap. Caden's presence was magnetic, pulling me in even as my mind screamed for caution. Just as I began to contemplate how to navigate the labyrinth of emotions between us, Tyler's interruption loomed large.

"Okay, I feel like I've walked into the middle of a soap opera," Tyler said, his smirk fading slightly as he read the room's charged atmosphere. "But it's time we stop playing around. Caden, spill it.

Whatever you're hiding, it's clearly not going away just because you've decided to play the noble knight."

Caden's jaw tightened, his gaze flicking to me, uncertainty dancing in his eyes. "It's not that simple, Tyler," he replied, his voice a mix of irritation and something softer, more vulnerable. "There are things I've done—things I thought I could outrun. I didn't want to drag you into it."

I crossed my arms, feeling a mix of frustration and concern. "And leaving me in the dark was supposed to protect me? Caden, it's exhausting to keep fighting for clarity while you're busy guarding your secrets."

Tyler leaned back against the wall, arms crossed, a knowing expression on his face. "Believe it or not, I'm actually on your side for once, Caden. Love is all well and good, but it won't hold when the weight of the past crashes down. You can't fix this without honesty."

I looked between the two men, my heart pounding. Caden seemed to shrink under the weight of their expectations, and my heart ached for the man who had once radiated confidence. "What do you mean, 'things you've done'?" I pressed, my voice steady, but internally, I felt like I was on the brink of a cliff, the ground crumbling beneath my feet. "What could possibly be so terrible that you thought it was better for me to remain clueless?"

The silence stretched, a taut string ready to snap. Caden's eyes flitted to the floor, and in that moment, I could see the cracks forming in his façade. "It's not just about me," he said quietly. "It involves others. People who have made choices that could hurt you."

"Others?" I echoed, the word feeling heavy as I thought of the network of lives intertwined with his. "Like who?"

He hesitated, as if weighing the gravity of his next words. "Like my brother, for starters. He's gotten involved in some shady dealings, and I thought I could shield you from it. I've been trying to keep him at bay, but he's gotten bolder, and it's not just my reputation at stake anymore."

The revelation hit me like a slap, and I took a step back, grappling with the sudden flood of emotions. "Your brother? Caden, I thought your family was behind you. Why didn't you tell me?"

"Because I thought it was over," he replied, a pained expression crossing his face. "I thought I could handle it. But now..." His voice trailed off, a flicker of dread igniting in the depths of his eyes.

Tyler cleared his throat, drawing our attention. "Whatever he's doing, he's clearly not done. You don't get involved with the kind of people your brother has without consequences. And now that you're back, he's likely to come sniffing around. You might want to be prepared for an unexpected visit."

The weight of his words settled heavily in the room, and I felt the chill of dread creeping in. "What are we supposed to do?" I asked, my voice trembling slightly. "Just wait for your brother to show up? I didn't sign up for this kind of danger."

"No, but you're already in it," Caden said, stepping closer, his presence both comforting and alarming. "I won't let him hurt you. Whatever it takes, I'll protect you."

My heart swelled with a mixture of affection and fear, but I couldn't shake the feeling of impending doom. "You've been trying to protect me this entire time by hiding the truth," I argued, my voice shaking with emotion. "You've put me at risk without even realizing it."

"Damn it, I was trying to keep you safe!" His voice rose, cracking slightly, revealing the raw frustration beneath the surface.

"Safe from what?" I demanded, the anger boiling over. "You can't just throw words around without giving me context! What's the point of love if it's wrapped in secrecy?"

Before he could respond, another thunderclap roared outside, shaking the room and sending the lights flickering. Tyler swayed, a dramatic gasp escaping him. "If that doesn't scream 'significant plot twist,' I don't know what does."

I couldn't help but let out a nervous laugh, the absurdity of the moment breaking through the tension. "Great, a literal storm and a metaphorical one. Just my luck."

Caden's expression softened slightly, a flicker of relief washing over him as he leaned closer, lowering his voice. "I promise I'll explain everything, but first, we need to figure out how to deal with my brother. We can't let him think he has any power over us."

As if on cue, the hotel room shook again, but this time, the sound didn't come from the storm. It was a loud crash, followed by frantic shouting from the street below. My heart raced as I glanced toward the window.

"What was that?" I asked, my pulse quickening.

Caden moved to the window, his body tense. "We need to see what's happening," he urged, stepping toward the glass, pulling back the curtain just enough to peer outside.

The scene unfolding before us was nothing short of chaos. A group of men—familiar faces from the shadows of Caden's past—were storming into the hotel's lobby, shouting and gesturing wildly. Panic surged through me as I realized this was more than just coincidence.

"What the hell is going on?" Tyler asked, moving beside Caden, his previous bravado fading into genuine concern.

Caden's eyes darkened as he turned back to us, urgency threading through his words. "They've found us. It's my brother's crew, and they're not here for a friendly visit."

My heart raced, adrenaline flooding my veins. "What do we do?"

Caden looked between us, determination igniting in his gaze. "We stand together. No more secrets. If they're coming for me, they're coming for you too. We'll face this together."

The door rattled ominously, the sound reverberating through the room like a countdown. My breath hitched, and with every second that passed, the tension coiled tighter. The stakes had never been higher, and as the door burst open, the figures silhouetted against the storm felt like a culmination of all our fears colliding in one chaotic moment.

And just like that, we were plunged into the unknown, teetering on the brink of a reality that threatened to shatter everything we'd fought for.

Chapter 17: Under Fire

The air was thick with tension, a palpable weight that hung in the dimly lit room like a storm cloud poised to break. I stood by the window, watching the rain streak down the glass like tears cascading from the heavens, mirroring my own inner turmoil. Each drop was a reminder of the chaos swirling just beyond my grasp, a turmoil I had hoped to escape when I made the decision to stay. The city was a relentless beast, breathing down my neck, and with each passing day, I felt its breath grow hotter, more insistent.

Victor's threats had morphed from veiled hints into bold proclamations, the kind that left bruises long after they were spoken. They had begun as whispers, ominous undertones in conversations I'd overheard, but now they echoed in my mind with unsettling clarity. "Caden is a fool to think he can protect you," Victor had said, his voice a low growl that sent shivers down my spine. "Sooner or later, you'll be the one paying the price for his arrogance." I shuddered at the memory, the echo of his words reverberating through my thoughts like a relentless drumbeat.

Caden had retreated into a world of shadows, his once warm demeanor replaced by a steely resolve that left me feeling isolated. I could sense the weight on his shoulders, a burden he refused to share. It was as if he had wrapped himself in a cocoon of solitude, hoping to shield me from the storm brewing outside, yet all it did was thrust me into a deeper darkness. I longed to reach out, to shake him from his reverie, but each time I opened my mouth, the words evaporated like mist in the morning sun.

"Hey, you okay?" Clara's voice pulled me from my reverie, a bright spark in the dimness that surrounded me. She stood in the doorway, her arms crossed and concern etched on her face. Her vibrant red hair tumbled over her shoulders like a fiery cascade, a stark contrast to the dull grays of the room. It was her usual entrance, a whirlwind of energy that brought a flicker of life into my otherwise stagnant world.

"Do I look okay?" I shot back, the frustration in my voice sharper than I intended. The moment it left my lips, I regretted it, the sting of my words hanging in the air like a weight I couldn't lift. Clara tilted her head, her expression softening as she stepped into the room.

"Hey, I know it's rough. But you can't shut everyone out, especially not me," she said, her tone gentle yet firm. "You need to talk about what's going on. Bottling it up won't help."

I let out a breath, frustration morphing into resignation. "It's just... everything is spiraling out of control, Clara. I don't know who I can trust anymore. Not with Victor lurking in the shadows, and the media sniffing around like starving wolves."

"Then let's put some distance between us and this mess." Clara's eyes sparkled with mischief, her hands gesturing wildly as if she were crafting an escape plan. "How about a girls' night? Just you and me. We'll grab some wine, watch terrible movies, and forget about everything for a few hours."

I couldn't help but smile, the corners of my mouth lifting despite the heaviness in my heart. "You really think a bottle of wine and a rom-com will fix this?"

"Hey, if they can make you laugh, they can definitely fix a few things. Plus, it'll give you a break. A breather, right? And who knows? Maybe we'll even come up with a plan."

Before I could respond, my phone buzzed on the table, a sharp sound that cut through the moment. I grabbed it, my heart leaping into my throat as I saw Caden's name flash on the screen. "It's him," I said, my voice barely above a whisper. "He never calls."

"Answer it," Clara urged, her gaze steady on me, a mixture of encouragement and caution in her eyes.

I hesitated, the weight of uncertainty pressing down on me. But I couldn't ignore the urgency in my gut. I swiped the screen and pressed the phone to my ear, the sound of his breathing on the other end sending a rush of emotions surging through me.

"Caden?" I breathed, the hope in my voice almost palpable.

"Where are you?" His voice was low and tense, tinged with an undercurrent of urgency that sent chills skittering down my spine. "I need you to be careful. Things are heating up, and I can't protect you if you're out in the open."

"What are you talking about?" I managed, a thread of panic weaving into my thoughts. "What do you mean, 'heating up'?"

"Just stay inside. Don't go anywhere without my say-so. Trust me, this is serious."

The line went dead, leaving me clutching the phone in a vice-like grip, my heart hammering against my ribs. I looked up at Clara, who wore an expression that mirrored my own shock. "What the hell just happened?"

"Did he say what's going on?" She stepped closer, her tone sharp and inquisitive.

"Not really. Just that things are getting serious." The unease bubbled within me, threatening to spill over as I racked my brain for clarity.

In that moment, the sound of shattering glass echoed through the apartment, a stark and jarring reminder that the outside world was indeed closing in. My heart raced, the adrenaline coursing through my veins as I exchanged a glance with Clara. The safety of our sanctuary shattered in an instant, replaced by a visceral awareness of the danger lurking just beyond the walls.

I shot to my feet, my breath catching in my throat as I turned towards the noise, adrenaline flooding my senses. Clara grabbed my arm, her grip fierce. "What was that?"

I didn't have an answer, but my gut told me it was no coincidence. Whatever was coming for me was already here.

The glass shattered, exploding into a million glimmering shards that danced through the air like deadly confetti. I froze, the adrenaline paralyzing me as I glanced at Clara, whose eyes were wide, pupils dilating with shock. The noise had come from the front of the apartment, and a deep instinct told me to retreat, to run and hide. But where could I go when every exit felt like a trap?

"Stay behind me," I whispered, stepping forward cautiously, as if the very air around me had turned toxic. My heart hammered in my chest, each beat loud enough to drown out any rational thought. I could feel Clara's breath against my back, her presence a reassuring warmth that clashed with the cold dread creeping through my veins.

Moving slowly, I edged toward the hallway leading to the living room, the floor creaking beneath my feet, each sound amplifying the eerie silence that followed the chaos. My fingers brushed against the wall, a futile attempt to ground myself, to remind my racing mind that this was still my home—at least, it had been.

As I rounded the corner, the scene unfolded in a grotesque tableau. The living room window was a jagged mouth, the shards of glass scattered like tiny stars on the floor, glimmering malevolently in the dim light. I took a tentative step inside, scanning the room for signs of life, or danger. The street outside loomed darkly, its familiar contours warped by the fractured glass. It felt wrong, as if my sanctuary had been tainted.

"What just happened?" Clara's voice quivered, barely above a whisper. She stepped up beside me, her bravado faltering in the face of reality. "Are we under attack?"

I hesitated, trying to process the chaos around me. "Maybe it was just an accident," I lied, desperation flooding my voice as I moved to check the window frame. "A rock, perhaps?"

"Or a warning," Clara shot back, her tone sharp as a glass shard. "We can't keep pretending this is just about Caden's business. Someone is targeting you, and we need to figure out who it is before it escalates."

"Okay, okay. Let's not panic," I said, though panic had already settled into the pit of my stomach like a stone. "I'll call Caden. He'll know what to do." I fumbled for my phone, my fingers trembling as I hit his number. My heart sank with every ring.

"Please pick up," I muttered under my breath.

Finally, his voice crackled through the receiver. "What's wrong?" he barked, urgency lacing his tone.

"Caden, someone just broke the window. I don't know if it was intentional, but Clara thinks—"

"I'm coming over." The line went dead before I could respond, the finality of his words sending a rush of unease through me.

"I wish he wouldn't be so dramatic," Clara muttered, her eyes flitting around the room as if expecting someone to leap out from the shadows. "I mean, I get it, but he's making it worse. Maybe we should call the police."

"Right. The police," I said, my voice dripping with sarcasm. "What do I say? 'Excuse me, officers, someone threw a rock, and I suspect my ex-boyfriend's shady business dealings are the cause?'" I ran a hand through my hair, frustration bubbling to the surface.

"Okay, fair point," Clara conceded, rubbing her temples. "But still, we can't just wait for Caden to show up like a knight in shining armor. What if he's too late?"

As if on cue, the sound of heavy footsteps echoed in the hall. My heart leapt into my throat. Caden burst through the door, his presence a mixture of strength and tension, eyes scanning the room like a hawk assessing its territory. "What happened?" he demanded, striding toward us.

"Glass everywhere," I said, gesturing vaguely. "I thought it might have been an accident."

Caden's expression darkened. "An accident doesn't cause this much damage. This is deliberate." He glanced at Clara, whose gaze flickered nervously. "Get your things. We need to move."

"Move? Where?" I asked, confusion mixing with dread.

"To a safer location," he replied, the determination in his voice an anchor in the storm. "I won't let anything happen to you. Victor is escalating things, and it's time to take this seriously."

"What about my things? My life?" I protested, the thought of uprooting everything sending waves of panic surging through me.

"Your life is more important than any of that," he said, his tone fierce yet comforting. "Trust me. We can figure out the rest later."

With a sinking feeling, I nodded, realizing the truth in his words. As much as I clung to my normalcy, it was slipping through my fingers like sand. "Okay, I'll get my bag."

Clara and I scrambled to gather my essentials, the urgency fueling our movements. I shoved clothes, toiletries, and my laptop into my backpack, trying to silence the chaos that threatened to consume me. My mind raced through a hundred scenarios, each one more terrifying than the last.

"Why didn't I see this coming?" I said, almost to myself.

"You weren't alone in this," Clara reminded me, her voice steady. "You're not to blame for his threats. You can't control other people's actions, only how you respond to them."

Just then, a noise echoed from the street below, a car screeching to a halt. My heart lurched. "Caden," I whispered, fear threading through my words.

He immediately tensed, his expression sharp. "Stay behind me."

We edged toward the window cautiously, my pulse pounding in my ears. From our vantage point, I could see a dark sedan parked haphazardly, the driver's door swinging open. A figure emerged, his posture tense and purposeful. As he stepped into the light, the streetlamp illuminated his face—Victor.

"Damn it," Caden muttered, turning sharply to me. "We need to go. Now."

The urgency in his voice pierced through the haze of panic, and I grabbed Clara's hand, our fingers entwined like lifelines. We bolted for the door, adrenaline propelling us forward. My heart thundered in my chest, a frantic drumbeat urging me to flee before the storm descended upon us.

As we slipped into the hallway, I glanced back one last time at the apartment that had felt like home just moments ago. Now, it stood as a reminder of how quickly everything could change, how swiftly safety could morph into danger. With Clara and Caden by my side, I dashed into the unknown, bracing for whatever lay ahead.

The hallway stretched before us, a darkened corridor filled with uncertainty and the faint scent of mildew that clung stubbornly to the walls. I could hear the rush of my own breathing, ragged and uneven, echoing in the silence that felt far too heavy. Caden moved swiftly, guiding us toward the stairwell, his back tense and alert, like a coiled spring ready to unleash. Clara's grip on my hand tightened as we descended the stairs, her knuckles pale against the fading light.

"Why did he have to show up now?" I muttered, the frustration bubbling just beneath the surface. "Can't he just let me live my life? What's the point of throwing rocks if you're not going to follow up with something more exciting?"

"Maybe he's hoping for a little drama," Clara quipped, forcing a smirk. "The kind you'd find in a bad soap opera. We could charge him for our services."

I couldn't help but chuckle, a brief reprieve from the fear wrapping around my chest like a vice. "Is it too late to get a refund on this life choice?" I asked, half-joking, half-serious.

"No refunds on bad decisions," Caden replied tersely, but the corner of his mouth quirked up in a ghost of a smile. "Only consequences."

We reached the ground floor, where the dull hum of the city life beyond the building beckoned like a distant siren. I could almost hear the clatter of coffee cups and the distant chatter of passersby, a stark contrast to the tension that enveloped us. Caden glanced at me, his eyes dark pools of concern. "We need to get to my car. Stay close."

The lobby was eerily quiet, and as we slipped outside, a gust of wind hit me, sharp and cold, ruffling my hair as if nature itself was trying to warn me. Caden led us to his car, a sleek, black sedan that seemed to blend into the shadows. He opened the back door, ushering Clara inside before sliding in next to her. I hesitated at the door, the weight of the world pressing down on me. "What if he finds us?"

"We'll be quick," Caden said, his voice a low growl that held an edge of determination. "We're not sticking around for a chat."

I climbed into the car, my body instinctively tensing as I slammed the door behind me. Caden's fingers danced over the keys, and the engine roared to life, vibrating beneath us. He peeled away from the curb, tires screeching, as if trying to escape the very ground that had felt like home just moments ago. The streets blurred past us, a chaotic tapestry of lights and shadows.

"Where are we going?" I asked, my heart racing faster than the car.

"Somewhere safe," he replied curtly, his jaw clenched as he navigated through the winding streets. "I have a friend who can help us."

"Great. I love mysterious friends," I said, my sarcasm acting as a thin shield against the rising tide of fear. "What kind of help are we talking about? Protection? An escape plan? A stash of chocolate?"

Caden glanced at me, and this time, there was no hint of humor in his expression. "All of the above. But let's focus on getting you safe first."

The city passed in a blur, the landscape shifting from towering buildings to quieter, more residential areas. I watched the familiar slip away, feeling as if I were losing pieces of myself with every turn. The sense of dread coiled tighter in my chest.

"Do you really think it's Victor?" Clara asked, her voice breaking the silence that had settled uncomfortably in the car. "I mean, there could be a hundred reasons someone would break a window. Maybe it was just kids throwing rocks?"

"Kids don't throw rocks through windows to send a message," Caden shot back, his tone leaving no room for doubt. "This is about more than just intimidation. This is personal."

A chill ran through me at his words, the implications echoing in my mind. It wasn't just about Caden's business dealings anymore; I was caught in a web spun from his past choices, ensnared in a danger I never asked for. "What do we do if he comes after us?" I asked, my voice trembling slightly.

"Then we're ready," Caden said, his gaze resolute as he maneuvered through the back streets. "But the best way to deal with someone like Victor is to cut off his options. I need you to trust me."

"Trust has been a tricky word lately," I replied, testing the waters of our fragile connection. "How do I know you're not leading us straight into a trap?"

He turned to me, eyes fierce yet softened with concern. "Because I won't let anything happen to you. I've made mistakes, and I'll own them, but I won't let this be another one."

The sincerity in his voice made my heart twist in an unfamiliar way. He wasn't just a man caught in a storm; he was a lifeline, offering me safety and, perhaps, something deeper. "Just so we're clear," I said, forcing levity into my tone. "If we survive this, I'm definitely going to need an explanation about your mysterious friend."

"Deal," he said, his lips curving into a small, genuine smile, and for a moment, the weight of the world felt lighter.

Before I could respond, Caden slammed on the brakes, the car skidding to a halt. My stomach lurched as I instinctively grabbed the handle, wide-eyed. "What is it?"

"Stay down," he instructed sharply.

From the corner of my eye, I caught movement—a figure emerging from the shadows, moving with a deliberate grace. My heart plummeted as recognition dawned. It was Victor, his silhouette sharp against the glow of the streetlight. He stood on the sidewalk, arms crossed, a predatory smile on his lips as if he had been expecting us.

"What do we do?" Clara's voice was a tight whisper, the fear threading through her words palpable.

"Stay quiet," Caden said, his voice low and steady. "Let me handle this."

Victor approached with an air of confidence, his eyes glinting like a predator's. "Well, well, look who we have here," he called out, his tone laced with mockery. "Didn't think you'd come out to play, Caden. And look at the company you keep. How charming."

"Back off, Victor," Caden warned, his hands gripping the steering wheel, knuckles white.

"Back off? Where's the fun in that?" Victor's laughter echoed through the night, a sound that sent chills racing down my spine. "I'm just getting started."

Before I could comprehend what was happening, a loud bang reverberated through the air, an unmistakable sound that sent my heart racing. My breath caught in my throat as the reality of the moment crashed over me like a tidal wave.

The window shattered beside me, raining glass like deadly confetti.

"Go! Now!" Caden shouted, his voice fierce as he swung the car into motion. The tires screeched as he accelerated, the vehicle lurching forward into the night.

I turned to look back, dread curling in my stomach as I caught a glimpse of Victor in the rearview mirror, standing there, a sinister smile still plastered on his face. He was a dark cloud looming over our escape, a reminder that danger was only a heartbeat away.

"Where to now?" I asked, panic rising as we sped through the deserted streets.

"Somewhere Victor can't find us," Caden replied, his expression grim, determination etched across his features.

And just as he spoke, the world around us erupted into chaos—headlights flared behind us, illuminating the darkness, a pair of vehicles barreling toward us, engines roaring like wild beasts.

"Caden, we're being chased!" Clara screamed, the realization dawning too late.

I felt my heart sink as the adrenaline coursed through my veins, pushing me to the edge of panic. "What do we do? What do we do?"

Caden's grip tightened on the wheel, his gaze locked ahead, unyielding. "Hold on tight!" he shouted as he swerved, the car narrowly avoiding a collision with the curb.

The pursuit was on, and as the darkness closed in around us, I knew we were on the brink of something monumental—an explosive confrontation that could change everything. As the vehicles drew closer, a sense of inevitability settled in my chest, intertwining with the thrill of the chase. The night had become a battlefield, and I was ready to fight.

Chapter 18: Crossroads

The air was thick with tension, a miasma of unspoken fears swirling around me like fog on a winter morning. I sat at my kitchen table, the remnants of breakfast scattered before me—crumbs from an uneaten croissant and a half-drunk cup of coffee cooling to an uninviting shade of lukewarm. I should have savored every bite, every sip, but the memory of the attack—sharp and searing—loomed larger than the sun filtering through the blinds. Each tick of the clock felt like a drumbeat, echoing the chaos that had erupted in my life the moment I let Caden into my world.

He was a storm, unpredictable and fierce, and I had danced right into the eye of it. The memories were fresh: shadows darting across my living room, voices that were a cacophony of anger and betrayal. In that moment, I had realized I wasn't just a bystander in Caden's tumultuous life; I was part of it now, woven into a tapestry of secrets and lies that threatened to unravel at the slightest pull.

I traced my finger around the rim of my coffee cup, thinking about the crossroads that lay ahead. I could feel my heart thrumming a restless rhythm, torn between my stubborn independence and the magnetic pull of a man who could either ruin me or save me. Caden's charm was intoxicating, but his world was a dangerous cocktail, mixing passion with peril in a way I was only beginning to understand.

The doorbell rang, pulling me from my spiraling thoughts. I hesitated, glancing at my reflection in the window—eyes wide, cheeks flushed. Whoever it was had come at an inconvenient moment, but I didn't have the luxury of choosing who entered my life anymore. I opened the door to find Victor, his presence imposing as he filled the doorway.

"Hey," he said, his voice low, an undercurrent of tension threading through the casual greeting. He stepped inside without waiting for an invitation, his brow furrowed as he surveyed the disarray. "You look like you've seen a ghost."

"Maybe I have," I shot back, crossing my arms defensively. There was an electric charge in the air between us, a mix of familiarity and hostility that made my skin prickle. Victor's eyes held a complexity I couldn't quite decode; they flickered with concern but danced dangerously close to something darker.

He ran a hand through his tousled hair, his gaze finally settling on mine, earnest and intense. "Listen, I know things have gotten complicated, but we need to talk about Caden."

The mention of Caden sent a jolt through me, a reminder of the choice I was grappling with. "What about him?" I said, trying to keep my voice steady, though it trembled on the edge of anxiety.

Victor stepped closer, invading my personal space with an urgency that left little room for pretense. "He's not what you think. He's tangled up in something much bigger than just a personal vendetta. You need to know the truth before it swallows you whole."

"Why do you care?" I challenged, my heart racing with a mixture of defiance and curiosity. "You've been just as much a part of this as he has."

"Because I care about you," he replied, the sincerity in his tone cutting through the tension like a knife. "You're in way over your head. Caden might think he can protect you, but there are forces at play that even he doesn't fully understand."

The vulnerability in his voice struck me, and for a brief moment, I saw the man beneath the bravado—the one who had always been lurking in the background, waiting for the right moment to step into the light. "What do you know?" I pressed, my pulse quickening.

Victor took a deep breath, his eyes locking onto mine with an intensity that made my stomach flutter and my instincts scream to run. "I've been following a lead. Caden's enemies are not just personal; they're connected to something much more dangerous—a syndicate that deals in shadows. If you're with him, you're a target."

"Is that why you're here? To scare me away from him?" My voice came out sharper than intended, but the protectiveness I felt for Caden clashed violently with the reality of what Victor was suggesting. I couldn't afford to lose him, not now when everything was so uncertain.

"I'm trying to keep you safe," Victor insisted, his tone softer now. "You deserve to know what you're getting into. If Caden finds out I told you, it could cost me more than just a friendship."

The weight of his words settled heavily between us, and I felt the walls I'd constructed begin to crack. I had been so focused on Caden, on the passion and intensity we shared, that I hadn't stopped to question the foundations of our relationship. Did I really know him? Or was I just in love with the illusion he had created?

"What do I do?" I whispered, the tremor in my voice betraying my fear.

Victor took a step closer, the warmth of his presence both comforting and unsettling. "You need to decide if you're willing to take that risk. Sometimes the truth is more dangerous than the lie."

His words hung in the air, and I felt my heart plummet into a chasm of uncertainty. It was a choice I couldn't ignore: a leap into the unknown or a retreat to safety, both fraught with their own consequences. I was standing on the precipice, and the choice before me felt like a riptide, threatening to pull me under.

The tension crackled in the air as I processed Victor's warning. His words seemed to hang there, heavy and charged, weaving an intricate tapestry of doubt and urgency. The kitchen felt smaller, the walls inching in as if they too were leaning closer to eavesdrop on this revelation. I could sense Victor's frustration, the way his fists clenched at his sides, his brows knitted in a way that suggested he had faced this turmoil before but wasn't entirely sure how to navigate it this time.

"Look, I know Caden can charm the skin off a snake," he said, voice steady but tinged with an edge of desperation. "But this isn't just a game. You've got to ask yourself what you really want. Is he worth the risk?"

"What risk?" I shot back, bristling at the challenge. "Isn't love inherently risky? What do you want me to do—run away just because his life is complicated? You don't even know him like I do."

Victor's expression hardened, and for a moment, I saw a flicker of hurt flash across his face, quickly masked by resolve. "That's just it. I've seen how things can spiral out of control, and I don't want you to be the collateral damage. You're worth more than being someone's pawn in a dangerous game."

"Collaterally damaged? Is that what I am to you?" I retorted, feeling an uncharacteristic bitterness spill from my lips. I hadn't meant to snap at him, but the rawness of my emotions was spilling over. The idea that anyone—especially Victor—might think of me as fragile was infuriating.

"You're not a pawn, but you're acting like one!" He took a step forward, his eyes darkening. "You're getting pulled into something you can't control. Caden is wrapped up in something deeper than you can see. I don't want to lose you to his world. You need to trust me on this."

"Trust?" I scoffed, folding my arms tightly across my chest, as if shielding myself from the weight of his words. "And what exactly has Caden done to earn my trust? For all I know, you're trying to protect your interests in all this."

The silence that followed was thick, a tangible pause filled with the unsaid. The way he looked at me made my heart ache. It was a look filled with concern, yes, but also regret. "You're not seeing the whole picture," he finally said, voice low and measured. "Caden's enemies are not the only threat. You need to prepare for what's coming."

"Prepare for what?" I shot back, eyes narrowing. The air was electric, and I felt the weight of every word in my chest. "More secrets? More chaos?"

"Yes," he answered, and the single word felt like a hammer hitting an anvil. "This is just the beginning."

I could feel my breath quicken, the urge to retreat surging within me. But instead, I planted my feet, refusing to back down. "Fine, tell me everything. I'm done being kept in the dark. If I'm going to face whatever this is, I need to know what I'm up against."

Victor exhaled, his posture relaxing just slightly as if the release of tension in my stance encouraged him to continue. "Caden's family is tied to a syndicate—money laundering, illegal trades, the works. And it goes deeper than anyone knows. They'll use anything or anyone to protect their interests, including you."

I felt the color drain from my face, the implications washing over me like cold water. "You think Caden is involved in that?"

"I don't think he's a puppet," he said carefully, "but he's tangled up in their web, and the more you stay in his orbit, the more likely it is that you'll get caught in it too."

The gravity of his words anchored me. My heart thudded in my chest, each beat resonating with the weight of what I was beginning to grasp. "And what makes you any different, Victor? Are you just another player on this board?"

His eyes flashed with something—determination, perhaps. "I've fought against them. I've lost people I cared about because of their reach. I know what they're capable of, and I won't let it happen to you."

"By scaring me away from Caden?" I challenged, my voice rising. "You think that will protect me? If I run, I might as well hand myself over to them."

Victor stepped closer, his intensity nearly overwhelming. "You're better than that. You don't need to entangle yourself in someone else's battles to prove your worth. You're strong on your own. It's time you remembered that."

The words rattled in my chest, igniting a fire I hadn't felt in a while. "Maybe I want to be entangled, Victor. Maybe I want to be in the thick of it, not on the sidelines."

He frowned, frustration etching lines across his forehead. "You think you can handle this? You don't know what you're asking for. Caden has a reputation—people will come for you just to get to him. You could lose everything."

"What is everything?" I challenged, my heart racing. "This career you keep talking about? A life devoid of passion? Or is it about safety, the comforting predictability of not having to confront your fears? Because honestly, that sounds so dull I could scream."

He took a breath, clearly grappling with his emotions. "It's not about dullness. It's about survival. I just don't want to see you lose yourself in this whirlwind. I care about you."

"I care about him too," I countered, the words spilling out before I could reel them back. "And it's not just about him. I've never felt this alive, Victor. You might not understand, but I want the full spectrum of life, the chaotic and the beautiful."

Victor's eyes softened, though a flicker of something darker remained. "And that's precisely what they prey on. Your spirit, your kindness. Don't you see? They'll use it against you."

I held his gaze, the heat of the moment wrapping around us like a cocoon. In that silence, an understanding began to form, fragile but potent. "Then I'll learn to fight back," I declared, my voice steady and unyielding. "If they think they can take me down without a fight, they're sorely mistaken."

The tension between us shifted, a new energy crackling to life. I felt empowered, filled with the fierce need to take control of my destiny, even if it meant navigating the treacherous waters ahead. In that moment, standing on the precipice of uncertainty, I knew I was ready to embrace whatever came next.

Victor's eyes held a glimmer of defiance as I locked onto his gaze, the weight of our unspoken truths swirling like a tempest around us. "You think being brave is just about jumping into the chaos? It's also knowing when to step back," he challenged, his voice barely concealing the frustration of a man caught between his protective instincts and the undeniable draw of something more.

"Stepping back means letting fear dictate my life," I shot back, my pulse quickening with each word. "You're acting like I'm some damsel waiting for a hero. I'm not afraid of the storm; I want to ride it."

Victor hesitated, uncertainty flashing across his features. "What if the storm consumes you?" he asked, a raw edge in his tone. "You don't know what you're playing with, and Caden? He's not who you think he is."

The sincerity in his voice tugged at something deep within me, a flicker of doubt that I had been ignoring. But my resolve remained unshaken. "Then I'll figure him out. I'd rather face the uncertainty than sit back and let it dictate my fate."

With a frustrated sigh, Victor ran a hand through his hair, the gesture betraying his growing exasperation. "You're as stubborn as they come," he muttered, half to himself.

"I prefer to call it determined," I quipped, a teasing smile breaking through the tension. The corner of his mouth twitched, as if my lightheartedness might just cut through the gravity of the moment. But as quickly as the smile appeared, it vanished, replaced by the seriousness of our conversation.

"I get it," he said, leaning in, intensity in every word. "You want to find your place in this, but Caden's world is not just filled with romance and adventure. It's dangerous, and there's a price for playing with fire."

I took a deep breath, steadying myself against the weight of his concern. "Maybe I'm already burned, Victor. But I want to know if it's worth the pain."

"You're playing with forces you don't understand." He stepped back, his tone shifting, bordering on pleading. "I've seen the aftermath of those who underestimate their opponents. You're too valuable to be collateral damage."

"Valuable?" I scoffed lightly, attempting to pierce the heaviness with humor. "I don't have a price tag, Victor. I'm not some object to be bartered."

"No, but you're a person," he replied, his voice firm yet softening. "And I refuse to let you become another casualty in this mess. Caden might be charming, but charm doesn't keep you safe when the bullets start flying."

The mention of bullets sent a chill racing down my spine. "So what do you propose? I just walk away and pretend none of this matters?"

Victor's gaze held mine, the weight of his words heavy between us. "I'm asking you to consider the consequences of your choices. If Caden is wrapped up in this, and if you stay, you'll get pulled into the crossfire."

"I can't unsee what I've seen. I can't pretend I don't feel this connection. It's not just a crush," I insisted, my heart pounding as the realization dawned on me. "And I'm not going to shy away from it because it's scary."

"Then you better learn how to fight," he said, a fierce glint in his eyes. "Because if you think this is just about romance, you're mistaken. It's a battleground."

With those words hanging in the air, the tension shifted. Suddenly, my phone buzzed on the table, shattering the moment like glass hitting the floor. I glanced at the screen, my heart dropping when I saw Caden's name flash before me. My finger hovered over the screen, the familiar warmth of his presence beckoning to me, but the cautionary voice in my head rang louder.

Victor's eyes narrowed as he caught the glimpse of my hesitation. "You can't answer that call. Not now," he warned, urgency clawing at his voice.

"What if he needs me?" I shot back, my heart caught in a frantic tug-of-war. "He might be in trouble."

"That's exactly what I'm talking about. You need to be smart about this. You can't just dive in blindly."

Ignoring his protest, I pressed the answer button, the voice I had come to crave filtering through the speaker like a siren's song. "Caden?" I breathed, trying to keep my voice steady.

"Where are you?" His tone was taut, laced with a tension that made my stomach drop. "I need to see you, now."

"Caden, I—" I began, but Victor stepped in, his eyes pleading with me to reconsider. "Don't, please," he urged silently, but I was already caught in Caden's pull.

"Meet me at the usual spot," Caden said, cutting off my hesitation. "I can't explain everything right now, but you need to trust me. It's urgent."

"Is it safe?" I asked, every instinct screaming for caution, but the urgency in his voice outweighed my doubts.

"Just meet me, please," he pressed, the vulnerability in his tone breaking through my defenses. "I'll explain everything when you get here. Just hurry."

As the call ended, the room felt charged with unspoken tension. I glanced at Victor, whose expression was a mix of concern and frustration. "You can't seriously be considering this," he said, disbelief coloring his voice.

"I have to go," I stated firmly, every part of me itching to rush into the storm that was Caden. "I can't leave him hanging."

"By running into a potential trap?" Victor stepped closer, his expression fierce. "I won't let you walk into danger."

"Then what do you propose I do? Just sit here?" The challenge sparked between us, a moment of heated intensity that felt almost tangible.

"Stay with me," he offered, his voice suddenly low and filled with urgency. "We can figure this out together. I can help you."

The pull of his words resonated within me, but I knew the choice was made. "I appreciate it, Victor, I do. But I can't ignore this. I have to see what he wants."

Before Victor could respond, I turned and rushed out the door, the weight of uncertainty pushing me forward. The chill of the evening air wrapped around me, invigorating yet terrifying. Each step towards the meeting place felt like an echo of my heartbeat, reminding me that I was teetering on the edge of something monumental.

As I approached the familiar spot, a secluded park illuminated by dim streetlights, the unease twisted tighter in my gut. I glanced around, searching for Caden, but the place was eerily silent. The shadows danced on the ground, creating ghostly shapes that shifted in the fading light.

And then I heard it—a sound that sent my heart racing: a sharp crack, followed by the unmistakable roar of an engine. Before I could react, headlights pierced the darkness, blinding me momentarily. The car sped toward me, a dark figure emerging from the chaos.

Caden.

But just as I registered his presence, another vehicle careened into the clearing, the engine revving as if hell-bent on destruction. My breath caught in my throat as the headlights swept across the park, illuminating the scene with a stark, harsh light.

I was standing at a crossroads, and the choice I had made was about to come crashing down around me.

Chapter 19: The Ultimate Sacrifice

The air was thick with tension, the kind that seeps into your bones and clings to your skin like a second layer. I stood at the precipice of my decision, heart racing as I faced Victor, his eyes glinting with a mix of satisfaction and malice. The dim light of the abandoned warehouse cast shadows that danced ominously around us, and every sound—every rustle, every creak—felt amplified, each whisper of the wind like a harbinger of the choice I had to make.

"Choose wisely, Anna," he said, a grin creeping across his lips as if the mere thought of my turmoil brought him joy. "Caden's fate hangs in the balance, and so does yours."

I shifted my gaze to the ground, focusing on the dust motes swirling in the narrow beams of light. The image of Caden flashed in my mind, his dark hair tousled, his smile that lit up even the darkest corners of my life. The laughter we shared, the late-night conversations that turned into dawn—it all felt like a distant dream now, tainted by the reality of our circumstances.

"I know you think you're strong, but everyone has a breaking point," Victor continued, his voice low, almost conspiratorial. "You can save yourself. Just turn your back on him. It's that simple."

Simple. The word hung in the air, mocking me. If only it were that easy. The thought of betraying Caden sent a shiver down my spine, an icy tendril wrapping around my heart. But the stakes were high, and the clock was ticking. With every second that passed, I felt the walls closing in, the enormity of the decision pressing down on me like a weight I couldn't bear.

"Caden believes he can fix this," I replied, my voice steadier than I felt. "He always has a plan. I trust him." I could see the disbelief in Victor's eyes, his amusement barely contained.

"Trust? That's rich, coming from someone caught in this web. Do you honestly think he would do the same for you?" He stepped closer, his presence overwhelming. "You're merely a pawn to him. And to me."

"No," I retorted, my voice rising, a hint of defiance igniting within me. "I am not a pawn. I am a player in this game, and I refuse to be manipulated by you."

Victor chuckled, the sound dark and twisted, reverberating off the concrete walls. "Players get eliminated, Anna. Choose your side carefully. Or better yet, choose yourself."

The notion of betrayal gnawed at my insides. Would saving myself mean losing a part of my soul? The love I felt for Caden was fierce and consuming, a wildfire that refused to be extinguished, but was it enough to withstand the trials we faced? Doubt crept in like a thief in the night, whispering insidious thoughts that made my heart race in fear. What if Caden couldn't fix this? What if trusting him meant sacrificing my own future?

"Why do you care so much?" I shot back, frustration bubbling within me. "What do you gain from this? You're just a ghost haunting my life, trying to stir up chaos."

Victor's eyes narrowed, a flash of annoyance cutting through his playful demeanor. "This isn't about me. It's about you and him, and the choices you make. You think love conquers all? Love is a distraction, and it makes you weak."

I clenched my fists, my nails digging into my palms as I wrestled with the tempest inside me. "Love doesn't make me weak. It makes me human."

With every heartbeat, my mind raced through the possibilities. What would Caden do if the roles were reversed? He would fight. He would sacrifice everything for me, without a second thought. The thought of his unwavering loyalty grounded me, reminding me of the man I fell in love with, the man who wouldn't back down in the face of danger.

But Victor was right about one thing: trust was a fragile thing, easily shattered. The lies that had spun around us, the secrets that felt like lead weights dragging us down, threatened to drown me in despair. My heart ached at the thought of betrayal, but the desperation to survive clawed at my throat like a chokehold.

"You're running out of time," Victor said, a smirk forming on his lips as he glanced at the digital clock flashing on the wall. "Make your choice, or I will make it for you."

The finality of his words sent a cold shiver through me. I glanced toward the exit, my mind racing with images of Caden—his strong arms wrapping around me, his warm breath against my skin, the promises he made that felt as eternal as the stars. Did I really want to walk away from that?

"Anna." Caden's voice cut through my thoughts like a knife, sharp and desperate. I turned, my breath hitching as I saw him standing in the doorway, his face set with determination, eyes blazing with a fierce intensity. "I knew you'd be here. I was afraid I'd lose you."

In that moment, the world faded around me, leaving just the two of us. Caden stepped forward, the warmth of his presence washing over me, banishing the cold shadows that Victor had cast. "I can fix this, I promise," he said, his voice steady but filled with urgency. "But I need you to trust me."

Victor's laughter echoed in the background, a reminder of the choice that loomed over us. My heart raced as I looked between the two men—one representing safety, the other a world of uncertainty. Would love triumph over the chaos that threatened to consume us?

I took a deep breath, the weight of the moment pressing down on me. Caden's eyes held mine, steady and true, and I could see the depth of his conviction shining through the turmoil. In that instant, the decision crystallized within me, the path forward becoming clearer, illuminated by the light of our shared moments and the unwavering belief in one another.

"Whatever happens, we'll face it together," I said, my voice steady now, emboldened by the conviction that had been rekindled within me. I felt the strength of our bond solidify around us, a shield against the darkness that threatened to engulf us both.

Victor's expression twisted, and for the first time, doubt flickered in his eyes. "You think this is over?"

"No, I think it's just the beginning," I replied, feeling the warmth of Caden's hand slip into mine, grounding me as we faced our adversary together. The weight of our love hung in the air, potent and undeniable, and with that, I made my choice.

The moment hung in the air, dense with unspoken fears and hopes. I could feel the crackle of electricity between Caden and me, a tether binding our hearts even as Victor loomed ominously behind us. The tension was palpable, thick enough to slice through, and I took a breath, steadying myself as the weight of my choice pressed down like a leaden cloak.

"Anna," Caden urged, stepping closer. His hand was warm in mine, anchoring me to the moment, to him. "You know I'd never let anything happen to you."

The sincerity in his voice washed over me like a balm, but doubts lingered, taunting me. Would I be a fool for trusting him again? The past few weeks had been riddled with lies and betrayals, each revelation a stab to my heart, and I couldn't shake the feeling that I was walking on the edge of a precipice.

"Enough with the theatrics," Victor interrupted, annoyance threading his tone. "Your little reunion is charming, but this isn't a fairytale. The clock is ticking."

"Then let it tick," I shot back, my voice firmer than I felt. "I'm done playing your games, Victor. You're right about one thing—love isn't a weakness. It's a choice."

Caden's grip tightened on my hand, a silent agreement, a vow to weather the storm together. "We're not afraid of you," he said, his voice steady, his gaze unyielding.

Victor's smile faltered for just a moment, a flicker of doubt crossing his features. "Bold words. But I assure you, love will not save you when reality comes crashing down."

"I've dealt with reality long enough to know that it's filled with choices," I replied, drawing strength from Caden's presence. "This is ours, and we choose to fight. Together."

The words felt like a rallying cry, echoing in the stillness of the warehouse, and I watched as Victor's bravado faltered. He was a puppet master, and I could see the strings beginning to fray. "You really think you can win? You're both in way over your heads."

"Maybe," I replied, heart racing as I prepared for the unexpected. "But at least we're in this together. You'll never understand what that means."

With a sudden movement, Victor lunged toward Caden, his intentions clear. Time slowed, a sickening sense of foreboding washing over me as I instinctively stepped in front of Caden, adrenaline surging through my veins. "No!" I screamed, my voice echoing off the concrete walls as I raised my arms, ready to shield him.

The world exploded into chaos, Victor's face twisting in rage as he swung at me. Caden's reaction was instinctual; he grabbed my waist and pulled me back, his strength radiating through me like a protective shield. "Stay behind me!" he shouted, his eyes fierce, igniting the spark of defiance in my chest.

The confrontation spiraled, Victor's anger spilling over like a boiling pot. The air crackled with tension, each second stretching into an eternity as we navigated the volatile landscape of our emotions. "You think you can protect her?" Victor spat, his eyes darting between us, searching for weakness. "You're a fool, Caden. You're nothing without me."

"Watch me," Caden shot back, his voice low and dangerous. In that moment, I saw the man I loved—the one who faced every challenge with unwavering resolve.

Victor lunged again, but this time, Caden was ready. He sidestepped, using Victor's momentum against him, and I could feel my heart racing as the two men clashed. The sound of fists meeting flesh echoed through the warehouse, and I took a step back, my breath catching in my throat as I struggled to comprehend the chaos unfolding before me.

"Caden!" I cried, desperation creeping into my voice. The thought of losing him sent a surge of panic through me, but he met my gaze with fierce determination, and I knew he wouldn't back down.

"Get to the exit!" he yelled, grappling with Victor, their bodies colliding with a force that rattled the very foundations of the building. I hesitated, torn between fear for Caden's safety and the instinct to run.

But running was not in my nature. I had fought too hard, endured too much to abandon him now. I squared my shoulders, channeling every ounce of courage within me. "I'm not leaving you!"

Victor's attention snapped to me, and I could see the flicker of surprise in his eyes. "You really think you're saving him?" he sneered. "You're only making it worse."

"No, I'm making it real," I retorted, taking a step forward. "You've lived in the shadows for too long. It's time to step into the light."

With a roar, Victor broke free from Caden's grip and charged toward me. I braced myself, ready to face whatever he threw my way, but just as he reached out, Caden tackled him from the side, their bodies crashing to the ground in a tangle of limbs.

"Anna!" Caden shouted, his voice fierce amidst the chaos. "Get out of here!"

"No!" I yelled back, my heart racing. "We do this together!"

In a split second, I noticed the glint of something metallic in Victor's hand—a knife, sharp and glistening. Panic surged through me, and I lunged forward, adrenaline propelling me as I grabbed a nearby metal pipe, my instincts kicking in. "Let him go, Victor!"

The world narrowed down to a single focus, the sound of blood pounding in my ears as I swung the pipe with all my might, connecting with Victor's arm. The knife clattered to the ground, and Victor howled in pain, momentarily stunned.

"Caden, now!" I shouted, my heart racing as I backed him up, the weight of the moment electrifying the air around us. Together, we pressed forward, our hearts synchronized in a rhythm of survival.

Victor's fury turned into desperation as he scrambled to regain control, but the fire in our resolve burned hotter. "You think you've won?" he spat, rage simmering beneath the surface. "This isn't over!"

Caden and I exchanged a glance, unspoken understanding passing between us. "No, it's just beginning," Caden said, determination etched into his features.

With one final push, we charged at Victor, our combined strength overwhelming him as we forced him back, ready to reclaim our future, ready to break free from the chains he had forged. The world was no longer a battleground for one; it was ours to fight for, side by side, and I felt the rush of hope flooding through me.

In the midst of the chaos, amidst the sweat and the struggle, I realized that love was not merely a shield. It was a weapon, a fierce declaration of who we were and what we stood for. And as we faced Victor together, I knew we were ready to embrace whatever came next, united in purpose, bound by love, and fueled by an unwavering determination to emerge victorious.

The cacophony of chaos enveloped us, a whirlwind of shouts and desperate struggles. Caden and I stood shoulder to shoulder, our hearts pounding in synchrony, fueled by a shared determination that burned brighter than the fear swirling around us. Victor was still on the ground, dazed but not defeated, his eyes narrowing with a mix of fury and desperation.

"You think this is going to end well for you?" he spat, the venom in his words echoing in the stillness that momentarily followed the fight. "You're playing a dangerous game, Anna. One you're not equipped to win."

"Funny," I replied, my voice steady, even as my heart raced. "You were the one who tried to take everything from me. I'm just here to reclaim it."

Caden shifted slightly, his body blocking mine from Victor's glare. "You're not going to intimidate us anymore," he asserted, his tone unwavering. "This ends tonight."

"Brave words from a man who's clinging to the past," Victor shot back, his composure returning, a predator licking his wounds. "You think you know love, but you have no idea what's at stake."

"You're right," I said, daring to step forward, my courage bolstered by Caden's presence. "I don't know what it means to betray someone I love. But you do."

Victor's laughter rang hollow, and it sent a chill down my spine. "You're all so naive. Love? It's a weakness, Anna. It clouds your judgment. It makes you blind."

"Then call me blind," I challenged, anger surging through me, mixing with the adrenaline. "Because I'm done letting you control me or my choices."

With that declaration, I felt the ground shift beneath me, a new resolve rising from the ashes of doubt. The air thickened, crackling with the tension of what was to come.

Victor surged to his feet, a dark cloud of rage gathering around him. "You don't understand the consequences of defying me!" He lunged, but I was ready.

"Caden!" I yelled, and in a heartbeat, we were a unit—twisting, dodging, and parrying like we'd practiced this in our minds a hundred times before. I swung the metal pipe again, catching Victor off guard. It collided with his shoulder, and he staggered, fury erupting in a strangled shout.

"Is that the best you've got?" he taunted through clenched teeth, his face twisted with pain. "You really think that little scrap of metal can stop me?"

"It's not just about the pipe," I said, voice steady as steel. "It's about the fire that fuels it. Together, we're stronger than you'll ever know."

For a split second, I could see the flicker of doubt in Victor's eyes. He had always underestimated us, always considered love a fleeting whim, a mere distraction. But now, faced with our defiance, it was as if the ground beneath his feet was shifting.

Caden surged forward, a whirlwind of movement. "We're not afraid of you!" he declared, pushing me behind him just as Victor charged again. The impact resonated, and for a moment, I held my breath, hoping Caden's strength would withstand the onslaught.

But Victor was cunning, his desperation morphing into calculated aggression. As he and Caden collided, I took a step back, trying to assess the scene unfolding before me. Caden was holding his own, but the intensity of the fight left me feeling helpless.

"Anna!" Caden shouted, his voice a mixture of command and concern. "Stay focused! Don't let him get into your head!"

"I won't!" I replied, my eyes darting around for something—anything—that could turn the tide in our favor. A glance at the remnants of crates scattered around the room sparked an idea. I was a strategist by nature; I could use this to our advantage.

While Victor had Caden temporarily distracted, I moved swiftly, picking up a handful of gravel from a nearby crate. "Hey, Victor!" I called, forcing confidence into my voice. "Bet you can't catch what you can't see!"

I hurled the gravel into the air, a cloud of debris obscuring his vision. For a heartbeat, it worked; he recoiled, blinking against the sudden assault, and Caden took advantage of the moment to shift his stance, using Victor's momentum against him once more.

"Now!" Caden roared, seizing the opportunity as Victor staggered back, blinded and enraged. I rushed forward, joining him, ready to put our plan into action.

Victor's fury morphed into panic as we advanced, two forces of nature determined to take back our lives. "You'll pay for this, both of you!" he bellowed, but there was a crack in his bravado now.

We fought like warriors, dodging and weaving, the metal pipe becoming an extension of my will as I swung it with all my might. Caden was relentless, a tempest of energy, his every movement fueled by the stakes of our struggle.

With a final, desperate push, I swung low, catching Victor off balance. He fell to one knee, gasping for breath, and I saw the moment when doubt crossed his face.

"Is this really how it ends for you?" I taunted, my breath hitching as the reality of the fight settled in. "You've lost control, Victor."

But in that split second of triumph, Victor's expression twisted into a mask of rage. "You think you've won?" He reached into his pocket, pulling out a small device that shimmered in the low light. My heart dropped as he pressed a button, and the air around us crackled ominously.

"What is that?" Caden shouted, eyes widening with alarm.

Victor's grin was manic, full of malevolence. "A little surprise. A farewell gift."

My stomach churned as the room filled with a low rumble, the ground shaking beneath us. "Caden!" I screamed, fear clawing at my throat.

In a matter of seconds, the world morphed into chaos once more. The walls began to tremble, debris raining down as Victor laughed, the sound echoing in my ears. "Enjoy your final moments together!" Caden pulled me close, his face a mask of determination. "We have to get out of here! Now!"

The urgency of his voice snapped me into action, but as we turned to flee, a deafening explosion rocked the warehouse, sending us both tumbling to the ground.

Darkness enveloped me, and I struggled to regain my senses, the world spinning as I pushed through the haze. But as I opened my eyes, a chilling realization washed over me: Caden was gone.

"Caden!" I screamed, panic flooding my veins. The air was thick with smoke, the remnants of our battle obscuring my vision. I crawled through the wreckage, searching for any sign of him, my heart pounding in my chest like a war drum.

The sound of crumbling concrete and distant sirens filled my ears, and the reality of what Victor had unleashed weighed heavy on me. I was alone, and the only light I had ever known was slipping through my fingers like sand.

"Caden!" I called again, my voice echoing into the dark abyss. But there was no answer, only the distant rumble of destruction and the suffocating silence that followed.

And just when I thought I couldn't bear it any longer, a shadow shifted in the smoke, and I felt a flicker of hope ignite within me.

"Anna..." a voice rasped, and I turned, desperately straining to see through the haze.

But the silhouette faded just as quickly as it appeared, leaving me grappling with uncertainty, the echoes of the past colliding with a terrifying present. I took a step forward, the ground shifting beneath my feet, and in that moment, I realized the battle was far from over.

Chapter 20: A Heart Divided

The steps beneath me are cool, the air thick with the scent of spring mingling with exhaust fumes and the faint trace of roasted chestnuts from a nearby vendor. As I watch the parade of people move past—each face a canvas of stories, hopes, and heartaches—I feel like a mere spectator in a play where the script has gone awry. My heart thrums with uncertainty, each beat a reminder of Victor's chilling ultimatum: choose, or lose everything. The weight of his gaze lingers like a shadow, reminding me of the dangerous game we've been playing.

When Caden finally arrives, his presence is like a breath of fresh air against the suffocating haze of my thoughts. He's disheveled, his dark hair falling into his eyes, giving him that rogue look I once found charming. As he approaches, the familiar warmth floods back, but it's tangled with the fear that he may be just another mirage in this desert of confusion. "You're late," I say, attempting a playful tone, but it falls flat. His smile doesn't quite reach his eyes.

"Had to dodge a couple of my 'friends,'" he says, running a hand through his hair, a nervous habit that doesn't escape me. "You know how it is." The casual tone contrasts sharply with the underlying tension that fills the air between us. I can't help but wonder just how deep he's in this time.

We settle on a worn bench, the kind that has witnessed countless whispered promises and silent farewells, and I focus on the pastel petals drifting down around us. They swirl in the breeze, fragile yet persistent, much like the emotions swirling in my heart. "I've been thinking," he begins, his voice low, "about us. About everything."

"Everything?" I echo, my brow furrowing. "Caden, it feels like there's been no 'us' for a long time." I want to sound strong, assertive, but my voice wavers slightly. The ache of what we once had is still there, an echo I can't shake.

"Let me prove it to you," he insists, his gaze piercing into mine with an intensity that ignites a flicker of hope buried beneath layers of doubt. "I'm getting out. I mean it this time." His words rush out like a lifeline, each syllable tugging at the fragments of my heart still yearning for the connection we once shared. "I've been talking to someone about a fresh start. A real one."

"Talking? Or doing?" I can't help the edge in my tone. Doubt has become my constant companion, and I'm not sure I can take another betrayal. Caden's expression falters for a moment, and I can see the familiar flash of frustration dance across his features, but it quickly gives way to something softer.

"Doing. I've got a plan," he says, his voice steady now, yet it trembles with the weight of his confession. "I'll have to make some moves, but it's possible. Just... trust me." Those two words—so simple, yet they claw at the jagged edges of my heart. Trust, after everything, feels like a luxury I can't afford.

"I don't know if I can," I whisper, the admission hanging between us like a fragile thread. "After everything you've done—everything I've been through with you..." I let the words trail off, feeling the sting of tears at the corners of my eyes. "You want me to leave everything behind, but what if it's just another lie? What if I'm running from one cage into another?"

"I'd never cage you, Eden," he insists, leaning closer, the warmth of his body igniting something dormant within me. "I want you to fly. To live without looking over your shoulder." His voice drops, laced with desperation. "To be free with me."

For a moment, the world fades—the chirping of birds, the laughter of children, the chaotic pulse of New York City. It's just us, caught in a moment suspended in time. I can see the sincerity in his eyes, but that nagging voice in my head whispers doubts louder than ever.

"What about Victor?" I ask, the name slipping from my lips like an unwanted truth. The thought of him sends a shiver down my spine, the reminder of his cold calculations and the way he had promised me security—a safety that felt more like a trap.

"Forget him. He's nothing compared to what we could have. I know he thinks he can control you, but he doesn't understand what we share. You belong with me." The intensity in Caden's voice is electrifying, and a part of me wants to believe him.

"Belong?" I scoff, the bitterness rising. "Isn't that what Victor is offering too? A sense of belonging?" The weight of my indecision hangs heavy, and I'm acutely aware of the way the cherry blossoms swirl around us like the conflicting emotions in my heart—fragile, beautiful, but ultimately transient.

"I can give you something real, Eden. I can change," Caden presses, leaning forward, his voice dropping to a conspiratorial whisper that sends a shiver down my spine. "I've already started. Just give me a chance to prove it. I need you."

The sincerity in his plea pulls at the strings of my heart, a melody I once danced to with abandon. But as I look into his eyes, searching for the truth beneath the surface, I'm reminded of all the broken promises, the shattered dreams. The path ahead is shrouded in uncertainty, and every fiber of my being screams for clarity.

I hold Caden's gaze, each heartbeat a quiet rebellion against the flutter of hope rising in my chest. The cherry blossoms drift around us, their soft pinks and whites a stark contrast to the tumult brewing within. "Caden," I start, my voice shaky yet resolute, "You can't just say you're out. It's not that easy. People don't just let you walk away from that life."

He opens his mouth to respond, but a sudden gust of wind scatters the petals around us, swirling them in a chaotic dance that mirrors the confusion in my mind. I can see the frustration boiling just beneath his surface, but there's something else too—a vulnerability that breaks through the bravado. "I know it's not easy. But you don't know what I've been through to make this happen. I have to try."

His words hang in the air like the scent of fresh rain on pavement, tantalizing yet elusive. I want to believe him. I want to close my eyes, lean into his words, and let myself be swept away into whatever future he's painting. But then there's the image of Victor, his presence looming in my mind, with his smooth charm and unsettling control. "And what about Victor?" I ask, the bitterness curling my lip. "What will he do when he finds out you're gone? He doesn't take kindly to people leaving his side."

Caden leans closer, the distance between us shrinking as he lowers his voice. "Victor's not as powerful as he thinks he is. He's got a tight grip on this city, sure, but I've been working on a plan to get back at him. If I can take away his assets—his connections—he'll be left scrambling."

"Assets?" I scoff, though my heart quickens. "You make it sound so simple. It's not just business; it's lives, Caden. My life."

"I'm not just thinking about business," he replies, his eyes dark and intense. "I'm thinking about you. This isn't just about freedom for me—it's about freeing you too. Don't you see? We can be together, far from all of this."

For a moment, the promise of a life beyond the chaos seems almost tangible. I picture us escaping to a quiet town, somewhere the noise of the city can't reach us—a cozy house with a garden, where we could drink coffee on the porch and feel the sun on our faces without the weight of the past dragging us down. But the fantasy slips away like the petals in the breeze, replaced by the sharp reality of my choices.

I take a deep breath, trying to steady my racing heart. "But how? How do we get away without him finding out? He's always watching."

Caden smiles, but it's a smile tinged with desperation. "I have a friend who can help. Someone who knows how to disappear. I just need to get my hands on some information, and then we can cut ties once and for all."

"You're asking me to trust you again. After everything." My voice softens, and I can feel the wall I've built around my heart starting to crumble. "What if it doesn't work? What if you're just leading me on?"

He shifts closer, resting his hand on my knee, his touch warm and grounding. "I know I messed up. But I'm not asking for blind faith. I'm asking for a chance. Just one chance to prove I can change."

As I look into his eyes, I see a flicker of the boy I fell in love with—a boy with dreams and ambitions. But the man before me is wrapped in shadows, a product of the world he's been in for too long. "And if you can't change? If this all falls apart?"

"I won't let that happen," he says, a fierce determination igniting his words. "I swear, I'll do whatever it takes to keep you safe."

Before I can respond, the atmosphere shifts like the sudden onset of a storm. A figure appears on the periphery of my vision, and my heart drops as I recognize the familiar silhouette. It's Victor, his presence commanding and oppressive as he strides toward us, a smile playing on his lips, though I know better than to trust it.

"Eden," he calls out, his voice smooth and deep, dripping with feigned charm. "What a lovely surprise to find you here." The words sound innocent enough, but there's an edge to them that sends a chill down my spine.

Caden's hand tightens on my knee, and I feel the tension radiating off him like heat from an open flame. "We were just—" he starts, but Victor's raised hand cuts him off.

"Just enjoying the beauty of spring, I see," Victor says, his gaze shifting between us, a predator sizing up his prey. "Caden, I didn't expect to see you here. Shouldn't you be working on our deal?"

Caden's face hardens, and I can almost see the wheels turning in his mind as he weighs his response. "I'm taking a break. Eden deserves that much."

Victor chuckles, a low, menacing sound that sends shivers through me. "Ah, Eden. Always the center of attention, aren't you? It's sweet that you're looking out for her, Caden, but we both know where your loyalties lie."

The atmosphere is thick with unspoken tension, the air crackling like the moments before a thunderstorm. I can feel the uncertainty seeping back in, suffocating the hope that had begun to take root. "Victor, I—" I begin, but he interrupts me, his gaze sharp as he focuses solely on Caden.

"Why don't you let me handle this, hmm? You know how things can get tangled when emotions come into play."

Caden stiffens, and the raw anger radiating from him is palpable. "I'm not letting you dictate my life, Victor. Not anymore."

"Oh, but you see, that's where you're mistaken," Victor replies, his tone deceptively casual. "You've made your choices, and I've made mine. If you think you can simply walk away from me, you're sorely mistaken."

The tension hangs heavy in the air, and I'm acutely aware of the choices I've made leading me here, to this moment where everything is hanging by a thread. My heart races as I watch the two men I've cared for face off, each representing a part of me I'm struggling to understand.

Victor's eyes narrow, and for a moment, the air between us thickens with tension, a taut line drawn between his calculated confidence and Caden's smoldering defiance. The city around us continues its chaotic symphony, oblivious to the silent war brewing just a few feet away. "You've made some very dangerous choices, Caden," Victor says, his voice low and laced with an unsettling calm that makes my skin crawl. "You know how this game is played. You can't just walk away without consequences."

Caden's jaw tightens, his defiance morphing into something more dangerous. "You don't scare me, Victor. Not anymore. You think you can just threaten me and walk away with Eden? You're mistaken."

I can feel the heat rising in the pit of my stomach as I watch the two men circle each other like predators. The stakes are higher than I ever imagined, and I'm the prize caught in their tug-of-war. "This isn't about you, Caden," I interject, desperate to reestablish some semblance of control. "This is about my life. My choices. Can't we just talk without all this hostility?"

"Ah, but Eden," Victor interrupts, his smile slick and disarming, "this is exactly how you need to look at it. Your life, your choices. You've tangled yourself with the wrong people. Caden is a reckless fool who will lead you straight to chaos."

"I'd rather take my chances with a fool than a man who wears a mask of civility while wielding a knife," I snap, feeling a surge of defiance. The words spill out before I can stop them, and the moment they do, I realize the audacity of my own stance.

Victor's expression shifts slightly, the veneer of calm cracking just enough for me to see the edge of anger beneath. "You're too caught up in the fairytale, Eden. Open your eyes. This is a game, and you're playing against someone who knows all the moves."

Caden steps forward, the protective instinct igniting in him like a flame. "You think I don't know how Victor operates?" he shoots back, his voice rising. "I've been watching him long enough to see through his charade."

My heart races as the confrontation escalates, the vibrant cherry blossoms swaying obliviously in the breeze. "This isn't helping!" I shout, but my voice feels swallowed by the weight of their animosity. "You're both playing with fire, and I'm going to get burned!"

Victor chuckles, but it's hollow, devoid of warmth. "You think you're the first person to try and escape this world? There's no exit, Eden. You're too deep. Caden can't save you from me."

A pulse of fury surges through me, and I turn to Caden, searching for the man I fell in love with—the man who promised me freedom. "Caden, please," I plead, but the unyielding grip of reality sinks in. "Can we just walk away? We don't have to do this."

"Walk away?" Victor's eyes gleam with amusement, as though he's just heard the most absurd joke. "You think you can just walk away from me? I built this empire, and I don't let people just leave. You're not just another pawn in my game, Eden. You're too valuable."

"What do you mean?" I ask, my voice barely above a whisper. The pit of my stomach drops as the realization washes over me. Victor is not just a man who threatens. He's a man who keeps score—a man who sees me as a bargaining chip.

He steps closer, invading my personal space, his presence overwhelming. "I've made investments in you, my dear. Time, resources. You're not just a pretty face. You're a part of my plans, whether you like it or not."

I feel the walls closing in, the weight of his words suffocating. "What are you talking about?"

"Let's just say, the stakes are higher than you think," he replies, his gaze piercing through me, a predator toying with its prey. "Caden might think he can protect you, but he has no idea of the game we're playing. And if he tries to take you from me, he'll regret it."

Caden steps forward, every muscle in his body tense as he confronts Victor. "You won't touch her. I'll make sure of that."

But the moment hangs heavy, thick with unspoken threats and raw emotions. I can feel the weight of my choices pressing down, the invisible strings tying me to both men drawing taut. "This isn't a game to me," I say, my voice trembling but resolute. "You're both playing with my life like I'm just a pawn."

"Life is a game, Eden," Victor replies, his smile unsettling. "You just need to learn how to play it well."

"Is that how you justify everything you do? You manipulate people, treat them like objects?" I challenge, my heart pounding in my chest, fear and anger intertwining.

"Not everyone is meant to be saved," he says simply, as if it's an accepted truth. "Some people are just collateral damage."

"Is that how you see me?" I whisper, feeling my throat tighten. "Just collateral damage?"

His eyes soften for a fraction of a second, a flicker of something—regret? Longing?—before he masks it with that same smug confidence. "You're too valuable to lose, Eden. I wouldn't dream of it."

Caden grips my arm, and I can feel the heat radiating from him, a fierce protective energy. "You don't get to dictate her life, Victor. You don't own her."

"Oh, but I do," Victor replies, his voice low and dangerous. "And when I want something, I take it. You'll learn that soon enough, Caden."

A chill runs down my spine, and the panic surges like a tidal wave, threatening to drown me. "You can't do this," I whisper, my voice shaking. "You can't control everything."

Victor's smile widens, a wolfish grin that sends a shiver through me. "I don't have to control everything. Just the people who matter."

At that moment, the world seems to tilt, the vibrant colors of Central Park fading to a muted gray as the weight of his words settles in. I'm trapped, caught in a web spun from their ambitions and my own misguided trust.

Just as the tension reaches its peak, a loud crash echoes through the park, drawing everyone's attention. A nearby vendor's cart topples over, spilling bright red apples across the pavement. The momentary chaos shatters the standoff, and Victor's eyes flash with annoyance. "This is not over," he hisses before stepping back, the smile wiped clean from his face.

"Eden," Caden breathes, his grip tightening as he pulls me closer. "We need to go. Now."

The urgency in his voice propels me into action, and I nod, but as we turn to leave, a dark figure emerges from the crowd, their face obscured. My breath catches in my throat, a new layer of dread unfurling within me. The stranger's presence feels ominous, their gaze locked on us with an intensity that sends a shiver down my spine.

"Not so fast," the figure calls, a voice deep and gravelly that pierces through the fading laughter and chaos. "I think we need to have a little chat, don't you?"

Caden's body stiffens beside me, and I feel my heart race as the implications of those words sink in. This moment is more than a simple confrontation; it's the beginning of a reckoning, one that will force me to confront the very essence of who I am and what I'm willing to sacrifice.

And in that moment, as the stranger steps closer, I realize I'm standing on the edge of a precipice, and I have no idea which way I'll fall.

Chapter 21: Shadows in the Light

I let the heavy wrought-iron gates swing shut behind me, the sound echoing like a closing chapter. The estate sprawled ahead, its elegant façade standing resolute against the lush greenery surrounding it. Caden walked beside me, his shoulders tense, his gaze flickering toward the horizon where the sun dipped low, casting an amber glow that transformed the world into a gilded dream—one I feared would shatter at any moment.

The first step onto the cobblestone path felt like entering another realm. Each stone beneath my feet whispered secrets, and the sprawling grounds unfolded like a tapestry, woven with wildflowers that danced in the soft evening breeze. I glanced at Caden, his features set in a grim determination that made my heart thud in unison with my worry. The crisp air tasted of uncertainty, laden with the aroma of jasmine that wrapped around us like a suffocating embrace.

"This is where I grew up," he said, his voice barely above a whisper, as if afraid the house might overhear. "It feels like a museum of my childhood—a beautiful facade hiding all the broken pieces."

"Isn't that just life?" I replied, attempting to inject a hint of levity, though my own insides were twisting in knots. "Pretty on the outside, messy on the inside?"

Caden chuckled softly, a sound that lifted my spirits momentarily. "You'd be surprised how much ugliness can lie beneath polished wood and manicured lawns."

He led me toward the grand entrance, the massive oak doors looming like sentinels guarding a treasure trove of memories and misdeeds. As we stepped inside, the cool air enveloped us, infused with the scent of aged books and polished mahogany, a potent mix of history and isolation. The foyer stretched out like a grand stage, adorned with an intricate chandelier that sparkled like a thousand tiny stars, illuminating the dust motes floating lazily through the air.

"Welcome to my family's legacy," he said, gesturing around. "Just don't be surprised if it tries to swallow you whole."

The walls were lined with portraits of solemn ancestors, their eyes following our every move, as if they were the guardians of Caden's past. I felt an odd chill at the nape of my neck, as if they were judging me. "Do they always watch like this?" I asked, a hint of humor lacing my words.

"They have a knack for making one feel unwelcome," he replied, his smirk betraying a trace of genuine affection for the bizarre sense of camaraderie we shared with the past. "But they won't be the scariest things in this house tonight."

I raised an eyebrow. "Please tell me that's just your way of building suspense."

"Not quite," he admitted, a shadow passing over his face. "There's a dinner tonight with my partners. I wanted to give you a taste of the life I'm leaving behind."

Tension crackled in the air as he led me down a long corridor adorned with more portraits, each one telling stories of ambition, betrayal, and loyalty. The walls seemed to close in, the weight of expectation suffocating, and I could feel the danger lurking just beyond the threshold of this world.

We reached a pair of double doors, gilded and imposing, leading into a dining room where the past would collide with our present. Caden paused, his hand resting on the doorknob. "You ready for this?"

"Do I have a choice?" I replied, a playful smile tugging at my lips, masking the unease coiling in my stomach.

He nodded, a flicker of admiration crossing his features, and pushed the doors open. The room opened up like a cavern, richly adorned with a long oak table set for too many. Candles flickered atop fine china, casting a warm glow that contrasted sharply with the chill in the air.

As we stepped inside, a silence fell over the gathering. The men at the table, all sharp suits and sharper gazes, turned their attention toward us. I could feel the tension in the room shift, like a taut string about to snap. Caden's partners were a formidable presence, their expressions a blend of curiosity and skepticism.

"Ah, Caden," one of them drawled, his voice smooth as silk, but laced with an edge that hinted at danger. "You finally decided to bring someone to join our little soirée. How... quaint."

"This is my partner," Caden replied, his tone firm but carrying an undercurrent of something deeper, something protective. "Julia, meet Thomas and the rest."

I forced a smile, trying to appear unfazed as I shook hands with the men, each grip firm and calculating, assessing. My intuition screamed at me—these were not men to be underestimated. The dinner began, and the conversation flowed as freely as the wine, but beneath the surface, I could sense the tension building like a storm on the horizon.

The banter danced dangerously close to hostility, Caden's attempts at humor met with veiled barbs, each retort igniting the atmosphere further. I leaned closer to him, whispering, "Is this what you meant by not being the scariest things here?"

"You have no idea," he murmured back, his voice low, his eyes scanning the table like a hawk, each flicker of his gaze betraying his inner turmoil.

The night wore on, laughter mingling with sharp words, a careful game of chess where no one dared to show their hand too early. I could see the stakes rising, the flicker of flames beneath the surface as Caden's resolve began to crack.

Suddenly, a loud crash echoed from the kitchen, shattering the facade of civility. Every head turned, surprise painted across their faces. I caught a glimpse of the kitchen staff scrambling, but my attention was drawn back to Caden. His expression shifted, a storm brewing behind his calm demeanor.

"What was that?" I asked, my pulse quickening, the reality of our situation sinking in like a stone.

Caden's jaw tightened, and he stood, a coiled spring ready to unleash its force. "Stay here. I'll find out."

"Not a chance," I replied, rising with him. The instinct to protect him surged within me, weaving through the trepidation gnawing at my gut.

Together, we moved toward the kitchen, the air thickening with an electric tension. Whatever lay ahead would require all of our wits, our courage, and the unpredictable bond we had forged in the shadows of this opulent prison.

The clamor from the kitchen rattled through the air, a stark contrast to the polished atmosphere of the dining room. I followed closely behind Caden, each step a calculated blend of anticipation and dread, the tension palpable between us. The scent of sautéed garlic and something sweet lingered, masking whatever chaos lay beyond the threshold.

As we pushed through the swinging door, the scene that greeted us was unexpectedly mundane yet unsettling. A young kitchen staffer stood in a flurry of movement, a pot of spaghetti splattered across the floor, the noodles pooling like an ill-timed metaphor. "Sorry! Sorry!" she blurted, her cheeks flushed, eyes wide with embarrassment. "I was just trying to—"

Caden waved his hand dismissively. "It's fine, Tessa. What happened?"

Before she could answer, a figure loomed behind her, a tall man clad in a crisp white apron that looked too pristine for the chaos. His face was an unreadable mask, but I caught the glint of something hard in his eyes. "I told you to be careful! We can't afford any mistakes tonight," he barked, the edge of his voice slicing through the warmth of the kitchen.

"Just—just clean it up," Caden snapped, tension coiling around us like a taut wire ready to snap. He turned to me, his expression shifting, revealing the cracks beneath his calm facade. "This isn't how I wanted you to see this place."

"It's not a crime scene, Caden. I promise I've seen worse," I replied, trying to inject some humor into the situation. But the gravity of our circumstances weighed heavily, and my words felt flat against the backdrop of their strained interactions.

The tension in the room was palpable, like the air before a storm. Tessa hurried to mop up the mess, her hands trembling as she tried to contain the chaos, while the man in the apron continued to scold her, his voice a relentless metronome of frustration.

Caden stepped closer to me, lowering his voice. "This is what I'm dealing with. My partners expect perfection, and the slightest slip can send them into a frenzy. I can't let them see any weakness."

"Then let's show them something different," I replied, emboldened by the intensity of the moment. "I didn't come all this way to watch you stand there while they pick apart your life."

His brow furrowed, surprise flickering across his features. "What do you mean?"

"Let's turn this chaos into our own version of a power play. If they're going to be ruthless, let's not give them the satisfaction of thinking they've rattled us."

Caden's lips twitched upward, caught between a smile and disbelief. "You really want to take on a bunch of sharks in suits?"

"Someone has to," I replied, my heart racing at the audacity of my words. "And besides, I've faced worse. Remember that time I stood up to my boss about that ridiculous deadline?"

A ghost of a smile broke through his stoic demeanor, a hint of the playful side I adored. "You do have a knack for trouble."

"Good trouble," I countered, stepping toward Tessa, who had finished cleaning up the remnants of her mistake. "Hey, don't worry about it. Everyone makes mistakes. Just make sure you keep that pasta al dente next time."

Caden snorted, clearly trying to suppress laughter. The tension in the air lightened a fraction as Tessa grinned shyly, relieved by the unexpected kindness.

"Thanks," she murmured, casting a furtive glance at her boss. The man in the apron shot me a bemused look, clearly unaccustomed to anyone breaking the mold around here. "I'll try my best."

"Great! We'll make a culinary masterpiece out of this chaos," I declared, feeling a surge of defiance. "Who knows? Maybe the best dishes are born from disasters."

Caden leaned closer, his voice dropping to a conspiratorial whisper. "What's your plan here?"

I glanced at the ornate clock on the wall, ticking away the seconds of our lives like it was counting down to something big. "We find a way to own this room. Let's not just blend into the wallpaper. We'll draw their attention away from the stakes and toward us. Get them talking, laughing—anything but plotting."

"Okay, I'm intrigued," he replied, a hint of admiration gleaming in his eyes. "But how do we get their attention?"

"Leave that to me," I said, an idea sparking in my mind. "We need a distraction. Something that makes this evening unforgettable."

As if summoned by fate, a bottle of wine caught my eye—one that glimmered with promise, its label ornate and tempting. "How about a toast? A grand entrance for our triumphant culinary adventure!"

Caden raised an eyebrow, the flicker of mischief lighting his expression. "You think that'll do it?"

"Watch and learn," I said, striding across the kitchen with a newfound confidence. I uncorked the wine with a flourish, the pop echoing in the room, and poured generous glasses for everyone, Tessa included.

"Ladies and gentlemen!" I called out, my voice ringing with an authority I didn't quite feel but embraced wholeheartedly. "A toast! To resilience and the magic of transforming disaster into delight! May our evening be filled with laughter and camaraderie!"

The partners exchanged glances, skepticism battling curiosity, but I pressed on, raising my glass high. "Let's drink to new beginnings! To culinary masterpieces and the unexpected joy of finding friendship in chaos!"

A moment hung in the air, then slowly, smiles broke across their faces, eyes brightening at the sheer audacity of it all. One by one, they raised their glasses, caught up in the spirit of the moment, and I felt a rush of triumph wash over me.

"To resilience!" they echoed, the room buzzing with a newfound energy.

As laughter and lighthearted banter began to fill the kitchen, I returned to Caden's side, a grin plastered on my face. "See? Not so scary now, right?"

He chuckled, shaking his head in disbelief. "You really do have a flair for the dramatic."

"Only when the moment calls for it," I replied, feeling emboldened. "Now, let's turn this place around."

The night wore on, the atmosphere shifting from tense to relaxed, the shared laughter forging connections where there had only been distrust. I watched as Caden gradually eased, his shoulders lowering, the weight of expectation lifting with each clink of glasses. We were no longer mere observers; we were participants in a delicate dance of power, reclaiming control.

But as the revelry unfolded, a lingering question clawed at the edges of my mind: how long could we maintain this fragile façade? I knew Caden was in deeper than he let on, and with each jovial laugh that echoed through the room, I couldn't shake the feeling that the shadows lurking beyond the light were waiting, ready to pounce when we least expected it.

The first evening at the estate is a symphony of shadows and moonlight, the grandeur of the place casting an ethereal glow that feels almost deceptive. I stand on the balcony, a glass of the estate's finest wine cradled in my hands, watching as the gardens sway gently in the breeze. There's a stillness here, punctuated only by the distant sound of laughter from the grand hall, where Caden's family and their guests swirl in a dance of privilege and pretense. I know I should feel enchanted, but instead, I feel like an intruder, an unexpected note in a well-rehearsed sonata.

Caden strides out onto the balcony, his presence a stark contrast to the tranquility surrounding us. His brow is furrowed, a subtle reminder that the man beneath the charm is still grappling with the weight of expectations. "You look like you're ready to bolt," he remarks, his voice playful yet laced with concern.

"Maybe I am. It's a bit hard to relax when I'm wearing designer heels that cost more than my rent," I quip, giving him a teasing smile. "You'd think a place like this would offer comfortable seating, not just uncomfortable furniture and worse decisions."

He chuckles, but the laughter doesn't quite reach his eyes. "You'll get used to it. Just wait until you see the way my mother decides to 'welcome' the guests tomorrow. You might want to stick to the wine."

"Ah yes, the charming family tradition of interrogation over hors d'oeuvres. What a delightful thought," I reply, rolling my eyes theatrically.

"Exactly! Just remember, when they ask about your career, 'employed' is the right answer. 'In hiding from impending doom' isn't quite the vibe we're going for."

I glance at him, noting the tension in his jawline, the way his fingers tap against the railing. "You're not just worried about your family, are you?"

He takes a breath, the vulnerability slipping through the cracks of his façade. "It's complicated. The business partners I'm trying to cut ties with? They're not the type to just walk away peacefully. They thrive on power and control, and I'm about to disrupt their delicate balance."

"Caden, you can't let them intimidate you. You're stronger than that," I assert, instinctively stepping closer, wanting to close the gap between us.

"I appreciate the vote of confidence, but strength sometimes looks like discretion, and I might need to lean into that," he murmurs, looking away into the shadows of the garden. "But if I'm being honest, I'm not just worried about myself. You're here now, and that complicates everything."

His words hang in the air, a weighty acknowledgment of the danger that lingers in the spaces between us. "I'm not afraid of a little drama. I can hold my own," I assure him, even as a flicker of uncertainty runs through me.

With a suddenness that surprises me, he steps back, breaking the connection. "It's not just drama, and it's not just about you or me. If things go south, they could come after you too."

I swallow hard, the gravity of his words sinking in like stones in my stomach. "What do you mean, 'come after me'? I'm just a—"

"Not just anything. You're my... well, you're important to me, and that makes you a target," he says, a thread of urgency weaving through his tone.

The night stretches before us, filled with stars and unspoken fears. I want to argue, to tell him I'm capable of handling myself, but the truth is, the stakes are rising, and I feel the chill of uncertainty creeping in. "What's the plan then?" I finally ask, my voice steadying, bolstered by the determination bubbling within me.

"We wait. I gather more information. I can't make any moves until I know their next steps. The last thing I need is to create a confrontation without a strategy."

He turns, the tension in his shoulders visible even in the dim light, and for a moment, I see a glimpse of the man I'm falling for—a mix of vulnerability and determination wrapped in a suit of armor.

"Caden, I can help. Just tell me what you need me to do."

His gaze sharpens, assessing my resolve. "I need you to stay close. If anything feels off, I want you to tell me. You're sharper than you think, and I can't afford to have anyone else—"

"Think of me as your extra pair of eyes?" I interject, raising an eyebrow, determined to lighten the mood.

He smirks, but it fades quickly. "More like my lifeline. If things go sideways, I need to know you're safe first. Then we can deal with whatever hell those men decide to unleash."

As we step back inside, the air is charged with uncertainty, every laugh and clink of glasses now tinged with the knowledge that the safety of our world hangs by a thread. The grand hall feels more like a stage than a sanctuary, filled with actors performing their roles under the watchful eye of the moonlight.

A slow dance begins, couples twirling in elegant harmony, but I can't shake the feeling of impending chaos. Caden scans the room, his posture stiffening as his eyes land on a figure across the hall.

"What's wrong?" I whisper, following his gaze, but the man standing there is obscured by shadows, a sense of danger emanating from his presence.

"Just someone I hoped wouldn't be here," Caden replies, his voice dropping to a whisper. "He's not supposed to be involved in this."

"Who is he?" I press, feeling the air shift around us, the tension palpable.

But before he can answer, the man lifts his glass, a mocking grin spreading across his face, and the smile is all wrong. It's the kind of smile that promises trouble.

And then, just as quickly as it began, the music stops, and a hushed silence blankets the room. My heart races as the moment stretches on, every eye now turned toward the figure in the shadows. The weight of the atmosphere is crushing, and I can feel the ground shifting beneath us, teetering on the edge of disaster.

"Caden," I breathe, my voice barely above a whisper.

He doesn't respond, his gaze locked on the man who just stepped into the light, and in that instant, I realize that the game has changed.

Chapter 22: A Dangerous Game

The mansion glimmered under the dazzling chandeliers, each crystal prism capturing the light and splintering it into a million tiny rainbows that danced across the walls. It was the kind of night where elegance felt like a costume, and every person in attendance was playing a role in a grand performance—Manhattan's elite draped in silk and satin, each laugh too polished, every smile too rehearsed. I stood at the edge of the grand ballroom, clutching a glass of something bubbly that tasted suspiciously like nostalgia mingled with danger. Caden's fingers grazed mine as he pulled me closer, his presence a comforting balm against the sparkling, yet suffocating, extravagance.

"Don't wander off," he whispered, his breath warm against my ear. "You're my good luck charm tonight."

A charming sentiment, but in the back of my mind, unease twisted like a serpent. I looked around, the faces of Caden's business partners lurking just beyond the throng, their expressions veiled yet watchful, as if each was a hawk and I the hapless mouse beneath their gaze. Caden, for all his warmth and charisma, was entangled in a web I couldn't quite see, and the strands of tension were beginning to tighten around us.

Victor, the man I hoped I would never see again, arrived uninvited, his dark silhouette cutting through the crowd like a knife. I caught a glimpse of his smirk, that disarming smile that had once made my heart flutter, now sent ice water rushing through my veins. It was the kind of smile that promised chaos, and as I stood rooted in place, I could feel the air shift, charged with unspoken threats. He hadn't come to mingle; he was here to disrupt, and he reveled in the chaos he sowed.

"Isn't this just delightful?" His voice dripped with sarcasm as he sidled up to me, the din of laughter and clinking glasses fading into a dull roar. "You clean up well, despite the company."

I shot him a glare, a weak defense against the rush of memories that accompanied him, but my heart was racing, adrenaline thrumming beneath my skin. "What are you doing here, Victor? This is a private event."

"Private? In this city? That's cute." He leaned closer, and the scent of his cologne wrapped around me—smoky, intriguing, a dangerous promise. "I couldn't resist the spectacle. You and your new prince charming—how charming indeed."

Before I could respond, a loud argument erupted from across the room, drawing the attention of every guest. Caden's voice, usually smooth and inviting, rose in intensity, each syllable laced with frustration. I turned just in time to see him facing off against a man I'd never met but whose reputation preceded him like a shadow. He was older, his face lined with the experiences of a life spent in the ruthless world of business. The tension crackled in the air, a tangible force that had everyone holding their breath, as if waiting for the moment when the storm would finally break.

"Caden, you can't just walk away. Not after everything we've built!" The man's voice boomed, shaking the very foundations of the laughter and music surrounding us.

"I'm not staying in this game any longer. You know it, and you know why." Caden's reply was sharp, slicing through the murmurs of discontent. I felt a sense of dread pooling in my stomach, like heavy stones sinking to the bottom of a river. This was more than a disagreement; it was a reckoning.

"Enemies are not so easily shaken off, my friend," the older man warned, his tone almost a hiss. "You think you can just turn your back and walk away? They won't let you."

The eyes of the room flicked between them, a sea of intrigue and silent judgment, and I could almost hear the whispers blooming like wildflowers—rumors sprouting from the seeds of uncertainty. With each word exchanged, the walls around me seemed to inch closer, the laughter dimming, replaced by the heavy weight of impending confrontation.

"Let them try," Caden shot back, his bravado defiant but tinged with an edge of desperation. "I'm not afraid of them anymore."

The statement lingered in the air, a challenge that hung like a ripe fruit ready to fall, and I couldn't shake the feeling that we were standing on a precipice. My heart raced, not just with fear but with an instinctive need to shield him from whatever darkness was lurking just beyond the party's glitzy façade. I stepped forward, my hand reaching for his arm, my voice trembling with urgency.

"Caden, maybe we should—"

He turned to me, his eyes fierce and unyielding. "No, Ava. You don't understand. I'm tired of being a pawn. They've used me for too long."

I could feel Victor's gaze lingering, a predatory gleam in his eyes, relishing the turmoil unfolding before him. He knew more than he let on, and the realization made my skin crawl. The stakes were rising, and I felt like a bystander in a dangerous game I never wanted to play.

As the argument escalated, the ballroom's atmosphere shifted from elegant to electric, the air thick with anticipation. It felt as if the party was merely a façade, a stage set for a drama that was about to unfold, one that threatened to unravel everything Caden had built, and in turn, everything we had begun to forge together.

"Why do I feel like we're in the middle of a storm?" I whispered, glancing nervously at the crowd, whose eyes were glued to the unfolding drama.

"Because we are," Caden replied, his voice low and fierce, a promise hanging in the air between us. "But I'll be damned if I let them take me down."

With every word, the stakes grew higher, and the fragile threads of our night began to fray, the opulent surroundings transforming into a battleground where every whispered secret felt like a bullet waiting to be fired. As the laughter faded and tension filled the space, I couldn't help but wonder—was I ready to stand by him as the storm broke, or would the tempest tear us apart before we had a chance to truly begin?

A sudden hush fell over the ballroom, thickening the air until it felt almost suffocating. Caden stood, resolute, his posture radiating defiance, and I could see the determination etched on his face, a stark contrast to the uncertainty swirling within me. The sharpness of the moment sliced through the haze of champagne and laughter, revealing the raw nerve beneath the evening's veneer of elegance.

"Caden," I murmured, my voice a soft plea against the rising tension. "Let's just go. This isn't worth it."

He turned to me, and for a fleeting moment, I saw vulnerability flicker behind his resolute gaze. "It is worth it, Ava. I can't keep running. I need to stand my ground."

Before I could argue further, the older man, whose name I still didn't know, leaned in closer, his voice low but venomous. "Your defiance is admirable, Caden, but naive. You think you can just sever ties without repercussions? You'll regret this. They won't let you walk away quietly."

A shiver ran down my spine. The threat lingered in the air, heavy and palpable, like a storm cloud ready to unleash its fury. I searched Caden's face for a glimmer of reassurance, something to tether me to the moment, but he merely squared his shoulders and clenched his jaw.

"Watch me," he replied, his voice steady yet laced with an undercurrent of tension that left my heart racing. I knew then that he was not just battling for himself; he was fighting for us, for the future we were cautiously building together. The revelation sparked a fierce resolve within me, and I took a step closer, willing to face whatever storm might come.

As if sensing my newfound determination, Victor smirked, sauntering over with the confidence of someone who thrived in chaos. "Caden, my friend," he said, his tone dripping with sarcasm, "are you really going to jeopardize everything for a fleeting dream? You think they'll just let you waltz away into the sunset with your little lady here?" He gestured to me with an exaggerated flourish, his eyes glinting with amusement, as if my very presence was a joke.

"Stop," I interjected, the word bursting forth before I could think. The entire room seemed to pause, curiosity rippling like a wave through the crowd. "This isn't about me, Victor. It's about Caden standing up for himself, for what he believes in. Something you wouldn't understand."

He raised an eyebrow, clearly taken aback. "Oh, darling, I understand power all too well. I just prefer to wield it from the shadows, unlike your brave knight here."

The taunt hung in the air, a challenge flung into the growing tension. Caden's jaw tightened, and I could see the battle brewing in his eyes. This wasn't just a confrontation; it was a declaration of war, and I was caught in the crossfire.

"Victor, you don't know anything about what Caden has sacrificed," I shot back, my pulse racing. "He's not the villain you think he is."

A small, knowing smile crept onto Victor's lips. "Ah, but every story needs a villain, don't you think? Someone to keep things... interesting."

Caden stepped between us, his presence a shield, and I felt a rush of gratitude mingled with anxiety. "Enough, Victor. You're not welcome here."

At that moment, the atmosphere shifted dramatically. A sharp, crashing sound echoed from the corner of the room—a champagne flute had slipped from someone's grasp, shattering on the marble floor like the delicate facade of the evening. Laughter abruptly ceased, and the whispers erupted into a chorus of alarm and confusion, the guests now all too aware of the storm brewing around us.

"Looks like your party is falling apart, Caden," Victor said, his voice silky smooth, laced with malice. "Perhaps you should reevaluate your choices."

I felt my heart race, a mixture of anger and fear boiling beneath my skin. "This isn't just a game to him," I said, my voice steady despite the chaos. "He's trying to change things, and it's not for you to mock."

The tension escalated, and I noticed several guests subtly shifting, inching away, as if the conflict was infectious. Caden's allies, once engaged in polite conversation, now stood as spectators, their gazes flicking between us, weighing the drama unfolding before them. I could see the stakes rising, the stakes shifting from personal conflict to a very public battle for Caden's future, and in that instant, I realized the truth: we were all players on this stage, each of us bound by the unseen strings of power and ambition.

"Is this how you want to be remembered, Caden?" Victor pressed, his tone a mixture of challenge and disdain. "As a reckless man willing to throw away his future over some misguided sense of loyalty?"

The questions hung heavy in the air, and Caden opened his mouth to respond, but the moment stretched, the weight of it pressing down on us all. I saw the flicker of doubt in Caden's eyes, a moment of vulnerability that sent my heart plummeting. Was this really worth the risk? Was he prepared to lose everything?

Then I stepped forward, my heart pounding with fierce determination. "You're not reckless, Caden. You're brave. You're choosing to fight for what's right, not just for yourself but for everyone who's been pushed aside. Isn't that worth something?" My voice, firm yet filled with emotion, seemed to pierce through the tension, capturing the attention of those around us.

The silence that followed was almost reverent. Victor's smirk faltered slightly, a crack in his armor, while Caden's eyes found mine, and I could see the fire reigniting within him. "You're right," he said, voice steady, no longer wavering. "I won't back down. Not for you, not for anyone."

"Then let's give them a show," I replied, a spark of mischief igniting in my chest. "If they want drama, we'll give them the performance of a lifetime."

Caden's lips curled into a grin, the kind that had the power to light up the darkest of rooms. "Alright then. But remember, once we start this, there's no turning back."

With a shared glance that held more promise than uncertainty, we stepped into the fray together, the crowd parting as we approached the man who had challenged him. The lights of the ballroom glimmered above us, but all I could see was the resolute spark in Caden's eyes, illuminating the path forward.

And as the murmurs began anew, electric with speculation and intrigue, I felt a thrill surge through me. The night was far from over, and this dangerous game had only just begun.

The atmosphere shifted as Caden and I approached the older man, a palpable tension weaving its way through the crowd. It felt as if the air itself had thickened, pressing down on us with the weight of unspoken words and hidden agendas. Guests formed a semi-circle around us, their faces illuminated by the glimmering chandeliers, but their eyes reflected something darker—curiosity mixed with malice, as if they were eager to witness a spectacle.

"Let's hear what you have to say, old friend," Caden said, a tightness in his voice that betrayed the bravado he tried to project.

The man regarded him coolly, his expression a mask of disdain. "You think you can just strut in here and make demands? You don't understand the game you're playing. You're merely a pawn."

I felt a surge of protectiveness for Caden, an instinct I couldn't ignore. "If he's a pawn, then you must be a relic," I shot back, surprising even myself with the sharpness of my retort. The words hung in the air, a challenge that shifted the dynamic in the room. "You're not the one who gets to dictate his choices anymore."

Laughter erupted from the crowd, and I could see the man's jaw clench, irritation flaring in his eyes. Caden's gaze flickered toward me, an appreciation shining in his depths. Maybe I had some fire in me after all.

"Let's not kid ourselves," the man replied, his voice lowering to a conspiratorial whisper that only we could hear. "You think you're helping him? You're only making things worse. You're a distraction, a liability."

The words stung, and I felt the heat rise to my cheeks. But Caden stepped closer, his presence a protective barrier against the cynicism swirling around us. "No, she's not a liability. She's my partner. Something you wouldn't understand," he shot back, the conviction in his voice striking a chord that resonated through the tension in the air.

Victor chuckled from the sidelines, his amusement laced with condescension. "Look at you, Caden. You're putting your faith in a dreamer. You're destined for failure."

I could feel the anger bubbling beneath my skin, ready to erupt. "Better to dream than to be a puppet on someone else's strings," I shot back, my voice steady. "At least we're brave enough to stand for something real."

The old man's expression hardened, and for a moment, I thought I saw a flicker of uncertainty cross his face. But just as quickly, it was gone, replaced by a sinister smile that sent a chill racing down my spine. "Then let the games begin," he said, his tone dripping with mockery. "You're in way over your head, both of you."

As he turned to address the crowd, the whispers intensified, a wave of speculation rising like a tide. I caught snippets of conversation—talk of alliances, betrayals, and power plays. The tension crackled, charging the atmosphere with an electric energy that made my skin prickle.

Caden's hand found mine, a solid anchor in the storm. "Stay close," he murmured, his voice low enough that only I could hear. "Whatever happens, don't let go."

I nodded, trying to suppress the whirlwind of anxiety swirling within me. We were standing on a precipice, and beneath us lay a churning sea of consequences. I had never wanted to be part of this world—the glitzy parties and hidden agendas. Yet here I was, tethered to a man who had thrown himself into the lion's den.

As the older man launched into a speech, touting Caden's "foolhardy ambition," I felt the weight of every eye upon us. The crowd was a sea of judgment, and I couldn't shake the sensation that we were the main event in a twisted theater, where the stakes were our lives.

"Enough of this charade," Caden interrupted, his voice cutting through the murmur of discontent like a knife. "I'm done playing your games. I'm leaving this life behind."

Gasps rippled through the audience, a collective intake of breath that signaled a turning point. The man's eyes narrowed, his mask slipping to reveal the simmering anger beneath. "You think you can just walk away? You're a fool. You're playing a dangerous game, Caden."

"I know exactly what I'm doing," Caden replied, his voice steady and unyielding. "I'm choosing to stand for something, to take control of my own fate."

"Your fate?" the man scoffed. "You think you're in control? You're a child playing with fire, and I'll make sure you get burned."

The crowd surged forward, the atmosphere electric with tension. I could feel the heat rising, the stakes escalating as whispers morphed into shouts. Caden's grip on my hand tightened, and for a moment, I reveled in the warmth of his confidence, the conviction that radiated from him.

But before I could voice my support, Victor stepped closer, his tone conspiratorial. "You've made a real mess of things, Caden. You have no idea what you're up against. You're not just battling one enemy. You're stepping into a war."

"What do you mean?" Caden shot back, his brows furrowing in confusion.

"Think about it. You think this man cares about your dreams? He's just the tip of the iceberg. There are others, far more dangerous, who will come for you once you make your move."

The revelation hit me like a punch to the gut, and I could see the dawning realization in Caden's eyes. The reality of our situation loomed larger than I had anticipated. A flicker of fear crossed his face, but he masked it quickly, returning to that fierce determination I'd come to admire.

"I'm not afraid of shadows," he declared, and I admired his bravery, even as my heart raced with apprehension.

But Victor only chuckled, a sound that echoed ominously through the crowd. "You should be. Shadows have a way of swallowing you whole."

At that moment, the atmosphere shifted again. The ballroom doors swung open, and a wave of fresh air swept through, mingling with the tension. But it wasn't just the air that shifted; it was the energy in the room. A group of men stepped inside, their expressions dark and predatory, like wolves entering a sheep's den.

I felt my breath hitch, the reality of danger crashing down around us like a tidal wave.

Caden's eyes widened as he took in the new arrivals, recognition flashing across his features. "What are they doing here?"

I turned to look, and the sight froze me in place. Each man carried an air of authority, their tailored suits and cold expressions indicating they were not here for pleasantries. They were here for retribution.

As they strode toward us, I could feel the palpable tension thickening, wrapping around us like a noose. This was no longer just a social gathering; it had transformed into a battleground where alliances would be tested, and lives might very well hang in the balance.

"Caden, we need to—" I began, but before I could finish, a shout erupted from the group.

"Caden! You have a choice to make," one of the men bellowed, his voice reverberating through the room, drawing every gaze toward us. "Join us or face the consequences."

A silence fell, heavy and ominous, as the world around us seemed to pause, teetering on the brink of chaos.

Caden looked at me, a mixture of determination and uncertainty in his eyes. "What do I do, Ava?"

I opened my mouth to respond, but the words caught in my throat, lost in the weight of the moment. The stakes were higher than I'd ever imagined, and now, with danger closing in, I realized that the choices we made tonight could alter the course of our lives forever.

As the shadows encroached, I grasped Caden's hand tighter, our futures intertwined in the flickering light of uncertainty, and I knew we were standing at the edge of a precipice—where one misstep could lead us spiraling into darkness.

Chapter 23: An Unexpected Ally

The café exudes an air of nostalgia, its weathered wooden beams groaning under the weight of countless stories. The scent of freshly brewed coffee intertwines with the sweetness of pastries, creating an atmosphere both inviting and oppressive. I sink into a corner booth, the cracked vinyl sticking to my skin as I glance out at the street, where the sun is setting, spilling molten gold across the pavement. It feels surreal to be here, amidst the ordinary chaos of life, while my own world teeters on the brink of disaster.

When Victor arrives, he cuts a striking figure, his tailored coat casting a shadow that belies the warmth of the café. His demeanor is one of cool confidence, his dark hair tousled in a way that looks effortlessly stylish. He scans the room, his eyes sharp and calculating, before settling on me with a look that stirs an unwelcome mix of anxiety and curiosity within. I shift uncomfortably in my seat, half-expecting him to slip back into the role of a menacing adversary.

"Thanks for meeting me," he says, his voice smooth, like whiskey poured over ice. "I know this is... complicated."

"Complicated is an understatement," I reply, crossing my arms defensively. "What do you want, Victor?"

He leans forward, resting his elbows on the table, his gaze piercing through the dim light. "I want to help you. Caden has made some dangerous choices, and if you stay with him, you'll get caught in the crossfire."

The mention of Caden sends a jolt through me. The image of his reckless grin flashes in my mind, juxtaposed with the weight of our recent chaos. "Help? Or control?" I counter, raising an eyebrow. "You have a funny way of showing concern for my well-being."

"Touché," he concedes, a flicker of admiration crossing his features. "But I'm not here to play games. Caden is spiraling. There are forces at play you don't understand. If I didn't think this was serious, I wouldn't have reached out."

The sincerity in his voice feels like a lifeline thrown into turbulent waters, but I can't ignore the inherent danger in trusting him. My instinct urges me to dismiss his offer, yet another part of me—perhaps the part that craves clarity in this storm of confusion—hangs on his words. "And how exactly do you propose to protect me?" I ask, my voice trembling with a mixture of hope and skepticism.

Victor hesitates, a shadow flitting across his features as he leans back. "I have connections. Resources. I can offer you a safe place until this blows over. You don't have to be tied to the fallout of Caden's decisions. You can walk away, start fresh."

The idea flirts with the edges of my mind, tantalizing and terrifying. My heart races at the thought of escape, a clean break from the tangle of loyalties and heartbreak. But there's a hitch, an unspoken question lurking beneath the surface: what does he want in return? "What's the catch?"

He smirks, a flash of something almost playful in his eyes. "No catch. Just a favor in the future. It's not as ominous as it sounds. Think of it as an insurance policy."

"An insurance policy," I echo, rolling the words around like marbles in my mouth. "What kind of favor?"

"I can't say yet," he replies, his tone shifting to something more serious. "But trust me, it won't be anything harmful. I just need to know you'll be there when I call."

The air between us thickens, a palpable tension laced with unspoken promises. I can't shake the feeling that there's more to this situation than meets the eye. A sliver of doubt twists in my stomach, but the allure of safety is potent, whispering sweet nothings that drown out the chaos of my reality.

"Why are you really doing this?" I challenge, unwilling to let my guard down completely. "You hardly seem like the type to play the hero."

Victor's expression softens, the corners of his mouth turning up in a half-smile that catches me off guard. "I guess you could say I have my own reasons. Let's just say I've seen the consequences of ignoring danger. I don't want that for you."

"Or for you?" I shoot back, a hint of steel creeping into my voice. "What's in it for you, Victor? You're not exactly known for your altruism."

He raises his hands in mock surrender, laughter dancing in his eyes. "Point taken. But I assure you, I'm not looking for some sort of twisted redemption. I've got my own battles to fight. I just don't want to add your name to the list of casualties."

The irony of his words isn't lost on me. Here he is, offering me an escape while also hinting that his own motives are tangled in a web of ulterior motives and power plays. I want to scream, to tell him to take his "help" and shove it, but deep down, I know I can't do this alone. The weight of the choices ahead presses heavily on my shoulders, each option feeling more fraught than the last.

"Let's say I consider it," I finally say, drawing a deep breath as I weigh the gravity of my decision. "What's the first step?"

He leans back, satisfaction flickering across his face, as if I've unwittingly walked into a game I didn't know we were playing. "Meet me tomorrow. I'll have everything arranged. You'll be safe, I promise. Just keep your distance from Caden for a while."

The words settle in my mind like a double-edged sword. I can't shake the feeling that this is a dangerous game, one that could easily unravel into chaos. Yet the prospect of stepping away from the life I've known, from the uncertainty that wraps around me like a noose, is intoxicating.

"Tomorrow, then," I say, and as the words leave my lips, I can't help but feel like I'm stepping onto a precipice, uncertain of where it will lead.

I wake the next morning to the soft glow of the sun streaming through my curtains, its warm light doing little to ease the unease that settles deep in my chest. The city hums outside, a symphony of honking horns, distant laughter, and the rhythmic thud of footsteps on pavement. It should feel comforting, but today it sounds like a warning bell, echoing the tumult of my thoughts. I run a hand through my disheveled hair, the remnants of sleep clinging to me like a stubborn shadow.

Coffee. That's what I need. I shuffle into the kitchen, the cool tiles beneath my feet grounding me as I prepare a much-needed cup. The ritual is familiar, each movement methodical: the scooping of beans, the grinding, the bubbling of the water. With each second that passes, the tendrils of doubt coil tighter around me. I can't shake the feeling that I'm standing at the edge of a precipice, and whatever decision I make today could send me tumbling into an abyss.

As I sip the rich brew, I try to push away the swirling thoughts. Victor's offer lingers at the forefront of my mind, a tantalizing thread that could lead to safety—or further chaos. The phone buzzes on the table, pulling me from my reverie. One glance at the screen sends a ripple of anxiety through me. It's Victor.

I take a deep breath before replying, my fingers hesitating over the keys. "I'm in." I hit send, the words flying into the void, and then immediately second-guess myself. What have I just committed to?

Half an hour later, I find myself standing outside a sleek building in the financial district, its glass façade reflecting the world around it like a polished mirror. I smooth my blouse and take a steadying breath. This place feels more intimidating than the café. As I step inside, I'm engulfed by an atmosphere charged with ambition and power.

Victor is already waiting in the lobby, his presence magnetic, drawing the eyes of passersby. He waves me over with a confident smile that seems to brighten the otherwise sterile space. "You made it!" he exclaims, genuine delight flickering in his gaze.

"Couldn't let you think I was all talk," I reply, trying to match his enthusiasm, though my stomach churns with uncertainty.

"Good. We need to move quickly," he says, shifting into a more serious tone. "Follow me."

As we walk through the building, I can't help but admire the modern artwork adorning the walls, each piece a bold statement, just like the people who bustle around us. Victor leads me to a sleek elevator, and we ascend in silence, the whirring machinery echoing our unspoken tension. When the doors slide open, I'm greeted by a corridor lined with glossy offices and glass-walled conference rooms.

We enter one of the offices, a space that feels both warm and imposing. It's decorated with dark wood furniture and artful touches that speak to someone who appreciates beauty but craves control. A sprawling view of the city sprawls beyond the windows, but my attention is drawn to a large desk where a man sits, poring over documents. He looks up as we enter, a frown creasing his brow.

"Victor," he says, his tone clipped. "You're late."

"Just catching up with an old friend," Victor replies smoothly, his voice betraying nothing. "This is our new ally, who's going to help us clean up the mess Caden's made."

The man studies me, his gaze piercing, assessing my worth in a split second. "I hope she's as capable as you say," he replies, the skepticism in his voice palpable.

"Trust me," Victor interjects, "she's more than capable."

I can feel the weight of their scrutiny, a silent contest playing out between them. "What exactly do you need from me?" I ask, trying to assert myself. "I'm not just a pawn in your game."

The man's lips curve into a faint smirk. "Smart. That's a good quality to have." He gestures toward a chair, and I take a seat, crossing my arms defensively. "Caden's actions have attracted attention—bad attention. We need to keep you safe, and to do that, we need to know everything you can tell us about him."

I hesitate, the thought of spilling my secrets feeling like opening Pandora's box. "What do you mean? I can't just lay everything out like that. You're asking me to betray him."

"Not betrayal," Victor chimes in, his tone soothing. "Survival. We need to understand what we're dealing with. You're the only one who can provide that insight."

The pressure in the room thickens, and I glance between them, weighing my options. "And if I refuse?" I ask, my voice steady despite the nerves churning in my stomach.

"Then you're at risk," the man says bluntly, his gaze unwavering. "Caden is reckless, and his recklessness has consequences. If you stay connected to him, you're walking a tightrope without a net."

"You don't have to decide right now," Victor adds, his voice a gentle reminder amidst the rising tension. "But I need you to understand the gravity of the situation. We're offering you a way out, a chance to step back from the chaos."

I take a deep breath, feeling the weight of their expectations pressing down on me. "Fine. I'll help. But I want assurances. I need to know that you'll protect me, no matter what."

"Absolutely," Victor says, his tone earnest. "That's what we're here for."

As the discussion unfolds, layers of tension unfurl like a tightly wound spring. I find myself drawing on an unexpected well of strength, realizing that in this dance of shadows and uncertainty, I'm no longer a mere spectator. I'm part of something larger, a chess game where every move counts, and I refuse to be a pawn.

Victor and the man exchange quick glances, their dynamic shifting as they begin to strategize. The conversation becomes a blur of names and numbers, the stakes rising with each mention of Caden's dangerous connections. I listen intently, piecing together a map of the world I've unwittingly stepped into—a world where every decision feels like a gamble, and the odds are stacked against me.

As they speak, I can't shake the feeling that I'm being drawn into a web of intrigue, my life entwining with forces far beyond my comprehension. But beneath the trepidation lies a flicker of exhilaration. In this chaos, I am finally taking control, forging a path through the unknown with each carefully chosen word. I may not know what lies ahead, but I'm ready to face it head-on, with or without Caden.

With every word exchanged in that glass-walled office, the air grew heavier, thick with the gravity of my decision. Victor and the man—whose name I still didn't know—mapped out strategies that sounded both thrilling and terrifying. They tossed around names I recognized only in whispers, dangers lurking like shadows waiting to pounce. My pulse quickened, a heady cocktail of fear and adrenaline coursing through me. This was my new reality, one where secrets were currency, and knowledge could either save or doom me.

"We need to set a plan in motion," Victor said, leaning over the desk with an intensity that made my heart race. "We'll need you to gather information from Caden without raising suspicion. It's critical we understand his next move."

"Gather information?" I echoed incredulously. "You want me to play spy? What do you think I am, a secret agent?"

"Not quite," Victor replied, a teasing glint in his eyes that momentarily softened the tension. "But you have an inside track, and that gives you an edge."

I crossed my arms, contemplating the absurdity of the situation. "And if Caden finds out? You think I could just charm my way out of that?" The idea was ridiculous, and yet it made a twisted kind of sense. He had to trust me, right? If only because I was as much of a pawn in this game as he was.

"Trust me, he won't suspect a thing," Victor said, his voice smooth as silk. "You know him better than anyone. Use that to your advantage."

"Easy for you to say." I couldn't hide the bite in my tone. "You're not the one who will be caught in the crossfire if things go south."

Victor stepped closer, his presence suddenly overwhelming. "I'll be there to back you up. You have to believe that."

A sudden pang of uncertainty gnawed at me, but his confidence was infectious. The fear of Caden's recklessness had begun to worm its way into my bones, chilling me. If there was even a small chance of protecting myself—and maybe even Caden—from this impending storm, I had to consider it. "Fine," I conceded, feeling the weight of inevitability settle on my shoulders. "But if anything goes wrong, I'm out. No second chances."

"Deal." Victor's smile was sharp, and the deal struck between us felt as binding as any contract.

As we moved forward with planning, my mind raced with the implications of what I was getting into. They discussed timing, locations, and potential allies, but my thoughts drifted to Caden. His laughter, his carefree attitude—how could he be so oblivious to the danger he was in? My heart twisted at the thought of deceiving him. Was I willing to sacrifice our connection for the sake of safety?

As if reading my mind, Victor leaned in, his voice lowering. "Caden may seem invincible, but even the strongest walls can crumble. You just have to make sure you're not standing in the rubble when it happens."

The metaphor struck a chord, and I nodded, steeling myself for what was to come. As we wrapped up our discussion, Victor handed me a small, sleek phone. "This is for emergencies. If you feel like you're in over your head, call me. No questions asked."

I stared at the device, suddenly aware of how entwined our fates had become. "I hope I don't have to use this."

"Me too," he replied, his expression softening for just a moment before a flicker of worry crossed his face. "Remember, the stakes are high. Trust your instincts."

The city hummed outside as I stepped back into the world that felt both familiar and foreign. The sun shone brightly, illuminating the chaos that lay ahead. I felt a mix of excitement and dread swirling within me, a cocktail of emotions that left me dizzy. I wandered the streets, lost in thought, trying to reconcile the betrayal I was about to enact against Caden with the potential safety Victor promised.

As I turned a corner, I spotted a familiar face in the crowd. My heart jumped as I recognized Lila, my friend and confidante, her vibrant personality as striking as ever. She was chatting animatedly with a group, her laughter ringing out like a beacon. I hesitated, torn between the urge to seek her out and the need to keep my distance. I couldn't risk involving anyone else in this mess, not when I was already playing with fire.

"Hey! Is that you?" Lila called, breaking free from the group and rushing over. "I haven't seen you in ages! What have you been up to?"

Her bright smile ignited a warmth within me, one that felt almost foreign given the tension I'd just navigated. "Oh, you know, just—surviving," I replied with a half-hearted grin, trying to keep the weight of my reality from spilling into our conversation.

"Surviving? Come on, you can't leave me in the dark! Spill!" She nudged me playfully, her eyes sparkling with curiosity.

"Really, it's nothing. Just a bit of... drama," I managed, the truth choking in my throat. The thought of laying everything out for her made me uneasy, but I also felt the familiar comfort of her presence tugging at my resolve.

"Drama? You know I live for that!" she teased, her enthusiasm contagious. "You have to tell me! Is it about Caden?"

A shiver shot down my spine at the mere mention of his name. "Uh, not exactly," I replied, the words feeling inadequate and hollow. How could I explain the convoluted mess of feelings and alliances without implicating her?

"Come on, you're acting super shady. What's really going on?" Lila leaned in, her voice dropping to a conspiratorial whisper, her instincts honed for detecting a lie.

"Nothing, I swear," I insisted, but my heart raced as I searched for an escape from the weight of my own deceit.

Just then, a commotion erupted down the street. A black SUV screeched to a halt, tires screeching against the pavement. My stomach dropped as I recognized the emblem on the side—a familiar logo that sent a jolt of fear coursing through me. The door swung open, and a figure stepped out, their posture rigid and menacing.

"What the hell is going on?" Lila asked, her eyes wide as she caught sight of the unfolding scene.

"I... I don't know," I stammered, every instinct telling me to run. The sudden shift in the atmosphere prickled my skin, a warning that something had just shifted irrevocably.

Before I could process the danger, the figure glanced in my direction, locking eyes with me. Recognition flickered across their face, and my heart raced as I realized who it was. I felt a surge of panic. Caden's world was crashing in on us, and I had just stepped onto the stage for a performance that promised to be anything but safe.

"Run," I whispered to Lila, but the words barely left my lips before the chaos erupted around us, shattering the fragile facade of safety I'd tried to maintain.

Chapter 24: The Storm Breaks

Rain lashed against the tall glass windows of Caden's penthouse, the sound echoing through the sprawling, minimalist space. I stood at the edge of the living room, my heart racing, feeling as if I was in the eye of a storm. The city sprawled out beneath me like a maze of glittering lights and shadows, but all I could focus on was the man in front of me—Caden, with his brooding gaze and that signature smirk that had once felt like a warm embrace now seemed like an unsettling mask hiding the truth.

I had played the role of the good girlfriend for far too long, turning a blind eye to the flickering shadows in his life. But tonight, there was no turning back. I had to confront him, had to peel back the layers he'd woven around himself like a protective shield. I had rehearsed this moment in my mind, but no amount of preparation could brace me for what was about to unfold.

"Caden," I started, my voice steady despite the tremor of uncertainty lurking beneath. "We need to talk."

He leaned against the sleek counter, arms crossed, his eyes darting to the city lights outside, avoiding my gaze. "Can it wait? It's a pretty terrible night to get into—"

"No, it can't wait!" I cut him off, the frustration spilling over like the storm raging beyond the walls. "I can't keep living like this, not knowing if I can trust you. I feel like I'm in a fog, and I need you to clear it. Please."

At my plea, the muscles in his jaw tightened. He finally turned to me, the storm reflected in his dark eyes, and for a moment, I saw the real Caden—the man beneath the layers of secrets and bravado. "You wouldn't understand," he said, his voice low, laden with an emotion that was equal parts frustration and fear.

"Try me," I challenged, stepping closer. "I'm tired of feeling like a pawn in your game. Just tell me the truth."

The weight of my words hung in the air, charged and heavy. He hesitated, his brow furrowing as if he were battling an internal war. The air crackled with tension, and just when I thought he might relent, he sighed deeply, running a hand through his tousled hair.

"Okay," he finally said, resignation painting his features. "But you have to promise me one thing."

"What?" I asked, anxiety prickling at my skin.

"Promise me you won't run away when you hear it."

I nodded, though dread pooled in my stomach like a lead weight. He pushed himself off the counter and paced the length of the room, his footsteps echoing against the polished floor. The rain drummed insistently against the glass, a chaotic rhythm that mirrored the turmoil swirling within me.

"I'm not who you think I am," he began, the words spilling out like a confession long overdue. "I didn't choose this life; it chose me. I was dragged into it, and I tried to pull you out, but it's too late for that now."

"Too late for what?" I pressed, my heart thudding in my chest. "What are you talking about?"

"I'm involved with people—dangerous people," he confessed, his voice cracking. "And I've done things. Things I'm not proud of, things that could put you in danger just by being near me. I thought if I kept you away from it all, I could protect you, but..." He paused, his eyes locking onto mine, a storm of emotion swirling within. "But I was wrong. You're already in it. We both are."

I felt as if the ground had fallen out from beneath me. The pieces of his confession crashed together in my mind, forming a horrifying picture. I had thought Caden was simply a man with a complicated past, but now I was staring into the abyss of his choices, realizing the depth of his entanglement.

Before I could process the magnitude of his words, the world outside exploded. The window rattled as thunder roared, shaking the penthouse, the air thick with electricity and the unmistakable scent of rain-soaked asphalt. A flash of lightning illuminated Caden's face, and I noticed the raw fear etched into his features.

"Caden?" I whispered, confusion and dread colliding within me.

"It's happening," he murmured, his voice barely above a whisper. "They've made a move. We have to go. Now."

I barely had time to react before he grabbed my wrist, leading me toward the elevator. My pulse quickened, not just from fear but from the realization that our world had just shifted irrevocably. The rain intensified, pouring down in sheets as if the sky were weeping for the chaos that had unraveled between us.

"Wait," I said, tugging at his arm as we reached the elevator. "What do you mean, 'they'? Who are we running from?"

Caden's gaze darkened, his jaw set tight. "Enemies. People who won't hesitate to hurt anyone I care about. We need to get out of here before they find us."

Before I could grasp the enormity of what he was saying, the elevator doors opened with a quiet ding, and he pushed me inside, his urgency palpable. As the doors closed, I felt the weight of the storm bearing down on us, not just outside but within the confines of our relationship. My heart raced, a wild drumbeat of fear and exhilaration as we plunged into the unknown.

With every floor we descended, the gravity of his revelations pressed down harder on my chest. It was like stepping into a different reality, one where trust was a fragile illusion, and the darkness loomed ever closer. The last remnants of my old life flickered away, swallowed by the storm that raged both outside and within my heart.

As we burst out into the rain-soaked streets, the city transformed into a blurred canvas of color and chaos. The storm wasn't just a backdrop; it was a catalyst, propelling us forward into the night, away from the familiar and into a realm of uncertainty. The pulse of adrenaline surged through me, mingling with the dread that clung like the wet clothes against my skin. With Caden by my side, I was no longer just a spectator in this world; I was inextricably tied to him, caught in a tempest of secrets and shadows, racing against the storm that threatened to consume us both.

We sprinted into the storm-soaked night, rain drenching us within moments, turning the streets into glistening rivers of chaos. The city felt alive, an electric pulse beneath the tempest, every heartbeat resonating with the thunder above us. Caden's grip on my hand was firm, a lifeline amid the swirling panic, but the questions roiling in my mind threatened to spill over like the rain around us.

"Where are we going?" I shouted over the wind, struggling to keep pace as he navigated through the darkened streets.

"To a safe place," he replied, his voice strained. "Somewhere we can figure this out."

I stole a glance at him, the fierce determination on his face mixed with a hint of fear, and it sent a shiver down my spine. The world I thought I knew was unraveling at breakneck speed, and with every step, I felt more ensnared in a web of his making.

"Caden," I pressed, fighting against the storm and the confusion swirling in my head. "You can't just drop a bombshell like that and expect me to run blindly into the night without answers. What kind of danger are we talking about?"

He paused, pulling me into a narrow alleyway, the slick brick walls glistening under the harsh neon lights from nearby bars. "You wouldn't understand. This is bigger than us. It's not just about you and me anymore."

"That's rich coming from you," I shot back, frustration bubbling up. "You dragged me into this without so much as a warning. Do you think I'm some delicate flower that can't handle the truth?"

His gaze softened momentarily, a flicker of remorse passing through his stormy eyes. "No, but I wanted to keep you safe. I thought I could protect you from my world."

I crossed my arms, letting the rain hammer down on my skin. "By lying to me? By keeping me in the dark while you play hero?"

The tension hung thick between us, mingling with the rain-soaked air. He ran a hand through his hair, looking both pained and resolute. "You're right. I should have told you. But it's complicated. I didn't want you to see me as—"

"As what? A monster?" I interrupted, my voice rising. "Because it sounds like you're in deep, and I'm not sure how much of this I can take."

His expression hardened, a mask of defiance replacing the vulnerability. "If you can't handle this, maybe it's better you don't know. I'm not going to let you get hurt because of my choices."

"Not let me get hurt?" I laughed bitterly, the sound harsh in the stormy silence. "Caden, I'm already in this mess! You think I'll just stand back and watch while you put yourself in danger? No. I want to know everything. If we're in this together, then you have to trust me."

We stood there, rain pouring down like a relentless barrage, our hearts pounding in unison. His eyes searched mine, looking for something—perhaps understanding, perhaps permission. Finally, with a resigned exhale, he nodded, albeit slowly.

"Fine. But you need to understand that once you know, there's no turning back."

"Isn't that the whole point?" I shot back, a strange mix of fear and resolve surging within me.

"Okay," he said, taking a step back into the alley, pulling me along with him, sheltered slightly from the torrential rain. "Let's find somewhere dry, and I'll explain. But promise me you'll be careful with what you say. There are ears everywhere."

With that, we continued through the alley, ducking into a dimly lit coffee shop. The place was nearly empty, save for a few patrons huddled in the corner, their conversations hushed as if they were part of some clandestine meeting. The aroma of freshly brewed coffee hung in the air, a comforting contrast to the chaos outside.

Caden led me to a corner table, the shadows offering a semblance of privacy. I sat, adrenaline still coursing through my veins as he paced back and forth, the tension palpable.

"Okay," he began, his voice lowered, the weight of his words heavy. "I'm part of a network. A group involved in things that..." He hesitated, searching for the right words. "Things that aren't legal. I got pulled into it a few years ago, and it's been a fight ever since to keep you away from it."

"Why didn't you tell me?" I pressed, the hurt spilling out. "I would have understood more than you think."

"Because I didn't want you to see me as anything but the man you fell in love with. I didn't want you to think of me as a criminal," he admitted, the vulnerability in his eyes almost breaking me.

"Caden, love is messy. It's not black and white," I said softly, the warmth of honesty pushing through the tension. "I wanted to know you, all of you. This... whatever this is between us, it deserves honesty."

He stopped pacing and looked at me, his expression shifting from anger to contemplation. "You're right. But knowing this puts you at risk. People are watching. If they think you're a threat..."

"What are they going to do?" I challenged, my voice steady despite the tremors of fear. "You think I'm just going to let you deal with this alone? No way. Whatever it is, I can handle it. We can handle it. Together."

The resolve in my voice seemed to reach him. For a moment, the storm outside mirrored the tumult within us, and in that quiet chaos, I could see the cracks in his facade beginning to splinter. "There are people out there who won't hesitate to hurt you just to get to me," he warned, his voice a low growl.

"Then we'll find a way to fight back," I said, my heart pounding with determination. "We'll find a way to keep each other safe, but I need you to trust me. And I need you to tell me everything."

He hesitated, but the steel in my gaze must have ignited something in him. He sat down across from me, the storm outside seeming to quiet for just a moment, the world narrowing down to the two of us in that dim coffee shop.

"Okay," he said, and I could see the burden on his shoulders shifting, a weight shared between us. "It started with a deal gone wrong. I thought I could play both sides—help people while staying out of trouble. But trouble found me. I became entangled with a group that doesn't play fair, and now..." He paused, swallowing hard. "Now they want their debts paid. And I don't know how far they'll go to collect."

The air between us crackled with intensity, and I felt the gravity of his words pulling me into a reality I had never expected. My heart raced not just with fear but with the adrenaline of the unknown. The storm outside raged on, but inside, amid the chaos, I felt a flicker of hope. If we were in this together, we could face whatever lay ahead.

And in that small, quiet corner of the world, the storm was just beginning.

The coffee shop felt like a refuge against the chaos outside, but I knew it was only a temporary reprieve. Caden's eyes held a storm of their own, swirling with emotion as he shared the depths of his secrets. The more he revealed, the more I felt the ground shift beneath me, as if I were standing on a fault line that could erupt at any moment.

"Who are these people, Caden?" I pressed, leaning forward, my voice a mixture of urgency and concern. "What exactly do they want from you?"

His gaze drifted to the window, watching the rain cascade down in a furious rhythm, as if it were trying to wash away our conversation. "They want the money I owe," he said, his voice laced with a quiet resignation. "But it's not just that. I've crossed some dangerous lines, and now they want more than just cash. They want power, control—and they'll stop at nothing to get it."

A chill swept through me, sharp and cold as the rain tapping against the glass. "Control? You mean... they're going to come after us?"

Caden turned back to me, his expression a mix of determination and regret. "They won't just come after me. They'll come after anyone I care about. That includes you."

"So, what's the plan?" I asked, trying to keep the rising panic at bay. "Are we going to hide in a bunker somewhere and live like hermits until they get bored? Because that sounds like a blast."

A faint smile flickered on his lips, but it quickly faded. "If only it were that simple. I have a contact, someone who can help us navigate this mess. But it's risky, and I don't want to put you in any more danger."

"Caden, I'm already in it," I insisted, my frustration boiling over. "You're not getting rid of me that easily. If we're going to face this together, then we need a plan. I'm not just going to sit here waiting for trouble to find us."

He ran a hand over his face, as if trying to wipe away the tension. "You're stubborn, you know that?"

"Stubbornness is my middle name," I shot back, allowing a wry smile to crack through the tension. "Just think of it as my superpower. Now, what's the next step?"

"First, we need to lay low for a while. Let the storm pass—figuratively and literally," he replied, glancing outside where the rain showed no signs of letting up. "Then we can reach out to my contact, but it won't be easy. I trust him, but there's always a risk involved."

"Great," I said, crossing my arms. "Risk. My favorite."

Caden chuckled softly, a sound that was both comforting and tense. "Okay, let's say we get in touch with him. He'll want to meet somewhere discreet. Somewhere we won't attract attention."

"Discreet," I repeated, letting the word roll off my tongue. "You mean like an abandoned warehouse? Because that seems like a prime spot for a horror movie."

He shot me a look, eyebrows raised. "You watch too many thrillers."

"Can you blame me? They always have better plot twists than my life," I replied, leaning back in my seat. "So, what's the game plan? We're just going to walk into a lion's den and hope they're in a good mood?"

"Something like that." His tone turned serious again, the weight of his reality returning to the surface. "I'll handle the conversation. You just need to stay alert and watch my back."

I nodded, the gravity of the situation sinking in. "I'm not afraid of getting my hands dirty. Just promise me you'll keep me in the loop."

"I promise," he said, his eyes locking onto mine, holding a depth of sincerity that gave me a flicker of hope amid the encroaching darkness.

The moment hung between us, charged with unspoken feelings, a fragile thread connecting our hearts amid the storm. But the tranquility was short-lived. A sudden commotion outside shattered the moment, breaking the spell as figures cloaked in shadows darted past the windows, their hurried movements hinting at something ominous.

"Caden?" I whispered, my heart pounding in my chest as I leaned closer to him.

He was already on his feet, his eyes narrowed, scanning the scene outside. "Stay here," he instructed, his voice low and tense.

I shook my head, my instincts screaming at me to stick close. "I'm not just going to sit here while you go investigate."

"Please," he urged, glancing back at me, the raw urgency in his voice making my stomach churn. "If they've found us—"

"Then I'll be right beside you. I won't let you face this alone."

There was a moment of hesitation, then Caden nodded, his expression softened by a flicker of gratitude. We moved toward the door, the rain continuing to hammer down outside as if the heavens were trying to drown the world below.

Stepping outside, we were immediately enveloped by the storm, the rain splashing against us in a relentless embrace. Caden pulled me close, his arm wrapped protectively around my waist as we navigated through the slick streets.

"What do you see?" I asked, straining my eyes to pierce through the darkness.

"There," he said, pointing to a shadowy figure slipping into an alleyway across the street. "We need to follow them, but quietly."

My heart raced as we moved, careful to keep our footsteps light against the soaked pavement. The figure ahead ducked further into the shadows, and my breath caught in my throat. Who were they? Were they friends or foes? My mind spun with possibilities, the adrenaline sharpening my senses.

As we turned the corner into the alley, I felt the weight of the world pressing down on me, a tangible fear mixed with an undeniable thrill. Caden and I exchanged a glance, an unspoken agreement passing between us—we were in this together, no matter where it led.

Suddenly, the figure stopped, turning abruptly to face us, the dim light barely illuminating their features. My breath caught as I recognized the unmistakable outline of someone I never expected to see.

"Caden?" the figure called, their voice thick with tension. "You shouldn't have come here."

My heart plummeted. This was not just a simple encounter; it felt like stepping into a minefield. With the storm still raging above and danger lurking just ahead, I could feel the ground shifting beneath us once more, and the sense that everything was about to change echoed like thunder through my veins.

Chapter 25: The Chase

The rain drummed relentlessly against the car roof, a frantic symphony that matched the racing pulse in my chest. I glanced over at Caden, his jaw set with determination, dark hair clinging to his forehead like he was in the middle of a storm of his own. The dashboard lights flickered, casting shadows that danced on his features, making him appear both heroic and haunted. It was disorienting, this duality of safety and peril, like being in a dream where the landscape morphed with each blink.

"Do you think we lost them?" I asked, my voice barely rising above the roar of the rain. It felt almost comical, the way the words hung in the humid air, heavy with doubt.

Caden's eyes darted to the rearview mirror. "I don't know, but we can't stop now. Not yet." His voice was steady, but there was an edge to it that told me he was just as nervous as I was.

The road snaked through dense woods, branches clawing at the sides of the car as if they were trying to pull us back into whatever nightmare we were escaping. I leaned my head against the cool glass, watching the blurry streaks of streetlights and trees pass by, feeling disconnected from the reality I once knew. The city, vibrant and chaotic, felt like a distant memory now, swallowed by the shadows of uncertainty.

We pulled into a small town nestled along the banks of the Hudson River. The flickering neon sign of a diner caught my eye, a beacon in the darkness that promised warmth and the possibility of a slice of normalcy, however fleeting. Caden parked the car behind the motel, a nondescript building that had seen better days, the paint peeling like forgotten dreams.

"Let's grab a bite," he suggested, his tone deceptively casual as if we were merely on a late-night adventure instead of fleeing for our lives.

I followed him, the rain finally easing to a soft drizzle that hung in the air like a promise. The diner was cozy, lit with a low glow that felt like a hug, and the scent of bacon and fresh coffee wafted through the air, inviting and strangely nostalgic. I settled into a booth while Caden ordered us two plates of fries and a couple of milkshakes.

"Your idea of a healthy dinner?" I teased, raising an eyebrow as he slid in across from me.

He chuckled, a warm sound that momentarily eased the tension. "What can I say? I'm a sucker for nostalgia. Besides, we need our strength."

As we dug into the food, I tried to push aside the weight of our reality. We shared half-hearted jokes, the kind that didn't quite reach our eyes, but I savored each moment. In the back of my mind, though, the knowledge that danger loomed just outside these walls gnawed at me.

Caden leaned forward, his expression shifting as he scanned the diner. "We need to be careful. If they find us here, it'll be all over."

I nodded, my appetite waning. "Do you think they're close?"

"Too close," he said, his voice low. "But let's not think about that right now. Focus on the fries."

I couldn't help but smile at his attempt to lighten the mood. We ate in relative silence, the clattering of dishes and murmurs of conversation filling the spaces between us. Outside, the rain resumed its drumming, a backdrop to our secret world.

A sudden crash of thunder rattled the windows, and my heart leaped into my throat. Caden's eyes snapped to the entrance, and I followed his gaze. A figure stood silhouetted against the dim light, shaking off raindrops like a wet dog. My stomach twisted as recognition hit me.

"Caden," I whispered, fear seeping into my words. "It's him."

Caden's body tensed, and for a heartbeat, the world fell silent. The man from the shadows—tall, with slicked-back hair and an air of menace—strolled in as if he owned the place. He scanned the room with unsettling calm, his gaze landing on us with unnerving precision.

"We need to go," Caden said, already sliding out of the booth.

I followed, my heart racing as I took one last look at the man, who now grinned like a predator spotting its prey. "What do we do?"

"Out the back," he instructed, his grip firm on my wrist as he guided me through the kitchen, the scent of grease and onions swirling around us.

I barely registered the clattering pots and the startled looks of the staff as we rushed past. We burst through the back door into the alley, rain drenching us instantly. The darkness felt thicker here, the kind that clung to your skin like a bad memory.

Caden looked around, scanning for any sign of escape. "This way!" He pulled me toward a narrow gap between two buildings, the space barely wide enough for us to slip through.

We squeezed into the shadows, my heart pounding in my chest as we pressed against the damp brick wall, the rain mixing with my unease. Caden's breath came in quick bursts, mirroring my own, and I could feel the tension radiating from him.

"Why did he come here?" I whispered, glancing back toward the diner.

"He must've tracked us," Caden said through gritted teeth. "He knows we're here. We're not safe until we get out of this town."

A sudden noise behind us—a splash, then footsteps. My stomach dropped. "Caden..."

"I know," he replied, voice tight. "Run!"

And just like that, we were off, racing through the rain-soaked alleyways, the cold biting at our skin as we sprinted toward an uncertain future. The world blurred around me, each step pounding a rhythm of fear and adrenaline in my veins. In that moment, all that mattered was the chase—the flight from shadows that seemed to grow longer with every heartbeat.

The rain continued to pour, but it felt like a different kind of pressure now, washing away the chaos of the city but also weighing heavily on my shoulders. Caden and I squeezed through the narrow alley, dodging puddles that splashed up like miniature geysers, the sound of our hurried footsteps swallowed by the rhythmic drumming of the storm. Each heartbeat echoed like a warning bell in my ears, a reminder of the danger lurking behind us.

"Turn left here!" Caden commanded, his voice barely above the patter of raindrops, urgency lacing his words. I nodded, my mind racing as we darted into another narrow passageway. My senses heightened; every shadow seemed to writhe with life, and every gust of wind carried with it a whisper of threat.

We emerged onto a small street lined with old brick buildings, their windows dark and uninviting. Caden glanced over his shoulder, scanning for pursuers, then fixed his gaze ahead, determination etched into his features. "There's an old boathouse down by the river. We can hide there until things calm down."

"Right," I said, though the idea of hiding made my skin crawl. The walls felt like they were closing in around me, and the weight of uncertainty was suffocating. "You really think they won't find us?"

"Trust me," he replied, his voice steady, but I caught a flicker of doubt in his eyes. "It's secluded, and we'll be able to see them coming."

We sprinted towards the river, the sound of the water crashing against the rocky banks blending with the relentless rain. The boathouse loomed in front of us, a skeletal structure with peeling paint and broken windows. It looked like something out of a horror movie, yet it was the best option we had.

"Home sweet home," I murmured, trying to inject some humor into the situation, though it felt forced.

Caden pushed the door open, the hinges groaning like an old man who hadn't seen action in years. Inside, the air was damp and musty, the scent of mildew mingling with the faint tang of the river. Caden led the way, shining his phone's flashlight across the dusty floorboards and cobwebs clinging to the rafters.

"Cozy," he said, smirking, and I couldn't help but chuckle. His attempts to lighten the mood were admirable, if futile.

As we settled into a corner, the sound of the rain became a comforting blanket, lulling my racing thoughts. I sank down onto a splintered bench, pulling my knees to my chest. "So, what now? We just wait?"

"Yeah, I'll keep watch." He leaned against the wall, his body tense as if he could feel the weight of every passing second.

The minutes stretched into what felt like hours. I tried to distract myself by thinking about the absurdity of our situation: hiding out in a boathouse while the world outside raged on. It was surreal, as if I were trapped in a movie plot designed by someone who'd read too many thrillers.

"Hey," Caden broke through my thoughts, his voice low, "I know this isn't ideal, but we'll figure it out. We always do."

I offered him a small smile, grateful for his optimism. "You say that like you've got a secret stash of plans up your sleeve."

"Maybe I do," he teased, his eyes sparkling in the dim light. "I've been holding out on you. I've got a whole folder labeled 'Escape Routes: 101.'"

I rolled my eyes, a laugh bubbling up. "Oh, great. Next, you'll tell me you're a former spy or something."

"Actually," he leaned closer, whispering dramatically, "I'm a former barista with a knack for latte art. My cover's blown."

We both laughed, the tension between us easing for just a moment. But that moment was fleeting, shattered by a sudden noise from outside—a branch snapping, perhaps, or a soft footfall. Caden's laughter died, his expression morphing into focus.

"Did you hear that?" he asked, his voice tense.

I nodded, straining to listen. The sound of the rain was louder now, but beneath it, something else crept into my consciousness—a rustle, perhaps, or a low murmur that sent chills down my spine.

"Maybe it's just the wind," I suggested, though I knew my voice lacked conviction.

Caden moved cautiously toward the door, peering out into the downpour. "I don't think so."

His eyes narrowed, and I could see the gears turning in his mind. "We need to stay quiet. If they're nearby, we can't give them any reason to suspect we're here."

I held my breath, my heart thudding like a drum in the silence that followed. Every instinct screamed at me to run, to hide, but I remained frozen, my eyes locked on Caden. His profile was sharp against the darkness, the phone light casting a halo around him, and I felt an overwhelming surge of gratitude for having him by my side.

Moments stretched on, each second heavy with uncertainty. Finally, Caden stepped back, his jaw clenched. "It was nothing. Just my imagination," he said, but the way his hands trembled betrayed him.

"Your imagination is scary," I replied, trying to lighten the mood again, but the smile fell away when I heard it—the unmistakable sound of tires crunching on gravel.

Caden's eyes widened, and I felt my stomach drop. "They're here," he whispered, panic flickering across his face.

"Can we get out the back?"

He nodded, and we made our way to a rickety door that led to a narrow path alongside the river. It would be risky, but staying put felt like a death sentence. As we slipped outside, the rain intensified, drenching us instantly, but I didn't care. I needed to put distance between us and whatever was coming.

We pressed ourselves against the side of the boathouse, breathless and listening. The sound of footsteps grew louder, and my heart raced. Just as we thought we might escape unnoticed, a voice cut through the storm, low and menacing.

"Caden! We know you're in there!"

I exchanged a glance with him, fear coursing through me like ice. Caden's grip tightened on my arm, his eyes narrowing in determination.

"We have to move," he said urgently.

With one last glance at the boathouse, we dashed down the muddy path, the rain blurring the world around us as we ran deeper into the unknown, the weight of our pursuers hot on our heels.

The rain was relentless, a curtain of water that obscured the world around us as we sprinted down the muddy path. Caden and I stumbled through the darkness, adrenaline coursing through our veins like wildfire. Every step felt like a gamble, each moment weighed down by the fear that we were just inches away from capture.

"Which way?" I panted, my breath coming in quick bursts, my heart racing like a runaway train.

Caden stopped for a moment, scanning our surroundings with the intensity of a hawk. "This way!" He veered to the left, pushing us into the underbrush that flanked the path. The branches whipped against my face, sharp as memories I wished I could forget. The ground was slippery, and I cursed under my breath as I stumbled, trying to keep up with him.

"Great hideout you picked," I quipped, forcing a grin despite the fear swirling in my gut. "Next time, maybe a hotel with less of a horror movie vibe?"

"Less sass, more running," he shot back, his tone playful, yet underlined with urgency.

We ducked beneath a thick canopy of leaves, the rain dampening our clothes and our spirits. The sound of footsteps on gravel echoed behind us, accompanied by voices that sent chills down my spine. They were getting closer.

"Caden!" I whispered urgently. "What if they split up?"

He shot me a look that could only be described as both exasperated and amused. "If they split up, it'll only make things more complicated. Stick together."

Just as he said it, a shout rang out, a harsh command slicing through the air. "They can't have gone far! Search the area!"

My stomach twisted in knots. "They're right on our tails!"

"Keep moving." His grip tightened around my wrist, leading me deeper into the thicket. The trees loomed like sentinels, shadows dancing eerily in the flickering light of distant flashlights. It was a race against time, and the stakes had never been higher.

As we pressed on, I could hear my heartbeat pounding in my ears, drowning out everything else. We dodged branches and weeds, slipping through the underbrush, our focus singular: escape.

"Caden, do you have any idea where we're going?" I asked, trying to peer into the darkness ahead, but the rain-soaked foliage blurred my vision.

"Not exactly," he admitted, his voice low and gravelly, but the hint of a smile tugged at his lips. "But it's an adventure, right? Just like we planned."

"Adventure? This isn't what I had in mind when I signed up for a quiet getaway." I managed to breathe out a laugh, even as my heart raced.

He paused, pulling me behind a tree trunk as the footsteps grew louder. "Shh! We need to be quiet. Let them pass."

We pressed ourselves into the damp earth, our bodies huddled together for warmth and security. The rain dripped from the leaves above, a rhythm that felt almost soothing, but the tension in my chest made it hard to relax. I could hear their voices now, clear and sharp.

"I swear they came this way!" one of the men said, frustration tinging his words.

"Check that path by the water. They might be trying to double back!" another shouted, and my breath hitched in my throat.

Caden's fingers tightened around my arm, his eyes wide as we waited, the darkness wrapping around us like a cocoon. The voices began to fade, but my heart was still in my throat, pounding like a drum.

After what felt like an eternity, Caden finally breathed out a sigh of relief. "I think they're gone."

"Or just regrouping," I said, trying to keep my voice steady.

"Let's move, then." He glanced around, searching for a way out. "We can't stay here."

We crept through the trees, the rain finally easing to a soft drizzle. I spotted a clearing up ahead, and Caden followed my gaze. "That might lead us to the river. We can use the current to our advantage."

"Great, but are you sure that's safe?"

"Safer than staying here."

We slipped into the clearing, the ground muddy and slick beneath our feet. The rain had turned the earth into a quagmire, but we pressed on, driven by the need to escape. The river roared nearby, a promise of freedom that felt tantalizingly close.

Just as we reached the water's edge, the sound of footsteps returned, louder this time. My heart sank. "Caden!"

"We need to go now!" He grabbed my hand, pulling me toward the riverbank. "Jump!"

Without thinking, we leapt into the frigid water, the shock of cold stealing my breath away. The current was stronger than I anticipated, pulling us downstream. Caden's grip was ironclad as we fought against the current, our bodies entwined as we fought to stay afloat.

"Hold on!" he shouted over the rushing water, his voice fierce and unwavering.

I nodded, my mind racing. The chaos around us blurred, but Caden was a steady presence, his determination like a beacon in the storm. "We can do this!"

The water tumbled around us, wild and unpredictable. I gasped as a wave crashed over my head, but Caden was right there, pulling me back to the surface.

"We've got to swim for that bend!" He pointed ahead, where the river curved and the trees offered a glimpse of refuge.

I kicked hard, the cold water numbing my limbs but igniting a fire of resolve in my chest. We fought the current together, driven by desperation and the will to survive.

With every stroke, I could feel the distance between us and our pursuers widening, yet the darkness that had chased us still loomed ominously at the edges of my mind. As we reached the bend, I could see the branches stretching out like welcoming arms.

"Just a little further!" Caden urged, his eyes fixed on our goal.

But just as we neared the bank, I heard the unmistakable sound of shouting from behind us. The voices pierced through the chaos, a reminder that we weren't free yet.

"Caden!" I gasped, panic rising in my throat. "They're still coming!"

"Keep swimming!" He urged, his grip on my arm firm.

We broke the surface, gasping for breath, and I fought against the current with every ounce of strength I had left. But just as we reached the shore, a flash of light illuminated the dark river, and I turned to see silhouettes emerging from the treeline, flashlights sweeping the area like searchlights in the night.

"Get down!" Caden hissed, pulling me close.

We ducked beneath the branches, hearts pounding as the voices grew louder, the threat of discovery hanging thick in the air. The rain softened to a gentle patter, but the sense of impending doom loomed larger than ever.

"I can't keep hiding like this," I whispered, fear twisting in my gut. "What if they find us?"

Caden's eyes met mine, a fierce determination burning in their depths. "Then we fight. We can't let them take us."

Just as the words left his lips, a flashlight beam swept across the bank, landing directly on us. My heart stopped, the light blinding and relentless, as the voice rang out once more. "There they are!"

A chill coursed through me as the realization hit. This was it. The chase was ending, but the outcome was uncertain. As the shadows closed in, the weight of our choices pressed down on us, and I held my breath, waiting for whatever came next.

Chapter 26: The Offer

The air in the dimly lit café was thick with the scent of freshly ground coffee and warm pastries, a comforting disguise for the tension that hung between Victor and me. I stirred my latte absentmindedly, the foam swirling like my thoughts—chaotic, unsure, caught between sweet comfort and bitter reality. Outside, the world bustled with the kind of ordinary chaos that felt utterly alien to me. People moved with purpose, oblivious to the tempest raging just beneath my skin.

Victor sat across from me, an immovable figure in a tailored suit that hugged his shoulders just right. He exuded confidence, his presence like a silent storm threatening to uproot everything I thought I knew. His smile was disarming, almost charming, but I had learned the hard way that charm could mask darker intentions. I glanced at the man who had become my captor, my tormentor, and yet, in some twisted way, he also held a piece of the key to my liberation.

"So, here we are," he began, his voice smooth as silk, yet edged with an undeniable authority. "You, caught in a web of choices. Me, offering a way out." He leaned forward, his eyes glinting with an intensity that made my skin prickle. "All you have to do is help me."

A lump formed in my throat, the enormity of his proposition pressing down like the weight of a thousand unsaid words. Betray Caden? The very idea felt like swallowing glass. Caden had become my refuge in a storm, a spark of light in the darkness that had threatened to consume me. I still remembered the first time we had met—his laughter, deep and rich, cutting through my despair like a warm summer breeze. It had been the beginning of something beautiful, something real, and now I was being asked to shatter it all.

"Caden is... complicated," I managed to say, my voice barely above a whisper. "He's not what you think." My heart raced, knowing I was grasping at straws to defend him.

Victor's lips curved into a smile that didn't reach his eyes. "Ah, but that's just it, isn't it? We all wear masks, darling. Yours just happens to be the most colorful of them all." He leaned back, surveying me with an expression that felt like a predator sizing up its prey. "And I'm offering you a chance to take it off, to shed those chains. Imagine it, Ella—a life free from fear, free from Caden's secrets."

The words tugged at something deep within me, a yearning for freedom I hadn't allowed myself to feel in far too long. The promise of liberation glimmered like a mirage in the desert, tempting and tantalizing, yet I knew better than to chase after illusions. "What's in it for you, Victor?" I asked, forcing myself to meet his gaze. "You're not known for your altruism."

He chuckled, a low, rich sound that rumbled through the air between us. "Touché. I'll admit, my motivations aren't purely philanthropic. But think of it as... an investment. Once Caden is out of the picture, I can take control of the territory he's been so careless with. It's a win-win, really. You walk away clean, and I get what I want."

His words slithered into my mind, wrapping around my conscience like a snake coiling around its prey. I could feel the pulse of my heartbeat echoing in my ears as I weighed my options. Freedom. That word was a siren song, pulling me closer to its rocky shore. But what did it mean to be free if I had to betray the one person who had seen the real me beneath all the chaos?

I shifted in my seat, my hands shaking slightly as I grasped my cup, desperately needing something solid to ground me. "And if I refuse?" I asked, my voice steadier than I felt.

Victor's expression hardened, the charming facade peeling away to reveal a steely resolve. "Then you remain in the same cage you've been in. Caden will continue to drag you through this mess, and I can assure you that it won't end well for either of you. You may think you love him, but in this world, love can be a liability."

His words pierced through the fog of my thoughts, and I struggled to catch my breath. I had never been a person to shy away from danger, but this felt different. This was not just about my safety; it was about the man who had captured my heart and the choices that would shape our fates.

"Caden might be hiding things, but he's not a monster, Victor. He's trying to protect me in his own twisted way," I countered, desperation creeping into my tone. "You think I don't see the good in him? I see it every day."

Victor's laughter was sharp, cutting through the air like a knife. "Protect you? From what? The truth? The life he's led? You're naïve if you believe he's capable of genuine protection. He's a part of a world filled with shadows and lies. You deserve better than that."

"Deserve better?" I echoed, my voice rising as frustration bubbled to the surface. "What do you know about what I deserve? You've spent years building your empire on the backs of people like Caden and me. You're the last person to lecture me on worthiness."

For a moment, silence enveloped us, thick with tension. I could feel the weight of our confrontation, a crackling energy in the air that had the potential to ignite. Victor's expression shifted, a flicker of something unreadable crossing his face. "You're fierce, I'll give you that," he admitted, the challenge in his tone almost begrudgingly admiring. "But fierceness won't save you from the consequences of your choices."

His words hung heavy in the air, a stark reminder of the ticking clock counting down the moments until I would have to make my decision. The café's ambiance faded into a blur, the laughter and chatter of patrons a distant echo as I grappled with the reality before me. In that moment, I knew I stood on a precipice, teetering between the life I had dreamed of and the treacherous depths of betrayal.

The silence stretched between us, an invisible thread laced with tension, fraying with every second I remained indecisive. Victor leaned back in his chair, studying me with an unnerving calm, as if he were waiting for a flower to bloom. "You're thinking too hard about this," he finally said, the hint of amusement dancing in his eyes. "Just imagine the possibilities if you took this leap. Freedom, Ella. The world at your feet."

His words were like honey dripping off a spoon—sweet and tempting but ultimately sticky, binding me to a decision I wasn't ready to make. I felt my heart race as images flooded my mind: the laughter we shared, the stolen moments with Caden when the world faded away. How could I trade that for freedom that felt more like a noose?

"Freedom to do what, exactly? To run away?" I countered, my voice steadying with the strength of my convictions. "To live in fear of what you might ask me to do next? That's not freedom. That's just another cage dressed up in shiny promises."

Victor's eyes narrowed slightly, a flash of irritation crossing his face before his composure returned. "You misunderstand, Ella. I'm offering you a way to break free from the chaos that's consuming you. Caden is a threat. To you, to everyone around him. You're just too blinded by your feelings to see it."

"Or maybe you're just too blinded by your ambition," I shot back, the words tumbling out before I could stop myself. "You think this is about what's best for me? This is all about you and your little power play. What happens when you've used me? Will I just disappear, like all the others?"

For a heartbeat, the air crackled with an electric tension as Victor's mask slipped for a fraction of a second. I saw a flicker of something vulnerable beneath his carefully curated exterior, a glimpse of a man not entirely convinced of his own grand vision. But then it was gone, replaced by the calculating gaze I had come to expect.

"Don't be naïve," he said, his tone clipped. "I won't harm you. You'll be free to live your life—just not with Caden." The finality in his voice sent a shiver down my spine, a reminder of the stakes at play.

The café around us buzzed with life, laughter echoing, clinking of cups, the hiss of steam from the espresso machine, yet I felt like I was in a soundproof bubble, a universe all my own, a conflict swirling at its core. I could feel the eyes of the barista, a young woman with a warm smile, glancing our way, as if sensing the undercurrent of tension. I tried to focus on her, on the scent of pastries wafting through the air, but my heart was a trapped bird, fluttering desperately against the bars of my conscience.

"Just think of it as a simple business transaction," Victor pressed, leaning forward, his elbows resting on the table. "You give me what I need, and I ensure you're taken care of. A simple trade. But if you refuse..." He let the words hang ominously, a chilling threat wrapped in silky undertones. "The consequences won't just affect you. You've already seen how far I'm willing to go."

I could almost hear my heart splintering at the thought of it. Caden's laughter echoed in my mind, the way he held me as if I were the most precious thing in the world. I was willing to fight for that, but could I face him with the weight of betrayal on my shoulders?

"What if I told you I'd rather face the storm than betray someone I love?" I said, the challenge bold in my tone, surprising even myself.

Victor's eyes flashed, something between admiration and irritation stirring within them. "Then you're choosing to drown."

"No, I'm choosing to swim," I retorted, my determination igniting a fire I hadn't realized had dimmed. "Drowning would mean giving in to fear. I refuse to let you dictate my choices."

His smile returned, but it felt more like a mask than before, brittle and thin. "You're stronger than I gave you credit for, Ella. But strength can be a double-edged sword. What happens when Caden's secrets come to light? What happens when the truth—your truth—exposes you both to danger?"

There was a moment of silence, the gravity of his words hanging heavy. I thought of Caden's guarded glances, the whispers of the past that he had tried to keep at bay. He was hiding something, and I knew it, but my love for him held me back from digging too deep. "Whatever it is, I'll face it with him. Together," I replied, my voice firmer than I felt.

Victor's gaze shifted, a flicker of something dark dancing across his features. "Together, huh? You think that will save you? It won't. You need to understand, Caden's world isn't meant for someone like you. You could get hurt, and I don't want that for you."

My resolve wavered, just a bit. The images of danger had a way of creeping in—sharp, unsettling, reminding me of the stakes. But then I thought of Caden, how he'd fought for me, how he'd embraced the chaos of his life while pulling me into the safety of his arms. I couldn't let Victor's threats shape my decisions.

"If you really cared, you'd leave me out of this," I said, forcing myself to meet his gaze. "You'd stop trying to manipulate me."

The silence that followed was thick with unspoken words, tension crackling like a live wire between us. Victor finally leaned back, crossing his arms, his expression unreadable. "You're a force, Ella. I admire that. But forces can be redirected. Don't underestimate what I'm capable of. You think this is just about you and Caden? It's so much bigger than that."

"Then make it bigger without me," I said, standing my ground. "I'm not your pawn."

His lips curled into a smile that didn't quite reach his eyes. "Very well. But remember, the world doesn't bend to your whims, darling. When the time comes—and it will—you'll wish you'd taken my offer."

With that, he pushed back his chair, the scrape against the floor jolting me from my thoughts. He rose, tall and imposing, a shadow stretching over the sunlight that filtered through the café windows. I watched him walk away, my heart a jumble of emotions—fear, anger, determination—but beneath it all, an undeniable spark of resolve flickered to life.

I wouldn't let him dictate my choices. Not now, not ever. As the café continued its mundane rhythms around me, I knew one thing for certain: the path ahead would be fraught with challenges, but I was ready to navigate it. I was stronger than I had realized, and I would fight for Caden, for us, no matter the cost.

The world outside the café seemed distant, a whirl of vibrant colors and muted sounds fading into the background as I wrestled with the storm inside me. I could feel the heat of Victor's departure lingering in the air, the scent of his expensive cologne mingling with the coffee's rich aroma. My heart raced, adrenaline coursing through me like a shot of espresso, and the cacophony of the café faded into a gentle hum.

I took a deep breath, trying to reclaim the pieces of my scattered resolve. Caden's face flashed in my mind, the warmth of his smile a stark contrast to the chill Victor had left in his wake. Was I really willing to risk everything for the promise of freedom? The thought sent my mind spiraling down a path of uncertainty. I reached for my phone, the device warm in my palm, and my fingers danced over the screen as I considered texting Caden. But what could I say? "Hey, I'm meeting with the devil's advocate and might have to turn you in"? No, that wouldn't do at all.

A movement caught my eye. At a table near the window, an older couple sat huddled over steaming mugs, their faces lit by the soft glow of the afternoon sun. Their laughter bubbled into the air, light and genuine, an easy reminder that love could be simple, uncomplicated. I envied them. In their world, choices were mundane, like which pastry to share or which park bench to sit on. My choices felt like navigating a labyrinth filled with pitfalls and monsters lurking just out of sight.

"Hey, Earth to Ella." A voice broke through my reverie, pulling me back to reality. I glanced up to find Sarah, my best friend, standing before me, hands on her hips, her curly hair bouncing as she leaned forward with an inquisitive expression. "You look like you've just seen a ghost. Or worse, like you've made a deal with one."

I managed a weak smile, grateful for her presence, but the weight of my thoughts pressed down heavily. "You might be closer to the truth than you know," I replied, gesturing for her to sit. "Victor was just here, and let's just say his offer was anything but benign."

Her brows knitted together as she perched on the edge of the seat, concern etched on her face. "What did he want this time? More threats? Or did he finally get bored of his own game?"

"Actually, it's worse than that. He wants me to betray Caden," I confessed, the words spilling out before I could filter them. "He thinks Caden is a threat, and he's trying to convince me that he's the only one who can save me."

"Ugh, I can't believe this guy," Sarah huffed, rolling her eyes. "Why does he think he gets to make your choices for you? You're not some pawn in his twisted game."

"I know," I replied, feeling the warmth of her support seep into my veins, but the doubt still lingered. "But what if he's right? What if Caden's secrets put me in danger?"

"Secrets can be dangerous, but so can giving in to fear," she countered, crossing her arms. "What do you really want, Ella? Not what Victor wants or what Caden might want, but you. Do you want to walk away from everything you have with Caden?"

The question hung in the air, shimmering with clarity and complexity. My mind raced with the memories we had shared: quiet moments in the kitchen, stolen kisses in the dark, and his laughter echoing against the backdrop of my insecurities. I couldn't just toss that aside because Victor waved a shiny promise of freedom in front of me. "No. I don't want to walk away. I just don't know if I can trust him anymore," I murmured, my voice tinged with vulnerability.

Sarah's eyes softened, understanding radiating from her. "Trust is a tricky thing, especially when it's been tested. But you can't let someone else dictate your story. You have to write it yourself."

"Easier said than done," I replied, the bitterness creeping into my tone. "What if I don't have the strength to fight this battle? What if I fail?"

"Then you'll get back up and fight again. That's what you do," she said, her conviction igniting something deep within me. "You're not alone in this. I'm here, remember? You have more strength than you realize."

As her words sank in, I felt a flicker of hope. Maybe I didn't have to navigate this dark labyrinth alone. Maybe together we could shed light on the corners that Victor would rather keep hidden.

Just then, my phone buzzed on the table, breaking the moment. I reached for it, my heart leaping as I saw Caden's name flashing on the screen. "Speak of the devil," I muttered, swiping the screen to answer.

"Ella?" His voice came through, low and laced with concern. "I've been trying to reach you. Is everything okay? You sound... off."

"I'm fine," I replied, forcing a cheerfulness I didn't quite feel. "Just at the café with Sarah."

"Good, good. I was just checking in. Can we meet? I need to talk to you about some things."

My heart raced at the urgency in his voice, the weight of unspoken words clinging to every syllable. "Sure, of course. When?"

"Now. Can you meet me at the park?"

The park. It had always been our place—lush, alive with color and the sound of laughter, a sanctuary amidst the chaos. But my stomach twisted with unease. "Okay, I'll be there soon," I said, already feeling the need to calm the rising tide of anxiety.

"I'll explain everything, I promise," he added, his tone softer. "I just need you to trust me."

Trust. The word danced on the tip of my tongue, as fragile as a butterfly's wings. But there was something in his voice, a depth of emotion that tugged at my heartstrings, making me want to believe him, despite everything.

"I'll try," I whispered, knowing the weight of that promise could shatter under the pressure of secrets and betrayals.

After I hung up, I looked at Sarah, who was watching me with an intensity that made my pulse quicken. "What is it?" I asked, feeling exposed under her gaze.

"Ella, be careful. If Victor is involved, you need to tread lightly. You don't know what he's capable of, and neither does Caden. Trust your instincts," she advised, her voice steady yet laced with urgency.

"Trust my instincts," I echoed, the phrase rolling over my tongue like a soothing balm. But could I trust them when they were so deeply entwined with love, fear, and uncertainty?

As I stood to leave, the weight of Sarah's gaze felt like armor, bolstering my resolve. I took a deep breath, summoning my courage, and stepped out into the bustling world beyond. The sun was shining, the sky a brilliant blue, but an undercurrent of darkness lingered, as if the universe itself was holding its breath.

As I made my way to the park, my mind swirled with questions, the echoes of Victor's warning still fresh in my thoughts. What would Caden reveal? Would it change everything? A sense of dread knotted in my stomach, yet a spark of defiance flickered to life within me. I wouldn't let fear control my choices.

Arriving at the park, I spotted Caden under the sprawling oak tree, his silhouette sharp against the vibrant backdrop of green. He turned as I approached, and the moment our eyes met, something shifted in the air, a current of emotion that tied us together even from a distance.

"Ella," he said, his voice tinged with relief. "I'm glad you're here."

But before I could respond, a sudden commotion erupted nearby, a cacophony of shouts and the screech of tires. My heart raced as a black SUV careened down the street, skidding to a halt mere feet from us. The door swung open, and out stepped a figure I hadn't expected to see—Victor, a predatory grin on his face, his eyes locked onto mine as he took a step forward.

"Looks like you found your little rendezvous," he called out, his voice dripping with mockery. "Mind if I join the conversation?"

My breath caught in my throat, and as panic coursed through me, I realized I had stepped right into a trap. The air thickened with tension, a sharpness that heralded chaos. I looked at Caden, his eyes wide with shock, and in that moment, I knew I had to make a choice. Would I stand and fight for the truth, or would I succumb to the shadows that loomed, threatening to consume everything I held dear?

Chapter 27: A Line Crossed

The sun dipped low, casting a warm, golden glow that spilled through the tall windows of my cramped apartment, illuminating dust motes that danced like memories in the fading light. I leaned against the cool granite countertop, the sharp scent of coffee mixing with the bittersweet tang of impending decisions, a blend that was both familiar and unsettling. Caden stood just a few feet away, his silhouette framed by the light, and I could feel the gravity of his gaze, heavy and unyielding. It was as if the world had narrowed down to this moment, our breaths hanging in the air, suspended like unspoken words.

"Are you really going to do this?" he asked, his voice low but edged with an intensity that made my heart stutter. He crossed his arms, a shield against the turmoil swirling around us, but I knew it wouldn't be enough to keep the truth at bay.

"I don't have a choice, Caden." I turned away, not wanting him to see the fear in my eyes, the doubt that gnawed at my resolve like a ravenous beast. My fingers traced the rim of my coffee mug, grounding me in the moment, but even that small comfort felt like it was slipping away. "Victor needs this. He's been pushing for weeks."

"Victor?" The way Caden spat out his name made it sound like a curse. He pushed off the counter, his body tense and rigid. "You're willing to risk everything for him? For that man?"

I clenched my jaw, biting back the sharp retort that hovered on the edge of my tongue. How could I explain? How could I make him understand the convoluted threads that tied me to Victor, the tangled web of desperation and loyalty? I poured a fresh cup of coffee, letting the steam rise between us, a barrier that seemed to mock our escalating tension.

"I owe him, Caden. You know I do." The words slipped out, weighted with the history that lay between us, the shared burdens that had shaped my choices. "He saved me once. I can't just turn my back on him now."

"Saved you?" Caden's voice cracked with disbelief. "Is that what you call it? Trading your soul for a favor? I thought you were stronger than that." His disappointment sliced through me, sharper than the knife I'd been using to chop vegetables earlier. I set the mug down with a thud, steam curling up like whispers of the past.

"Stronger? Or just naïve?" I snapped, and the air crackled with our unspoken frustrations. "Maybe I'm just trying to survive in this mess of a life. Maybe we all have our lines, and I'm willing to cross mine if it means saving what's left of my sanity."

His silence felt like a physical blow, and I could see the internal struggle playing out on his face, each muscle tensing, then relaxing, as if he were fighting against some unseen tide. "You think this will make you feel better? That doing this for him will erase everything he's put you through?"

I turned away, unable to meet his piercing gaze, feeling the walls of my own resolve beginning to crumble. "I thought you'd understand. You're the one who always said we should take risks, that life is too short to live in fear."

"Taking risks is one thing, but throwing yourself to the wolves is another." His tone was softer now, a thread of concern weaving through the harshness. "What happens if Victor decides he's done with you once you've given him what he wants? What then?"

The question hung in the air, heavier than the mug I'd abandoned on the counter. I bit my lip, the taste of iron and uncertainty flooding my mouth. "I don't know," I admitted, my voice barely above a whisper. "But I have to try. I have to believe it will lead to something better."

He took a step closer, the warmth radiating off him pulling me in like a moth to a flame. "And what about us? What happens if you cross that line? What if there's no coming back?"

"Us?" The word felt foreign on my tongue, as if I were speaking a language I hadn't mastered. "Caden, this isn't just about us. It's bigger than that. It's about my life, my choices."

"And it's about your heart," he replied, his voice tinged with a fierce tenderness that ignited a spark of hope deep within me. "You're a fighter, but you're also human. You don't have to bear this weight alone."

In that moment, the world outside my apartment faded into a blur of colors and sounds, the reality of our lives constricted into this small space where everything hung in the balance. Caden reached out, his fingers brushing against my arm, a fleeting touch that sent shivers down my spine. "I can't lose you to this, whatever this is. Don't let Victor drag you into his darkness."

I could see the storm brewing in his eyes, a tempest of emotions crashing against the barriers he'd built to protect himself from my choices. But what he didn't understand was that I was already lost in the darkness, and this was my chance to find the light again, even if it meant navigating the treacherous waters of Victor's demands.

"I have to go," I finally said, the words spilling out like a confession. "I'll meet with him tonight. Just to hear him out, to see what he wants. That's all."

Caden's expression hardened, his mouth tightening into a thin line. "And if it's more than that?"

"Then I'll figure it out," I shot back, the defiance bubbling up inside me, a shield against the encroaching fear. "I promise."

But as I turned to leave, a flicker of doubt gnawed at the edges of my resolve, whispering that the line I was about to cross could alter everything—not just for me, but for Caden, for the fragile bond we'd built amid chaos. The weight of my decision felt heavier than any burden I'd ever shouldered, and I couldn't shake the feeling that, in seeking my freedom, I was stepping into a trap of my own making.

The sky darkened as I navigated the winding streets, the fluorescent glow of city lights illuminating the pavement in patches. Each step felt heavier, as if the weight of my decision had manifested into a physical force pulling me down. I wrapped my arms around myself, the crisp evening air biting at my skin, a stark contrast to the warmth I'd just left behind. The haunting memory of Caden's disappointment lingered in my mind, gnawing at the edges of my resolve like a persistent shadow.

My phone buzzed in my pocket, a small reprieve from the tension that coiled within me. I fished it out, seeing Victor's name flash across the screen. My pulse quickened. The conversation I was about to have with him felt like stepping onto a tightrope, the ground far below obscured by fog. I hit "accept," and his voice crackled to life, smooth and persuasive, like honey sliding down a throat that yearned for sweetness.

"Are you on your way?" he asked, the warmth of his tone wrapping around me, tempting me to believe that this was just a casual catch-up, nothing more than two friends meeting for a drink. But deep down, I knew better.

"I'm almost there," I replied, trying to keep my voice steady. "Just needed to clear my head a bit." I was aware that I was lying, a practiced deception that twisted the truth into something more palatable.

"Good. I'll order us a couple of drinks. You know I like the usual." He paused, the silence stretching between us like a chasm. "I really appreciate you coming. I promise, it's worth your time."

"Right." I hesitated, my stomach knotting in anticipation. "See you soon."

As I entered the dimly lit bar, the ambiance shifted around me, enveloping me in a cocoon of muted voices and clinking glasses. It was the kind of place where secrets lingered in the corners, and the air buzzed with unspoken promises. The rich scent of aged whiskey and the lingering hint of spiced rum filled my lungs, grounding me for just a moment before the gravity of my situation took hold again.

Victor sat at the far end of the bar, a lone figure draped in shadow, his sharp features illuminated by the soft glow of the overhead lights. He raised a hand in greeting, and I felt an involuntary shiver race down my spine. As I made my way to him, I could feel the weight of his presence pressing against me, a reminder of the tangled history we shared.

"Glad you could make it," he said, his voice low and smooth, like silk brushing against skin. He gestured to the empty stool beside him. "I was beginning to think you'd change your mind."

"Trust me, that thought crossed my mind." I slid onto the stool, and Victor chuckled, a sound that echoed with both charm and mischief. "But here I am. So what's so urgent that I needed to drop everything?"

He leaned closer, the scent of his cologne—a mix of cedar and something darker—filling the space between us. "I've got an opportunity for you. One that could change everything."

I narrowed my eyes, skepticism threading through my thoughts. "You know I'm not interested in anything illegal, Victor."

"Nothing illegal," he assured me, raising his hands in mock surrender. "Just a chance to be part of something bigger. A project that could put you back on the map. It's... well, let's just say it involves a lot of resources and a little bit of risk."

"Risk is your middle name, isn't it?" I shot back, trying to keep the banter light even as the gravity of his words settled around us like a thick fog. "What's the catch?"

He smirked, an expression that hinted at secrets untold. "You always were too clever for your own good. The catch is simple: you have to trust me. I need someone with your skills to help pull this off."

I scoffed, trying to mask the flutter of curiosity that sparked within me. "And what exactly am I supposed to do?"

Victor leaned back, studying me as if I were a puzzle he was determined to solve. "You've always had a knack for navigating tricky waters. I need you to gather intel, make some connections, maybe even play the role of the innocent bystander. You know, charm the right people."

"Right," I said, rolling my eyes. "Because that sounds completely aboveboard."

He laughed, a low, melodic sound that filled the space between us. "You're too much fun to toy with. But think about it. You'll have access to the kind of power and influence that can launch your career to the next level. No more scrappy freelance gigs, no more hustling for scraps."

I hesitated, the allure of his words wrapping around me like a vine, intoxicating and dangerous. "What's in it for you, Victor?"

He tilted his head, the smile fading as he regarded me with a seriousness that sent a shiver through my spine. "I have my reasons, believe me. But I can assure you, this is a win-win. You help me, and I'll make sure your skills don't go unnoticed. You've worked too hard to stay in the shadows."

My heart raced, caught between temptation and caution. I could feel the line blurring further, the choices spiraling like a wild dance. Just as I opened my mouth to reply, the sound of laughter erupted nearby, slicing through the tension. I glanced over to see a couple at the next table, wrapped in each other's warmth, oblivious to the world around them. Their joy felt like a stark contrast to my own internal chaos, a reminder of everything I longed for but felt I could never grasp.

"Don't let distractions pull you away," Victor said, his voice low and conspiratorial, pulling me back into the moment. "You have a chance here. A chance to reclaim your life, your dreams."

The weight of his words pressed down on me, swirling in my mind like the dark liquid in my glass. My decision loomed, a storm on the horizon. Could I really trust him? Did I have the strength to navigate the waters he was suggesting, or would I drown in the very depths I sought to escape?

"Think about it," he continued, leaning forward with an intensity that made my breath hitch. "You're smarter than this. Don't let your fear dictate your future."

I could feel the heat rising in my cheeks, a mixture of anger and frustration. "You think I'm scared?"

"Not scared," he replied smoothly. "Just cautious. And that's wise. But there's a fine line between caution and complacency, my dear."

I swallowed hard, the weight of his words hitting me in a way I hadn't expected. Perhaps he was right. Perhaps I had been playing it safe for too long. But the notion of leaping into the unknown with Victor felt like jumping off a cliff with no idea of what lay beneath the surface.

I leaned back, searching his eyes for sincerity, trying to decipher the man who had always walked the line between ally and adversary. "And if I say yes?"

Victor smiled, a glimmer of mischief sparking in his gaze. "Then we embark on an adventure that could reshape your destiny. You'll be in the driver's seat, I promise."

Just then, the bartender approached, placing our drinks in front of us with a nod. I picked up the glass, the cool surface a stark contrast to the warmth of my skin, and took a slow sip. The whiskey burned pleasantly, a reminder that even the most uncomfortable paths could lead to unexpected warmth.

"Let's toast to new beginnings," Victor suggested, raising his glass with a flourish.

"To new beginnings," I echoed, the words tasting bittersweet on my tongue. I clinked my glass against his, feeling the weight of the moment settle over us like a heavy quilt. I had crossed a threshold, and now there was no turning back. I was standing on the edge of a precipice, staring into an abyss that promised both danger and possibility. The thrill of the unknown called to me, and though my heart raced with fear, I couldn't ignore the allure of what lay ahead.

The moment the glasses clinked, a bubble of tension popped between us, and I felt a rush of adrenaline course through my veins. I hadn't expected to feel so alive, so acutely aware of every sensation—the coolness of the glass against my palm, the warmth of Victor's presence beside me, and the buzz of conversation swirling around us. But beneath that exhilarating rush was an undercurrent of dread, a nagging voice whispering that I was in over my head.

"I can't believe you're actually considering this," I said, trying to keep my tone light, though the weight of my decision hung heavily in the air. "What if I end up being your personal errand girl?"

Victor chuckled, his laughter smooth and inviting, but there was an edge to it, a hint of the predator lurking beneath the surface. "Hardly. Think of yourself as my secret weapon. You have a way of getting people to talk, and let's be honest—you could charm the skin off a snake."

I couldn't help but roll my eyes. "Flattery will get you nowhere."

"Flattery is just the appetizer. The main course is what I'm offering," he replied, his voice dipping into a conspiratorial whisper. "Imagine walking into those rooms with power, influence, and the kind of opportunities you've only dreamed of. You'd be a player, not a pawn."

"Sounds enticing," I admitted, the words tumbling out before I could catch them. "But at what cost?"

Victor leaned closer, the air thickening between us as he laid out the details with a flourish that made my heart race. He painted a picture of high-stakes negotiations and clandestine meetings, of my skills transforming into leverage in a game played by the elite. The prospect of finally breaking free from my self-imposed limitations sent shivers of excitement down my spine, even as a gnawing doubt simmered just beneath the surface.

"But what if I don't want to be a player?" I countered, my voice firmer than I felt. "What if I just want to live a quiet life?"

He snorted, his expression a mixture of amusement and incredulity. "A quiet life? You, of all people? I've seen you in action, and let me tell you—your life is anything but quiet. You thrive on chaos, on challenge. Why not embrace it?"

The corners of my mouth twitched upward, despite myself. "You make it sound like I'm some sort of thrill-seeker."

"Maybe you are." His eyes sparkled with mischief, and I could feel the energy crackling between us, an undeniable chemistry that tugged at the edges of my resolve. "But you're also cautious. You won't jump in without a parachute."

"Maybe I've just been careful," I shot back, crossing my arms defensively. "You know how it is. There are risks in everything."

"Exactly. But this is a risk worth taking." He paused, his gaze penetrating as he studied me. "You've spent too long hiding behind what ifs and maybes. It's time to grab life by the reins, don't you think?"

For a moment, I considered his words. The idea of finally breaking free from the shackles of my self-doubt and mundane routine was intoxicating. Yet, the specter of Caden's disappointment loomed large, a reminder of the lines I was prepared to cross. The stakes felt higher than ever, and I wasn't sure I could afford to gamble with my heart.

"You make it sound so easy," I replied, a hint of sarcasm creeping into my voice. "What if I can't do it? What if I screw everything up?"

"Then we fix it," he said, his tone resolute, almost comforting. "That's the beauty of this game. You learn as you go. And believe me, I won't let you fall. I'm not in the business of losing my most valuable asset."

At that moment, the world outside faded into a soft blur, the flickering lights of the bar and the laughter of patrons morphing into a distant hum. It was just the two of us, the weight of possibility thickening the air around us. But as alluring as his offer was, my heart raced with the knowledge that stepping into this new reality meant leaving behind everything I'd known—everything that had defined me.

"I need to think," I finally said, the words heavy with uncertainty.

"Take your time, but not too much," Victor replied, raising an eyebrow. "The clock is ticking, and opportunities like this don't wait around forever. You know that better than anyone."

His words wrapped around me like a warm embrace, both comforting and suffocating. I knew he was right; life had a way of slipping through your fingers if you weren't willing to grasp it firmly. But as I stared into the depths of my drink, the amber liquid swirling like the chaos in my mind, I couldn't shake the feeling that I was standing at the precipice of something monumental—something that could either elevate me or plunge me into the depths of despair.

"I'll think about it," I said finally, trying to inject some conviction into my voice.

"Good. Just remember, hesitation is the enemy of progress." He raised his glass, and I mirrored his action, the clinking of glass punctuating the tension that hung in the air. "To new adventures, whatever they may hold."

"To new adventures," I echoed, though my heart felt heavy with doubt. As I drank, the whiskey burned down my throat, igniting a fire in my belly. The thrill of what could be coursed through me, a heady mix of fear and excitement, but just as I began to contemplate the possibilities, a sudden commotion erupted nearby.

A group of patrons stumbled into the bar, laughter spilling over as they pushed through the door. Among them, I recognized a familiar face—Caden. My breath caught in my throat as his gaze swept the room, landing on me with a shock that mirrored my own. The warmth in his eyes turned to ice, and I felt a jolt of panic as I realized the precarious situation I had found myself in.

"Caden," I whispered, feeling my heart drop into my stomach. What was he doing here? This wasn't how I'd wanted our paths to cross—not like this, not after our earlier conversation.

Victor followed my gaze, a smirk creeping across his lips. "Looks like your past just walked in. Timing really is everything, isn't it?"

I shot him a warning look, my mind racing as I grappled with the implications. Caden moved closer, his expression shifting from shock to something unreadable, a storm brewing behind his eyes. I could feel the weight of unspoken questions thickening the air between us.

"What are you doing here?" Caden's voice was steady, but the intensity of his gaze bore into me, making my skin prickle with anxiety.

"I—" I stammered, the words sticking in my throat like a stubborn lump. I had crossed a line, one I had promised not to, and here he was, my past crashing into my present with a vengeance.

"I thought we were done with secrets." Caden's words were sharp, a knife that cut through the haze of my confusion. "What's going on, really?"

I opened my mouth to explain, but Victor's laughter echoed in the background, a taunting reminder of the choices I had made. Caden was right; I had been hiding, but now I was caught in the web of my own making, and I wasn't sure how to untangle it without losing everything.

"Caden, wait," I finally managed to say, desperation creeping into my voice as I reached for him, but the moment hung precariously in the balance. Just then, a loud crash broke through the air, drawing our attention to a commotion at the entrance. The sound reverberated through the bar like a gunshot, drawing gasps and murmurs from the crowd.

In an instant, chaos erupted, and the atmosphere shifted from casual to frenzied. My heart raced as I turned to see what had happened, and as the adrenaline surged through my veins, the enormity of my situation hit me like a freight train. In that one moment, as Caden and I locked eyes, I knew that whatever lay ahead would change everything.

But before I could process it, the shadows began to shift, and the danger I had invited into my life was about to reveal itself in a way I had never imagined.

Chapter 28: The Fall

The sun hung low in the sky, a fiery orb bleeding its warmth into the horizon, casting long shadows that danced across the cobblestones of the town square. I stood there, the chill of the evening settling into my bones, and watched as the townsfolk bustled about, their laughter a distant echo, a mocking symphony to the chaos unraveling in my heart. The air was thick with the scent of baked bread and roasted chestnuts, but all I could taste was the bitterness of regret.

Caden's empire, once vibrant and thriving, lay in ruins, the debris scattered like the broken pieces of my own resolve. I could see the remnants of what we had built together—those vibrant banners that once fluttered in the wind now hung limply, their colors dulled by the dust of despair. Each gust seemed to carry whispers of our dreams, mingled with the heavy thud of my betrayal, a symphony of destruction that played on repeat in my mind.

I had thought I was so clever, maneuvering through the intricate web of loyalty and ambition. But now, as I surveyed the wreckage from a distance, I realized that in my quest for freedom, I had unwittingly shackled myself to a fate far worse than the one I had sought to escape. Freedom tasted sour on my tongue, a cruel joke wrapped in irony.

Caden had always been the sun in my life, warm and radiant, illuminating the shadows I had lived in for so long. His laughter had been a balm, a reminder that even amidst the chaos, joy could thrive. But now, the sun was eclipsed, and the darkness that enveloped me felt inescapable. I glanced around, hoping to find solace in the faces of those I had once called friends. Instead, their gazes turned away, filled with disappointment and betrayal, as if I were a ghost haunting the very ground I had once claimed as my own.

"Look at you, like a lost puppy," a voice cut through the fog of my thoughts. I turned to find Lena leaning against a nearby fountain, arms crossed and eyebrows raised in that familiar arch of judgment. "You're not going to wallow in self-pity, are you?"

I offered a weak smile, my insides churning like a tempest. "Just enjoying the view," I replied, the words dripping with sarcasm. "You know, the ruins of my life."

She pushed herself off the fountain, her dark hair cascading around her shoulders like a waterfall of shadows. "You're a mess, you know that? Caden's not the only one suffering from this. You're dragging down the entire town with your guilt."

"Is that what you think?" I shot back, my voice rising. "That this is about me? I didn't ask for any of this."

"Neither did he," she snapped, her eyes flashing with an intensity that made me take a step back. "He trusted you, and you just... you threw it away. For what? A moment of weakness? Did you think Victor would actually give you the freedom you crave?"

I pressed my lips together, biting back the retort that threatened to spill forth. "I thought I could take control. That I could change my fate."

"Control?" She laughed, a sharp sound that felt like shards of glass. "You've lost everything, haven't you? And now you're standing here pretending it doesn't matter. Get it together. You owe it to him to face what you've done."

Her words sliced through me like a knife, exposing the raw, aching truth I had tried so hard to ignore. I didn't want to face it. The thought of Caden, his blue eyes clouded with betrayal, made me sick to my stomach. I could still hear his voice, the way it trembled when he had confronted me, the disbelief etched into his features as the reality of my actions sunk in. I had wanted to explain, to justify my choices, but the words had failed me, leaving only the silence that stretched between us like a chasm I could never bridge.

"I'm not going to just stand here and let him ruin everything," I said, a fire igniting within me. "I'll fix this. I have to. I can't let him win."

Lena narrowed her eyes, a flicker of concern breaking through her tough exterior. "You think you can take on Victor alone? He's not some petty rival. He's ruthless, and he won't stop until he has everything he wants, including you."

"Maybe that's exactly what I need," I replied, the determination hardening my resolve. "I won't let him take what's left of my life, or Caden's. I'll find a way to make this right."

"Be careful," she warned, her voice softening slightly. "You're playing a dangerous game, and the stakes are higher than you realize."

With that, she turned and walked away, her silhouette blending into the throng of people, leaving me standing alone at the edge of the square. I took a deep breath, trying to steady the whirlwind of thoughts racing through my mind. The challenge loomed ahead, a daunting mountain I would have to climb alone, but the fire of determination flickered anew within me. I had to face Victor, had to confront the tangled web of my choices and find a way to unravel the chaos I had created.

The sun dipped below the horizon, casting the world into a twilight that felt heavy with promise and danger. As I set my sights on the path ahead, I couldn't shake the feeling that my true battle was just beginning, and for better or worse, I was ready to fight.

The streets grew quieter as dusk settled over the town, casting a soft, golden light that felt like a cruel reminder of the warmth I had once known. I turned my back on the square, the echoes of laughter fading into a whisper behind me, and headed toward the only place that felt remotely familiar—the old coffee shop on the corner. The scent of freshly brewed coffee mingled with the rich aroma of cinnamon pastries, a small comfort in a world that felt increasingly foreign.

As I pushed open the door, a small bell chimed, its sound a fragile reminder that life still buzzed around me, even if I felt like a ghost haunting my own existence. I slid into a booth in the corner, the vinyl cracked but welcoming, a sanctuary from the chaos swirling in my mind. The barista, a young woman with bright blue hair and an impressive array of piercings, gave me a sympathetic smile as she approached, her name tag reading Luna.

"You look like you could use a double espresso with a shot of optimism," she said, her tone light but probing, as if she sensed the weight of my despair.

I couldn't help but chuckle, despite myself. "Make it a triple, and I'll consider it."

She raised an eyebrow, then nodded. "Coming right up. And maybe a pastry on the side? You know, to soak up all that angst."

"Perfect choice. I'll take whatever you recommend."

As she disappeared behind the counter, I leaned back in the booth, watching the world outside through the large window. The streetlights flickered on, casting long shadows and illuminating the faces of passersby. Each smile, each carefree moment, felt like a punch to the gut, a stark contrast to the turmoil within me. I was trapped in a nightmare of my own making, and there was no escape.

When Luna returned with my order, she placed the steaming cup and flaky pastry in front of me with a flourish. "Here's your fuel. Don't drown in self-pity; it's not worth the calories."

"Thanks, Luna. You have a gift for unsolicited wisdom," I replied, taking a sip of the bitter coffee, the heat seeping into my chest like a feeble attempt to warm my cold heart.

"I like to think of it as my superpower," she said with a wink. "So, what's the deal? You look like someone who just found out her favorite sweater has a giant hole in it."

"More like I've just burned all my sweaters and the house along with it," I said, laughter bubbling up even as the truth felt more like a weight pressing down on my shoulders. "I messed up. Big time."

Her expression softened. "You're not alone in that. I think everyone has that one moment that sends everything spiraling. But you can either wallow in it or turn it into a stepping stone."

"Easy for you to say. You're not the one who—" I stopped, biting my tongue. Talking about my mistakes felt like slicing open a fresh wound. "You don't know what it's like to betray the one person who trusted you."

"Trust is a fragile thing," she said, her tone shifting to something deeper, more thoughtful. "But you know what? People are also resilient. You might be surprised by how forgiving Caden could be. If you want to mend things, maybe you should start by being honest. With yourself and with him."

"Honesty? Right now, that feels like the worst idea I could entertain," I said, rubbing my temples as if that could relieve the headache forming there. "He deserves better than my half-hearted apologies."

"Maybe," she replied, leaning closer. "But think about it. What do you have to lose at this point? You're already on the floor; the only way to go is up."

I considered her words, the truth of them settling like a stone in my stomach. Luna had a point. Caden might hate me now, but I had to try. I couldn't just walk away from everything we'd built—our dreams, our plans. I took another sip of coffee, feeling its warmth seep through the cracks in my resolve.

"I need to find him," I said suddenly, determination igniting within me. "I have to face the music."

"Now you're talking," she replied, her eyes sparkling with encouragement. "But remember, it's not just about you. You'll need to listen, really listen. A heartfelt apology is one thing, but understanding where he's coming from is another."

"Thanks, Luna. I think you should be a therapist instead of a barista," I said, grinning.

"Just doing my part to keep the world caffeinated and emotionally intact," she shot back, her smile wide.

With renewed energy, I finished my coffee, the caffeine coursing through my veins like a jolt of lightning. The weight of my decision pressed against me, but it felt less suffocating now. I paid the tab and stepped outside, the night air cool against my skin, a stark contrast to the warmth radiating from within.

I made my way toward Caden's place, the familiar path lined with flickering lamplights guiding me through the darkness. With each step, I rehearsed the words I would say, the way I would explain myself, hoping against hope that he would listen, that he would understand the fear that had driven me to betray him.

As I approached his door, my heart raced, anticipation and dread intertwining. I raised my hand to knock, hesitated, and then pressed my palm flat against the wood, the barrier between us feeling more like a fortress than a home. In that moment, I realized the magnitude of what I was about to do. I had to be brave, to let my vulnerability shine through even if it meant risking everything.

With a deep breath, I knocked, the sound echoing through the quiet night like a heartbeat. I stood there, anxiety coursing through my veins, waiting for the door to swing open, knowing that whatever happened next would change everything.

The door swung open, and there he was—Caden, a silhouette framed by the warm glow of the interior lights. His expression was unreadable, a tight line of uncertainty carved into his handsome features, and for a moment, I was frozen, caught in the tension that crackled between us. I could see the faint shadows under his eyes, a reflection of sleepless nights spent wrestling with betrayal and loss, and it made my heart ache in a way I hadn't anticipated.

"Why are you here?" he asked, his voice steady but laced with a tremor that hinted at the storm brewing just beneath the surface.

"I came to talk," I managed to say, my throat suddenly dry as desert sand. "I know I don't deserve it, but I need to explain. Please, just give me a moment."

He stepped back, allowing me to enter, yet his gaze never left mine, as if I were a puzzle he was trying to solve. The familiar scent of sandalwood and cedar enveloped me, reminding me of evenings spent curled up on the couch, our laughter echoing off the walls. Those memories felt like daggers now, piercing through the layers of time that had accumulated since my betrayal.

"What could you possibly say that would make this any better?" Caden's words were sharp, yet I could see the flicker of pain in his eyes, and it was that flicker that gave me hope.

"I know I've hurt you. I can't change what happened, but I want to make it right," I said, my voice trembling. "I need you to understand why I did it. It wasn't about you; it was about me and my fears."

He crossed his arms, the muscles in his jaw tightening. "So this is about your freedom again? Because that's what you keep coming back to, isn't it? What about us? What about everything we built?"

"I thought if I could gain control—if I could make a choice—it would give me the strength to fight for us. But I was wrong. So wrong." My heart pounded as I searched for the right words, my breath catching in my throat. "I thought I could handle it, but I underestimated Victor. I didn't realize how far he'd go to ruin us."

Caden's expression softened slightly, but he still stood his ground, a fortress fortified against my attempts to breach his defenses. "And what? You thought you could just play both sides?

That you could betray me and still come back like nothing happened?"

"No," I whispered, feeling the weight of his disappointment crush me. "I never meant to hurt you. I was just trying to survive."

A long silence stretched between us, thick with unspoken words and shattered dreams. I could see the flicker of conflicting emotions in his eyes—anger, sadness, longing. He wanted to believe me, but the hurt ran deep, and I was acutely aware of the chasm that had opened between us.

"I want to believe you," he finally admitted, his voice barely above a whisper. "But trust doesn't come easy, and you've broken it. What makes you think you can fix this?"

"Because I want to try," I said, stepping closer, the urge to reach out to him overwhelming. "I'm here, Caden. I'm willing to do whatever it takes to prove I'm not the person you think I am. I want to fight for us."

His gaze flickered to the floor, and I could almost see the gears turning in his mind. "And what if it's too late? What if you've already ruined everything?"

"Then let me take the first step," I urged, my heart pounding against my ribcage. "I'll show you that I can be trusted again, that I can be the partner you deserve. Just let me in."

There was a hesitation, a tiny crack in the armor he had built around himself. "You're asking for a lot," he said slowly.

"I know," I replied, my voice steadying. "But I'm asking for a chance. Please."

He studied me for a long moment, and I could feel the tension mounting as if the very air around us held its breath. Then, suddenly, the moment shattered. A loud crash echoed from outside, followed by a frantic shout, jolting us both from our fragile connection. Caden's expression hardened, and he moved toward the window, peering out into the darkening street.

"What was that?" I asked, my heart racing again, this time with a fresh wave of fear.

"Stay here," he commanded, his tone brokering no argument.

I watched him slip out the door, my pulse quickening as dread washed over me. I didn't want to be left alone, not now, when everything was hanging by a thread. I followed him out, stepping into the night just in time to see a figure stumbling away from Caden's property, clutching something shiny that glinted in the streetlight.

"Hey! Stop!" Caden shouted, his voice laced with urgency.

Before I could grasp what was happening, the figure turned and bolted down the street, disappearing into the shadows. Caden took off after him, the determination in his stride making my heart race with a mixture of fear and concern. I hesitated, torn between the impulse to follow him and the desire to stay where I was, safe and out of harm's way.

Then I noticed something lying on the ground where the figure had been—something small and metallic, glinting ominously. I knelt to pick it up, my fingers wrapping around it, the cold surface sending chills up my spine. It was a small device, and as I turned it over in my hand, a chilling realization hit me.

It was a tracking device, the kind Victor used to keep tabs on people.

A scream of alarm surged in my throat as I glanced in the direction Caden had gone. I had a moment of panic, a rush of dread that perhaps I hadn't escaped my past after all. The implications of what I held in my hand settled like lead in my stomach. I was the reason Victor was here, the reason Caden was in danger. I had to warn him, but he was already racing down the street, and I was left standing there, my heart in my throat.

"Caden!" I shouted, the urgency of his name tearing from my lips.

But the darkness swallowed my voice, leaving me alone with the weight of my mistakes and the haunting fear that we were already too late. The shadows deepened, and the night felt suddenly alive with danger, a web of chaos spun around us, threatening to ensnare everything we had left. As I turned to run after him, my pulse pounding in my ears, I couldn't shake the feeling that this was just the beginning of a much darker game, one I wasn't sure we could win.

Chapter 29: A Fragile Hope

The sun dipped below the horizon, casting an amber glow across my cluttered studio, where scraps of fabric danced in the soft breeze, whispering secrets of designs yet to be born. I stood before my sewing machine, fingers poised over the fabric like a pianist ready to strike a chord. The rhythmic hum of the machine filled the air, a comforting melody amidst the vibrant chaos of sketches and color swatches scattered about like the remnants of dreams yet to be realized. Each stitch I made was an attempt to sew together the tattered remnants of my heart, a heart that still bore the scars of a love both intoxicating and tormenting.

I let out a breath I didn't realize I'd been holding, staring at the floral pattern taking shape beneath my hands. This particular fabric had a richness to it, deep blues and greens swirling together like the ocean on a stormy day. It was my favorite; a reminder of those fleeting moments when life felt like a painted canvas, each day a brushstroke of possibility. But beneath the surface of my creativity lay an undercurrent of longing, a wistfulness that refused to be washed away. Caden was the ghost haunting my creations, and no matter how hard I tried to push him away, he lingered like a shadow, a reminder of what once was.

I shifted my focus, forcing myself to remember the joy of creating. The flutter of excitement that bloomed within me as I envisioned the perfect dress for a client, the way their eyes lit up at the mere thought of wearing something crafted with love and intention. I often poured my soul into each piece, hoping to transcend the personal pain with every stitch, but Caden's absence loomed large, a specter that made every accomplishment feel incomplete.

The door swung open with a creak that sliced through my concentration. My heart raced, an instinctive response to the intruder, fingers trembling over the fabric as I turned to face whoever had dared to disturb my sanctuary. It was then that I froze. Caden stood there, framed by the warm glow of the setting sun, his silhouette a powerful contrast to the soft hues of my sanctuary. Time seemed to suspend itself, the world outside fading into insignificance as my eyes locked onto his.

He looked different, the years having added a subtle maturity to his features, a weight of experience reflected in his gaze. The casual confidence that had once charmed me now seemed tempered, like a fine wine aged too long. I searched his eyes for answers, for a spark of the man I had once known, but all I found was a deep well of emotions, swirling with unspoken words and unresolved tension.

"What are you doing here?" I managed to croak out, my voice barely a whisper as if the very sound might shatter the fragile atmosphere. The space between us felt electric, charged with the possibilities of the past and the uncertainties of the present.

He stepped forward, his movements deliberate, as though he were afraid of breaking the delicate thread that connected us. "I... I saw the sign outside. Thought I might find you here," he replied, his voice low and rich, wrapping around my heart like a familiar embrace. "I've missed you, Jess."

Every syllable ignited a flurry of emotions within me—hope, anger, longing—all vying for dominance in my heart. I felt my pulse quicken as I searched his face for sincerity. "You've missed me? After everything? How could you?" The words tumbled out, sharp and laced with bitterness, but my heart screamed for something more, something deeper.

He took a deep breath, running a hand through his hair, a gesture I remembered all too well. "I know I messed up, but I've thought about you every day since. I came to apologize, to explain."

I was torn between wanting to hear his explanation and the fear of being swept back into the emotional whirlwind that was Caden.

"Apologize? After months of silence? You think that's enough?" My voice trembled, betraying the whirlwind of emotions I struggled to contain.

His eyes softened, and he stepped closer, reducing the distance that felt insurmountable only moments ago. "I know I don't deserve your forgiveness, but I want to make things right. Can we at least talk? Just give me a chance to explain."

The plea in his voice wrapped around my heart, pulling me toward him like a moth drawn to a flame. My resolve wavered, the walls I had painstakingly built beginning to crumble. The memory of laughter shared, secrets whispered, and dreams woven together surged forth like a tidal wave. I had fought to forge a new identity without him, yet here he stood, an undeniable force stirring up emotions I thought I had buried.

"Fine," I said, the word escaping before I could fully process it. "But only for a little while." I motioned for him to sit at the small table littered with my sketches, the remnants of my life laid bare before us. As he settled in, the air crackled with tension, the silence stretching between us like a taut string, ready to snap at any moment.

"Where do I even start?" he began, his voice thick with emotion. "When I left, I thought I was protecting you, protecting us. But in trying to shield you from my world, I only pushed you away. I was scared, Jess. Scared of what I felt and scared of losing you."

The weight of his admission hung in the air, and I felt my heart thud painfully in my chest. The truth of his fear resonated within me. I had faced my own demons, battling the insecurities that came from loving someone who danced with shadows. I had thought he'd chosen his world over me, but perhaps I had misread his intentions, wrapped in my own hurt and anger.

"But it's too late now," I whispered, though part of me wanted desperately to believe that it wasn't.

"No, it's not," he insisted, leaning forward, his intensity capturing my gaze. "I've changed. I'm ready to fight for us. I want to be the man you deserve."

The sincerity in his voice clawed at my heart, and for the first time in months, a flicker of hope ignited within me, fragile and uncertain. But it was there, breathing, alive, and longing for the possibility of what could be.

I studied him, letting the moment stretch like taffy, each second a sticky blend of sweetness and tension. Caden shifted in his seat, his hands fidgeting on the table, the silence heavy between us. I could see the resolve in his eyes, a flicker of the boy I once knew, but I also sensed the man he had become, forged in the fires of his decisions.

"Why now?" The question slipped out, sharp as a needle, and I felt a rush of vulnerability. "Why not before?"

He ran a hand through his hair, his familiar gesture sending a wave of nostalgia crashing over me. "I thought I was protecting you," he replied, his voice steady, yet it trembled with the weight of his admission. "I was caught up in my own world, Jess. I didn't realize until it was too late that love isn't about protection; it's about trust and openness."

I couldn't help but chuckle, a mix of disbelief and bitterness. "So you thought ghosting me was the best option?"

His lips twisted into a wry smile, one I recognized from years gone by. "Clearly, I wasn't thinking clearly at all."

We shared a fleeting moment of laughter, but the gravity of our conversation loomed over us like an ominous cloud. "I've spent months rebuilding my life," I said, my voice faltering. "Finding myself outside of us. And now you're here, stirring everything back up."

"I didn't come to complicate your life," he said, his eyes earnest. "I came to apologize and to tell you that I'm still here, if you'll let me."

That hope flickered again, delicate yet persistent. I felt the pulse of possibility thrumming in the air, and I wanted to grasp it, to clutch it tightly against my chest like a cherished secret. Yet the scars of our past were not so easily forgotten. "You think you can just waltz back in here and expect me to forget everything?" I challenged, crossing my arms defensively.

"I don't expect anything," he said quietly, his gaze unwavering. "But I want to try. I miss you, Jess. I miss us."

I studied him, caught between the memories of our laughter, our shared dreams, and the pain that had driven a wedge between us. Could I really allow myself to believe in us again? "What's changed?" I pressed, unable to hide the skepticism in my voice. "How do I know you won't just run away again?"

"I'm ready to fight for this, for you. I know what I lost, and I'm not about to let it slip away again." His sincerity tugged at my heartstrings, urging me to let down my guard just a fraction.

"Fighting doesn't guarantee victory," I countered, but the truth was, I was hungry for his words. "And I'm not sure I'm ready to risk it again."

He leaned in, lowering his voice as if sharing a secret. "What if we take it slow? I don't want to pressure you. Let's just... see where this goes."

I met his gaze, seeing the earnestness behind the familiar boyish charm that had once captivated me. He looked older, worn by life, but that same spark of mischief glimmered in his eyes. The tension between us shifted, becoming less a battle and more a tentative dance—a slow exploration of what had once been lost.

"Okay," I said, the word barely above a whisper. "But slow means no grand gestures, no sweeping declarations. Just... coffee and conversation."

A grin broke across his face, and I couldn't help but feel a flutter of excitement. "Coffee sounds perfect."

As we settled into an easy rhythm, the conversation flowed like an unhurried river, each word washing away the barriers that had built up over the months. We talked about everything and nothing—my designs, his work in finance, the mundane happenings of our lives that had unfolded separately. The air crackled with a sense of familiarity, but I also felt a newness, a rediscovery of who we were now.

Yet beneath the surface, I sensed the unspoken questions simmering between us. What had happened in those long months apart? What had changed so fundamentally that we could even consider navigating this fragile terrain?

As the sun dipped below the horizon, casting golden rays through my studio window, Caden's gaze lingered on a sketch pinned to the wall—a dress I had designed for a summer gala that now felt distant, a vestige of the life I had imagined without him. "You still have that fire," he remarked, his voice soft yet vibrant with appreciation. "I remember how you used to pour your soul into your designs. It's beautiful to see."

"Thanks," I said, a blush creeping up my neck. "I had to find that fire again. It wasn't easy."

He nodded, understanding flickering in his eyes. "I can't even begin to imagine how difficult it was. You always were stronger than me."

"Strength isn't just about bravado," I replied, a hint of defiance in my tone. "It's about overcoming the things that threaten to break you. I learned that the hard way."

The air thickened with emotion, and I saw him process my words, each one landing like a pebble tossed into still water, creating ripples that spread between us. "I wish I could take back the pain I caused you," he said, his voice heavy with regret. "But I can't. All I can do is try to be better."

"Better is a start," I conceded, feeling a flicker of hope intertwined with my trepidation. "But you can't expect me to just forget the past. Trust isn't easily rebuilt."

"I understand," he replied, his expression earnest. "I'm not here to rush you. I just want the chance to show you how much I've changed. How much I want to be part of your life again."

I couldn't deny the longing that bubbled up inside me. His words wrapped around me like a warm blanket on a cold night, inviting me to step back into the comfort of what we had once shared. Yet the fear of being hurt again loomed like a shadow in the corner of my mind, waiting to pounce at the first sign of vulnerability.

As we settled into a comfortable silence, the only sound the distant hum of the city outside, I wondered if this fragile hope could grow into something more substantial. Could we truly build a bridge over the chasm that had formed between us? Or were we destined to stumble, forever haunted by the ghosts of our past?

As the shadows deepened in the studio, I couldn't shake the feeling that this conversation was a delicate dance, each step uncertain yet electrifying. The air was thick with tension, a palpable energy humming between us, igniting memories of laughter shared in quiet corners of cafés, and whispered secrets beneath a blanket of stars. But lurking beneath that warmth was the ever-present fear of being burned again.

Caden leaned forward, his expression earnest, the remnants of our past swirling in his gaze. "What if we don't think about the 'what-ifs' for now? Let's just enjoy this moment. I'd like to rediscover who we are, separately and together."

"Rediscover? That sounds a little too philosophical for a Tuesday evening," I teased, allowing a smile to break through my apprehension. "Are we supposed to hold hands and frolic through meadows next? Because that's not my idea of a good time."

"Why not? I hear the flowers are lovely this time of year," he quipped, his eyes dancing with mischief. "But seriously, I'm not expecting anything grand. Just... let's explore this new terrain, see where it leads us. Maybe we'll find a few flowers along the way."

I rolled my eyes playfully, trying to mask the way my heart fluttered at his words. "Fine, Mr. Philosophical. But no flower-picking until we're sure we won't trip over our own feelings and fall into a thorn bush."

"Deal," he said, the corners of his mouth lifting into a smile that made my stomach flutter with something akin to hope.

For a moment, the room transformed. The clutter of sketches and fabric seemed to fade, leaving only the two of us suspended in a bubble of tentative exploration. We began to recount our lives in the months apart, the mundane details that made up our daily routines, each revelation drawing us closer, stitching the fabric of our separate worlds back together, stitch by stitch.

I told him about my recent successes, how my designs had been featured in a local showcase, drawing admiration and interest from new clients. His pride in my achievements radiated from him, and I felt a warmth bloom in my chest. "I knew you'd make it big," he said, a gleam of sincerity in his eyes. "You've always had that fire."

"And what about you? How's the world of finance treating you?" I asked, genuinely curious despite the knot of jealousy twisting in my stomach at the thought of him thriving without me.

He shrugged, a light chuckle escaping his lips. "It's the same old grind, filled with numbers and suits. I've learned to appreciate the small wins, like finishing a complex spreadsheet without losing my mind."

We shared a laugh, the sound echoing like a melody through the room, but beneath the surface, I could sense the seriousness of our situation lurking. Every shared smile felt like a fragile promise, and every joke served as a brief respite from the underlying uncertainty.

But as we drifted deeper into conversation, an unexpected tension crept into the atmosphere. I watched as the laughter in his eyes dimmed slightly, replaced by a flicker of hesitation. "There's something I haven't told you," he said, his tone shifting to one of gravity.

My heart raced, apprehension tightening around me like a vise. "What is it?"

He took a deep breath, as if summoning the strength to reveal a truth that hung heavy in the air. "After everything, I thought I could step away from my old life. But the truth is, I'm still tied to it, whether I want to be or not. I've had to deal with some... complications."

"Complications?" The word slipped from my lips, the weight of it heavy, echoing in the growing silence.

"Yeah. I didn't come back just to reconnect with you. I've been dealing with some serious fallout from my past decisions, and it's starting to catch up with me."

I leaned closer, my heart pounding. "What do you mean?"

He hesitated, searching for the right words, and the air between us thickened with uncertainty. "It's about my father and the family business. Things are getting out of control, Jess. I thought I could handle it, but I need your help."

"Help? What do you mean?" My mind raced, trying to process the implications of what he was saying. "You want me to step back into that world?"

He nodded slowly, pain evident in his expression. "I don't want to pull you into it, but I can't do this alone. I need someone who knows me, who understands the stakes."

My heart sank, a heavy stone settling in my stomach. The world I had worked so hard to escape, the chaos and drama that had consumed our lives, was knocking at the door again. "Caden, I—"

"Please," he interrupted, his voice a mixture of desperation and determination. "I wouldn't ask if I didn't think it was necessary. I've been trying to keep you out of it, but things have escalated. I can't afford to lose you again."

A part of me wanted to refuse outright, to draw a line in the sand and declare my independence from the life that had once entangled us. But the way he looked at me, that blend of hope and fear, tugged at something deep within. "I don't know, Caden. You're asking a lot."

"I know, and I'm sorry," he said, his voice dropping to a near whisper, "but I wouldn't ask if it wasn't serious. You're the only one I trust to help me navigate this mess."

I felt the weight of his words, the unspoken bond of trust tethering us together once again. "What exactly are we talking about?"

"There's a situation with a business deal gone wrong—threats have been made, and I need someone who can think on their feet. You're resourceful, you can help me strategize."

"Are you saying you're in danger?" My voice was tight, the fear surging through me as I processed his words.

He met my gaze, his expression grave. "Not just me. You're part of this now, whether you want to be or not. I can't let you walk away again."

The finality of his statement struck me like a thunderclap, the storm brewing between us both exhilarating and terrifying. As I considered the magnitude of his request, I felt my pulse quicken. Could I really step back into that life, back into the chaos that had threatened to consume me before?

Just as I opened my mouth to respond, the studio door swung open with a crash, the hinges groaning in protest. I turned to see a figure silhouetted in the doorway, the light casting a harsh shadow across the room. My breath hitched, heart racing as I recognized the unmistakable outline of a man whose presence sent a chill down my spine.

"Caden," the intruder's voice boomed, cutting through the tense atmosphere like a knife. "We need to talk."

The room went silent, the weight of impending danger hanging thick in the air, and as Caden's expression shifted from surprise to dread, I knew that everything was about to change.

Milton Keynes UK
Ingram Content Group UK Ltd.
UKHW032321221024
449917UK00001B/91

9 798227 639318